Kate Charles and her husband live in a large Victorian house with their two dogs – one white, one black. Her previous novel, *Unruly Passions*, followed her series of popular ecclesiastical mysteries.

STRANGE CHILDREN

KATE CHARLES

WARNER BOOKS

A *Warner* Book

First published in Great Britain in 1999
by Little, Brown and Company

This edition published by Warner Books in 2000

Reprinted 2001

A CIP catalogue record for this book
is available from the British Library.

ISBN 0 7515 2542 1

Typeset by Solidus (Bristol) Ltd, Bristol
Printed and bound in Great Britain by
Mackays of Chatham plc, Kent

Warner Books
A Division of
Little, Brown and Company (UK)
Brettenham House
Lancaster Place
London WC2E 7EN

www.littlebrown.co.uk

For Marcia, the best of best friends.

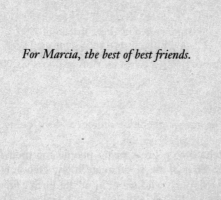

Acknowledgements

I am indebted to a great many people for their help with this book. First of all, to Marcia Talley, Deborah Crombie and Terry Mayeux, who were 'in at the birth'. For specialist knowledge readily shared: Suzanne Clackson, Dr Andrew Gray, Sandra McClelland, and the Reverend Nicholas Biddle, among others. For constant encouragement and advice: Ann Hinrichs. For editorial input: several of the above, plus Lucy Walker, Carol Heaton, and the incomparable Hilary Hale.

And to Rory, for everything.

*As soon as they hear of me, they shall obey me: but the strange
    children shall dissemble with me.
The strange children shall fail: and be afraid out of their prisons.*

Psalm 18: 45–46

Chapter 1

They met at a wedding, or more accurately at a wedding reception. That they were seated next to each other at the reception was deliberate, a bad joke on the part of the bride and groom. And it seemed that everyone else at the table was in on the joke, for they were observed covertly and with some interest.

Characteristically, it was Rob who spoke first, shortly after they'd sat down and before the first course was served. 'You're not a friend of the bride?'

Tessa, not meeting his eyes, shook her head a shade too emphatically for disinterest or a neutral denial. 'No. I'm not,' she said in a soft, flat voice.

'A friend of the groom, then,' he surmised.

She clamped her mouth together to keep her lower lip from trembling, but he continued to regard her with interest and seemed to expect some sort of response from her. 'Not any longer,' she managed at last, toying with the stem of her champagne glass. It was still mostly full; Tessa had no appetite for champagne on this occasion.

'Then why are you here?' Rob persevered.

Still she kept her head averted, like some great drooping flower in desperate need of watering. 'I had to come. I had to see for myself, to be sure . . .' Her voice tailed off.

Rob might have turned away then, might have entered into a

light-hearted conversation with the pretty brunette in the flame-coloured dress on his left. But he was in no mood for light-hearted conversation himself, and so he persisted. 'Tell me,' he said. 'Surely it's not so bad as all that.'

His voice was gently teasing, and it was the gentleness in it that captured her attention at last; she raised her head and looked at him for the first time.

He was good-looking, her mind registered with detachment: handsome in a long-jawed English sort of way. Like a somewhat overgrown public-school boy. Black hair, straight and thick, parted off-centre and falling artistically over his brow; eyes of a deep and penetrating blue. Lean face, prominent cheekbones. Like a young Rupert Everett, she thought. Not like Ian; he looked nothing at all like Ian. At the moment that was very much in his favour.

She would tell him, she decided. 'Ian,' she tried to say, but the name stuck in her throat. 'The groom,' she said instead. 'He's . . . We used to . . .'

Comprehension widened his eyes. 'You and Ian.'

The table fell quiet, as everyone strained to hear what would come next. But the hush was unnatural and couldn't last; the brunette turned to the man on her left, speaking in a bright voice, and the rest of the table followed suit.

Rob's gaze hadn't left Tessa's face, as he searched out the pain that was revealed there. 'They've done this on purpose, you know,' he told her quietly.

'What?'

'They've seated us together. Bastards,' he added viciously, swivelling his head to look towards the top table where bride and groom reigned in splendour. But when he turned back to Tessa, he was smiling.

'I don't understand.'

'Their idea of a joke, I suppose.' Rob's mouth twisted. 'Don't you see? We're the rejects.'

*

Rob and Amanda had met at work, a classic office romance. As neither had any other attachment at the time, it was straight-forward.

They encountered one another in the lift on a regular basis; Rob couldn't help noticing the striking redhead, always dressed in dark suits and laden down with a massive briefcase. At first he contented himself with making brief eye contact and smiling at her; when he realised that the smile she returned held interest, he told her his name. After that they chatted between floors on an almost daily basis, and one day he asked her to join him for a drink after work, at a watering hole popular with young City professionals.

The relationship progressed fairly rapidly. They went out for a few meals, went to the cinema once or twice, slept together.

The latter, in particular, was more than satisfactory, so after a few months they moved in together. More accurately, Amanda moved in with Rob. She had been living in a tiny studio flat which was convenient for work but not really suit-able for a young woman on her way up – and that Amanda certainly was. A true yuppie, she made no secret of her ambitions to rise within the company.

Rob owned a house. It was not a large house, nor was it in a fashionable part of London, but Islington was even then on its ascendency towards trendiness, and the house was more than adequate for two people, with good tube connections into the City.

The arrangement suited them both very well. Very quickly they stopped going out – admitting to one another that they both loathed the cinema – and settled down into a routine. Amanda, on a fast management track, worked much longer hours than Rob did, often not returning home until late in the evening, but this didn't bother him; he preferred, in fact, to spend his free time alone, in the room of his house which he had turned into his sanctuary. This was his computer room, equipped with the latest state-of-the-art computer hardware and loaded with the most up-to-date software. He could happily spend hours there, playing extended and complex simulation games and 'surfing the Net'.

When, eventually, Amanda would return home, he would manage to tear himself away from his computer, and they would share a meal. Needless to say, Amanda was not in the least interested in the trappings of domesticity, and cooking was not even a word in her vocabulary. Rob could cook if he had to, but he didn't often bother: there were so many convenient take-away places – Chinese, Indian, pizza, kebabs, chicken – in the Holloway Road, and a Marks and Spencer as well, where tasty and nutritious meals were available in abundance, ready to be popped into the microwave. Amanda could, at a pinch, handle the microwave.

And then to bed. That was what made the relationship worthwhile, what kept it going for over six years. They were wonderful together in bed, and the excitement never palled. Amanda, insatiable, found Rob an inventive lover, and he was constantly aroused by her desire for him.

Marriage wasn't an issue, at least as far as Amanda was concerned. There was no reason why they should marry, she often said. There was no question of them having children – babies were not part of her life plan, now or ever. That included Rob, who knew better than to expect Amanda to baby *him*.

Just occasionally, Rob raised the subject of marriage – the idea of a permanent and legal attachment to a compatible sex partner appealed to him. But such suggestions were always firmly quashed by Amanda.

They never argued; they didn't have rows. Perhaps Rob knew that it would be a waste of time: Amanda would always have her way in the end, so why bother? At any rate, it wasn't his style. On those rare occasions when their wishes were in conflict, Rob would retreat to his computer room and shut the door; even Amanda knew better than to violate the sanctity of his private hideaway.

And so they went on for six years and a few months, in a settled routine which was comfortable and satisfactory for both of them.

Until the day that Amanda announced that she was going to marry Ian.

Tessa had known Ian for ever, or at least it seemed that way. They'd met at school, at the local comprehensive in the town where Tessa's father was the vicar of the parish church. She couldn't remember a time when she didn't think that Ian was the handsomest, the most vital and fascinating person in the world.

Unfortunately Ian had not, from the beginning, reciprocated those feelings. Not that he thought much about Tessa at all in those early days. He was a popular boy at school: sporty, well-built, good-looking. And Tessa was – well, she was just *there*. Quiet, shy, academic. Her nose always stuck in a book, and without anyone who could be called a friend. A solitary girl, too tall, and habitually hunched over to minimise her height. Colourless, with pale hair and pale skin; her best feature was a pair of large grey eyes. Not, in short, the sort of girl that Ian would take any notice of.

But she noticed Ian. In the classroom, moving about the school, laughing with his friends, on the rugby field and the cricket pitch. He lived a few streets away from the vicarage, and sometimes Tessa would follow him home. The first time had been an accident; she just happened to be leaving at the same time as he did. But after that she waited, hanging about the school gates until he emerged, usually surrounded by a crowd of friends; then she would skulk home behind him, hunching over even more than usual in an effort to be inconspicuous.

Ian's friends began to tease him about the pale shadow who trailed his steps; that was when he first became aware of Tessa's existence. His feelings towards her at that time were chiefly scornful, dismissive, with a pinch of pity mixed in. He was flattered, of course, but Ian was used to being admired by his fellows, and in any case he liked to be the one who made the running.

They ended up at the same university, perhaps by chance and perhaps not. Ian's popularity continued; there were scores of girls who fancied him, and he had his pick of the lot.

But Tessa was there as well, in the background, adoring him silently and from afar.

And then one day he spoke to her. They were in the library, where Tessa was reading a book, all the while aware with every fibre of her being that he was in the same room. Ian needed to find a particular book for one of his lectures, and as there was no librarian in evidence, he stopped by the table where Tessa sat and asked her to help him to locate his book. She found it for him straight away, and moved by some sentiment of gratitude, he invited her to join him for coffee.

Tessa accepted. And though in her imagination she had carried on countless scintillating conversations with Ian, on every topic under the sun, she found herself tongue-tied at the critical moment.

It didn't matter. Ian was quite capable of delivering a monologue, and he discovered that he rather enjoyed doing so with such an appreciative audience. Tessa hung on his every word, rapt with adoration.

Ian had only just broken up with his latest girlfriend. In a generous moment, he asked Tessa to accompany him to a party in place of the ex-girlfriend.

At the party he met another girl, the girlfriend of one of his mates, someone more exciting than Tessa. But excitement wasn't always what a chap needed – even a chap like Ian – and after that relationship ended, he found himself ringing Tessa and telling her about it, encouraging her sympathy for his solitary state.

She invited him to her lodgings for a home-cooked meal.

He accepted that, and everything else she had to offer to him, until someone else came along a few weeks later.

It became a pattern. Ian would have an intense and usually short-lived relationship with someone, and then he would come back to Tessa until he found someone else.

For Tessa it wasn't the most satisfactory arrangement in the world, perhaps, but it was enough. To know that Ian would always return to her meant everything. One day, she told herself, he would come to his senses, would realise that she was right for him all along, that no one could love him as she did, or lavish devotion upon him as she always had done.

During their second year at university, Ian had a particularly intense fling with the daughter of an earl; he moved in exalted company, ignored his studies, skipped his lectures. And failed his exams just at the time that the affair fizzled out.

Tessa hadn't seen him for weeks when he turned up on her doorstep, feeling extremely sorry for himself. Their reunion was a blissful one for her; this time, she was sure, he would stay.

But Ian had other ideas in the wake of his failure. University wasn't for him, he now decided. What he'd always wanted was to be a policeman, and he certainly didn't need a degree to do that. So he left university, got an entry-level post with the Metropolitan Police, and moved to London.

Tessa went with him. It would have been unthinkable not to do so, when he needed her so badly. Her own studies weren't important when weighed against Ian's needs, she told herself.

It was good at first, and lasted longer than any of their previous reunions. Tessa found a job, bought a flat, cosseted Ian and looked after his every need.

Then he met a sparky young WPC, and moved out. This absence, too, was longer than any to date, but eventually he returned. The pattern continued for years: he might be away from Tessa, with another woman, for weeks or even months, but she knew that he would always be back.

Until the day she learned that Ian was going to marry Amanda.

He didn't even have the decency to tell her face to face; she discovered the horrible truth when she opened the wedding invitation which he had so thoughtfully sent to her.

The prawn cocktail arrived and was served with due ceremony. 'I'm called Rob, by the way,' Tessa's companion said quietly as their inquisitive tablemates tucked into the mounds of soft pink.

She moistened her lips and swallowed, offering him a tremulous smile. 'Tessa.'

'A pretty name. Tell me about yourself, Tessa.'

'There's not much to tell.' She stuck her miniaturised spoon into the prawns – pink shrouded in pinkness – but knew that she was incapable of eating; as she twisted the spoon round she could hear in her head her father's sharp voice: *Don't play with your food, Tessa*.

Inspired, perhaps, by that image, she began to recite the bare bones of her life. 'My father is a vicar,' she said. 'My mother is . . . dead. I work at an advertising agency in London, as a copy writer.' *And sit up straight*, continued her father's voice in her head. *Be proud of your height*.

Tessa straightened her back, deliberately. For a woman she was exceptionally tall: slender and striking, when she wasn't trying so hard to be self-effacing. Her finely textured pale blonde hair was worn short, and ruffled out round her head like feathers, or dandelion down. Today she was wearing, in complete variance with her mood, a turquoise slip dress which complemented her pale colouring and showed off her slim body and her long legs. The dress had been her one gesture of defiance, bought specially for the occasion, and she wasn't at all sure that it hadn't been a mistake.

She couldn't think of anything else to say about herself, not without mentioning Ian. And she would not mention him, not now. 'And that's about it,' she said. 'Tell me about you,' she added with some effort, and it seemed important to finish with his name, 'Rob.'

'I work with computers.' He conveyed a spoonful of glistening prawns to his mouth. 'IT.'

'That sounds boring,' Tessa said without thinking, before she could stop herself, then widened her eyes in horror at her gaffe.

He seemed amused rather than offended. 'Not at all. I love it. Computers are . . . predictable. By and large. Not like people.'

At that statement, both of them turned, drawn by an irresistible urge, to look towards the top table, where the bride and groom were spooning prawns into each other's mouth and laughing uproariously.

'I met Amanda at work,' Rob said, though he hadn't really intended to mention Amanda.

Amanda. She looked incredibly beautiful, thought Tessa. Of course, all brides were meant to look beautiful, but Amanda's beauty wouldn't be removed with the confection of a wedding dress, as was the case with so many others. She was a redhead of the rich coppery sort, with thick glossy curls piled on her head and escaping in artful tendrils beside her cheeks. Her complexion was creamy, enhanced by the ivory of her gown. And she was petite, small of stature but with voluptuous breasts, all too evident in the *décolletage* of creamy lace and pearls. In the receiving line, when it had been Tessa's turn to shake the bride's hand, she'd towered over the tiny Amanda, feeling gawky, giraffe-like, monstrous in the presence of such miniature perfection.

The wedding was the first time she'd glimpsed Amanda, and the need to see her was the main reason that Tessa had come, in spite of her instincts. All Tessa had really wanted to do today was to curl up in a foetal ball in her bed, but she was driven to see the woman that Ian had chosen, the woman for whom he'd left her for the final time.

And the reality of Amanda was even worse than Tessa had feared. It would have been bad enough if she'd been vaguely like Tessa only prettier, but she couldn't have been more unlike Tessa in every way. She certainly didn't need to ask herself what Ian could see in a woman like Amanda when he could have married her instead; it was all too obvious what he'd seen in her.

Tessa knew that other people considered her foolish – a doormat, a victim – for continuing to take Ian back, time after time. But it was a deliberate choice to do so. One day, she'd always felt sure, he would realise that she was the one who could make him happy. After all, the good times, when they were together, were very good indeed – enough and more to make up for the times in between. And the fact of the matter was that she loved Ian, with all of his failings, and she wanted him, on whatever terms she could have him.

But he had married Amanda. That was the thing that hurt. Not just that it meant he wouldn't be coming back to Tessa, not ever again, but that he had *married* her. Made a lifetime commitment to her, to have and to hold. From this day forward. Words from the marriage service, so recently performed, echoed painfully in Tessa's head. Marriage was not to be undertaken 'unadvisedly, lightly, or wantonly'. And it was 'ordained for the procreation of children.'

Amanda would have Ian's children. That, perhaps, was the most painful thing of all. The one thing Tessa yearned to give him, after she had given him everything else that she could possibly offer.

But he hadn't wanted that.

Tessa had turned thirty that year, and her biological clock had gone into overdrive. She wanted to marry Ian, and she wanted to bear his child.

When, during their last long extended period together, she'd approached the subject, tentatively, Ian had laughed. Marriage was not for him, he'd said. And as for children –

forget it. 'Can you imagine me as a father?' he'd said with disbelief.

She could. But he had married Amanda, and now it was Amanda who would give him babies.

From their exalted position at the top table, Amanda and Ian smugly surveyed the guests: their friends and relations who had been gathered together in this place at such short notice.

The wedding had been arranged with what some might consider unseemly speed. Ian, in the clueless way of bridegrooms, took it all for granted, not realising the frantic machinations that had taken place behind the scenes; having landed him, Amanda was going to take no chances that he might slip off her hook, so she gave him very little time to do so. Ordinarily, the wedding venue, a posh country house hotel in Hertfordshire, was booked up at least a year in advance, but Amanda's father, an influential solicitor in nearby Harpenden, had managed to pull a few strings, and here they were.

'Poor old Rob and your Tessa seem to be getting on together,' Amanda pointed out with a malicious smile. Seating them together had been her idea, but Ian had agreed that it was a splendid one, a good joke. Now, feeling vaguely guilty about it, he wasn't so sure. He was fond of Tessa, in his way: she was a good kid, a real brick. She'd always been good to him, had never reproached him when he'd strayed, like most women would have done. And they'd had some good times together, there was no doubt about it. At times he had thought he would probably settle down with Tessa eventually. It was only just at the end, when she'd started nagging him about getting married, that he'd known he had to get out. Not just marriage, but babies, for Chrissakes. Tessa wanted a bloody baby. That was the last straw.

And then he'd met Amanda. He turned and looked at her now with dazzled pride. His prize, his wife.

They had met just a few months ago, in the line of duty for

Ian. Amanda, leaving work late one evening after an extended working day, had been mugged on her way to her car. Ian, responding to the call, had been the police officer to whom she had given the account of her frightening ordeal.

He remembered her now as she had been when he had first seen her: not triumphant in her wedding dress, but terrified and vulnerable, her eyes enormous with shock, a scratch on her cheek where she'd been shoved to the pavement. Ian had felt protective, had wanted to catch the bastard who had done this to her and break his neck.

Of course, the mugger had never been caught. But Ian found that he couldn't get the beautiful victim out of his mind. He had her phone number amongst the paperwork. One day, when Tessa's ruminations about a baby were really getting to him, he rang Amanda at work and invited her out for a drink.

She'd said no at first, and again the second time he rang her. She was living with someone, she told him. Not available. But something in her voice gave him hope. He persisted, and eventually she agreed to meet him after work for a drink. Just a drink, nothing more, she emphasised.

They had their drink, and that was it. A week later, when he was finally able to persuade her to repeat the experience, things progressed no farther. A drink, and then she was off home to Rob.

Ian knew that he was good-looking, well-built and attractive to women. He was not used to women who found his charms resistible, and the more Amanda resisted, the more determined he was to break down her resistance. For weeks he tried to get her into bed, and for weeks she held him at arm's length. She would see him occasionally, yes, but that was it.

He was obsessed by her, maddened, inflamed with desire for her. Unattainable, she was all he wanted.

And then it had all happened with such dizzying speed. She had finally gone to bed with him – at the flat of an accommodating friend, one unforgettable afternoon – and it had been beyond his wildest dreams. The next thing Ian knew, they were looking in jewellery shop windows at engagement rings, and scarcely more than a few short weeks later here they were, the solitaire sapphire which matched her eyes joined by a gold band to signify that she was his wife.

His wife. Ian didn't quite know how it had happened, but at the moment, smiling at her, stroking her wrist in a pro- prietorial way, he considered himself the luckiest man on earth.

'Do you think it will last?' The brunette in the red dress, who happened to be a cousin of Ian's, was in the ladies' room, re-applying her scarlet lipstick. The meal had been con- sumed, from prawn cocktails through veal cordon bleu to brandy-snap baskets with strawberries; soon it would be time for speeches, toasts, cutting of the wedding cake, and dancing. She addressed her question to the woman next to her at the long mirror, a blonde dressed as a bridesmaid, who was teasing her careful coiffure into shape with her fingers.

It was the sort of remark, flippant and cynical, that one made at weddings. But the blonde considered it seriously, tilting her head to one side and meeting the other woman's eyes in the mirror, though they had been strangers till that moment. 'Well, that depends,' she said. 'If Amanda really wants it to, it will.' She was, in fact, Amanda's oldest friend; they'd grown up together in Harpenden, and she knew Amanda probably better than anyone did. She understood, for instance, that her own pale leaf-green bridesmaid's dress had been chosen by Amanda with the utmost care, in a colour flattering as a backdrop to Amanda though unbecoming to its wearer, and cut in a simple style that posed no danger of upstaging the bride.

'What do you mean?'

The reply was succinct, and delivered with a knowing smile. 'Amanda always gets what she wants. She always has.'

'And Amanda wanted Ian?' the brunette extrapolated.

'She got him, didn't she?'

The brunette leaned closer to the mirror and inspected her lipstick minutely, pursing her lips, then licking them. 'Now, that's interesting,' she said to her own reflection. 'Because I've known Ian all my life, and he's only interested in things that he can't have.' She capped the tube of lipstick and dropped it into her tiny bag, then turned to her companion. 'I remember when we were kids, he always wanted my toys. I had a stuffed dog once,' she recalled. 'He fancied it and wanted me to give it to him. He was desperate to have that dog – he begged, he cried, and finally he gave me all his pocket money in return for it. And as soon as he had it, he lost interest. He played with it for about ten minutes, then left it out in the rain, and never gave it another thought.'

The blonde was quick on the uptake. 'That *is* interesting,' she agreed, looking at the other woman with raised eyebrows. 'So I suppose the answer to your question is: wait and see.'

Tessa found talking to Rob surprisingly easy. He was a good listener, and she told him a great deal more about her relationship with Ian than she had intended. He told her about himself, as well: about his job, and his computers, and his life with Amanda. Though his delivery was unemotional, the muscles of his face very much under control, empathetic Tessa glimpsed behind that controlled mask a vulnerability which made her like him rather more than she had expected to. By the time they reached the end of the meal, she felt as if she had known him for a long time.

Now it was time for the speeches and the toasts: the groom's toast to the bridesmaids, the best man's tribute to the bride, and the bride's father's encomium to the happy couple. Tessa knew that these would be difficult for her to listen to, and thought about leaving at that point, but realised that her departure would be marked. During the final toast, at one particularly fulsome phrase delivered by the jowly red-complexioned man who was Amanda's father, Rob caught her eye with a wink and she felt oddly cheered. After all, she thought, he was suffering too, and if he could put a brave face on it, so could she.

The cake was cut with due ceremony, and the band tuned up for the first dance. Later there would be a disco, stretching late into the night, with loud music and strobe lights, but for now there was a traditional live combo, primed to play the old favourites. Amanda and Ian glided on to the dance floor, the tall muscular groom and his petite red-haired bride. The long lace train of her dress was looped to her wrist; she had shed her veil, and she looked exquisite. Ian smiled down at his bride, his prize, as though all the treasure of the world was there in his arms.

Rob watched the lone pair on the dance floor, his face devoid of emotion. Then he turned to Tessa abruptly. 'Come on – let's join them.'

She stared at him, uncomprehending.

'I'm asking you to dance with me, Tessa.'

She shrank back. 'But we can't, Rob. The first dance is just for the bride and groom.'

For just a second she saw a flash of some strong emotion cross his face, to be instantly replaced by the controlled mask. 'Bugger the bride and groom,' he said in a soft voice that nonetheless carried to the people at their table and beyond. His eyes locked with Tessa's, challenging her.

Something of the spirit of defiance that had led her to buy the turquoise dress surged in her unexpectedly. Tessa straightened her shoulders and rose from the table, giving Rob her hand. 'Bugger the bride and groom,' she repeated, head held high, as he led her on to the dance floor.

As a gesture it was magnificent, and if Rob's idea had been to get attention, he succeeded splendidly. Everyone was talking about them, and those who had been unaware of their mutual status as the rejected ones were soon filled in by others.

They made a very striking couple on the dance floor, well matched in height: Rob was as tall as Ian, which is to say just a shade taller than Tessa, and his slim frame was more suited to dancing than Ian's muscularity was. Inspired by Rob's confidence as a dancer, Tessa forgot to be self-conscious and self-effacing; instead of hunching over she stood straight. The turquoise dress showed off her figure and her colouring to great advantage, and the contrast between the two heads of hair – hers pale and feathery, his smooth and dark – was remarkable, and pleasing. Altogether, people agreed, they made a most handsome pair. And how appropriate, how fitting that they should.

Tessa felt, as she danced with Rob, as if she were another person; it was as though the real Tessa were sitting on the sidelines, watching this other woman whirling about the dance floor with such aplomb. It was a strange feeling, of being disembodied, and unlike anything she had ever experienced before.

And for that brief time, dancing with Rob, she knew herself to be happy. The realisation astonished her.

Too soon, though, the band departed and the DJ arrived for the disco. The lights were dimmed, the coloured strobe lights began flashing, and the music screeched out of the gargantuan speakers at ear-splitting volume. Tessa's euphoria was immediately replaced by a pounding headache.

Now, she thought, was the time to leave. She had stayed a respectable length of time, and now could make her escape under the cover of darkness and perhaps no one would even notice.

The music was too loud for conversation, too loud even for a shouted goodbye. Tessa picked up her handbag and pantomimed to Rob that she was going. 'Thank you,' she mouthed, knowing that it was inadequate as an expression of her gratitude to him, but hoping he would understand.

'You're going?' he mouthed in reply.

Tessa nodded, and rose from the table. Rob rose too, following her out of the room and out into the gathering twilight of late spring. After the oppressive heat of the crowded room, the evening air was like an exotic balm, and the sudden silence was blissful. The bass thump of the music was still audible, but the difference was so marked that the noise of the disco now seemed like a bad dream.

Tessa gulped in lungfuls of the refreshing air and felt her headache easing. 'Whew. That's better,' she breathed. 'I'm sorry – I just couldn't cope any longer.'

'You did very well,' Rob said softly.

'Thanks to you.'

They smiled at one another.

'Well, it's been nice meeting you,' Tessa said awkwardly, after a moment. She realised, as she turned from him, that they were out in the country, there were no taxis available, and she would have to go back inside to phone for one.

'Wait,' Rob said. 'You didn't come by car, did you?'

'No, I don't drive,' she admitted. 'I came up by train.'

'Then let me take you home,' he said.

'Oh, no. It would be out of your way. But you could', she added, 'give me a lift to the station at Harpenden. That is, if you're ready to leave. I don't want to take you away from the party if you're not ready to go.'

Rob took her arm and led her through the car park to his car. 'I insist on driving you home,' he said. 'I'm more than ready to leave, and it won't be far out of my way.'

'But I live near Victoria, and you live in Islington,' she protested; this much they had established during their conversation. 'It's miles out of your way. Just drop me at the station, and I'll be fine. The Thameslink trains go straight through to Blackfriars, and from there it's only a short tube journey on the Circle Line.'

'Methinks thou dost protest too much,' Rob grinned. He

unlocked the car and held the door open for her. 'And there's no use arguing, because I insist.'

When they got to her flat, nearly an hour later, by some miracle there was a parking place right in front. She invited him in for coffee.

He stayed for breakfast.

And a few weeks later, as soon as the arrangements could be made, they were married.

Chapter 2

Tessa and Rob's wedding was a small, private affair, at the opposite end of the spectrum from Amanda and Ian's gala matrimonial celebration.

They were married at a register office, on a Friday morning. The two witnesses were also the only two guests. One was the registrar's wife, and the other was Andrew Darling, a work colleague of Tessa's.

Tessa had invited her father, but at such short notice he had been unable to come. She was not surprised; parish duties had always been his top priority. When she had rung him with the news, and the invitation, there had been a long pause at the other end of the phone. 'You're not being married in church?' he'd asked. Tessa knew that she had disappointed him; in fact he would most certainly have expected her to have the wedding in his church, or at the very least would have expected her to ask him to come and perform the ceremony in London. But a church wedding was not what Rob wanted, and Tessa was used to disappointing her father. She still, after all these years, minded.

Tessa also minded that Rob's parents were not present, and had not even been invited. She had been looking forward to meeting her new in-laws, and was surprised when Rob shrugged off her questions about them.

His parents were divorced, he told her. A long time ago,

when he was still at school. His father, a doctor, had remarried and emigrated to New Zealand; Rob hadn't seen him in years.

And his mother he refused to talk about. Yes, she was still alive, but he had no contact with her. He didn't know how she was, and didn't want to know.

This was something that Tessa couldn't understand, hard as she tried. Her own mother had died when she was quite young, and the ache of losing her, of growing up without a mother, had never gone away. The idea that Rob could turn his back on his mother horrified her.

There had to be a reason for it, she knew. Perhaps Rob blamed his mother for the break-up of the marriage, for driving his father to the other end of the earth. But when she asked him about it, in those weeks before the wedding, his face grew tight-lipped and his eyes opaque. He would not discuss his mother.

And so the wedding was a quiet affair. After the short and unceremonious ceremony, the bride and groom repaired to a nearby McDonald's for the wedding breakfast, taking their witness Andrew with them. There were awkward silences over the Egg McMuffins; it was the first meeting for Andrew and Rob, and they found that they had little to say to one another. That left Tessa, as a bridge between the two of them, to make whatever conversation there was, and though she tried, her heart wasn't really in it.

This was not, somehow, what she had ever imagined her wedding breakfast would be. The fact that she had always expected Ian to be the one sharing it she put resolutely out of her mind; Ian was now ancient history, and she had no intention of beginning her marriage with regrets on that score. But to be sitting on a moulded red plastic chair in McDonald's, her modest bouquet wilting on a Formica table which was embellished with the grotesquely smiling face of Ronald McDonald and strewn with polystyrene cartons and cardboard coffee cups – somehow it didn't seem the ideal start for what she promised herself would be an ideal marriage.

Before long Andrew made his excuses, averring that he had to get to work. He shook Rob's hand, congratulating him in a formal manner, then took Tessa's hand. 'I'll see you soon,' he said, looking into her eyes. 'After the honeymoon.' He held both her hand and her eyes a fraction longer than politeness dictated, then gave her a quick peck on the cheek.

Friday morning was always a busy time for Linda Nicholls. She had, as usual, spent the first part of the week doing the laundry – all of those bedlinens, and the other things as well – and on Fridays she had to think about food. Buying it, preparing it. Before they'd opened the Asda supermarket in Southgate, not far from her house, she'd had to go farther afield for the shopping. After all, she had lived many years in Southgate and was known by sight, if not by name, to the local merchants, and she couldn't take the chance of awkward questions about the contents of her shopping basket. The Asda was suitably anonymous, and even if she saw someone she knew – which wasn't likely, as Linda didn't really have close friends, and kept herself to herself – she could make up some excuse, laugh it off as a joke.

Sometimes of late, she'd had a bit of help with the shopping, the laundry, and other things. Geeta Patel, a girl who worked at the residential care home just down the street, had been willing to take on the extra work, fitting it in amongst her hours at the nursing home. Geeta was glad of the extra income, as she was helping to support a large family of younger brothers and sisters, and Linda paid her generously. She was a bright girl, and hard-working; she'd been a god-send, as Linda's business seemed to be booming these days, and Geeta's skills and experience fitted right in with Linda's needs.

But today was one of those days when Geeta was tied up at

the nursing home, so Linda had to do all of the shopping and preparation herself. A bit later in the day, help of a different sort would be forthcoming from Greg Reynolds, the man whom Linda called, in her own mind, her boyfriend, but whom others, in view of Linda's age if not Greg's, might more accurately have described as her lover. His regular job was as a fitness trainer at a gym, so he had flexible hours, in addition to a flexible body, and both could come in handy on a Friday, when there was so much to be done.

Coming out of the house, Linda was disconcerted to see her next-door neighbour, Hilda Steggall, already in the adjacent front garden, watering her beloved herbaceous borders. But she hid her dismay behind a neutral, neighbourly smile. 'Good morning, Mrs Steggall,' she said; though they'd been neighbours for years, they'd not progressed to a first-name basis.

'Good morning, Mrs Nicholls. It's going to be a fine day.' Hilda Steggall glanced upwards at the cloudless blue sky with a smug smile, as though she had personally ordered the day up, and was taking full credit for it.

'It certainly looks that way.' Linda opened the garage door; though the Asda was only a few minutes' walk away, she would take the car. The shopping would be too heavy to carry.

Mrs Steggall watched her neighbour's back as she disappeared into the garage. Linda Nicholls cut a trim figure; she was small-boned and short of stature, and kept herself in shape. Black-haired and blue-eyed, she was possessed of a rather brittle prettiness, and the lines etched round her thin lips in repose – lines which suggested that her mouth was often pursed, as if bestowing chaste kisses – were the main indicators that she was not as young as she might have appeared at first glance. Linda was nearly fifty, not all that many years younger than Hilda Steggall, but with her sleek black bob and her short straight skirt showing off her attractive legs, she might have passed for forty or even thirty-five. 'Mutton dressed as lamb,' Mrs Steggall murmured to herself; it was one of the kinder epithets she applied to her next-door neighbour. Stand-offish, unneighbourly, and, Hilda Steggall was all too afraid, no better than she should be.

The honeymoon was wonderful: two weeks of bliss. They spent it in the Azores, at a secluded and luxurious resort hotel.

Rob had often holidayed abroad, sometimes with Amanda, and when she couldn't spare the time from her job, by himself. He didn't mind being on his own, and travelling held no terrors for him. The choice of honeymoon location had been his idea.

Tessa's travel experiences were far more limited: limited, in fact, to just one foreign holiday. That had been several years ago, a cut-price package tour to Greece with Ian, and it had been a disaster.

She had looked forward to it so much, her only fear at the time being that Ian would go off with someone else before the holiday came round, and the whole thing would be cancelled.

But Ian had stayed, and the long-anticipated holiday turned into a nightmare. It started at the airport, when the ancient charter plane was grounded for several hours with mechanical problems. By the time it took off, bad temper and tiredness prevailed amongst the passengers; Ian had passed the time drinking, which when done in excess always put him into a foul mood.

The hotel turned out to be filthy and cramped, virtually uninhabitable, serving vile food. The beach was dirty and crammed with loutish British holidaymakers. And on the very first day, unused to the Mediterranean sun and its effects, Tessa, with her fair English skin, spent the day on the beach in a bikini, receiving such a severe sunburn that it was agony even to be touched by Ian. That put paid to the anticipated delights of the holiday; she spent the rest of the fortnight in misery, watching wretchedly as Ian drank too much and flirted with other women.

She had never wanted to repeat the experience.

But the honeymoon was different. The location was like paradise, with warm blue waters and a beautiful secluded beach. This time Tessa had learned her lesson: she slathered herself with high-factor sunscreen and wore a wide- brimmed straw hat, and was thus able to spend hours on the beach and in the water. They swam, they lazed in the sun, they ate delectable food and sipped ambrosial drinks, they hired a car and explored the surrounding countryside.

And they made love. Several times each day, several times each night. Sometimes urgently, other times lazily, but each time it was a revelation, and a joy. Their pleasure was mutual and reciprocal; Tessa found Rob a considerate lover, as concerned for her pleasure as his own, and that was so far from what she had known with Ian as to constitute a different sort of experience altogether, one that turned 'making love' into more than a euphemism for something cruder. Rob's delight in her was evident as well, and it thrilled Tessa to be the instrument of his gratification.

Inevitably, though, after a fortnight of romance and ecstasy the honeymoon was over, and with regret they left it behind them, and returned to London to begin their new life together as man and wife.

To their relief, neither the romance nor the ecstasy ended with the honeymoon, which is not to say that a certain amount of adjustment wasn't required.

Tessa put her flat on the market and moved her possessions into Rob's house. They both agreed that it made sense: his house was more than adequate for the two of them, and though there was some merit in the idea of selling both properties and buying something a bit larger, there was no point in both of them uprooting themselves when it wasn't necessary.

That was the theory. Tessa had no qualms about leaving

her flat, with its memories of Ian, behind, and was delighted with Rob's small Islington house. It was only after she moved in that she discovered it to be haunted by Amanda's ghost. Though Amanda had in fact not spent very much of her time in the house, it had been her home for some six years, and Tessa was hyperconscious of the little things that spoke of her presence: the arrangement of the furniture in the front room, the sleek metal blinds at all of the windows, the half-used bottle of shampoo in the shower that she hadn't felt worth taking with her when she moved out. Amanda had slept in this bed, on these sheets, thought Tessa, and even the empty half of the wardrobe exuded a faint hint of her perfume.

Tessa also had to adjust to Rob's solitary habits, his need for privacy. Each evening between supper and bedtime, he retreated to his computer room, shutting the door behind him and leaving her to fend for herself. While she tried not to mind, and spent the evening hours reading books – an activity of which she never tired – she couldn't help feeling a bit hurt; after all, those hours were, apart from the weekends, supper-time and the hours spent in bed, the only time that they had together. Rob refused to discuss it: it was not negotiable, he said. It didn't mean that he didn't love her, or want to be with her, and at least he was in the house – wasn't it better than skiving off down to the pub with his mates every night like other men did?

Ian, for example, he might have said but didn't. Early on in their relationship she had told him of her frustrations with Ian, one of which was the way he took off for the pub each evening. Rob had said, self- righteously, that he would never do that. Tessa didn't really see the difference; the result, for her, was the same.

The biggest adjustment, perhaps, was the fact that Tessa now had to commute to work. The chief attraction of her flat, in a distinctly unposh road near Victoria – which some dignified by referring to as Pimlico, though that was stretching things a bit – had been its proximity to her work. She'd been no more than a ten-minute walk from the building housing the advertising agency where she'd worked since her arrival in London, and that had suited her very well. Tessa, vaguely claustrophobic, disliked the Underground, and found the bus system confusing and slow; since she didn't drive, that left her few options.

Her commute now involved a fifteen-minute walk to the tube station at Caledonian Road, a change from the Piccadilly Line to the Victoria Line at the always-crowded King's Cross station, and a five-minute walk at the other end. She hated it: hated the descent into the bowels of the earth, the dirty trains, the rush-hour crowds pressed cheek-by-jowl. On a bad day, at the height of rush hour, it could take nearly an hour to traverse London in this way.

Each evening she complained about it to Rob over supper, recounting the horrors of that day's journey: a broken-down train at Hyde Park Corner, necessitating a long wait for the next one; a throng of shoppers embarking at Oxford Circus, one of them whacking her with an unwieldy parcel and leaving a massive bruise; a 'security alert' at King's Cross, closing the station and forcing her to take an expensive taxi all the way to Victoria; a smelly man who leered at her and fondled her bottom when they were crushed in uncomfortable proximity during the evening rush hour.

Rob exhibited a certain degree of sympathy for these indignities, but grew impatient at their repetition. In the way of men, he failed to understand that the telling was sufficient therapy in itself, and tried to seek solutions. 'If you hate it so much,' he said on several occasions, 'why don't you give it up? After all, Tessa, you don't *need* to work.'

That much was true: there was no financial necessity for Tessa to continue working. They could live quite comfortably without her wages. Rob owned the Islington house outright, with no mortgage – his absent father had bought it for him when he turned twenty-one – and he himself earned a handsome salary, more than enough to support the two of them.

When he had made this suggestion several times, the idea took hold. Tessa enjoyed her job, but her affection for it fell short of passion. And the vision of domesticity held a certain appeal for her. She could make a proper home for Rob, look after him and pamper him. Most important, she could have a baby . . .

Rob's baby. Her biological clock ticked with more urgency than ever.

Tessa handed in her notice, and worked out her time.

On Tessa's final day of work, her colleagues held a small farewell party for her, with cake and drink and cards and a leaving gift. Tessa was touched.

She had worked at the advertising agency for ten years. That was not an inconsiderable time to be in one place, and it would have been expected that she would have made some close friends amongst her colleagues. But that had not really been the case: Tessa was shy, and held herself back from their joint plans and activities. Convinced that she was uninteresting, she rebuffed any advances as being evidence of kindness or even pity rather than real interest. All of her colleagues liked and respected her, and would have welcomed the chance to know her better, but she'd never given them that chance.

Andrew Darling was the one near-exception. He worked in close proximity to her, in the next cubicle, and perhaps he had persevered harder than the others. At any rate, he and Tessa had developed, over several years, a good working relationship which almost verged on friendship. It had never been evident to Tessa that Andrew would have wished for more than that, and had once had hopes that, Ian out of the way, he might stand a chance with her.

Andrew had been the one who, the night before Ian's wedding to Amanda, had taken Tessa out for a drink after work, had fortified her courage by urging her to go to the wedding, and to wear the turquoise dress. 'Get him out of your system, once and for all,' he'd said, proffering a handkerchief for her tears.

She had followed his advice, and had been grateful to him ever since. After all, Tessa realised, if she hadn't gone to Ian's wedding, she would not have met Rob.

Andrew's window of opportunity had been extremely small, and he had missed out. He was all too aware of that as he lingered behind on that last day, watching as Tessa cleared out her desk and packed her personal belongings in a couple of carrier bags. 'Come out for a drink with me?' he suggested. 'One last time?' The night before Ian's wedding had been the first time he'd asked her out, the first time he'd felt it appropriate to do so, to provide friendship and solace. Perhaps if he'd made the offer earlier, and more frequently, they wouldn't be in this situation, with her leaving, and him facing the prospect of not seeing her again.

Tessa thought about the long commute, about Rob waiting at home for her, waiting for his supper. 'No,' she said. 'No, thanks.'

'Listen,' he said awkwardly. 'You'll stay in touch, won't you?'

The others had all said the same thing. But Tessa's mind had already moved on, away from the world of advertising and into the beguiling world of prams and nappies. 'Yes, of course,' she said, not believing that he really meant it, knowing that she wouldn't.

'Because,' he went on, looking down at his hands rather than at Tessa, 'I feel responsible for you. After all, I *was* the witness at your wedding.'

She smiled at him: dear kind Andrew, the closest she'd had to a friend for years. He was certainly no figure of romance, shorter than she by a couple of inches, ordinary-looking, with earnest brown puppy-dog eyes and sandy hair parted at the centre and drawn back behind his ears in a neat pony-tail. And he favoured baggy trousers, denim shirts, and outrageous ties – a far cry from shining armour. But he *had* rescued her from that particular predicament, and Tessa was grateful. Asking him had been a spur-of-the-moment thing; she hadn't known whom else to ask. 'Yes,' she agreed. 'I appreciated that. It was good of you to take the morning off work.'

'Just remember, if you ever need me,' he continued, 'you know where to find me.' He looked up then, engaging her eyes. 'I mean, if things go wrong . . .'

'Don't be silly,' Tessa said lightly. 'What could go wrong? I love Rob. He loves *me*.' She paused, and went on in a different voice, almost a whisper, not quite sure why she was confiding this to Andrew. 'And don't tell anyone this, not yet, but I'm going to have his baby.'

'Then you're . . .'

'Not yet,' she said. 'But soon. Soon.'

There was a long pause. 'Remember what I said,' Andrew repeated. 'If you ever need me, I'm here.'

On that same Friday, Linda Nicholls again carried out her Friday routine, though this time she managed to go out to do her shopping without being observed by Hilda Steggall.

It was just as well, because on that day she was also making her monthly trip to the recycling centre, and in the garage she loaded the boot of the car. There were boxes and boxes of jars and bottles; it was safer to take them to the recycling centre than to put them in the bin for the rubbish collectors. And there were newspapers as well. Saturday papers, Sunday papers, though she wasn't much of a newspaper reader herself.

At the recycling centre she was alone, and could take her time disposing of her detritus, unobserved. Linda enjoyed pushing the jars one by one through the round opening of the collecting bin, listening to them shatter as they hit the bottom. Then the bottles, and finally, less satisfyingly, the newspapers, which made only a muffled thumping noise as they went through the slot and fell within.

But one newspaper caught her eye as she collected an arm-load from her boot, and the name NICHOLLS jumped off the page at her. Wedding announcements, she noted, and looked at the date of the paper: it was several weeks old, and the date given in the announcement was older still. Robin John Nicholls, it said, to Tessa Catherine Rowan, in London.

For a long moment she stared at the words, as their meaning sank in. Then, thoughtfully, Linda tore the page from the paper, folded it, and put it in her pocket.

The excitement, the anticipation, were almost too much for Father Theo. Sweat sheened his brow, his breathing was shallow, and the last thing that he was thinking about was the prayer that came so easily, so routinely, to his lips.

It was always thus on a Friday afternoon. The congregation for evensong was small, as ever: two or three elderly ladies at the most. Father Theo could say the service – the words so familiar – without being conscious of it at all.

On Sunday morning it would be different, of course. Sunday would find him back here in his stall, sick with shame and guilt. It was the same every week. But this was Friday, and between now and Sunday . . .

After evensong, Father Theo stood at the back of the church, managing with difficulty to hide his impatience with his departing congregation. If only they would go. Just go, and let him get on with things. But Miss Smith, as always, seemed to take forever to gather up her shopping bags and her stick, and Mrs Cater would inevitably linger to tell him of her latest aches and pains. Any other time he would listen to her, and willingly; Father Theo was a good priest, a loving shepherd of his flock. But this was Friday.

Friday. Friday. The word beat in his head as, the congre-

gation finally dispatched and the church locked, Father Theo
hurried back to the clergy house.

Mrs Williams, the housekeeper, was nowhere in sight, for
which Father Theo was enormously grateful. If only he could
manage to get back out again without being intercepted
by her, he would save precious minutes. Father Theo was a
somewhat heavy-set man, but he negotiated the stairs quickly,
light-footed and silent. At the top of the stairs he turned the
knob of his bedroom door and slipped inside; the room wasn't
locked, as Mrs Williams needed access to clean it.

But the bottom drawer of his chest of drawers *was* locked.
Father Theo fumbled in his pocket for his keys and inserted
the proper one into the lock, bending over to pull the drawer
out. Then he opened his ornate antique wardrobe and
retrieved the large black holdall from where he'd stashed
it the week before: at the bottom, beneath the row of black
shirts and dark suits, behind his extra pair of neatly polished
black shoes. The holdall was empty, innocent in itself; even if
Mrs Williams snooped in his wardrobe as she hung up his
newly laundered and pressed shirts, she would find nothing
exceptional about the holdall.

He heaved it out on to the bed, and with a nervous glance
at the door lest Mrs Williams choose that moment to come
in, he filled it with things from the bottom drawer. It didn't
take long; everything he needed to take with him was in that
drawer, and packing quickly had become part of his weekly
routine.

Father Theo snapped the holdall shut, re-locked the bottom
drawer, and closed the door of his room behind him. Down
the stairs, then; the front door was in sight. But Mrs Williams
caught him just as he reached for the knob. 'You're off, then?'
She stated the obvious, her black eyes taking in the holdall,
Father Theo's stealthy tread and the start he gave as she spoke.

'Why . . . yes.' He tried to keep his voice steady, betraying
neither irritation, defensiveness, nor guilt.

'And you'll be back tomorrow night?' she probed.

'Or Sunday morning at the latest.' He *would* stay till Sunday morning, he had already determined, even though it meant a very early start. 'I'll be back in time for the eight o'clock Low Mass.'

Mrs Williams didn't believe his story that each weekend he visited a priest in south London, an old friend from theological college days. He knew that she didn't believe him, but he didn't care; there was no way, short of having him followed, that she could disprove his story. Saturday was his day off, and what he did on his day off was his own business. He'd even bought a mobile phone so that he could be reached in an emergency; he certainly wasn't going to take the chance of giving Mrs Williams – or anyone else – a contact number.

Father Theo turned the knob and opened the front door, then slipped through and pulled it shut behind him. He was free. He was on his way. The weight of the holdall was as nothing to him as anticipation sped his footsteps towards the bus stop.

Chapter 3

Tessa's childhood had not, in its entirety, been a happy one. That is to say that her childhood was divided into two distinct periods: before her mother's death, and after. The first few years, while her mother was alive, Tessa had known herself to be a loved and cherished child. Her mother had instilled in Tessa her own love of books, reading to her from the time she was in her cot and teaching the little girl to read herself long before she reached school age. She had always been there, available for her only child: reading to her, making up stories for her, playing with her, taking her on outings, surrounding her with love.

And then her mother had died. Suddenly, tragically. To this day her father refused to talk about the circumstances of her mother's death, but Tessa knew, had always known – as one does know these things, even at a young age – that her father blamed her for it, that she was somehow responsible. One day her mother had been alive, vital, loving, and the next day she was gone. Tessa couldn't remember what had happened in between. She just knew that it was her fault; the reproach was there, silent, whenever her father looked at her.

He had always been a conscientious vicar, lavishing his time and his energies on his parish. But after his wife's death, Tessa's father had thrown himself into his work with renewed passion, as if by staying away from the vicarage, now bereft of his wife's presence, he could somehow avoid the fact of her death.

A housekeeper had been taken on, and it was that house-keeper who had brought Tessa up from that time onwards. She was not an affectionate woman, nor an imaginative one, and Tessa was not her idea of what a little girl should be. Her nose always stuck in a book, she grumbled. Quiet, shy. How was she ever going to get on in the world?

Tessa's mechanism for survival was retreat. She spent much of her time shut in her room, avoiding the housekeeper, using books to shield her from the world. In her room, reading a book, she could forget for a time that her mother was dead, that her father was not there either.

Her mother had been a paragon of domesticity, the supreme vicar's wife, and had she lived, Tessa would have grown into that as well. But her mother's death had changed the pattern of Tessa's life beyond recognition, and though that domestic spark had never quite gone out, she had directed her energies in other directions, just as her father had.

Now, though, things were different. Domesticity beckoned Tessa, its siren call irresistible to her. At last she had her own house, her own family of sorts, and she could be to Rob – and to the children that they would have – the sort of nurturing force that her mother had been to her and her father.

As soon as she'd quit her job, she plunged into it head first, virtually wallowing in domesticity. She bought a thick cookery book and began working her way through the recipes, she re-arranged the furniture in the front room, she even took up gardening.

Rob's house – now her house as well – was not large, but in Tessa's eyes it was perfect. A Victorian mid-terrace, it was deep and narrow, the rooms running back and accessed by a corridor. Three floors: the ground floor held a front room with a bay, looking on to the road; a dark dining room in the centre; and a kitchen at the back, opening into a small garden, overgrown but full of potential. On the first floor, reached by a steep and rather narrow staircase, were two bedrooms, with a bathroom in between. Theirs was the front room, and the back room was Rob's computer hideaway. The floor above was really no more than a high-ceilinged attic, unfinished; the previous owners had filled it with unwanted rubbish which they'd not bothered to clear when they moved out, and Rob and Amanda had added to that in some small degree.

Most of the house had not been decorated in years. Rob had started with good intentions when he'd moved in; he had painted the front room, fixed up the computer room, then run out of steam. Amanda's main contribution had been the choosing of the metal blinds which adorned the windows instead of curtains.

Tessa hated the blinds, finding them fiddly to operate and sterile in appearance. She was determined to replace them, throughout the house, with curtains. And furthermore, she would make the curtains herself. Somehow, she felt, when she had done that, she would have reclaimed the house as her own, and banished the ghost of Amanda once and for all.

She went to John Lewis and chose the fabrics, bringing home samples for Rob's approval. Then she created a work-room for herself, in the little-used dining room.

One of the few things of her mother's that she owned was her sewing machine – a machine on which her mother had made clothes for the young Tessa. She remembered standing beside her mother, watching, rapt, as bits of fabric turned into dresses in her mother's expert hands.

She had always kept the sewing machine, as a sort of talis-man of her mother's memory, but she had never used it, had never wanted to use it. Now she wanted to; now was the time. She set it up on the dining room table, read the instruction manual, followed the directions for the complicated thread-ing procedure, oiled it carefully, and discovered that it worked. That first practice seam, carried out on one of the fabric samples, was marvelled over, and spurred her on.

First the bedroom, she decided; it was right that Amanda should be banished from the bedroom first of all. She chose, with Rob's agreement, a sprigged fabric, cheery without being too feminine. After the initial terror of cutting into the bolt of fabric, it was easy, and by the next weekend their bedroom had new curtains.

Tessa felt an enormous satisfaction in the accomplishment, and admitted to herself that she had done a good job.

After just a few weeks of sewing, cooking, gardening, and pottering round the local shops, she wondered how she had managed to waste so many years going off to work every day. This was so satisfying, so elemental somehow. Taking care of her husband, as he deserved to be taken care of.

Her husband: the words still gave her a little thrill of pleasure, tinged with disbelief. He was her husband. Hers, and not Amanda's.

Tessa was deeply in love with Rob. The long days at home gave her plenty of time to think about him, and each day, as her thoughts dwelt upon him, she missed him and loved him even more. Each day she could scarcely wait for his return home, and she usually met him at the front door with a kiss which did nothing to disguise her love for him, her desire for him. She discovered his favourite foods and learned to prepare them, making sure that not a day passed without serving him at least one of them. And on one of her trips to John Lewis she visited the knitting wool department, chose some wool of a blue which matched Rob's eyes, and taught herself to knit. She would make a jumper for him, to keep him warm next winter, with love knitted into every stitch.

Rob, naturally, was delighted with the newly domestic Tessa. Though it had been his idea for her to give up her job, he was surprised at the enthusiasm with which she had embraced her altered lifestyle. He benefited from it directly, of course: from the cooking and the decorating, and the attention which she lavished upon him each evening. The pampering, the nurturing: he'd never been looked after like that by Amanda.

Over a few weeks' time, under the force of Tessa's relentless domesticity, the pattern of their evenings altered. Often their reunion at the front door would lead them swiftly to the bedroom, making dinner late. Neither of them minded the delay. And after a delicious meal, when Rob would ordinarily have retreated to his computer room, he discovered himself lingering behind, basking in the glow of Tessa's love for him. As the nights drew in, he found himself spending much of the evening with her, sitting in the front room and watching her, in a soft pool of lamplight, her head bent over the blue wool and the needles clicking as she knitted a jumper for him. And when he did eventually go off to his computer room, where he used to remain sometimes until late at night, he now emerged in plenty of time to go to bed at a decent hour, to enjoy the delights that Tessa had to offer him.

She was happy. He was happy. They were happy together. Now, thought Tessa, just one thing was missing.

And so she stopped taking her birth control pills.

Linda Nicholls found, as the days and weeks passed, that she couldn't get that wedding announcement out of her mind. It caused her to think about things she had managed to suppress for years, and it made her conscious, in a way she had never been before, of her age.

She would be fifty next year. She sat at her dressing table and examined, in her magnifying mirror, the signs of encroaching age. Her hair was still as glossy and black as ever, with a bit of help from the bottle. But the grooves around her mouth seemed to have become more deeply etched, and had been joined by a pronounced web of lines below her eyes. Were her eyelids sagging? The flesh at her jaw line?

Would Greg still want her when she was fifty?

And in her line of work, it just wouldn't do to look old. Mature was all right, but not old and saggy.

She needed, Linda decided, a bit of judicious attention from a plastic surgeon. Nothing flashy or too obvious: a nip here, a tuck there, a few collagen injections to smooth things out.

But that sort of thing, done well, cost money. And she wasn't exactly rolling in it. The house was expensive to keep up, and there were a great many business expenses, including Geeta's wages.

She would have to find a way to supplement her income, to raise a bit of spare cash. Linda's eyes met those of her reflection in the mirror and nodded thoughtfully.

Tessa sensed the changes in her body immediately, and knew she was pregnant, even before she'd missed her first period, even before she did the test. Not for her the uncomprehending morning sickness, the slowness to grasp the truth. The test was nothing more than a confirmation of a fact she was already sure of, but nonetheless she trembled with excitement as she watched for the test strip to change colour.

Change it did, and at that moment Tessa felt her life turn upside down, the patterns rearranging themselves like the colours of a kaleidoscope.

She was having a baby. Rob's baby. Their lives would now be different, irrevocably, but in the very best way.

Tessa would now be utterly fulfilled, with a baby to love and care for. She would be everything to her baby that her mother had been to her. And Rob, she knew, would be a wonderful father. Together they would be a family. She wasn't greedy; more children would be nice, but she would be satisfied if this were the only one. Her baby. Their baby.

She stood in front of the mirror, that morning after she'd done the test, and looked at her body, at her flat stomach. Though she felt completely different already, she looked just the same as always. Strange to think that soon her body would change, would grow as her baby grew.

Her immediate impulse was to ring Rob at work, to blurt out the wonderful news to him before another moment passed. But she checked herself, and changed her mind, deciding not to tell him straight away. It was as if she needed some time, not to get used to the idea, but to hug it to herself. Soon she would share this baby with Rob, and they would enjoy it together, but for now she needed to commune with it herself, to accustom herself to its hold on her body.

It. Him. Her. Funny to think that even now, even when her baby was little more than a cluster of cells, its sex had already been determined. Tessa wouldn't know for a while, but already it was a him or a her.

She would be happy with either – delighted – but Tessa admitted to herself that she would prefer a girl. She didn't know much about little boys, and a girl would give her a chance, somehow, to redeem the unhappiness of her own childhood. And Rob would be wonderful with a little girl.

She couldn't go on thinking of her baby as *it*. From now on, Tessa determined, she would think of it as *her*.

Several weeks passed. If Rob noticed any change in Tessa, he attributed it to her continuing adjustment to the marriage and to staying at home. He certainly wasn't complaining: her nurturing behaviour increased, and so did her libido. If she wasn't plying him with his favourite foods, she was luring him to bed. Marriage suited them both very much, Rob decided, satisfied with himself and with her.

And then Tessa's body began subtly to change, though her stomach remained flat. Her small breasts swelled, like buds on a tree just before spring, and became tender; her skin took on a glow. There was some morning sickness and nausea, and in the afternoons, alone in the house, she felt increasingly tired, as though the baby growing inside her was sapping all of her energy. Still Rob noticed nothing, though by now she expected daily that he would put two and two together, or at least mention something.

By now she was beginning to feel that she'd left it too long to tell him. She had enjoyed, in a way, keeping the secret, but it was becoming embarrassing. And he had a right to know, to share her excitement and her joy.

So she planned a special evening. All of his very favourite foods for dinner: steak and kidney pie – though handling the slippery kidneys made her feel quite queasy – heaps of mashed potatoes, apple crumble with home-made custard. The table laid in the dining room rather than the kitchen, with candles and fresh flowers.

She met him at the door with a kiss, dressed in one of her best frocks, and with expensive scent dabbed behind her ears.

After the kiss, Rob held her at arm's length and observed her. 'You're looking rather smart tonight. And you smell wonderful. What's the special occasion? Are we going out? Have I forgotten something, then?'

Tessa gave a mysterious smile. 'You'll see. But we're staying in.'

'Oh, good.' He ran his hands over her breasts, anticipating pleasures to come. She had never looked so lovely to him as she looked then, her skin with a delicate flush and her eyes sparkling. How she had bloomed since their marriage! He noticed that her frock strained over her breasts, and desire stirred in him strongly.

She stepped back, away from his insistent hands. 'Dinner first, bed later,' she demurred.

His temporary disappointment faded when he saw the candles, the flowers, the steaming steak and kidney pie. The pie, in its own way, smelled almost as good as Tessa. 'My favourite,' he said.

'Yes.'

There was a bottle of wine on the table, a rather good

claret. Tessa, who didn't know much about wine, had asked the advice of the man at the wine merchant's in the Holloway Road, and this had been his recommendation. He'd even told her to let it breathe, so she'd opened it some time ago. Rob picked up the bottle and looked at the label with an approving nod, then extended it towards Tessa's glass.

She covered the glass with her hand. 'None for me.' Tessa hadn't been drinking alcohol at all since she'd known about the baby, but as she'd never been much of a drinker, Rob hadn't really noticed. Now he gave her a curious look. He filled his own glass, sat down, and raised the glass to his wife. 'Here's to whatever it is we're celebrating.'

By now she was feeling very nervous; she was sure that the deliberate spurning of alcohol would have given the secret away, if nothing else had. But she went ahead and served the pie, and Rob helped himself to a mountain of mashed potatoes.

'Aren't you going to tell me what this is all about?' he urged, when he'd taken a sip of his wine and a bite of the pie.

'Haven't you guessed?'

Rob shook his head. 'I'm not a mind reader.'

Tessa took a deep breath and plunged in. 'I'm pregnant. I'm . . . we're . . . having a baby.' Suddenly shy, she looked down at her plate, awaiting his whoop of delight. Thus she missed the expression of utter horror which froze his face for a split second.

By the time she looked up at him, smiling tremulously, he had rearranged his features in a semblance of neutrality. 'Are you sure?' he asked, his voice steady.

It wasn't the response she'd expected. 'Yes, I'm sure.'

'But you can't be,' he went on in a flat, reasonable tone. 'You're on the Pill.'

Tessa gulped. This was not going at all as she had imagined. 'I stopped taking it,' she admitted.

'Without telling me?'

She nodded, knowing suddenly that she'd been wrong not to tell him. 'I wanted to surprise you,' she said in a small voice.

'You've done that, all right.' For a moment he was silent, observing her impersonally, as a doctor might, looking at her flat stomach and her flushed cheeks. 'How far along are you, then?' he asked, still in the same detached tone.

'Nearly eight weeks.'

'Not too late to get rid of it, then.'

He'd said it in such a reasonable, unemotional way. Tessa gasped and stared at him, feeling as though she'd just been kicked in the stomach. Her baby – their baby – get rid of it? When she'd waited so long, and wanted it so badly? How could he say such a thing? It was monstrous, it was cruel. It was impossible that Rob, the man she'd married, the man she loved, was suggesting that she get rid of their baby.

She knew now that she should have told him she was going off the Pill, should have told him much sooner about the baby. She deserved his anger for that, and if he had raged at her, shouted at her, she could have borne it, knowing that she deserved it. But this calculating, heartless, impassive face which looked back at her across the table – across the steak and kidney pie and mashed potatoes – was the face of a stranger. Her eyes swam with tears; his features blurred. 'I'm not getting rid of our baby,' she managed to say.

'Very well.' Rob lined up his knife and fork, precisely, on the edge of his still-full plate, and pushed back from the table. 'I'll be in my computer room. And I don't wish to be disturbed.'

'But Rob,' Tessa wailed. 'You can't go now, before you've had your dinner. And there's apple crumble and custard.'

'You can eat it, then,' he said. 'All of it. I'm not hungry. And you're eating for two. Isn't that what they say?'

Tessa spent the evening alone, in floods of tears, until her throat hurt and her eyes were nearly swollen shut. She knew that she should try to remain tranquil, for the baby's sake, but she felt as if her world were crashing round her ears.

Midnight came and went, and still the door to the computer room was shut. Tessa got ready for bed, determined to stay awake until Rob joined her. But she drifted off to sleep, eventually, exhausted from crying, and when she woke in the morning, feeling nauseous, the other side of the bed was cold, the pillow undented. Rob had not come to bed.

It was a Friday. Malcolm Hogg was at his desk, as he usually was on a Friday afternoon, casting his eye over important paperwork.

Malcolm Hogg was an important man, a bank manager. Employees deferred to him, and customers feared him. He had power over their lives: power to say yea or nay as to whether they would have a new car, a foreign holiday, or even a new television set. It was true that these days, by and large, the decisions were out of his hands; there were now computer formulae which determined whether or not a loan or an overdraft was viable. But he didn't tell people that: still he revelled in the sense of power that surged through him like a drug as he faced a supplicant across his broad desk, in the hushed atmosphere of his private office. He enjoyed listening to their explanations, their fervent pleas, and then delivering his verdict. Sometimes it was fun to say yes; more often it was enjoyable to say no.

Usually Friday afternoons were busy – the busiest time of the week, as people tried to secure financing before they went off at the weekend to look at new cars or holiday brochures. Today was no exception, but Malcolm Hogg found a few moments in between his paperwork and the next customer appointment to flip through a holiday brochure himself. He had called in at the travel agent's over his lunch hour and picked up several brochures; now he was eager to see where he might spend a fortnight of holiday. Not in England: Mother had always insisted on going to the same seaside resort, to the same hotel, year in and year out. But Mother was dead now, and Malcolm could please himself. He *would* please himself; he would go abroad.

The idea had occurred to him that morning, as he packed his holdall for the weekend: he would go abroad. Perhaps to Spain. Perhaps to Italy. Maybe even to Africa, or Australia, or America. On his own, or on one of the luxury package holidays that he was always telling other people they couldn't afford.

He could afford it. Mother had left him the house, and all of her money. She'd had no one else to leave it to, not after her beloved Gerald had died. Malcolm had no illusions: if Gerald, the favourite son, had lived, he would have inherited the lot, and Malcolm would have been left without a ha'penny. Even though Malcolm was the one who'd looked after her, who'd taken her on her annual holidays to the seaside, and Gerald had merely deigned to ring her once a week and to visit her once a year, at Christmas.

Mother had loved Gerald; Gerald's untimely death had killed her. Without him, she had lost the will to live. She had died of grief.

But Malcolm had the house, and the money. It might not have been an adequate substitute for Mother's love, but it was better than nothing.

His secretary buzzed to tell him that his next appointment had arrived, was waiting. Malcolm took his time in putting the holiday brochure away, then straightened the papers on his desk, squaring them up with the front edge, before indicating that she should send the supplicant in. It didn't hurt them to wait a few minutes, he always thought; that way they came into his office suitably nervous, and knowing who was boss.

Malcolm Hogg might have been boss, but he was hardly a prepossessing sight for the loan-seeker who came through the door of the office. His eyes were small, like flinty marbles behind oversized square tortoiseshell spectacles. Equally small was his mouth, lipless and prissy. His complexion was oily, of a shade that might be described as swarthy, and even at this hour of the day, well before teatime, he had a heavy five o'clock shadow. His hair was his pride and joy – still dark, as Mother's had been till the day of her death, and still thick. Though the eminence of his job demanded fairly short back and sides, he wore the top on the long side, to emphasise its abundance: parted with military precision and held precisely in place with a great quantity of hair oil. The hair oil and the greasy skin gave him a somewhat oleaginous appearance, complemented by the shininess of his green suit.

Rising from behind his desk, he moved to the door to shake hands with the loan-seeker. He had a peculiar walk, singularly upright, as if he had a poker up his fundament, and he moved with quick, light-footed steps, his toes pointed outwards.

The loan-seeker subsided into a chair as, across the desk, Malcolm Hogg consulted the paperwork. Malcolm took his time, frowning and clicking his tongue against his teeth. That, he knew, always enhanced their nervousness; sometimes he even shook his head and sighed.

The paperwork before him was in fact quite straight-forward: the man wanted a loan to buy a second-hand automobile. After a few minutes the man began, stumblingly, to offer an explanation. 'There's this car, see. Just what I need. And if I don't buy it this weekend, it will be gone.'

Malcolm Hogg quelled him with a look. 'Yes, I see.' The computer had indicated that the man was a good credit risk, and that the loan should be granted. Malcolm rather wished that he could turn him down, but there was some compen-sation in magnanimity. 'Yes, you may have the money,' he said, his small mouth lifting in a semblance of a smile. After all, it was Friday, and he always felt in a good mood on a Friday afternoon, full of the milk of human kindness. The holdall was in the boot of his car and the weekend lay before him, with all of its promised satisfaction.

Rob had left the house before Tessa woke on that Friday morning. Through the day she was in a state, not knowing what to say to him when he returned. *If* he returned, she said to herself, fearing the worst. That he should leave her was unimaginable; yesterday she would have said it was impossible. But the stranger who had faced her so calmly across the table last night, the stranger who had suggested getting rid of her baby, might do anything.

She couldn't bear to stay in the house, so she went out and walked aimlessly and for hours, through streets of houses and commercial districts and public parks. Though autumn was just round the corner, and the leaves were already beginning to come off the trees, it was one of those cloudless September days when the warmth of the sun brought faint memories of a summer now past, and it was not uncomfortable to be out all day in a lightweight jacket or cardigan. But even if it had been bitterly cold, Tessa would not have noticed.

One thing she did notice. Everywhere she went, it seemed, she saw babies: babies in prams, babies in pushchairs, babies in the arms of their mothers. Babies laughing, babies crying, babies sleeping. Had there always been this many babies? Odd that she had never noticed them before. Each time she saw one, Tessa stopped and looked into its face, hungrily. This time next year she would be pushing a pram with her baby in it; the reality of that seemed suddenly overwhelming. She ached to hold her baby; that ache kept at bay, as much as was possible, her tortured memories of the night before.

But her anxieties intensified as the time approached when Rob usually arrived home from work. What if he didn't come? And if he did – of course he would – should she meet him at the door as usual? She dithered in the kitchen, putting together a simple meal of cold meat and salad, and when she heard his key in the lock she remained where she was, as if frozen to the floor. Would he be angry, and shout at her, insisting that she get rid of the baby? Or would he be contrite, sweeping in with a bunch of flowers and an apology?

Rob did neither. He came into the kitchen and gave her a

peck on the cheek. It didn't have the warmth of his usual passionate greeting, and he made no move to urge her upstairs to bed for a pre-dinner session, but apart from that he was much the same as always. Through dinner he chatted about his day at work; he didn't refer to her pregnancy, or to what had happened the night before. Tessa, deciding it was best to leave well alone, followed suit.

After dinner Rob helped her to clear the table and load the dishwasher. But then, instead of following her into the front room for coffee, he disappeared upstairs, retreating to his computer room for the rest of the evening.

Tessa spent the evening alone, attempting to read but finding it impossible to concentrate, and when she tried to knit, her fingers seemed all thumbs; the yarn tangled and she dropped stitches. Finally she went to bed, put on her sexiest night dress – one that never stayed on for very long – and waited up for her husband, pretending to read a book.

She waited a long time. It was gone midnight when he left his computer room and came into the bedroom. For the first time since she'd known him, he went to a drawer and took out a pair of pyjamas, undressed and put them on. And when he got into bed he gave her a chaste kiss on the forehead, then pulled up the covers and settled down to sleep, his back turned firmly towards her.

Chapter 4

They didn't discuss it: not the baby, nor the fact that their lovemaking had come to an abrupt end. Rob showed no inclination to mention either matter, and Tessa was afraid to do so, afraid of provoking a confrontation in which they would both say things that they would regret.

Tessa keenly regretted the cessation of the lovemaking, which she had always enjoyed and participated in with eagerness. Even more, perhaps, she missed the closeness that had always followed it, the drowsy lethargy in which they held each other and whispered endearments. She had always loved going to sleep in Rob's arms, his bare skin warm against hers as they drifted off to sleep, nestled together like spoons. It made her feel cherished; it made her feel married.

Now, though, Rob invariably wore pyjamas, a layer of cold stiff cotton between them. And he always turned his back to her, hugging the edge of the bed. She might snuggle up next to him, but it wasn't the same.

Sometimes, late at night while Rob slept, Tessa lay wakeful, thinking about her baby and thinking about her marriage. Occasionally she gave in to the tears that always seemed to lurk just below the surface these days; they trickled silently from her eyes, wetting her pillow.

Tessa knew that her pregnancy was making her more emotional than usual; she told herself that it was a natural thing that she should feel depressed and weepy. It was her hormones. Rob would come round eventually: he had to. The baby was a fact, not to be wished away or ignored indefinitely. Tessa longed for her pregnancy to show; then, she thought, he would have to acknowledge it, and discuss it. And when the baby was born, and he held his daughter in his arms, he would feel differently. Of course he would. Then things between them would return to normal, would be the way they'd been before. The same, only even better, because they would have the baby to put the seal on their marriage, to make them a real family.

During the day, Tessa continued her nest-building activities, making more curtains and starting to look at patterns for sewing baby clothes. But the house which had seemed so perfect for two people suddenly seemed less perfect as a third entered the equation. The stairs were steep, potentially dangerous for a baby or small child, and then there was the question of where to put the nursery. The house had only two bedrooms, and it was out of the question that Rob should give up his computer room. That left the attic room. It would do, Tessa decided; it could be made quite comfortable, with a bit of effort. They would need to clear the rubbish, of course. Then, with a coat or two of paint and a bit of carpet and some cheery curtains, it would be well on the way. She would talk to Rob about it. Soon. Not yet.

She began to read books about pregnancy and birth and babies, finding the subject fascinating. Poring over photos of developing foetuses, Tessa marvelled to think that her own baby was growing like this, inside her body. Already she had tiny hands with tiny fingers, and little black eyes like the eyes of a king prawn. Looking, come to think of it, more prawn-like than human altogether at this point, Tessa realised as she studied the photos. It was miraculous that this alien creature would very soon develop into something recognisable as a baby.

And, in spite of herself, Tessa found herself thinking more and more about her own mother. Had her mother sat in the chair which Tessa still remembered clearly from her childhood, rocking dreamily and looking forward to Tessa's birth? Had she, too, imagined what her daughter looked like as she grew in her womb? She wouldn't have had the photographs that modern technology made possible, but her imagination would have supplied the details of the tiny hands and little eyes. Her mother would have looked forward to her birth with anticipation, loving her already.

Tessa missed her mother, with a sharpness she hadn't experienced for some years. Her loss felt fresh, raw, unassuaged. It was so unfair that her mother wasn't here to share this time with her, to relate to her the stories of her own pregnancy, to reassure her that all would be well, and eventually to hold her granddaughter in her arms. It was unfair for Tessa, unfair for her mother. And unfair for the baby who would never know her grandmother.

Thoughts like these led her, in time, to realise that her baby *did* have a grandmother: Rob's mother. This shadowy woman began to take on a new and renewed importance for Tessa; not only was she Rob's mother, and thus her own mother-in-law, but she was also her baby's grandmother.

What was she like, Rob's mother? Tessa began to think about her quite a lot, in parallel with her grieving thoughts of her own mother. She tried to imagine what she might look like, and to fathom what strains might have existed in her relationship with her son to drive such a wedge between them.

A determination grew in her that her baby would know her only surviving grandmother. It would be too cruel to deprive her of both grandmothers. The loss of one was beyond Tessa's control, but the other was still alive. It would be difficult, with the way Rob felt about his mother, refusing even to talk about her. Tessa wished that she knew what had happened between them; it would make her feel more equal to the task of convincing Rob that his mother, wherever she might be, needed to be told that she was to be a grandmother.

She *would* talk to him about it. She would make him see that his mother had a right to know.

And perhaps, Tessa acknowledged to herself, getting to know Rob's mother might help to fill up that emptiness – that mother-shaped hole – that had existed in her own heart for so many years.

In October, Tessa visited her GP. She entered the waiting room nervously, not knowing quite what to expect, yet excited that she was about to acknowledge her pregnancy publicly.

She was not the only pregnant woman in the waiting room of the surgery; there were two women sitting in close proximity who were very visibly in that condition. Shyly, Tessa chose a seat across from them.

One of the women was delivering a monologue to the other. 'I keep telling Trevor that he'd better get busy painting the baby's room,' she said. 'He's going to be early. I just know it. Kayleigh was early, and Kyle will be even earlier. See if I'm not right.' She patted her unwieldy bump. 'A proper little kicker, he is. Can't wait to get out and start playing football.' She laughed at her own joke.

Tessa observed the women out of the corner of her eye. The one who had spoken, and who carried on speaking, was a bit younger than Tessa, perhaps in her late twenties. Her mouth was her most prominent feature, wide with rubbery lips and an abundance of large teeth. Perhaps, thought Tessa, the mouth's size had developed with exercise, like a muscle; its owner seemed incapable of silence.

The other woman, nodding sympathetically, appeared rather older, nearer to forty than thirty. She had a pleasant, comfortable face with warm brown eyes, and her hands were folded protectively over her distended abdomen. She was not as far along as her companion, it appeared, as her bump was smaller.

'Are you pregnant?' asked the younger woman. That seemed a rather odd question to Tessa, when the other woman so obviously was; then she realised that the speaker was addressing her, looking across at her in a speculative way.

'Yes,' Tessa confirmed, casting her eyes down shyly. 'But how did you know?'

'Oh, I can always tell,' stated the woman with a smug smile. 'I knew it as soon as you walked in the room. Is it your first, then?'

'Yes.'

'You're in for it, then. Morning sickness – I suppose you've had that already, haven't you?' Not stopping for an answer, she went on. 'Getting fat.' She patted her stomach. 'Your husband won't fancy you much when you're as fat as this. You're married, are you? Trevor says he fancies me as much as ever, but I don't believe him. Mind you, my boobs are enormous, which suits him just fine – ha ha. Anyway, then you have the birth to look forward to. I was in labour for fifty-three hours with Kayleigh. Can you believe it? The midwife thought she was never going to come out. "Too comfortable in there", she said to me.' The woman laughed. 'It was awful. Tore me up something terrible. Even though she was early, she weighed over eight pounds. Eight pounds, two ounces! Kyle's going to be even bigger. He's probably eight pounds already, and I have nearly two months to go! Anyway, the birth was awful. You can't even imagine the pain. I told Trevor, while it was going on, that I would never have another one. I meant it, too. "That's it, mate," I said. "You're sleeping in the guest room from now on." Ha ha. But Trevor just can't keep his hands off me, and that's a fact. And I'm just one of those fertile women. We were being careful, just like we were the first time, but it didn't make any difference. Kayleigh's only two, and here I am again.'

'JoAnn Biddle,' announced the nurse.

The woman who had been speaking struggled to her feet. 'My turn. See you, then.'

When she'd gone, Tessa looked involuntarily across at the other woman. The woman was smiling, and she raised her eyebrows at Tessa. 'I'm sorry you should have been subjected to JoAnn like that, without any warning,' she said. 'She's not really so bad – she means well. But she can be a bit overwhelming the first time you meet her.'

Tessa responded to the woman's smile. 'I felt as if I was supposed to know who Trevor and Kayleigh were,' she said.

'JoAnn is like that. She assumes that the rest of the world is clued in to and fascinated by the minutiae of her life. I'm Melanie, by the way,' she added. 'Melanie Maybank.'

'Tessa.'

'It's nice to meet you, Tessa.' Melanie leaned over the bulk of her stomach and extended her hand. Tessa shook it.

'Does she know that her baby's a boy, then?' Tessa asked.

'Oh, yes. If she'd had longer, she would have told you about her scan, and how it left no doubt that it was a boy.' Melanie smiled again, ironically but without malice. 'It's one of her favourite stories, so I'm sure you'll hear it the next time. If you're lucky, she might even show you the scan photos.'

'What about you?' Tessa nodded towards Melanie's bump. 'Girl or boy?'

'Girl, almost certainly.' She shook her head with a rueful smile. 'I had my first scan a few weeks ago. They can't tell for sure with girls, of course, like they can with boys. And I told them I didn't want to know, even if they *could* tell. But I have three girls already, and I don't have any reason to suppose that things will be any different this time.'

'Three girls?'

'Eight, ten and twelve,' confirmed Melanie.

It seemed unlikely, then, that this baby had been planned. 'Does your husband mind?' Tessa asked, thinking of Rob's reaction to the unexpected news.

Melanie misunderstood. 'Oh, I'm sure he'd like a boy. But he insists that another girl would be just fine.'

'I'm hoping for a girl,' Tessa confided shyly. 'Though of course I wouldn't really mind, either way.'

'It's your first, you said?'

'Yes.' Unconsciously Tessa rubbed her flat stomach, observing the size of Melanie's distended abdomen. Would she really look like that in a few months' time? 'When is your baby due, then?'

'February.' Melanie's smile widened. 'Valentine's Day, to be exact. Maybe I'll call her Valentine. What about you? When are you due?'

'Sometime in May. I haven't seen the doctor yet, so that's just my own reckoning.'

'They can tell on the scan,' Melanie informed her. 'They can give you an exact date. But you won't have that for a few weeks yet.'

'It's all so new to me. I've been reading some books,' Tessa said.

Impulsively Melanie leaned over and touched Tessa's knee. 'Listen,' she said. 'Why don't you come to our next NCT meeting? National Childbirth Trust,' she amplified. 'I've been involved in the organisation for years, since before Helena, my eldest, was born. It's a nice bunch of women, and a great support group. If you have any questions, someone there is bound to know the answers.'

Tessa's natural diffidence and reserve took over. 'Well, I don't know.'

'Here,' Melanie went on, tearing a strip of paper from the edge of an old magazine and pulling a pen from her handbag. 'Let me give you the date of the next meeting, and my phone number.'

Tessa took the proffered scrap of paper, knowing that she would be very unlikely to take up the offer, but touched by the other woman's kindness. 'Thanks.'

'Melanie Maybank,' intoned the nurse.

Unhurriedly, Melanie rose to her feet. 'Well, my turn.

Give me a ring, Tessa. And it was nice to meet you. I hope to see you again.'

'Yes,' said Tessa.

A few minutes later Tessa was called into the doctor's consulting room herself. Her GP was a woman, young and competent. 'So, you're pregnant,' she said, not wasting any time.

'That's right,' confirmed Tessa. 'Do you have to do a test or anything?'

'No, I'll take your word for it. Now,' the doctor went on, 'we have some boring paperwork to deal with.'

That took some minutes. 'The hospital will notify you of the date for your first scan, between sixteen and twenty weeks, depending on when they're able to fit you in,' said the doctor at the end. 'They'll send you an appointment card, in due course. You'll go to the hospital for that. All of your other antenatal visits will be dealt with here, at the clinic. Friday mornings we see our mums – makes it easier that way. Usually you'll just see Stephanie, the midwife, though sometimes you'll see me as well. And of course you mustn't hesitate to get in touch at any time, with me or Stephanie, if you have any problems or questions. We want you to have a healthy baby, Tessa.'

Tessa nodded, overwhelmed yet reassured.

The doctor put her pen down and leaned back in her chair. 'Do you have any questions, then? Since it's your first, you must have one or two things on your mind that I could help you with.'

Most of Tessa's questions had already been anticipated and answered by the doctor, and the ones that hadn't were beyond her ability to articulate. But she didn't want to miss out on this opportunity for experienced professional advice. She looked down at her fingernails. 'Well . . .'

The doctor had seen enough pregnant women, and endured enough embarrassed silences, to know what wasn't being said.

'Is your sex life all right, then?' she asked in a professional yet warm voice.

Tessa bit her lip. 'Not really,' she admitted. Now that it was out in the open, she decided she might as well be honest. And the doctor seemed very understanding, not at all threatening or judgemental. 'My husband hasn't touched me since . . . well, since I told him I was pregnant.'

'Oh, dear.' The doctor clicked her tongue against her teeth. 'It's very common, that reaction,' she went on reassuringly. 'I see it all the time. He's afraid of hurting you, of harming the baby. Suddenly he feels he has to treat you like a cut-glass ornament. Suddenly his lover has changed into a different sort of creature, has become the receptacle of something precious and fragile, and he doesn't know how to deal with that.'

Letting out her breath in a sigh of relief, Tessa smiled at the doctor. How marvellous to know that Rob's reaction was normal, that other men felt and behaved the same way.

'You've probably felt rejected, have thought that it must mean he doesn't love you, when what it really means is that he loves you very much, and just doesn't want to do anything to harm you.'

Tessa nodded thoughtfully. 'But what should I do?'

The doctor smiled back at her. 'Talk to him, of course. Tell him that you won't break, and that he can't hurt the baby. It's perfectly safe – and perfectly normal – to make love right up to the very end. Mind you, by the end it may require some contortions, but it *can* be done.'

'Yes,' said Tessa. 'Yes, I'll tell him.'

She left the doctor's surgery feeling as if an enormous weight had been lifted from her shoulders.

That afternoon, Tessa had a phone call. She recognised the voice even before he identified himself. 'Tessa, it's Andrew.'

Andrew, she thought guiltily. She had promised to keep in touch, and she hadn't rung him even once in the months since she'd left work. 'Hello, Andrew,' she said with warmth, surprised at how pleased she was to hear his voice.

'How are you?' he asked; she was relieved that he didn't sound reproachful.

'I'm fine. I'm . . . having a baby. In May.'

There was a pause on the other end of the phone. 'Con gratulations, Tessa,' he said at last. 'It's what you wanted, isn't it?'

'Oh, yes.' Her enthusiasm overcame her guilt. 'I'm so excited about it.'

'And Rob?' he asked. 'Is Rob excited as well?'

It was Tessa's turn to pause. Loyalty to her husband warred with her natural impulse towards honesty; in the end she reached a compromise between the two and went for the middle ground. 'He's . . . getting used to the idea.'

'I see.' There was another pause, then Andrew went on. 'Listen, Tessa. I'd like to see you sometime. Have a nice long chat, face to face.'

'Why not?' She thought about it for a moment. 'Maybe you could come here to dinner one night. A Saturday night, perhaps. Or to Sunday lunch, if that's more convenient. Rob would like to see you too, I'm sure.' They hadn't done any entertaining at all since they'd been married; perhaps, thought Tessa with a burst of enthusiasm, it was time to start, and where better to start than with non-threatening Andrew?

'That would be lovely,' he said, though it wasn't at all what he'd had in mind. 'Shall we set a date now?'

'I'd better consult Rob,' she backtracked. 'Ask him to check his diary. Why don't I ring you next week?'

'Yes, all right.' Andrew paused again. 'Tessa, I *am* pleased about the baby,' he said, awkwardly.

Tessa smiled into the receiver, and though it wasn't something she'd thought of until that moment, she said, 'You could be godfather. Would you, Andrew?'

'I would be honoured. And delighted,' he replied in a solemn voice.

'Oh, good. I'll tell Rob. And I'll ring you next week.'

'I'll look forward to it,' said Andrew.

On Friday afternoon, Harold Dingley put on his white uniform and got ready to go to work. He wished he were not going to work. It wasn't that he didn't like his job: being a hospital porter gave him a great deal of satisfaction in many ways. He liked the contact with people, and the feeling that he was performing a service for them. He enjoyed chatting with the patients as he wheeled them down for x-rays and other tests – he learned a lot about other people's lives that way, and that always interested him. And when he wheeled them upstairs to the operating theatre, sometimes he could provide a bit of comfort to them, a word of cheer.

He took pride in his job, and the way he performed it. But there were two drawbacks to his job, and ones that were especially irksome to him on a Friday: it was not at all well paid, and it involved shift work.

There was a place he would far rather be going to on a Friday afternoon than to the hospital. But even if he hadn't had to work on that particular night shift, he wouldn't have been able to afford to go. No, he would have to save up for at least a fortnight before he could once again indulge himself in his favourite recreational pastime. It didn't come cheap, that pastime, and it was becoming more expensive all the time. That meant a fortnight without any frivolous expenditures; it meant watching every penny. Sandwiches from home rather than eating in the canteen, and no trips to the pub after his day shifts.

Not that Harold was ever a great one for the pub. Sometimes his workmates invited him along for a drink, out of kindness, but he didn't really care much for beer, and the cost of a round of drinks horrified him, when he was so used to being careful with his money. And to be honest, Harold never really fitted in with the others, who worked hard and afterwards enjoyed the simple pleasures of a pint and a chat with their mates, discussing the latest football scores.

Harold didn't follow football. He'd never been sporty, even at school. He was, in fact, one of those boys who had always been left on the sidelines, the last one chosen when drawing up teams.

It wasn't that Harold was clumsy, or fat. He was just soft. In his white uniform, there was something slightly indistinct about him, a bit out of focus, like an underdeveloped photograph. The outlines were blurred. His nondescript-coloured hair hung down in a lank clump over one pale eye; most of the time he couldn't be bothered to brush it out of the way. In his movements he was languid, where most of the other porters were brisk and businesslike.

The patients liked Harold, though. He was a good listener, so they talked to him, and he liked that.

It gave him some things to tell Bunny about, when he got home from work. Bunny always enjoyed hearing his stories. She worked in an office, with the same people every day – boring people, she said, and she had already heard all of the stories that they had to tell.

Not that Bunny was nosy. She never asked questions about where he went on those Friday nights, and he never told her. There were some things you just didn't talk about with your sister, no matter how close you were.

In fact Harold and Bunny were extremely close; they always had been. It was only natural, when there were just the two of them, and scarcely more than a year between them.

Harold was the elder. Mummy had laughed at him when he'd said that he could remember the day that Bunny was born. He'd only been a baby himself, she'd said. How could he possibly remember? But it was true: he did remember. He remembered how Mummy had cooed over the cot on the day she'd brought Bunny home from hospital. A girl, she'd said joyfully. Mummy liked girls better than boys; she'd never said as much, but Harold knew. And he'd been dispossessed from the cot from that day. He remembered, all right.

Now Mummy was gone. She'd died a few years ago, of breast cancer, when she was barely fifty. Harold and Bunny's father was dead as well, some years since, so now the siblings lived alone together in the house where they'd always lived.

The arrangement suited them both very well. Harold was the tidy one; working shifts, as he did, he was able to keep the house in order. He did the laundry, and especially enjoyed ironing. Bunny did most of the cooking, and the shopping. She was a good cook, like Mummy, and was able to create tasty meals with a minimal outlay of the housekeeping money.

It was Harold's fear, articulated to himself in his darkest moments, that Bunny would upset the status quo one day, would find herself a man and decide to get married. After all, that wouldn't be such an unusual thing for a woman of twenty-eight to do. Bunny was a pretty enough girl, if a bit plump, and though she never talked about it, surely she would welcome the opportunity to marry if a man were to come along and ask her. And then where would Harold be? He couldn't afford to keep up the house by himself, on his meagre wages, and he certainly couldn't afford to buy out Bunny's share. They would have to sell the house; he would have to move.

There didn't seem to be any indication that such a thing was imminent, though Harold was always alert to any possibilities. He questioned her minutely about her co-workers, asking about their ages and marital status. Most of them were women, Bunny told him, and all of the men were married, and old. That was a relief, if not a guarantee; Harold had seen enough of the world to know that married men had affairs, and even left their wives for other, younger women.

And as for Harold, there was no chance that he would marry. He liked women, but apart from Bunny he was not comfortable with members of the opposite sex who were anywhere close to his own age, and he was aware that they did not find him attractive. When, on rare occasions, he went to the pub with his fellow porters, he envied them their easy banter with the nurses at the next table, their casual conversations about their casual sexual encounters. Such things were not for him, and he knew it.

There were compensations: he had Bunny, and he had his Friday nights, once or twice a month.

And even on this particular Friday, when he was going to work rather than packing his holdall, he had things to look forward to. The night shift was in many ways preferable to the day shift: not so busy, leaving him more time to chat with the patients. Of course, there were no scheduled operations at night so, apart from the odd emergency, the main activity was provided by the births of babies – no respecters of schedules, they. Every night several of them were born, and the very best part of Harold's job, day or night, was wheeling the new mums back from the delivery rooms to the wards. They were usually tired, sore, but euphoric, and often they let Harold hold their babies. Tiny scraps of humanity, pink and wrinkled, wearing impossibly diminutive nappies. Some screamed lustily, outraged at their precipitous entry into the world, while others slept, exhausted by their ordeal. Holding them, when they were so freshly emerged from the womb, was the greatest privilege that Harold could imagine, cradling them in his arms and breathing in their distinctive scent of talc mingled with something sweet and almost other-worldly. It was the very best thing of all.

Tessa had decided to talk to Rob over dinner about her visit to the doctor, and the conversation they'd had. But at the last minute she lost her nerve, and instead retreated to the subject of Andrew and his phone call.

'I was thinking that we might have a dinner party,' she said as she spooned the casserole on to their plates. 'It would be fun do to some entertaining, and we could invite Andrew.'

'But who else would we invite?' Rob queried.

That was a point, Tessa acknowledged. They didn't have any friends as a couple. Rob had acquaintances at work, though no one he would count as a friend, and she only had Andrew. There was always Amanda and Ian, she reflected, but that was ludicrous, not even to be contemplated. For a moment she thought of Melanie Maybank, with her kind brown eyes. She had seemed very nice, and had even given Tessa her phone number. But they'd only just met, and what would she think if she had a phone call out of the blue, inviting her to a dinner party?

'Andrew doesn't even have a partner, does he?' Rob went on. 'He's not married, doesn't live with anyone?'

'Not that I know of.'

'One person doesn't make much of a dinner party,' he pointed out, not unkindly.

'Maybe Sunday lunch would be better,' Tessa decided.

Rob pushed some of the casserole on to the back of his fork. 'Whatever,' he said, indifferently.

Now was her opportunity to mention the baby, Tessa thought; that could then lead into the subject of her visit to the doctor. She took a deep breath. 'I've asked Andrew if he'll be the baby's godfather,' she brought out with studied nonchalance. 'He said he would be delighted and honoured. Or maybe it was honoured and delighted. You don't mind, do you?'

'If that's what you want,' Rob said in a neutral tone.

It wasn't exactly wild enthusiasm, but at least she'd broached the subject. 'I went to the doctor today,' she went on.

'Oh?'

Then she lost her nerve. 'The doctor says I'm doing well,' she said lamely. Later, she decided. They could talk about it later.

*

Later turned out to be in bed, in the dark. She moved close to him, snuggled up against his impassive back, and insinuated her hand under his pyjama top, stroking his chest. He twitched, as though a pesky insect had landed on him.

'Rob,' she whispered.

'What?'

'I went to the doctor today.'

'You said.'

It was now or never. She whispered into his neck, feeling a stirring of desire at the nearness of him, the scent of him. 'The doctor says that we don't have to be afraid of making love. It won't hurt the baby.'

He lay very still for a moment, then switched on the bedside lamp, turned over and stared at her, his eyebrows raised in amazement. 'Is that what you think? That I'm afraid of hurting the baby?'

Confused, she nodded. 'Or hurting me, maybe.'

Rob gave a mirthless laugh. 'Oh, that's rich.'

'Then why?' Tessa choked, her eyes filling with tears and her voice raw with pain, the words ripped out involuntarily. 'Why won't you touch me? Oh, Rob. It was so wonderful. We were so good together. And now it's as if you think I have some disease.'

Without moving, he seemed to distance himself from her. 'If you must know,' he said unemotionally, 'it's very simple. Making love to you now would be like sleeping with my mother.'

Tessa gasped, unable to comprehend what he was saying; she fastened on to the one thing she understood, and said the first thing that came into her head. 'But why do you hate your mother so much?'

'I've told you before: I don't want to talk about my mother,' he said in an icy voice, his tone indicating finality.

'But she's our baby's grandmother, Rob! The only grandmother our baby will ever have! I don't know what she's done to you, but it can't be that bad. Please, Rob – our baby needs to know her. And she deserves the opportunity to get to know her grandchild.'

'She – deserves – nothing,' Rob said through clenched teeth. 'Discussion closed.' He switched off the bedside lamp and turned his back to her, as remote as if he were sleeping on another continent.

Chapter 5

The next day, a Saturday, Rob behaved as if nothing had happened; after breakfast, at which he was perfectly amiable, he retreated to his computer room, leaving Tessa to mooch about the house and try to amuse herself.

There had been a time, not that far distant, when they had always spent Saturdays together, in bed, making up for the time they'd lost during the week. Tessa realised, with regret, that those days were over for good, even if their lovemaking resumed after the baby came – and she had every expectation that it would; she knew enough about babies to know that their schedules did not permit their parents to spend entire days in bed, whether they wanted to or not.

But at least she would have the baby to keep her company and pass the time. The morning dragged on; Tessa leafed through one of her books, then picked up her knitting. On her last trip to John Lewis she had bought some primrose-yellow wool, gossamer-fine, and had started on a tiny cardigan. She'd thought it would knit up quickly, but it was on such small needles, and incorporated such intricacies as cables, that it was taking longer than expected.

It was while she was puzzling over an arcane instruction in the pattern that she first felt a twinge in her lower abdomen, in the region where she knew the baby to be. The pain wasn't severe, but it was unexpected, and she caught her breath in surprise. The twinge that followed on, a few seconds later, was considerably sharper.

Tessa put down her knitting and stood up. The pain didn't go away; if anything, it was more intense. She tried walking round the room, but that didn't help either.

From her books, Tessa was all too aware that a quarter of pregnancies end in miscarriage during the first trimester. She was still within the danger zone, and the fear that assailed her was even stronger than the pain.

Rob had made it clear that he was never to be disturbed during his sessions with his computer, by anything short of an announcement that the house was on fire. Tessa, holding her stomach, was beyond rational assessment of the importance of this emergency as she pulled herself up the stairs and moved down the hall to the door of Rob's room. Still, though, at the door something held her back from just barging in. Instead she knocked on the door. 'Rob!' she cried urgently.

'What is it?'

A particularly strong twinge almost doubled her over, and she gave an involuntary moan. 'I think I'm losing the baby!'

He was out in an instant, guiding her down the hall and into the bedroom, urging her to lie down on the bed, where she immediately curled up into an agonised ball.

Rob rang the GP from the bedside phone. 'The doctor says to bring you in straight away,' he told Tessa. 'Come on, my love. I'll help you down the stairs.'

An hour later they were back home: it was a false alarm. The doctor explained that this was quite a common phenomenon, as the ligaments in the abdomen stretched to accommodate the baby. Nothing to worry about at all, she assured them.

Tessa, enormously relieved but tearful and exhausted by the intensity of her fears, slept through the afternoon. Rob stayed with her, holding her hand and stroking her hair.

She woke just once, in the middle of a bad dream, and said

something that she would not have dared to articulate in a more wakeful state. 'You would have been relieved if I'd lost the baby,' she murmured.

'Don't be silly,' Rob assured her, giving her hand a squeeze. 'I do love you, you know.'

She had always known that he would come round, and somehow this incident, this scare, seemed to have made a difference. Now Rob was solicitous of Tessa's health, and began to take an interest in the baby.

He helped her to clear the rubbish from the attic room; one weekend he took her shopping to look at cots and nursery furniture, and together they pored over wallpaper books and paint chips.

It was just like it should be, Tessa thought with satisfaction: the two of them, looking forward together to the birth of their baby.

Only one thing was not quite right. Still Rob wore his pyjamas each night and slept with his back towards Tessa, and his kisses were not those of a lover. He never mentioned it again, and neither did she; everything else was perfect, and she wasn't about to spoil it by bringing up this one niggling disappointment. It wasn't that important, she told herself; when the baby came, things would be different.

Tessa had yearned, almost from the beginning, for her pregnancy to show, and quite soon after this it began to do so. She was so slender that it didn't take long for a small bulge to appear, a bulge that began to grow into something rather more noticeable.

She went shopping for maternity clothes, and began to wear them, though she certainly could have managed without them for another month or two. But she was proud of her baby, proud of her little bump, and she wanted to flaunt it, wanted everyone to know.

*

In all of the excitement of the false alarm, and the changes that followed, she had forgotten all about her promise to ring Andrew back and fix a date for a get-together. And so when he rang her, about a fortnight later, she reacted once again with guilt.

'I'm so sorry. But . . . well, things got a bit complicated,' she explained.

'Good complicated or bad complicated?' he asked, concerned.

She smiled into the phone. 'Mostly good. Very good, in fact. Oh, Andrew, you should see me!' she enthused. 'I'm getting so fat. It's wonderful!'

Andrew laughed. 'When *can* I see you, then?'

'Soon.' This Sunday, she recalled, they were going to make a trip to Ikea, so that was no good. On impulse she said, 'Why not tomorrow? I'm going to be in town, doing a bit of shopping, and we could meet for lunch. If you're free.'

He agreed instantly, and they fixed a time and place.

Andrew was the first one there, a few minutes early, just to be on the safe side, and waited for her outside of the restaurant.

'Here I am,' she announced as she arrived, spot on one o'clock.

'Tessa – how wonderful to see you.' He kissed her cheek. 'And you look . . . blooming.'

He wasn't exaggerating; there was a sparkle in her eye and a becoming flush on her cheek that he'd never seen before.

Tessa turned sideways and stuck out her stomach for emphasis. 'And just look how fat I am.'

Andrew could barely discern a bump, but it was obvious that it was important to her that he should agree. 'You must have a monstrous baby in there,' he laughed. 'My godson is going to be a real bruiser.'

'Goddaughter,' Tessa corrected him demurely as they went into the restaurant and found a table.

'Do you know that for sure, then?'

'No,' she admitted. 'But I just feel it.'

The waiter materialised and asked for drinks orders.

'I'm going to have a glass of your house red,' said Andrew. 'Tessa? Will you join me?'

She shook her head. 'Mineral water for me.'

'Of course.' He smiled at her approvingly. 'You're taking good care of my goddaughter.'

'I'm trying to.'

'I want you to know,' Andrew went on, 'that I plan to take my responsibilities as a godfather very seriously indeed. Not just a cheque at birthdays and Christmas. When I stand up in church at the christening and swear to renounce evil on her behalf, and to encourage her faith by my prayers, example and teaching, I won't just be saying those things. I intend to carry them out.'

Tessa looked at him curiously. 'You know an awful lot about christenings. Do you have other godchildren, then?'

'No. But my father is a vicar.' He smiled. 'I grew up in church, and it's gone rather deep.'

'Really!' Tessa was amazed; in all the years she'd worked with Andrew, she'd never known that they had this in common. 'Me, too! That is to say, my father is a vicar as well. But I don't go to church any longer,' she admitted. 'I had rather enough of all that when I was growing up.' She'd gone every Sunday; it was the only time she could be sure of seeing her father.

'Well, you know what they say about vicarage children,' said Andrew. 'They either turn out very good, or very bad. There doesn't seem to be a middle ground.'

'And which are you then, Andrew?' asked Tessa in an un-characteristically teasing way.

He grinned across the table at her, delighted to see her in such high spirits, and responded in the same vein. 'That, Tessa, is for me know and for you to find out.'

*

At sixteen weeks Tessa went back to the GP for her monthly antenatal checkup, feeling wonderful, proud of her growing bump. She walked into the waiting room with confidence this time, and crossed to where she'd sat before. Both Melanie Maybank and JoAnn Biddle were there, both looking considerably larger than they had a month before.

'Well, hello, Tessa,' smiled Melanie. 'I'd been wondering whether we would see you again.'

'You're really starting to show,' declared JoAnn. 'Of course, you're skinny to begin with, so you *would* show early. But I'll bet you'll have a big baby. Like me! Sometimes I think I'm going to have a monster, not a baby.' Smugly she patted her now-enormous girth. 'Less than a month to go now, and Kyle just can't wait to get out. Kayleigh was the same. And she had an enormous head. Stephanie said she'd never seen a baby with such a big head. Of course, Trevor's got a big head too, or at least that's what I tell him. Ha ha.' She laughed, but scarcely paused to draw breath before she went on. 'And my second scan showed that Kyle's head is even bigger than Kayleigh's. I don't know how he's going to get out of there. I was in labour for fifty-three hours with Kayleigh, and I don't look forward to *that* again, thank you very much!' As she talked, she rummaged in her handbag. 'I have the photos from my scan. Just wait till you see how big Kyle's head is.'

'JoAnn Biddle,' called the nurse.

'I'll have to show them to you next time,' JoAnn promised, struggling to her feet with some difficulty. 'That is, if I'm still here next time. Ha ha.' She turned to the corner of the waiting room, where, unnoticed by Tessa till now, a toddler was playing with a set of blocks. 'Kayleigh, you just stay there till Mummy is finished. Mummy won't be long.' To Melanie and Tessa she added, 'Keep an eye on her, won't you? She'll be fine. I had to bring her this morning because Trevor's mother couldn't have her. The silly cow had fixed an appointment to have her hair done. I ask you! Wouldn't you think that looking after her granddaughter would be more important than getting her hair done?'

Kayleigh looked at her impassively, but as soon as JoAnn had disappeared through the door of the consulting room, the child opened her mouth and let out a yell. 'Mummy!' Her face creased in dismay. 'Mummy, Mummy!'

'Mummy will be back in just a minute,' Melanie said to the little girl. Kayleigh, ignoring her, picked up a block and hurled it across the room. She screamed louder and louder, as her face turned bright red and she launched into a full-scale temper tantrum. Heads all over the waiting room turned, staring disapprovingly at the child and the two women nearest to her.

Melanie got up and went to Kayleigh, lifting her in her arms. She carried the child back to her seat and settled down with her on her lap, in spite of her intrusive bump. 'There, there,' she soothed.

Kayleigh's screams diminished in volume and intensity, then stopped altogether. She put her thumb in her mouth and nestled her tear-stained face against Melanie's breast.

Tessa was impressed. If she'd been here by herself she wouldn't have known what to do, but Melanie had dealt with the situation calmly and without any fuss. Having three girls already, she must be quite used to such things, must have seen innumerable temper tantrums. And, thought Tessa, she seemed a naturally motherly person; in fact, she reminded her a bit of her own mother.

And Tessa realised, looking at the now-tranquil Kayleigh, that her dreams of the future had somehow stopped with the baby; she had not imagined as far as a toddler. But her baby would grow into a toddler one day, and then into something bigger. A screaming toddler, an unhappy child, an angst-ridden teenager. Was she really up to the task of motherhood? Her confidence abruptly evaporated as she acknowledged to herself the depth of her ignorance and inexperience, and she felt herself to be utterly inadequate to take on such an awesome responsibility. But it was too late now to change her mind.

Her thoughts must have shown on her face; Melanie smiled across at her, a lovely crooked smile, and said, 'Don't worry, Tessa. I've had a great deal of practice, but you'll find that it all comes naturally.'

Tessa wasn't so sure. She wished, suddenly and absurdly, that *she* could climb up on Melanie's lap, suck her thumb, and feel those motherly arms around her.

After lunch on that Friday, as on every Friday, James Wooldridge went home to his large executive mansion in one of the suburbs comprising Milton Keynes, and packed his holdall. He owned the company; it was his right and privilege to leave early on a Friday if he wished to do so. Traffic was so bad on the motorway on a Friday, he had found, that if he didn't leave by mid-afternoon, he would get caught up in the rush hour, and what should be a journey of an hour and a half could easily take twice that long.

His wife Felicity was not at home; James supposed that she was out shopping, as it was not yet time for her to collect the children from school. Not that there was much for her to do at home: the cleaning lady came in every day and looked after the house.

If Felicity minded his trips to London every Friday, she never said so. It was true that she sometimes complained that he was not there on a Saturday afternoon, that he missed Geoffrey's soccer matches or Emma's ballet recitals. But Felicity was not really the complaining sort, and at any rate she was mostly relieved that he was making the trip on his own, discharging his responsibilities without requiring that she be involved.

The excuse that James used for his Friday trips was that he needed to visit his mother. He was particularly proud of this excuse, for several reasons: firstly, it was not altogether a lie, and secondly, it meant that there was no danger that Felicity would ever suggest that she and the children might go with him. Felicity had never liked James's mother.

He always did call in on his mother, during these trips. She lived near St Albans, just off the motorway, so if things were going smoothly on a Friday, if he got away from home in good time and didn't get caught up in traffic, he would stop by for a cup of tea before completing his journey. And if he happened to be running late on Friday, he would call in on Saturday instead, on his way back home.

His mother didn't mind that his visits were brief and per-functory. She was fond of James, in her way, but she had never been a clingy sort of mother, and their family was not a demonstrative one. She was quite content to see him for three-quarters of an hour, once a week.

It all worked very neatly, and it never would have occurred to Felicity – who was very close to her own mother – that he was being less than truthful. James was afraid, sometimes, that it worked *too* neatly, and that one day something would happen and he would be caught out. One day Felicity would need to get in touch with him: Geoffrey or Emma would have an accident, or the dog would get hit by a car, or the house would burn down. Felicity would ring his mother's, and he would not be there.

But it hadn't happened yet, and James told himself that he would cross that bridge when he came to it.

He snapped his holdall shut. It was an expensive holdall, leather with a designer label.

Felicity was coming in the door, laden with shopping, as James went out. He stopped long enough to give her a kiss. 'See you tomorrow, then,' he said.

'Give your mother my love,' she replied, unconvincingly.

'I will.' It was a ritual exchange.

James Wooldridge put his holdall in the boot of his BMW,

pulled out of the long drive of his executive home, and headed towards Junction 14 of the M1.

Tessa had never considered herself to be a jealous person, but Amanda was a special case. After all, their lives were doubly entwined: Amanda had taken Ian from her, and Amanda had been Rob's lover before her. The very thought of Amanda was enough to arouse all of Tessa's deep-seated insecurities; she tried, for her own peace of mind, to banish Amanda from her thoughts.

On Saturday, though, Tessa answered the phone, and Amanda's richly timbred voice asked to speak to Rob. She recognised the voice instantly, though Amanda didn't bother to identify herself; sometimes, still, Tessa heard that voice in her dreams.

Rob took the call in his computer room, and it seemed, to Tessa, to go on for quite a long time. She stood in the corridor outside the door, hating herself for doing it, and though she couldn't make out his words, she could hear the relaxed tone of Rob's voice, his easy laughter. Surely *she* never made him laugh like that, or at least hadn't done so for quite some time . . .

By the time the call was over, Tessa was busying herself with some task downstairs. She was determined not to quiz Rob about the call, but looked up as he entered the room, and the words came out in spite of herself. 'What was that about, then?'

Rob shrugged, smiled. 'Nothing very much.'

Tessa continued to look at him expectantly, so he elaborated. It was something to do with Amanda's accounts, he explained patiently, and with a touch of condescension. In spite of the fact that Amanda was a wonder-woman at her job, clever and ambitious, she just couldn't get her head round doing her own accounts. Rob had always done them for her, on his computer spreadsheet. She just needed to check one or two figures with him, and to ask him to transfer the information to a floppy disk for her.

It was all very plausible, and Rob didn't seem to attach any importance to it, but it niggled at Tessa for days afterwards. Could Amanda, not content with having taken Ian from her, now want Rob back as well? Tessa tried to tell herself that she was succumbing to emotional paranoia; still, she couldn't help fretting about it.

The following week a letter arrived in the post, addressed by hand to Rob. Tessa looked at it curiously, not able to identify the handwriting but recognising it as unmistakably female.

In view of the recent phone call, it was not surprising that her thoughts went to Amanda. Could Amanda be writing to Rob for some reason? The postmark was London; there were no other identifying marks.

Tessa didn't think that she'd ever seen Amanda's writing, or if she had, she couldn't remember it. The letter *could* be from Amanda. If not Amanda, then who?

She set it aside, and gave it to Rob when he got home that evening. He looked at it, then put it in his pocket without opening it.

'You're not going to open it?' Tessa couldn't help herself asking.

Rob shrugged. 'It's nothing important. What's for supper, then? I'm starving – I had a long meeting this morning, and missed lunch.'

And so, when Tessa was emptying the bins on the morning before the rubbish collectors' weekly visit, she did something she most certainly would not have done under ordinary circumstances.

Usually Rob's computer room was sacrosanct; she didn't go in there, even to empty the bin, unless she was invited to do so. But on that day something impelled her to be thorough in her job. She wasn't exactly looking for anything in particular, but when she caught sight of the envelope in his bin, scrunched into a ball, she recognised it immediately. After only a brief battle with herself, she retrieved it and smoothed it out. The envelope was not empty; though it had been opened, she could see that the letter was still inside.

Still, though, it was several more hours before she succumbed to the temptation to look inside the envelope. She'd put the envelope on the hall table, where it caught her eye each time she went by, and all the while it occupied her thoughts. At last she could resist no longer; she made herself a cup of tea, took the envelope through to the front room, and held it in her hand, smoothing the creases from it as she pondered the unfamiliar writing.

She had come this far, Tessa told herself; she may as well be done with it. With fingers that trembled slightly she pulled the letter from the envelope and unfolded the single sheet of writing paper.

The address was written in the upper right-hand corner in the same female hand: 27 Chase View Road, N14.

She thought, from something that Rob had said, that Amanda and Ian were living in Docklands, but she wasn't at all sure about that. They might be anywhere in London, even N14.

'*Dear Robbie,*' the letter began. Did Amanda call him 'Robbie'?

Tessa's eyes moved down the page.

'*It has been far too long since we have seen one another, or even spoken.*'

Not Amanda, then. Did Rob have some pre-Amanda girl-friend that Tessa hadn't even heard of?

'*I understand that you have a new wife – I should very much like to meet her.*'

Not an old girlfriend, unless she was a masochist.

'*Things have not always been easy between us, Robbie, and for that I accept much of the blame. But perhaps it's time to make a fresh start. After all, I am your mother.*'

Tessa drew in her breath sharply, feeling faint. Rob's mother!

Rob's mother had been in London all along, and Tessa hadn't even suspected; Rob had never said anything to indicate her whereabouts, but Tessa had imagined her living far away, in some unspecified corner of the country, or even abroad. But London! And N14 at that.

When Tessa's breathing had returned to normal, and she had begun to take in the implications of the letter, she got up and found her London A–Z, then, with the help of the index, located Chase View Road, N14. Southgate, it was. Tessa had not, to her recollection, ever been to Southgate, in the northern suburbs of London, though she knew vaguely where it was. She consulted the Underground map on the back of the A–Z: Southgate, she discovered, was on the Piccadilly line, eight stops up from Holloway Road.

Rob's mother, so long imagined and yearned for, was just eight tube stops away.

Without thinking about what she was doing, Tessa got her coat, and, armed with the A–Z, she left the house and headed for the Holloway Road.

The journey on the Underground took scarcely twenty minutes. Tessa passed the time by studying the map of Southgate in her A–Z, memorising the way from the station to Chase View Road. It wasn't far: certainly within walking distance, most likely closer to a five-minute walk than a ten-minute walk.

And as the train approached Southgate, it emerged from the tunnel and travelled above ground, giving Tessa a glimpse of substantial white houses across a stretch of green playing fields, and a church spire in the distance.

When Tessa emerged from the station, though, in spite of her preparations it took her a moment to get her bearings. The station, she discovered to her surprise, was round, a futuristic yet curiously old-fashioned building which looked as if it had strayed from some 1950s science-fiction film; it seemed, in character, far more than eight tube stops from the Victorian gloom of Holloway Road, lined with dark green tiles like an old-fashioned fireplace.

The late November sun was already hovering near the western horizon, pointing the way. West, then south. Her steps took her through a bustling parade of shops, then suddenly into a quiet residential street. This was suburbia, the houses sitting on plots of ground with a bit of elbow room between them, nothing at all like the crammed-together terraces of Islington.

One turn, then another. Chase View Road. Carefully she counted the houses. One, seven, fifteen, twenty-three.

Number 27 was, like its neighbours, a substantial detached house, set back from the road and gleaming white in the gathering dusk. Above, it was decorated with black half-timbering, in a vague 'Tudorbethan' way, and, below, it boasted a pair of post-Edwardian rounded bay windows. The result, though, was not as incongruous as it might sound; the house had a sort of dignity about it, by virtue of its size, and underpinned by its similarity to the other houses in the road.

Tessa's intentions, when she'd left home so abruptly, had been unformed; she had acted on instinct, not really sure what she was going to do. Now that she was here, she paused. Did she intend to march up to the door of number 27, to ring the bell and introduce herself to Rob's mother?

Perhaps that was what she had intended. But her courage failed her, and she lingered for a moment on the pavement, taking in the house and imprinting it in her mind, then she turned and slowly walked back through the darkening streets of Southgate towards the station.

By the time she got home, though, Tessa's resolve had hardened. Without giving herself time to think about it – to consider how Rob would feel about what she was about to do, or to ponder the consequences – she got out the telephone directory.

There was an entry for an L. Nicholls, in Chase View Road.

With fingers trembling slightly, she punched in the numbers.

'Hello?' The voice that answered was cool, female, middle-class.

Tessa opened her mouth, but found herself suddenly breathless; it was a few seconds before she was able to get the words out. 'Is this Mrs Nicholls?'

'Yes, I'm Mrs Nicholls,' the woman confirmed, with a hint of wariness born, no doubt, of having heard this question so many times on the lips of double-glazing telephone salesmen.

'And do you have a son called Rob?'

'Who is this?' the voice demanded. 'Has something happened to Robbie?'

'No, no. Rob is fine,' Tessa said quickly. 'I'm . . . his wife.'

There was a pause on the other end. 'So, you're Tessa,' said the woman at last, with more warmth in her voice.

'Yes.'

After that the conversation became easier; they talked for several minutes. Linda Nicholls reiterated what she'd said in her letter: that she very much wanted to meet Tessa. And Tessa, overwhelmed, told her, rather shyly, about the baby, and her hopes that her child would have a relationship with her grandmother. Not admitting to her mother-in-law that she had already made a preliminary trip to Southgate, she offered to visit her at the earliest opportunity.

They must meet, Linda agreed, and soon. But not at the weekend. She suggested the following Tuesday, in the afternoon. Could Tessa come to her then, for tea? Bringing Robbie, if he would agree?

Tessa could, Tessa would. And she *would* bring Rob, of that she was determined.

Anxious as she was to meet Rob's mother, the woman who would be like a mother to her, and her baby's grandmother,

Tessa didn't mind the delay too much. It would give her time to approach the subject delicately with Rob, to bring him round, to make him see that whatever had happened between him and his mother, it was in the past, and nothing could change the fact that she *was* his mother.

Chapter 6

As it turned out, Tessa spent the entire weekend trying to think of a way to broach the subject of his mother with Rob. It was a delicate and difficult issue: he seemed to be in a particularly good mood that weekend, and she was loath to spoil that by bringing up a topic which she knew he would not welcome.

So it was Monday evening, at dinner, by the time she mentioned the by-now imminent planned visit to his mother.

Tessa had been right to be worried about it; she had never seen him so angry. In fact, Tessa realised, she had never really seen him angry at all, had never heard his voice raised in fury. His displeasure had, in the past, taken the form of withdrawal, as he shut himself in his computer room and remained there until he had returned to a better humour.

This was different. Still he didn't shout at her, at least not at first, but his lips were compressed into a thin, hard line, his eyes narrowed, and he bit off each word as though it were poisonous to the taste. 'You went through my rubbish?'

'Not exactly,' she tried to explain. 'I just happened to see—'

'And you rang my mother. Without asking me, without telling me!'

Tessa hung her head meekly. 'Yes. I knew you wouldn't want me to.'

'But you did it anyway! Tessa, this is insupportable!' His

voice went up in volume, and he slammed his hand down on the table, making the cutlery jump.

She looked across at him with tears in her eyes. 'Rob, I'm trying to make you understand. It's really important to me to get to know your mother. It's important for the baby's sake, and it's important for me as well.'

'My mother', he said, and he spat out the words, 'is a bitch. If only you knew.'

'But you won't tell me,' she pointed out. 'You won't talk about her. How can I understand if you won't tell me?'

'If I tell you,' said Rob, a bit more quietly, 'tell you about the sort of bitch my mother is, will you promise that you'll forget about meeting her?'

Tessa thought about it for a moment. 'No,' she said at last. 'I can't promise that. It's too important. And anyway, Rob, when I talked to her, she sounded perfectly normal. Very nice, in fact.'

He snorted in disgust. 'So you're determined to meet her?'

'Yes,' said Tessa, quiet but certain.

'Then it's on your head! I can't stop you. *You* can meet her – I'm certainly not going.'

'I wish you would change your mind,' she said.

'Bloody hell, Tessa!' he shouted. 'When are you going to learn to leave well alone?' And with that he shoved back his chair, picked up his glass and hurled it at the opposite wall, then stalked out, not to be seen again that night.

Tessa swept up the slivers of glass carefully, too numb for tears. She *knew* that she was doing the right thing.

That conviction was borne out the next morning, at breakfast. Rob was still by no means his usual self – though his voice had returned to its normal level, his lips were still tight, and he wouldn't meet Tessa's eyes – but he apologised for throwing the glass. And, more importantly, it seemed that overnight he had changed his mind about seeing his mother.

He asked Tessa what time she was planning to go, and she told him that they had been invited to come for tea.

'But what made you assume that I could get away from work at that time?' he pointed out in a reasonable voice.

'Well, I did think of that. And I suggested that we might come at the weekend instead. She said that the weekend wouldn't be convenient.'

Rob snorted knowingly, but refused to explain.

'You *will* come?' Tessa pressed him. 'It would mean so much to me if you would come with me.'

'I can't promise that I can get away from work. But I *will* try.' Still he wouldn't look directly at her. He would, he explained, if he could manage it, meet her at his mother's house. Tessa wasn't to wait for him; she was to make her own way there, and he would meet her if he could. It wouldn't be difficult for her to find, with the help of the *A–Z*. And if she thought it was going to be a problem, she could always take a taxi.

Tessa didn't tell him that she had already been to Chase View Road. Yes, she agreed, she could find it. A taxi wouldn't be necessary. And she would meet him there.

All morning she was in a state of high excitement. At last, at last, she kept saying to herself. At last she was about to acquire a mother. She couldn't settle to doing anything, wandering the house from one end to the other.

Finally, unable to wait any longer, she set out for the Holloway Road tube station. It was barely past lunch-time, but she was drawn as if by invisible strings towards Southgate; she could always, she told herself, pass the time there, and explore the lay of the land. On her first visit she had hurried through the town itself, intent on her goal. Now she could remedy that.

Southgate, she discovered, was a sizable place, with plenty of scope for exploration. There were the usual High Street shops and fast- food outlets, but much else of an individual character: several antiques shops, upmarket eateries, charity shops, estate agents, pubs, hairdressers, newsagents, butchers, greengrocers. There was even a small shop selling baby things, and of course she couldn't resist going in, fingering the tiny frilly dresses with a thrill of anticipation. Next door was a bookshop – an independent one, not a chain – and Tessa was able to spend nearly an hour in there, browsing the shelves under the benign eye of the proprietor.

The time went more quickly than she had expected; she looked at her watch and realised that she just about had time to buy some flowers before making her way to Chase View Road. There was a convenient florist's shop, and she selected deep red roses.

Past the police station she walked, remembering vaguely that once, a few years ago, Ian had been stationed there; the name had not meant anything to her at the time.

Now it seemed very familiar to her already, as she hurried through the streets to Chase View Road. Again it was that time in a November afternoon when it suddenly became more dark than light, the night drawing in rapidly as shadows fell; people switched on lights and drew curtains, lit fires and heated kettles for tea. A cosy time, for those within, and Tessa's anticipation heightened as she walked past lights going on and curtains twitching shut.

But there were no welcoming lights in the windows at 27 Chase View Road, and the curtains in the front bays were still open, showing dark within. Tessa paused on the pavement, checking her watch. Perhaps she was a bit early, or maybe tea was laid out in some room at the back of the house.

There was no sign of Rob. Tessa, not exactly uneasy but thrown off balance by the lack of lights in the house, decided to wait a few minutes for him. He *would* come, she had convinced herself.

And sure enough, a moment later his car drew up at the kerb.

Rob got out of the car; his face looked white in the blood-draining glare of the street lamp. 'Tessa – where have you been?' he demanded. 'I was trying to ring you at home, but there was no answer. Where were you?'

She went to him, concerned. 'What's wrong? What's the matter?'

'Nothing is wrong. It was just that I found I had a meeting this afternoon, and didn't think I was going to be able to get out of it. I was hoping you would be able to reschedule this for another day.'

'I'm sorry,' she said contritely. 'I left the house early. But you're here, so you must have been able to get out of your meeting.' Tessa smiled at him, gratified that he had gone to such trouble; he must truly have had a change of heart, she thought. 'Come on then,' she added, taking his hand. 'Your mother will be waiting for us.'

Together they went to the front door; Tessa was the one who rang the bell, awkwardly, with the hand in which she held the roses. This was the way she had dreamed it would be, the way she wanted Rob's mother to see them: together, standing hand-in-hand.

And in Tessa's dreams, Rob's mother had had many different faces. Now, Tessa told herself, she was about to see the real one.

But there was no answer to the bell. Tessa pressed it again, and heard it peal inside the house.

'She's not here,' said Rob. 'She must have forgotten.'

Tessa would not, could not believe that. 'No,' she said stubbornly, trying the bell again. 'Perhaps she just didn't hear the bell. Maybe she's upstairs and didn't hear it. Or maybe she's on the phone.'

Still there were no footsteps, no indication of anyone within.

Rob dropped Tessa's hand and took a step backwards. 'Let's go,' he urged. 'We can't stand here all night, Tessa.'

'I'm not going.' Tessa had begun to feel uneasy: the house

was so very still, so dark. 'Rob, maybe there's something wrong. Maybe she can't get to the door. Perhaps she's fallen down the stairs and has hurt herself.' She *wouldn't* forget, Tessa added to herself. Something had to be wrong.

'Don't be silly, Tessa.' Rob's voice was impatient rather than indulgent. 'Let's go home. It's too cold to stand here any longer.'

It *was* cold. Tessa realised suddenly that her hands felt like ice, as she cupped them both round the bouquet of roses. At the same instant she noticed that the front door was minutely ajar, as if the Yale lock had failed to engage. With one of her cold hands she pushed on the door and it swung open.

'What the hell are you doing?' demanded Rob, taking another step away from her.

'Rob, something is wrong,' she insisted. 'She may need our help.' Through the open door she shouted, 'Hello? Is anyone there?'

Still there was no answer. Tessa stepped over the threshold, spurred by her concern; Rob had no choice but to follow. 'Hello?' he shouted in his louder voice.

They were in a large entrance hall, with stairs going up in front of them. Tessa started towards the stairs, pursuing her theory of a fall, then noticed that the door to the left was half open.

Rob went through the door first, almost stumbling over one of the fireplace irons, which was lying on the floor near the door. Automatically he picked it up, then stopped. 'Don't come in here, Tessa,' he said in a stricken voice, turning and raising his arms to shield her from the sight of what lay beyond.

It was too late; Tessa was right behind him, and she saw. The roses, red as blood, fell from her slack fingers and scattered on the floor.

Southgate police station was normally a fairly quiet place; traffic violations and burglaries were their main stock in trade.

So it was inevitable that when the call came through that there had been a murder, the news should spread quickly.

Perhaps it was a coincidence that Sergeant Douglas Coles was standing by the desk, passing the time of day with the desk sergeant, when the telephone rang.

'Murder,' said the desk sergeant, looking up and raising his eyebrows at Doug Coles. 'Just round the corner – 27 Chase View Road.'

Coles felt his muscles constrict; he wanted to sit down. He wanted to throw up. Instead he said, with a show of nonchalance, 'I'll go, shall I?'

'All right, then,' his colleague agreed. 'Find yourself a constable and get over there smartish. And take a WPC as well,' he added. 'Seems some family members found the body, and they'll want looking after.'

So Sergeant Douglas Coles went to 27 Chase View Road. He knew the way.

The family members who had found the body – a son and daughter-in-law – were, as instructed, sitting in their car outside the house. They were, understandably, in no fit state to talk about what they had seen, so Coles left them in the care of the WPC and went into the house. That was just as well; he had other things on his mind.

The constable he left guarding the front door. Soon the house would be swarming with police: scene-of-crime officers, a photographer, a doctor to certify death, the CID. But Doug Coles was the first through the door, and that gave him just a few minutes alone at the crime scene. A gift.

Linda Nicholls, dead.

For a moment he looked at her body with regret. But he was a realist, not a sentimentalist, and he knew he didn't have time to waste with cheap emotion. There were other things that needed to be done – things that just might save his own skin.

It was all part of his philosophy of life: looking out for Number One. Numero Uno. That was his motto, learned at his father's knee.

His dad had been a bitter man, even more cynical than Doug Coles. But then he'd had good reason. Doug's mum had run off with the bloke next door, leaving his dad to bring up five kids, the youngest of them – Doug himself – still a baby.

It hadn't been a very good start in life. His dad had done the best he could, but it wasn't the same as having a mum. And it had soured Doug Coles's attitude to women, at least as far as marriage was concerned. He had his women, all right. As many as he wanted, for Coles was an attractive man in a beefy, rough-diamond sort of way. But it was always on his terms: love them and leave them, hurt them before they could hurt you.

Then he'd met Linda Nicholls, and she had changed his life. She'd been different from the rest – so different. She'd given him what he'd never had from any other woman, what he'd never dreamed he could find.

And now Linda was dead.

Life, thought Doug Coles, before he went to work, was a bitch.

At the window of number 25, Hilda Steggall was having a wonderful time. Even with all of the comings and goings next door over the years, she had never seen anything like this before. Blue lights slashing through the dark, police cars in profusion, men and women in uniform and plain clothes, eventually the mortuary van. When the latter arrived, she could wait no longer. Agog with excitement, she put on her coat and went out into the road, where she stood for a moment to size things up. Then, choosing her target, she marched up to the uniformed constable who guarded the entrance to the front garden of number 27. He was young, tall, and had the sort of almost transparent skin that colours easily.

'I'm sorry, ma'am, but I can't let you pass,' he said in a conscientious but polite tone, his face flushing with the responsibility. His mother had brought him up well, Hilda Steggall thought approvingly.

'Just doing your job,' she agreed; she had expected this, fond as she was of police programmes on the telly. But there were ways of getting information. 'Someone's dead, then?' she asked, nodding in the direction of the mortuary van.

The constable hesitated, but saw no harm in confirming the obvious. 'That's right, ma'am.'

'Who is it, then?'

'I'm afraid I can't discuss that information, ma'am.' Now the tops of his ears were bright red.

Hilda was not deterred. 'It's her, isn't it? That Linda Nicholls?'

After a moment the constable nodded. He'd been ignored, treated like a gatepost, by all of the bigwigs who were coming and going from the house; here at last was someone who wanted to talk to him, who was deferring to him as a source of information. The temptation was just too great to resist. 'Her son identified the body,' he offered.

'Her son!' Now here was a turn-up for the books; Hilda Steggall hadn't seen Linda's son in years.

'He and his wife were the ones who . . . found her,' the constable added.

So the son – Robin – had a wife, and they had been here. This was something for Hilda to chew over later on. But she couldn't allow herself to be deflected. 'She was murdered, then?'

He had come this far; he saw no reason to stop now. In for a penny, in for a pound. 'That's right. Bashed with a poker, or some such.'

Hilda tried to compose her face into a semblance of regret. But all she managed was an expression of smug self-righteousness. 'I can't say I'm surprised,' she said. 'The way that woman lived.' She shook her head. 'Oh, I could tell the police a thing or two. If they cared to have a word with me. I live next door – number 25. Mrs Steggall. You'll tell them?'

'I'll tell them.'

The WPC drove Tessa and Rob home to Islington in their own car, judging that he was not fit to drive. She accompanied them into the house, made them mugs of strong sweet tea – in time-honoured tradition – then offered to ring their GP and ask her to prescribe a sedative. She also warned them, in a gentle way, that the police would want to talk to them, a bit later but before the day was over. They had found the body; they were the chief witnesses. And at this point the police had nothing else to go on, no one else to talk to.

They were both in shock; the enormity of what they'd seen, and what it meant, had scarcely begun to sink in. The arrival of the CID, later that evening, was like a physical assault. Rob withdrew into himself, and Tessa reacted with anger.

'Can't you just leave him alone?' she demanded. 'His mother has been murdered! He just wants to be left alone to grieve!'

Detective Inspector Tower had heard it all before; it was an occupational hazard. He was sympathetic, of course, but he had a job to do. 'Just a few questions,' he said quietly but firmly.

They sat hand-in-hand on the sofa as he led them, step by step, through the events of the afternoon, culminating in the finding of the body. At this point Rob seemed to break down, slumping over and covering his head with his arms, though he still hadn't shed a tear.

DI Tower pressed on, as soon as Rob had regained a measure of composure. 'So you picked up the poker, Mr Nicholls. Why did you do that?'

'Because it was lying on the floor and I didn't want to trip over it.'

'Did it seem odd to you that a poker was lying on the floor?'

Rob frowned. 'Of course it seemed odd. My mother was a

very tidy person – she wouldn't have left a poker on the floor.'

The Inspector nodded. 'So you picked up the murder weapon, and obliterated any fingerprints that the murderer might have left on the handle.'

'I didn't know it was the murder weapon, did I?' Rob snapped.

'Didn't you?'

The Inspector's implication penetrated the numbness in which Tessa had wrapped herself to get her through the ordeal of the interview. 'Are you suggesting that my husband murdered his own mother?' she cried.

'I'm not suggesting that at all, Mrs Nicholls,' said the Inspector, though it appeared to Tessa that his expression was at odds with his words. 'But it does seem peculiar to me that he should pick up what was so clearly the murder weapon.'

'I picked it up before I knew there had been a . . . murder,' Rob explained wearily. 'Before I saw . . . the body. My mother's body. I saw the fire-iron on the floor, and I picked it up. End of story.'

But it wasn't the end of the story, as far as DI Tower was concerned. He asked each of them for a detailed account of their whereabouts and activities for the entire day.

Rob went first. He'd been at work, he said, until it was time to leave for Southgate and the scheduled meeting with his mother. He'd come by car, and joined up with Tessa there. Tessa had arrived first.

Tessa explained that she had been at home in the morning, by herself, and had spent a couple of hours in Southgate in the afternoon before going to Chase View Road. She had no real alibi, she said defiantly, just in case the Inspector thought that she had murdered her mother-in-law. The ticket inspection booth at Southgate station had been unmanned, and the only person she'd spoken to all afternoon was the proprietor of the bookshop – Winston, he was called.

It was all duly noted down by Sergeant Doug Coles, who

up to this point had been silent but watchful, waiting for his chance. 'And before today, when was the last time you saw your mother, Mr Nicholls?' he said suddenly.

The Inspector shot him a look, but nodded at Rob to answer.

'I don't know . . . exactly,' Rob said, looking at his hands.

'Approximately, then,' urged the Inspector.

Rob bit his lip and shut his eyes. 'About . . . seven years ago. Or eight.'

DI Tower's eyes widened. 'You hadn't seen your mother in seven or eight years?'

'No.'

'Could I ask you why?'

'That', said Rob viciously, 'is none of your bloody business.'

The Inspector went on as though this exchange had not taken place. 'Does that mean, Mrs Nicholls, that you had never met your mother-in-law?'

Tessa gulped. 'No. I mean yes. I mean, I had never met her.'

'She was a stranger to you.'

'Yes.'

'But', the Inspector probed, 'you were going to have tea with her.'

Tessa explained, as calmly as she could, that she had spoken to Linda Nicholls on the phone, that she had wanted to meet her husband's mother, and that she wanted their baby to know her grandmother. This was all the truth, of course, but there was much that Tessa didn't say: she didn't tell him how she and Rob had quarrelled over his mother, more than once, or how adamant he had been that he didn't want any dealings with her. She didn't recount her subterfuge in finding Linda Nicholls, or the fact that she had initiated the contact without Rob's knowledge or consent.

She *knew* Rob, knew that he had nothing to do with his mother's death, but she was beginning to be afraid of how it would look to the police. The less said, the better.

The Inspector asked Rob another question. 'If you hadn't seen your mother in that many years – seven or eight years, you say – does that also mean that you had not been to the house at 27 Chase View Road during that time?'

'Yes, of course.'

'But you *had* been there in the past?' he pursued.

Rob answered with deliberate patience, masking contempt, as though he were talking to a halfwit. 'Of course I had. I grew up in that house. Lived there for years, except when I was away at school.'

Tessa's gasp of surprise at that information was not lost on the Inspector, but he didn't pursue it. 'So,' he said, 'you were familiar with the house, and knew where the fire-irons were.'

'What the bloody hell are you getting at?' he lashed out. 'What are you implying?' Tessa, holding his hand, could feel the tension which held his body rigid, like a piano string that had been tightened almost to breaking-point.

She reacted more quickly than the policeman. 'Inspector,' she said firmly, surprising herself as much as him, 'my husband has just lost his mother, in a horrible way, and he is quite naturally upset. He has answered all of your questions. Now I think that it's time for you to go, to leave us alone. If you have any further questions, I'm sure they can keep till tomorrow.'

Caught unawares by her determination, DI Tower gave in with good grace and retreated. 'I *will* be back tomorrow,' he promised at the door.

Doug Coles, following him, turned back to look at Rob, his eyes narrowed. Neither Rob nor Tessa noticed.

Ministering to Rob, concentrating on his needs, was the only way that Tessa got through that evening. If she thought about Rob, and what he was going through, she could hold at bay the memory of that hideous moment, that instant of utter horror before Rob's encircling arms had blocked her view.

Later, too, there would be her own more complex

bereavement to deal with. But for now she must think only of Rob.

He had lost his mother; he had seen her dead, savagely murdered body.

And inevitably the knowledge of the years of estrangement must give him an extra burden of guilt. All of those 'what ifs . . .

No matter what had happened between him and his mother to cause them to be estranged, she had still been his mother, and that was a bond that could never be completely broken. But the incontrovertible fact was that now she was dead, and there would be no mending of fences, no reconciliation. And all of those years had been lost for ever.

Tessa knew and understood all of these things. Rob was frozen, locked in a torment that she could not share or take away from him. But she could be there for him, and she was determined to reach him somehow.

He refused food, he refused drink, he refused a sedative. Still he held himself rigid, unwilling or unable to cry for the woman who had given him birth.

Tessa led him upstairs to the bedroom and settled down with him on the bed, encircling him with her arms.

Suddenly Rob broke down. One tear trickled down his cheek, followed by a flood. He sobbed in Tessa's arms, clinging to her like a drowning man. 'Mummy! Mummy!' he cried over and over again, his voice thick with pain. Tessa stroked his hair, cradled his head on her breast, shared his agony.

When, after a time, the flood had subsided, and the tears reduced to a trickle, something unexpected happened. Rob's head was still cradled on Tessa's breast, and he began to unbutton her blouse. Without waiting for either of them to undress, he made love to her swiftly, urgently, with a single-minded fierce intensity such as she had never experienced before.

After that he fell asleep immediately, and heavily, as though drugged, half on top of her, their clothing in uncomfortable disarray.

Tessa did not sleep. She held her husband in her arms, triumphant and relieved that he had somehow returned to her, yet ashamed at her feeling of satisfaction, in view of the circumstances that had brought it about.

His mother was dead, and he was shattered.

The police would be back, with more questions designed to entrap him: they had no other leads, no other suspects, and would not leave Rob alone.

Tessa would protect him. She wouldn't let the police bully him.

She had to be strong, for his sake.

These were the thoughts that occupied her wandering mind into the night. She would *not* think about what she had seen; she would *not* think about what she had lost. Least of all would she think about her own guilt, that implacable inner voice that said: *your fault*.

But when she closed her eyes at last, she dreamed of those roses, strewn on the carpet, as red as blood.

Chapter 7

Father Theo Frost always began his day by saying Morning Prayer. A shave, a quick shower, then across to the church for Morning Prayer, followed, most days, by a celebration of the Mass. Daily celebration: that was one of the tenets of his Anglo-Catholic faith, and he carried it out with conscientious reverence. No one else ever attended, not even the handful of old ladies who came to evensong, but he was scrupulous about beginning at the advertised time, just in case. It was his discipline, and much as he would have enjoyed a lie-in, every now and again, he forced himself to get up when the alarm rang.

The year was drawing to a close; today was the first of December. Advent already, and soon it would be Christmas. The darkest time of the year; when Father Theo's alarm sounded it was pitch black inside and out, and it was only barely light when he locked up the church behind him and returned to the clergy house for his breakfast.

That breakfast was his reward for being up and about so early. Mrs Williams, his housekeeper, shared his philosophy about breakfast, and it was her joy as well as her duty to provide it for him. A fry-up, always: egg, bacon, sausage, mushrooms, tomato, and fried bread, and on high days and holy days black pudding as well. Terrible for his arteries as well as his weight, and Father Theo knew that he ought to be eating

All-Bran and dry brown toast instead, but breakfast was his one indulgence. Almost, he told himself, his only one.

Lunch would be more austere – perhaps no more than a bowl of soup. And his evening meal was often taken in haste, sandwiched between meetings and other commitments. So it was important, he told himself, that he breakfasted well, got the day off to a good start.

And Mrs Williams would be so disappointed if he didn't have his cooked breakfast.

Fresh coffee, strong and hot, was waiting for him on the scrubbed pine table, next to his morning paper, when he came in, his pink face even pinker than usual from the cold of the December morning. Mrs Williams always managed to time the coffee perfectly so that it was ready when he arrived, giving him a few minutes to enjoy it with the paper before his breakfast was presented to him.

So on Wednesday morning he settled down as usual, took a sip of coffee, and unfolded *The Guardian*.

The murder was on the front page. Murder in London, in Southgate. 'Southgate Woman Slain', said the headline. Father Theo shook his head in automatic sympathy, then looked more closely at the blurred photo of the victim. A passport photo, or something similar, and not a very good likeness. But he drew in his breath sharply as he recognised her: Linda Nicholls. There was no mistake about it.

Mrs Williams heard the intake of breath, saw the dismay on his face. She shook her head. 'It's a wicked world we live in,' she intoned.

Father Theo scarcely heard her as he scanned the article. The details were sketchy, but he could imagine it all too well: the drawing room, the fireplace irons. Linda. His vivid imagination combined the familiar elements and produced a horrifying mental picture.

Linda's son and his wife had found the body. 'Oh, the poor creatures,' Father Theo said aloud.

Mrs Williams scooped the last mushroom out of the frying pan on to his plate and brought it to the table, presenting it to him with a flourish.

'No thank you, Mrs Williams, I couldn't possibly,' Father Theo said, rising from his chair. 'I must go back to the church. To pray.'

'Well!' Astonished, she watched as he hurried from the kitchen, fumbling in his cassock pocket for his keys.

Inside the church, Father Theo didn't bother with the lights; he knew his way. His first stop was the candle stand before the statue of the Virgin and Child. With shaking fingers he struck a match, lit a candle, stuck it into one of the holders. 'Mother of God,' he breathed aloud. 'Have mercy on her soul. Rest eternal grant unto her, and let light perpetual shine upon her. May she rest in peace and rise in glory.'

The statue looked down upon him with a fixed, inscrutable smile.

He repeated the words several times, until they ceased to have any meaning.

Then he went into the chancel, to his stall in the sanctuary. The light was just beginning to glimmer through the east window as he knelt in his stall. There, fixing his eyes on the great gilded crucifix on the altar, he prayed for the son, for the daughter-in-law. For everyone who had loved Linda Nicholls, and now had lost her. For himself.

After a good many minutes had passed and he had finished his prayers, he remained on his knees as his thoughts charged ahead to the implications of Linda's death.

The son and the daughter-in-law. They would need help, spiritual and practical. There would be arrangements to be made, technicalities to be looked after. A funeral.

Someone would have to take the funeral, though Linda had by no means been a religious woman.

Should he offer to do it? *Could* he? Father Theo knew that he ought to make the offer, but he wasn't sure that he had the courage. To call attention to himself – questions might be asked. Questions that he couldn't answer.

That unleashed a whole flood of unwelcome thoughts. Someone, he realised suddenly, had killed Linda Nicholls. Not just wished her dead, but murdered her. Was it someone that he knew? Possibly, even probably.

He didn't have to ask himself *why* someone had killed Linda. That was obvious.

And then an even more chilling thought: Linda had kept records. Thorough records, he was sure. That meant that it could be only a matter of time before the police came to him. Then it would be all over for him. Exposure, humiliation, shame. And he would have to leave the Church, to give up his true vocation.

Shivering in the cold church, Father Theo bowed his head over his clasped hands and prayed for courage. Courage to do the right thing, courage to face the inevitable.

The kitchen where James Wooldridge ate his breakfast had very little other than its function in common with the one in Father Theo's Victorian clergy house: his was a modern kitchen, in a modern house, equipped with every convenience. The coffee – decaff, of course – was made in an electric drip machine, and kept warm on the integral hotplate.

The coffee was the only thing hot about James Wooldridge's breakfast. And there was no Mrs Williams to prepare it for him. Felicity had put the coffee on to brew before going out to take the children to school, but the rest was up to him.

Not that it was difficult. Bran flakes, followed by brown toast. Every day, the same. The only difference was that on a Monday, Wednesday and Friday – the days that Felicity visited the health club for an hour-long workout and swim after dropping the children off – James allowed himself a spoon-ful of marmalade on his toast. Felicity, who had decreed the bran flakes and brown toast, didn't approve of marmalade:

not good for teeth or figure. But James was partial to marmalade, and in a rare gesture of defiance, he bought it in secret and ate it when Felicity was out. Guiltily, but he ate it.

This was a Wednesday, so the marmalade jar came out of hiding, joining the bran flakes and the rack of toast on the chrome-and-glass table. James, freshly showered and dressed in a bespoke suit and expensive silk tie, poured himself a cup of coffee, regretting – as he occasionally did – that it contained no kick of caffeine, and took it to the table, where his papers waited for him. Felicity arranged them for him each morning before she left: the *Financial Times* on top, the *The Daily Telegraph* underneath.

He picked up the salmon-coloured *FT* and leafed through it while he sipped the coffee and poured a splash of milk on his bran flakes. Mergers and acquisitions, profits and losses – appropriate, somehow, to accompany the tasteless crunch of bran flakes.

Then he opened the marmalade jar, spooned some on to his toast, and unfolded *The Daily Telegraph*.

It was the picture that he saw first, rather than the headline. The blurry passport photo, vaguely familiar. 'Oh, God,' he said aloud as he read the caption, identifying the subject of the photo, and then the headline: 'Death in Suburbia'.

'Oh, God. Oh, God. Oh, God,' he repeated over and over to himself as he scanned the article. Not much detail, but enough. Linda Nicholls was dead. Linda Nicholls had been murdered.

That was all that James Wooldridge needed to know. The details weren't important; the fact itself was.

With the quick mind and ability to get to the heart of things that had made him a successful businessman, James Wooldridge grasped the implications immediately.

He was about to become, if he wasn't already, a murder suspect.

Linda had been no fool, no sentimentalist. In spite of what he – and the others – chose to think of her, James knew that she had been a businesswoman first and foremost. She would have kept records. And even if they were coded, it could only be a matter of time before someone found him.

Because who else could have – would have – killed her, if not one of them? She'd given them reason enough, and no one knew that better than he. The police weren't stupid. They would work that out.

James folded the paper carefully and returned it to its spot on the table. There was nothing he could do – nothing but wait. No one he could contact, no strings he could pull. What would happen would happen; things were out of his control.

It wasn't until he was at work, sitting at his vast desk, that he remembered something important: he had left the marmalade on the table. James Wooldridge groaned and covered his face with his hands. Felicity would kill him.

Harold Dingley had been working the night shift at the hospital, and it had been a good night: three babies born, and he'd been able to hold two of them. So he was feeling tired but pleased as he made his way home in the morning.

He was hungry; Harold was often hungry. He didn't want to spend any of his hard-earned money to buy himself something to eat – after all, Friday was now only two days away – but he knew that by now his sister Bunny would have gone to work and would not be at home to give him breakfast. Anyway, he was almost sure that she wouldn't have bought the sort of food he liked to eat at this time of day: sweet things. For breakfast he liked sugary treats like Pop-Tarts and pastries, but Bunny somehow never remembered to buy them on her trips to the grocery store.

There was a doughnut shop near the tube station, and Harold decided to drop in there. He could get a doughnut and a mug of sweet tea, and it wouldn't set him back much more than a quid. And he could read a newspaper while he was eating, which would save him buying one.

He selected a large sugary doughnut from the case, and a *Daily Mail* from the rack of newspapers. Bunny liked the *Daily Mail*, and if they ever had a paper at home, that's what it would be. 'Terrible about that murder,' said the girl behind the counter in a chatty sort of voice. She knew Harold by sight – he often stopped in for a doughnut in the morning – and she liked to have something to say to him.

'Murder?' said Harold. He took his breakfast and the paper to one of the Formica tables.

It dominated the entire front page. 'Why did she die?' shouted the headline in large bold type, above a huge blown-up photo, a close-up of a face, blurred even more by the enlargement. 'Tragic Linda', proclaimed the caption.

Harold recognised the face, in spite of the poor quality of the photo. Still he didn't grasp what had happened. He read the words, but they didn't make sense to him.

'Linda Nicholls lived alone, in a quiet suburban street in Southgate, north London,' said the *Daily Mail*. 'Her neighbours describe her as a private person, keeping herself to herself. Yet yesterday afternoon someone killed Linda Nicholls, brutally, beating her to death with the poker from her own fireplace. Did she interrupt a burglary in progress, or was she murdered by someone she knew?'

She was dead. As the meaning of the words penetrated Harold's brain, he gave a little cry. Abandoning paper and doughnut, he blundered out of the shop, his thoughts focused on that one terrible fact.

He didn't know where he was going, what he was doing; there was no room in his brain for conscious, rational thought. Without making any deliberate decision about it, he went down into the Underground. There was only one place he could go right now, and his body was taking him there.

Southgate. Chase View Road. His feet carried him down the familiar streets. All the while he moaned, making little whimpering noises like an animal in pain.

A mistake. There had to be a mistake. It was someone else who was dead: some other Linda Nicholls, who looked a bit like her and lived in Southgate.

But as he approached number 27 he saw the blue-and-white crime scene tape blocking off the entrance to the front garden.

No mistake. Harold stopped, clung to a bit of wall, and burst into tears. Noisy, extravagant tears, uncontrollable and uncontrolled, such as he hadn't wept since his mother had died.

Sergeant Doug Coles picked up a newspaper on his way to the police station that morning. The *Sun*. 'House of Horror', shrieked the front-page headline, in huge fat type. They alone of the papers featured a photo of the house, taken in the dark and thus intensifying its demonic atmosphere.

When he got to his desk, with the greasy bacon butty he'd collected from the police canteen – his customary breakfast, though once in a while he varied it with a sausage butty or a chip butty instead – he settled down to read the story.

'*Sun* Exclusive', it trumpeted. After it had dealt with the facts of the story – the who and where and when – it entered into the realms of the why and wherefore. 'Sources inside the police describe the murder as "horrific" and a "bloodbath", and tell the *Sun* that there was no sign of forced entry. This leads police to believe that Linda Nicholls might have been slain by someone she knew. The *Sun*, on behalf of its readers, calls on the police to catch this maniac! Get him off the streets!!'

Sources inside the police: Doug Coles liked the sound of that. That was him, of course. He'd even been paid a bit of money for the information, which made it all the better. Just as long as no one found out, and there was no reason why they should.

No reason why they should find out about the *Sun*, or about anything else. Why would they even suspect?

He was still eating his breakfast when the young constable who had guarded the entrance to the crime scene came into the office, the tips of his ears pink with the importance of his task. 'The woman next door,' he said. 'She asked me to tell someone involved in the investigation that she might have some information that would be relevant.'

'And you're telling me,' Coles stated.

The constable nodded conscientiously. 'I've written it all down here on this bit of paper – her name and her address.'

Coles reached for the paper. 'Thank you very much, Constable. Good work.'

Nodding and blushing, the constable retreated. As soon as he'd gone, Coles tore the paper into tiny fragments and dropped them into the bin, smiling a private smile.

Doug Coles was well pleased with himself as he finished his bacon butty and wiped the grease from his fingers. He had saved his skin, saved his career and his reputation, and that was the most important thing.

His optimism was confirmed a bit later, as he joined everyone else for a briefing by Inspector Tower. They had no leads, Tower told them; they were no closer to making an arrest than they had been yesterday afternoon. Yes, it was true that there had been no forced entry – and at this Tower glared round the room, as if trying to pick out the Judas who had passed that information on to the *Sun* – but there was also no forensic evidence that had got them any farther along. Plenty of fingerprints all over the place, but the only ones on the murder weapon were those of the son, who had so carelessly picked it up and thus obliterated any prints that might have been left by the murderer.

It seemed, Doug Coles told himself, that this was one murder that would never be solved. A few weeks of police time wasted with frantic rushing about, a mountain of paperwork accumulating, then it would all just go on to the back burner, where it would stay. And that suited him just fine.

*

When Tessa woke, she was alone in bed. Rob, showered and shaved and dressed, stood in front of the mirror, concentrating as he tied his tie.

'What are you doing?' Tessa asked groggily.

Rob's reply was patient. 'My tie.'

'But why? Where are you going?'

'To work, of course.' He consulted his watch. 'And if the traffic isn't too bad, I ought to make it on time.'

She sat up in bed. 'But you can't go to work! Your mother is dead!'

Rob pressed his lips together, spoke deliberately. 'And how will my going to work change that? If I stay at home, will she be any less dead?'

'But the police! They said they would be back today, that they'd have more questions.'

'The police can wait,' he stated, turning back to the mirror. 'And if they want me badly enough, I'm sure they'll find me.'

Tessa subsided back on to the pillows. 'What about your breakfast?'

'I'm not hungry.' Rob leaned over the bed and gave her a perfunctory kiss. 'Try to get some sleep. I'll unplug the phone by the bed.' He knelt down and disconnected the jack from the extension box.

It seemed to Tessa that she was conversing entirely in questions. 'Why are you doing that?'

'Because,' Rob explained succinctly, 'the press will be trying to ring. Wanting some nice juicy quotes on how it feels to find your mother murdered.'

Tessa shuddered. How could he speak about it so dispassionately?

In a moment he was gone; Tessa heard the front door click behind him.

She felt stiff, as though she'd slept in an uncomfortable position. And she was still wearing her clothes from the day before, she realised. She ought to get up, have a nice hot shower, change her clothes. It would make her feel better.

But if she got up, she would have to think, and Tessa didn't want to do that. She didn't have the will or the energy to get out of bed, or even to get undressed and put on something more comfortable.

She pulled the covers up round her shoulders, turned and buried her face in the pillow, and slept.

When she woke again it was afternoon, judging from the angle of the light that filtered through the curtains. She didn't want to get up, but she discovered that she needed to go to the loo, and she had an overpowering desire to talk to Rob, to hear his voice. So she went into the bathroom, and splashed some cold water on her face before returning to the bedroom and reconnecting the phone.

Someone else answered his phone – screening calls from the press, Tessa surmised. But when she had identified herself, he came on the line straight away.

'What's going on?' he asked.

'I just needed to hear your voice,' she explained feebly. 'How have you been? Don't you think you ought to come home early?'

'I'll be all right.' The stoicism sounded not at all forced. 'Have you been getting some sleep, Tessa?'

'I haven't done anything *but* sleep,' she admitted. 'And I haven't even thought about food. About what to make for dinner, or anything.'

'Don't worry about that. I'll bring something home,' Rob stated. 'A takeaway. Some Chinese. Or would you rather have a pizza?'

'I don't care.' Tessa wasn't hungry; she was only concerned for Rob.

'I'll see you at the usual time then,' he said, ringing off.

Tessa restored the phone to its cradle and sat on the edge

of the bed, trying to summon the energy to decide what to do next. Back to bed, or get up and have a shower?

The phone rang, almost immediately. She picked it up and answered. 'Hello?'

'Mrs Nicholls?' enquired a smooth voice, unfamiliar to her. 'Yes . . .'

'I'm from the *Sun*, Mrs Nicholls. I wondered if I might have a word.' He went on quickly, not giving her time to reply. 'Our readers would be very interested in your story, Mrs Nicholls. How you felt when you discovered your mother-in-law had been murdered, that sort of thing. An exclusive. You wouldn't have to write anything yourself, of course. Just talk to me and tell me your story, either on the phone or face to face if you'd find that easier. And we would pay you rather well.' Without pausing for breath, the voice adopted a more unctuous tone. 'And, by the way, may I offer you my deepest sympathy on your very great loss?'

Tessa squeezed her eyes shut. 'How could you?' she demanded, slamming the phone down.

She was afraid to pick it up when it rang again, a moment later, and her hand hesitated over the receiver. But she had an almost superstitious fear of leaving a phone unanswered. It could be Rob, it could be the police. It could be something important, or even urgent.

'Tessa?' said a voice that she recognised immediately.

'Andrew!' She relaxed back on to the bed, her tension dissolving in a warm feeling of relief.

'I've been trying to reach you all day,' he said. 'Tessa . . . I just don't know what to say. I'm so sorry.'

She could picture him, sitting at his desk, as she'd seen him there talking on the phone so many times, and the familiarity of the imagined picture brought her an obscure – and unexpected – sort of comfort. 'Thanks, Andrew,' was all she could manage.

'I know you're not all right, so I won't even ask. And I don't suppose that there's anything I can do. But if there were, you would tell me, wouldn't you?' The concern in his voice was sincere.

'I . . . suppose so.'

'Because you know that I'd do anything I could. For you, for the baby. And for Rob,' he added in what sounded almost like an afterthought.

The baby. She'd scarcely thought of the baby in nearly twenty-four hours, Tessa realised with a shock. Instinctively, her arm curled round her abdomen.

'Are you managing to eat anything?' Andrew went on, adding, 'I could do some shopping for you, if you like.'

'I'm not hungry,' she said automatically.

'That's not surprising. I'd feel the same, I'm sure. But you have to think about the baby, Tessa. You have to eat something, keep up your strength, for her sake.'

The baby. She would not, after all, know her grandmother.

Perhaps it was Andrew's evident empathy that undid Tessa. She closed her eyes, and in spite of herself, two fat tears squeezed out from the corners and trickled down her cheeks.

For several minutes after she'd finished talking to Andrew, Tessa cried into her pillow. This time she was crying on the baby's behalf, rather than Rob's: still not for herself. Her own grief was walled up somewhere deep inside.

She had stopped crying, and blown her nose, when the phone rang again.

'Mrs Nicholls?' enquired another unfamiliar male voice, tentative and soft-spoken.

Surprised at her own firmness, Tessa stated, 'If you're from the press, I have nothing to say to you.'

'Oh, no,' he said quickly. 'I'm not from the press. I'm a priest.'

'A priest? A Catholic priest?' Though Tessa's father was a clergyman, his churchmanship was very middle-of-the-road;

he would never have called himself a priest, and the usage confused her.

'*Anglo*-Catholic, not Roman.' The voice had a nice touch of humour, as though he were smiling at the question, and had heard it before. 'I'm called Father Theo,' he added belatedly. 'I know . . . knew . . . your mother-in-law. Linda Nicholls.'

'Oh!' Tessa swallowed. 'I didn't know that she went to church.'

The humour was there again, just a glimmer of it. 'She didn't. That's really why I'm ringing. Have you . . .' He paused, then went on in a different tone of voice, sombre and concerned. 'Have you and your husband made any arrangements yet for the funeral?'

'Funeral!' Oh, God, thought Tessa. She hadn't even begun to consider the idea of a funeral, or the fact that they would have to make the arrangements. There was no one else to do it. 'No,' she faltered. 'I hadn't thought . . .'

'It won't be for a week or so,' he said comfortingly. 'There will be . . . other formalities. I suppose there will have to be an inquest, and so forth.'

'Of course,' she realised, fresh despair overwhelming her.

'But I just wanted to offer my services, if you feel it's appropriate. To take the funeral, or help in any other way that I can. Linda wasn't a churchgoer, as you said. Her parish priest wouldn't know her, though he would of course conduct her funeral, and hold it at the parish church, if that was what you and your husband wanted. But if you would rather have someone who knew her, I would be very happy to do it here at my church – St Nicholas, Hoxton.'

'How did you know my mother-in-law?' Tessa asked with a flicker of curiosity. There was so much she didn't know about Linda Nicholls, so much she wanted to know, and here was someone who could tell her. 'Since she wasn't a churchgoer, I mean.'

Father Theo paused, then said in a neutral voice, 'We . . . were friends. I was very fond of her.'

Someone who had known Linda Nicholls, and had been fond of her. 'Oh, yes,' said Tessa. 'Of course we'd be delighted if you could take the funeral. Perhaps we could meet soon. Talk about it.'

'If you think that your husband would agree . . .'

That brought Tessa up short. *Would* Rob agree, if he knew that this Father Theo had been a friend of his mother's? Her husband's feelings about his mother were so complicated, but surely, now that she was dead, things would be different. Now he could come to terms with their relationship – now that it was too late to change anything. Too late.

Chapter 8

The next few days passed in a merciful blur for Tessa. The police came and went, several times. An inquest was opened and adjourned. Through it all, Rob professed a smooth indifference which Tessa suspected masked deep grief and regret at a relationship that could never, now, be put right.

She was worried about him. After that one night of extravagant mourning, he seemed to have shut down his feelings, and that could not be healthy. He should be raging, shouting, weeping. Instead he was placid, almost sanguine.

And, she admitted to herself, it must seem very strange indeed to the police. He had told them his story several times, and now he could relate it calmly, with no show of emotion.

He had left it to her to make the funeral arrangements, which she had done with the very welcome help of Father Theo. The priest had been wonderful, taking much of the burden from Tessa's shoulders; he'd even seen to the placing of the notices in the papers.

And now, here they were at the funeral. Tessa had feared that, at the last minute, Rob would refuse to attend, but he had come. Dressed carefully in a dark suit, white shirt and the black tie which she'd bought for him, he sat beside her in the front pew of the church, looking grave and very handsome. He was sombre, and Tessa was on edge: would he break down?

Her attention was focused on him, rather than on the other mourners. There were not many of them, and they were all sitting behind her, but she registered, dimly, that most of them were male. Men of all ages, on their own, with seemingly little in common between them. Among them were one or two policemen, out of uniform, who looked familiar to her; that, Tessa supposed, was not surprising, given the manner of Linda Nicholls's death.

Father Theo, wearing a black cope, preceded the pallbearers and the simple pine coffin into the church, intoning the burial sentences. '*I am the resurrection and the life, saith the Lord* . . .'

Tessa took Rob's hand. It was cold, lifeless. Her heart ached for him.

'*We brought nothing into this world*,' boomed Father Theo in a sombre voice, '*and it is certain we can carry nothing out. The Lord gave, and the Lord hath taken away* . . .'

For a brief instant Tessa allowed herself to think of her own loss. She had not attended her own mother's funeral, so in a sense this moment stood for that as well. She'd had her own mother for a few brief – all too brief – years, then her mother had been taken from her. Linda Nicholls, the mother who would have been, she'd lost before she could even claim her. Suddenly she realised the extent, not just of her loss, but of her anger with God. How could He be so cruel?

Her anger did not extend to Father Theo, who was now facing them from the front of the church with benign sorrow. Tessa wrenched her thoughts back to the present, back to Rob's cold hand and Father Theo's sad visage.

Thus far her contact with the priest had been on a purely practical level; he had guided and helped her with the funeral arrangements, and that was all. Tessa was aware that he was willing and available to talk about spiritual matters, should she wish it, but she had deliberately resisted that. She wasn't ready.

Nor had she been ready to talk about Linda Nicholls: about the brief glimpse she had had of her in death, or about what she might have been like in life. Father Theo had known her; he had described her as his friend. Looking at him now, Tessa wondered about that friendship. How had they met? What had they shared in common? What could he tell her about the woman who had given birth to Rob? The woman whose mortal remains lay in that pine box, just in front of her. Tessa mustn't allow herself to think about that, to feel Linda's presence. Instead she focused on Father Theo, on the earnest round pink face below the balding dome of a forehead, the light glinting from his steel-rimmed spectacles, and on the sound of the words that he spoke.

Churchy words, meaningless to her. Psalms and prayers and readings from the Bible. She had heard them all before, or interchangeable ones just like them, glib words from the mouth of her father.

Now his words changed, and the tone of his voice changed: the sermon. Rob had been invited to say a few words about his mother, and had refused; Father Theo was to speak about her instead.

Tessa sat up straight and listened.

'We are here today,' said Father Theo, 'to celebrate the life of Linda Nicholls. To remember her, as we knew her. Our friend.' He looked at Rob and Tessa. 'Our mother. Some of us have known her for very many years, others of us not so long. But she has affected each one of us, or we would not be here today.' He paused, then went on. 'Linda was a woman of unusual gifts. We've all experienced that, in different ways. We shall all miss her very much, and carry with us for ever our memories of what she has meant to us. We shall not forget her.'

'The manner of her death was horrible. But what we must remember about Linda is not her death, but her life. She lived her life in her own way, on her own terms, overcoming difficult circumstances through her own strength of character, yet always giving of herself to others.'

There was more, but Tessa's attention shifted to her husband. Beside her Rob was rigid. She could feel the tension in his body, coiled like a steel spring. How painful it must be for him, when he had been estranged from his mother for so many years, to hear about what she had meant to other people. Why? Tessa wondered, not for the first time. What silly, inconsequential thing had come between this man and the mother whom he had obviously loved so deeply? And why couldn't he – wouldn't he – talk to her, his own wife, about it?

After the sermon came a few more prayers, then Father Theo spoke the stark words of the committal: 'earth to earth, ashes to ashes, dust to dust'. There would be no graveside service; the coffin would be taken from the church to the crematorium. This was the end.

As the coffin began its last journey from the church, on the shoulders of the professional pallbearers, there was a cry from behind. Tessa turned to see a man move to the end of the aisle, putting his hand out to touch the coffin as it passed. He was weeping extravagantly, his face distorted in pain; a youngish man, though it was difficult to tell his age, looking as though he was not used either to being in church or to wearing the tie which, awkwardly tied, seemed to strangle him. Who was he, and why was he grieving so?

A few minutes later, as Tessa and Rob moved towards the church door, Tessa became aware of a woman hovering just inside the door. A respectable-looking, middle-class woman, the far side of middle age, neatly dressed in conspicuous black – black coat over black dress – and wearing a black hat perched on brown hair which was far too uniformly-coloured to be natural. 'Robin?' said the woman as they approached. 'I'd like . . .'

Rob looked at her coldly and walked straight past.

Tessa was torn between her desire to follow him and her

embarrassment at his rudeness, and desire to put it right, coupled with curiosity: who was this woman who knew Rob by name? Momentarily the latter won out, and she paused. 'I'm so sorry,' she said. 'My husband is very upset.'

The woman smiled ingratiatingly. 'I understand, my dear. You're the new wife, then.'

'Yes, I'm Tessa.'

'And I'm Mrs Steggall. Hilda. Linda's neighbour,' she said, claiming an intimacy in death that she had not had in life, and put out a black-gloved hand.

Tessa took her hand. 'Oh – how do you do, Mrs Steggall.'

'And I just wanted to offer my condolences to you and your husband.' She gave an ostentatious sniff, fumbling in her coat pocket for a tissue. 'Very sad. Such a bad business.'

'Yes,' Tessa said inadequately, thinking that she ought to catch up with Rob.

'And if you ever want to talk, my dear, you know where to find me. Number 25. I'm almost always there.'

'Thank you,' Tessa responded. 'And if you'll forgive me, Mrs Steggall, I must go.'

She found Rob waiting on the pavement outside. 'What did you have to go and talk to that old bag for?' he said.

Tessa was shocked by his tone of voice as much as by his words. 'Rob! She just wanted to offer her condolences.'

'Wanted to ingratiate herself, you mean,' he said dismissively. 'Nosy old cow. Probably thought we'd invite her to join us for the funeral baked meats or something.'

'There aren't any funeral baked meats.'

'Oh, my literal Tessa.' Rob took her hand. 'It's one of the many things I love about you. Let's go home.'

'But shouldn't we—'

He cut across her words. 'Let's go home. Now.'

All of those men. It worried at the edges of Tessa's consciousness through the day, conveniently keeping her thoughts away from the crematorium. She refrained from mentioning it to Rob, but it nagged at her. Why had Hilda Steggall been virtually the only female at the funeral?

In the middle of the night she awoke, overheated, and with an answer shrieking in her head.

Lovers. Linda had had lovers.

It would explain so much.

All of those men.

It would even explain why Rob had been estranged from his mother, if he had not approved of her promiscuous life-style. Rob was no prude, but he had standards.

And if she had taken lovers, had affairs, while she was still married to his father, Rob could blame her for the break-up of the marriage, for the fact that his father was now living on another continent.

Why had this not occurred to her before? Tessa knew that she was naive, but now that she had thought of it, it seemed so very obvious. Linda must have been an attractive woman, and not all that old. All of those men.

Including Father Theo?

Tessa shied away from that. Surely not. He was a priest.

She couldn't – daren't – ask Rob for confirmation of her theory. And perhaps, after all, she couldn't ask Father Theo either. Just in case.

Then another thought came to her, unbidden.

Someone had killed Linda Nicholls. No arrest had been made, and up to this point all the police seemed to have done, as far as Tessa knew, was to question her and Rob, to go over and over the same ground until it ceased to have any meaning.

There was, it would seem, no sign of forced entry into Linda's house. No evidence of robbery, or intent to rob. Linda had, presumably, been murdered by someone she knew, someone she had let in, someone she had trusted.

One of her lovers.

*

The next day, a Saturday, the police were back. Detective Inspector Tower and Sergeant Coles. This time, they said, it was to deliver Linda Nicholls's keys to them. The keys to her house, to her car. They'd been found in her handbag. The police had finished with them, had completed their forensic searches, and the keys ought to go to the next of kin. Rob. Now he could do what he liked with them.

'Thanks,' said Rob indifferently, taking the keys and tossing them on the table in the hall.

'Can you tell us anything?' Tessa asked. 'We deserve to know.'

'No arrests have been made,' DI Tower stated in an official voice.

'But don't you have any leads? Any suspects? Please tell us.'

The policeman's eyes moved to Rob. 'Our investigations are still under way,' he said. 'We'll be in touch.'

Doug Coles smiled, showing his teeth.

For the rest of the weekend, the keys remained where Rob had tossed them, and each time Tessa passed through the hall, she was acutely conscious of them, though she resisted the urge to pick them up and examine them. They were just keys, after all, and Rob might notice if they'd been moved.

But on Monday morning, after Rob had left for work, her curiosity overcame her better judgement, and she held the keys in her hand. There were not enough of them to be called a bunch: half a dozen or so, on a key-ring with a plastic tab. 'Southgate Gym and Fitness Centre' said the tab.

For several minutes Tessa stood in the hall, feeling the weight of the keys in her outstretched palm.

She had gone this far; how could she stop now? It was too much of a temptation, and Rob need never know.

Tessa put on her coat and let herself out of the house, dropping Linda's keys into her coat pocket.

As she walked towards the Holloway Road tube station, she tried to justify it to herself.

The police, it was clear, still suspected Rob of being implicated in his mother's death; so ran Tessa's thoughts. It was absurd, impossible, yet they didn't seem to have any other suspects. If there were any, surely the police would tell them; they were the next of kin, and ought to be told.

Perhaps she, Tessa, would find something at the house which the police had missed and which would lead to finding the killer.

She owed it to Rob, she told herself, jamming her hands in her pockets and feeling the cold metal of the keys.

The Holloway Road was hung with Christmas lights, and out of the shops, as Tessa walked past, wafted the jangly tones of Christmas muzak. Rob had already mentioned getting a tree. Their first Christmas together, he had said. Something to celebrate, something to remember.

Tessa felt strangely reluctant. She had never been all that keen on Christmas, when it came right down to it. Christmas had always been one of the busiest times of the year for her father, naturally enough, and that meant that Tessa had seen even less of him than usual. And after her mother died, he hadn't even bothered to put up a tree or decorate the house. Christmas, apart from the obligatory hours spent in church, had been just like any other day, only colder and more lonely.

Perhaps it *was* time to wipe out those memories, to start afresh. Yes, Tessa told herself firmly. She and Rob would start their own Christmas traditions, with a fragrant tree decorated with fairy lights and shiny balls and a tinsel garland; holly on the mantelpiece, mistletoe hung from the overhead lights; a wreath on the door; presents beneath the tree. So many things she could buy for Rob, and wrap in pretty paper: a new shirt, a dashing silk tie, a pair of silver cufflinks, some leather gloves, a book on computers, a box of chocolates.

And next year . . .

Tessa's hands went to her expanding abdomen. Next year there would be the baby, and Christmas would be even better: a tiny stocking, toys under the tree, all sorts of lovely little presents.

By the time she got to Southgate, and yet more shops alive with Christmas cheer, she was feeling more sanguine about the prospect. It *would* be good, her first Christmas with Rob. Outside the station a man was selling Christmas trees; Tessa stopped to examine them, touching their spiky needles and inhaling their sharp piney scent.

'Looking for a tree, love?' said the man, rubbing his gloved hands together. 'I can do you a nice one, any size you like.'

Tessa smiled at him. 'Maybe later,' she said, then turned and continued on her way to Chase View Road.

She stopped on the pavement outside number 27, as she had done before, and for a moment her courage failed her. How could she overcome the horrific memories of that last time? In her determination to come back, she hadn't even thought of that.

She must, Tessa told herself. She had to do it some time, and it wouldn't get any easier. She was doing it for Rob.

That thought galvanised her. She marched up to the front door, drawing the keys from her pocket. The Chubb lock, and then the Yale: it only required a couple of tries to find the right keys, and the door swung open.

Tessa took a deep breath and stepped over the threshold. The house was cold; someone – the police? – must have turned off the heating. Closing the door behind her, she searched for the thermostat. It was in the hall, and she turned the dial up, then looked round her.

The sensation that assaulted her was almost like a physical blow, and as unexpected. Linda Nicholls. Not Linda dead, but Linda alive.

Linda Nicholls had lived in this house for almost thirty

years. She had come to it as a very young bride, scarcely out of her teens. In this house she had raised her child, had seen her marriage disintegrate – for whatever reason – and had continued to live here. She had died here. Tessa was trespassing not just in another woman's house, but in her life.

If Amanda had impressed her personality on Rob's house, Tessa said to herself in that breathless moment of surprise, how much more had Linda Nicholls impressed herself into the very walls of this house?

And yet . . .

And yet it was not as clear as all that. Linda was all around Tessa, yet her essence eluded her.

It wasn't just that the police had been in. They had tidied up after themselves admirably; there was no indication that they had dusted everywhere for fingerprints, had been through the house with a fine tooth-comb.

Perhaps, thought Tessa, it was to do with the excessive neatness, with the 'just so' feel that underlaid it all.

The entrance hall was spacious, as befitted a house of that size. It could have made a bold statement, with stripy Regency wallpaper marching up the stairs to the landing above. Even magnolia-painted wood-chip would have been making a statement of sorts. But the paper was a neutral, inoffensive dove grey which said precisely nothing about the woman who had chosen it and had lived with it.

Likewise the things hanging on the wall. If Tessa had hoped for photographs – for snapshots of a little Robbie, or even school photos documenting his yearly increments of growth – then she was disappointed. The framed prints on the walls might have adorned any doctor's waiting room, any hospital corridor. Not quirky, not personal: just something to fill up space.

And the only furniture was a table, polished and bare except for an arrangement of pink and burgundy silk flowers.

Perhaps, Tessa told herself, the rest of the house would be different.

She avoided the left-hand front room – that she wasn't ready for, and might never be. Instead she went into the corresponding room on the right. It was a large dining room, furnished traditionally with solid wood furniture: a table, eight chairs, a sideboard. The furniture wasn't antique, nor was it noticeably new. And again the décor was of an almost excessive neutrality, a slightly darker grey than in the hall, with burgundy velvet curtains. The room certainly didn't feel as if it were ever used; no jolly family holidays had left their mark on it, no elegant dinner parties with clinking champagne glasses and sparkling conversation.

The room behind seemed at first glance to be more promising: a breakfast room attached to a kitchen. Stretching back, it was a huge room, and seemed to have been extended into the garden, but the only furniture was a Welsh dresser with neatly arranged plates and bowls and cups on its shelves – a matching set, white with a criss-cross pattern of red lines – and a long pine table and chairs. There would have been space in that room for at least two more tables of that size, but the vast floor – white vinyl with a grey fleck in it – stretched emptily towards the French doors which opened into the garden.

Tessa moved to the doors and looked out. The garden was, of course, locked in the grip of winter, but the beds were tidy and well-kept. No rogue vines or rambling rose bushes marred its symmetry, and Tessa could imagine how it would look in summer: the grass trimmed short, and flowers in orderly rows. Nothing at all like her own little jungle of a garden, which she'd only begun to tame into some sort of submission.

Linda had been a fastidious person, then, Tessa told herself as she progressed into the kitchen; that much, at least, was clear. The kitchen was to the side of the breakfast room, and joined to it by an island with cabinets above, forming a large open hatch.

Immaculate white worktops ringed the kitchen, and there was a professional-looking cooker and an enormous American-style fridge. Cooking utensils hung from a metal grid on the wall.

And on one of the worktops stood heart-stopping evidence that the police had left things as they had found them: a tea tray, laid out in readiness for the anticipated visit of Tessa and Rob, with plates, cups, saucers, spoons, a sugar basin and a milk jug.

For a moment she stood still, staring at it, tears welling in her eyes. She couldn't bear it; she wouldn't allow herself to think about it. Tessa moved on without exploring the contents of the cupboards and the fridge. That could wait for another time, when she felt a bit stronger, and when such an action would seem less like trespassing.

Tucked behind the kitchen was a utility room with industrial-sized washing-machine and tumble-drier, and a walk-in larder. After a quick peek, Tessa went back into the hall. There were three more closed doors leading off it. One proved to conceal a cupboard for coats and a vacuum cleaner, and one opened into a powder-room, immaculate and smelling strongly of air freshener.

The third door led into a small room which was furnished as an office, with a desk and a filing cabinet. Half-guiltily, Tessa pulled open the top drawer of the filing cabinet.

It was empty.

That seemed odd, and odder still that the other three drawers were likewise empty. Why have a filing cabinet if there were no files in it?

Then she realised, with a jolt, that perhaps the police had taken the files away with them, as evidence. And maybe that was good: maybe the files would lead them to the killer.

The desk yielded little more than the filing cabinet:

a drawer with pens and pencils and paper-clips, and one containing blank paper. Nothing else.

Puzzling over the empty office, Tessa went upstairs. She was still in pursuit of the elusive personality of Linda Nicholls, though she was beginning to form a picture of a woman for whom tidiness had been a way of life. Everything in its place, and surely that had not been effected merely for the anticipated visit of Rob and Tessa.

That theory was borne out by the rooms upstairs, which presumably Tessa and Rob would not have seen had the visit taken place as planned. They were equally neat and well-kept, and on the whole utterly without personality.

Four bedrooms. Quite a lot, thought Tessa, for a woman living on her own. Three of them were furnished as guest rooms, each with a single bed and a wardrobe, each with bland wallpaper and neutral curtains and insipid pictures on the walls.

One of these rooms, Tessa told herself, must have been Rob's when he was a boy. It was impossible to tell which: none had been kept as a shrine to a departed son, as so often happened, with every evidence of schoolboy interests and passions retained as though preserved in aspic. No model aeroplanes, no sporting trophies, no shelves of well-thumbed adventure novels.

In fact, Tessa realised suddenly, no books at all. That was one of the things that had been bothering her, sub-consciously, about this house: there were no books. Tessa couldn't imagine living without books. Apparently Linda had not felt the same way.

There was a bathroom, large and well-appointed, and then there was Linda Nicholls's bedroom, at the front of the house.

Linda's bedroom was feminine, but not in a flouncy or romantic or even comfortably cluttered way. Its walls were a cool pink, with curtains to match, and the furniture was of good quality. There was a double bed with a padded head-board and a duvet, a wardrobe, a chest of drawers, a dressing table with neat rows of bottles on top, and a bedside table with a telephone. An *en-suite* bathroom was attached, equally well-ordered. Not exactly a torrid love-nest, thought Tessa.

It just didn't add up. Tessa pondered the enigma of Linda Nicholls as she went back on to the landing, back to the small staircase which led up to another floor. She climbed the steps carefully.

There was a door at the top, and it was locked.

Tessa twisted the knob one way, then the other, just to be sure. Then she took Linda's keys from her pocket and tried them, one by one.

None of them worked.

For some reason it seemed very important to Tessa that she should be able to open this door, to complete her pre-liminary examination of the house. That it was locked, delib-erately, was an outrage. All of the clues she'd been seeking to Linda Nicholls's personality – to her killer, even – might be lurking behind this door. Impotently she thumped on it, knowing that it would do no good. Then, defeated, she went back down and returned to the bedroom, something half-noticed tugging at her memory.

The bedside telephone. It had several speed-dial buttons, and two of them were labelled. 'Greg – work' said one, and 'Greg – home' the other.

Greg. Who was Greg, then?

Without giving herself time to think about it, Tessa lifted the receiver and punched the top button.

Chapter 9

'Southgate Gym and Fitness Centre,' announced a chirpy female voice at the other end of the phone. 'Can I help you?'

That had a familiar sound; Tessa felt in her pocket for the keys and looked at the plastic tab. 'Could I speak to Greg?' she said with a boldness she didn't feel.

'Greg's not here right now. He doesn't come in till this evening.' Helpfully the chirpy female added, 'You could try after six, or you might try him at home.'

'Thank you,' Tessa said, disconnecting, then pushing the second button.

This time she was more successful; a man answered on the third ring. 'Hello?'

'Is this Greg?' asked Tessa.

'Yes, I'm Greg,' he confirmed. The voice was flat and classless. Vaguely London, but without a strong accent.

In the brief pause that followed, Tessa tried to think what to say, and wished that she'd worked it out before taking such precipitate action. 'My name is Tessa Nicholls,' she said.

There was an intake of breath on the other end.

'Linda Nicholls was my mother-in-law,' Tessa rushed on. 'I believe that you knew her?'

'Yes.' Just that one syllable, unreadable.

Now what? thought Tessa. 'I wondered,' she improvised, 'if we might meet. I'd like to talk to you about her.'

Another pause. 'Yes, all right,' he agreed.

'Soon? Today?' Tessa suggested boldly.

'All right.'

He was not a man of many words, evidently, and Tessa found herself trying to compensate for that. 'I'm in Southgate,' she said. 'At her house. Would it be convenient for you to come here, or would you prefer it if I came to you?'

'Not there,' Greg said, then made a suggestion: the café across from the tube station. In twenty minutes.

Tessa was there first, waiting by the door and wondering how she would recognise him. Could he possibly be the weeping man she'd noticed at the funeral? His voice – what she'd heard of it – had sounded young, as young perhaps as that man had been. None of the other men at the funeral had impressed themselves upon her to the extent that she felt she would recognise them.

She scanned the faces of the men who approached. A few teenaged lads, skiving from school, swaggering about in their leather jackets, went past her into the café. Then a swarthy old man leaning on a stick, and a businessman in a pinstriped suit. None seemed even vaguely possible candidates to be Greg.

Her attention was distracted by the efforts of a young woman to wangle a pram through the door. Tessa held the door for her, and bent over to examine the baby inside.

When she straightened up, he was standing in front of her. 'Mrs Nicholls?' he said awkwardly.

'Please, call me Tessa,' she said, adding, 'You must be Greg.'

'Greg Reynolds.'

Not the weeping man, then. He wasn't tall – Tessa had to look down at him – but he was heavily muscled, especially through the upper torso; his jacket strained across broad muscular shoulders. It was a bomber jacket, and below it he wore jeans and trainers. His age was difficult to determine: he was obviously young, but perhaps not quite so young as his baby face suggested. In an effort to add some years to that face, he cropped his gingery hair short, and cultivated a heavy walrus moustache. The results were not entirely successful; the moustache, several shades darker than his hair, and luxuriously thick, only managed to look false, as though it were part of a disguise or a theatrical costume.

He nodded towards the door, and they went into the café. It was evidently run by Greeks, or maybe Turks; the display case was full of delectable-looking pastries in which honey featured as a main ingredient. 'I can't resist that baclava,' said Tessa.

'Don't you want some lunch?' Greg suggested, indicating the sandwich case.

Tessa looked at her watch in surprise: it was indeed lunch-time. She had spent the whole morning on her quest. And she suddenly discovered that she was very hungry. 'Yes,' she said. 'I'll have tuna mayonnaise on a baguette. *And* the baclava. And some fizzy water.'

'Just cappuccino for me,' ordered Greg, then led her to a table which was just being vacated by two heavily made-up teenaged girls.

They sat and looked at each other, waiting for the food. When it seemed that neither of them would ever speak, Tessa took the initiative and started with something safe, a repetition of her question on the phone. 'You knew my mother-in-law, then?'

'Yes,' said Greg. 'She was my girlfriend.'

If Tessa had been eating, she would have choked on her food at that: the word seemed so wildly inappropriate, the idea almost ludicrous. Girlfriend? A woman of almost fifty? Tessa didn't know what to say. But she realised that if she didn't say something, the conversation would die. 'Had you known her for long?' she managed.

'About two years.'

The food and drink arrived then, giving Tessa time to think of her next question. She felt like an inquisitor, drawing out information bit by bit, and wished that he were more forth-coming.

'We met at the gym, where I work,' he volunteered, taking a sip of his cappuccino.

'The Southgate Gym and Fitness Centre,' Tessa prompted. She wished she hadn't ordered a baguette; it was going to be difficult to eat without making a mess.

'That's right. I'm a fitness instructor.' He said it with pride, unconsciously flexing his shoulder muscles. Then Tessa's prayers were answered: he began to talk, without prompting. 'Linda used to work out at the gym. That's how we met. She was very fit.'

Tessa gave him an encouraging nod, and tackled her baguette. It was delicious, and she was hungry, so there was a double incentive to carry on with it.

'After a while,' Greg went on, 'we started seeing each other. Outside of the gym, I mean. We went out a few times. For a meal, that sort of thing.'

Tessa looked across the table at him. He was absorbed in his story, unaware of the cappuccino foam which adorned the bottom of his moustache. 'Just a few times?' she said.

'Mostly we stayed in,' he amplified. 'After we got to know one another better. We never lived together or anything like that,' he added, seeing Tessa's expression. 'But I'd go round to her place, two or three times during the week, when I got off work. That is, when I worked days – then I usually finish at about six. So I'd stop and get some food – a pizza, or a Chinese take-away, sometimes a curry – and go round to Linda's. We would eat, watch some telly or a video. And . . . you know. Bed.'

The words, and his tone of voice, were matter-of-fact rather than coy; he met Tessa's eyes candidly as he spoke. She was the one who was embarrassed, and didn't press him to elaborate.

'If I didn't have to start work early the next morning, sometimes I'd stay the night,' he continued. 'But I have my own place. A flat, not far away.' He seemed to run out of steam after that, and lapsed into silence, sipping his cappuccino.

Tessa tried to get him started again; she didn't want to put words in his mouth, but there were things she needed to know. 'So you and Linda were . . . fond of each other,' she said carefully.

His reply was prompt. 'Oh, yes,' he said. 'I told you – she was my girlfriend.' Defensively he added, 'I know she was older than me. But she was good fun. And she was in great shape.' Again he flexed his shoulder muscles.

'So,' said Tessa, after a pause in which she finished her baguette. 'Did you have . . . plans? The two of you?'

'Plans?' he echoed blankly.

'For the future, I mean.'

Greg shook his head. 'It wasn't like that with Linda and me. I'm too young to settle down.'

'Did you have . . . other girlfriends, then?' Tessa asked.

He shook his head once again. 'No,' he stated. 'Linda was the only one. I work hard at the gym, and in my time off, I like to relax. I don't go in for the club scene, and I don't hang out down at the pub.' He patted his rock-hard abdomen. 'I have to keep in shape, you know, and too much beer is bad for you. So it suited me, going to Linda's of an evening. I could relax with her.'

'And this was – what did you say? – two or three evenings a week?'

'That's right,' he confirmed, nodding. 'That's what my schedule is like. Sometimes I work days, and sometimes I work evenings.'

Looking at the crumbs which she'd distributed on the table rather than at him, Tessa asked her next question. 'And what about Linda? If she only saw you two or three times a week, did she have other . . . um . . . boyfriends?'

He wasn't angry at the question, as she'd feared, only puzzled. 'No. Nothing like that.'

Tessa was not ready to give up her theory of Linda's multiple lovers; that theory still explained so much that was otherwise inexplicable. 'Was it *possible* that she had someone else, and you just didn't know about it? On the other nights of the week, when you weren't around, or during the days when you were working?'

'I would have known. She would have told me.' His voice was confident. 'Listen, Mrs . . . Tessa. Our relationship suited both of us, Linda and me. But if she'd wanted to see someone else, she would have told me.'

He was telling the truth, Tessa perceived, or at least the truth as he believed it. There was no point in alienating him by pursuing it any further, so she changed the subject. 'When was the last time you saw Linda?'

Greg looked over Tessa's shoulder, towards the steamy café windows, and spoke softly. 'The night before. The night before she . . . died. It was a Monday night.'

'Go on,' she encouraged him, when, after a moment, it seemed as if he'd said all he intended to say.

Still he gazed towards the windows. 'I got off work at six. I went home and showered and changed, then I stopped and got a pizza – pepperoni and extra cheese. Linda liked pepperoni.' It was obvious that he'd relived this in his mind since then, but it didn't have the feel of a practised story. He went on, 'We ate the pizza. There wasn't much on the telly that night, so we watched a video.' Greg turned and looked directly at Tessa. 'You and your husband – her son – were coming the next day, for tea. She was so excited about it, so pleased. I helped her to . . . get a few things ready. Then we went to bed, but I had to start early the next morning, so I didn't stay.'

Tears welled in Tessa's eyes at the thought of Linda's careful preparations for their visit; she blinked them away. She mustn't allow herself to get distracted. 'So you didn't have a row or anything?'

'A row?' Greg sounded baffled. 'Why would you think

that? Linda and I never rowed.' Then the penny dropped; his brows drew together. 'Wait a minute! You don't think I killed her, do you?'

'Why . . . no,' Tessa said hastily. 'But I just wondered. Have you talked to the police at all? Have you told them any of this?'

'The police?' He shook his head. 'What does it have to do with the police? Why do they need to know that Linda liked pepperoni on her pizza?'

'You saw her the night before she . . . died,' Tessa pointed out. 'The night before . . . she was murdered. You might be able to tell them something important. Something that would help them to find the person who . . . killed her.'

'And have them ask the same sort of questions you've been asking me?' he challenged her, defiant. 'I've seen those cop shows on the telly. I know how they can twist things round. First thing you know they'd have me in gaol. They'd say I killed her.'

'And you didn't kill her,' Tessa stated, meeting his eyes.

'I didn't kill Linda.' His voice dropped, lost its belligerence. 'I couldn't have done. In the first place, I was at work. And in the second place . . .' Greg hesitated, as if admitting some frightful weakness, or even confessing some heinous crime. 'In the second place, I loved her.'

Looking into those sad eyes, Tessa believed him.

She believed that he'd loved Linda Nicholls, but did she believe that he hadn't killed her?

As she made her way home, emerging from the tube to the yuletide-decorated Holloway Road, she pondered the question.

He had seemed utterly sincere. But there was something about his story that didn't add up. In any case, it didn't fit in with Tessa's firmly held belief that Linda Nicholls had not been a one-man woman.

Suppose, Tessa said to herself, he had killed her *because* he loved her. Suppose he *had* found out that there was another man, or more than one. Suppose he had dropped in that lunch-time to retrieve something he'd left behind the night before, and had somehow discovered that he wasn't her only 'boyfriend'. He might have been so angry, so inflamed with jealousy, that he had . . .

But the poker from the fireplace scarcely seemed his sort of weapon. No, thought Tessa. A frenzied attack with a poker was just not his style. If he had wanted to kill Linda, in a moment of blinding rage, he would have used his bare hands. She remembered those powerful shoulders, and imagined – all too vividly – his hands round a slender white neck, squeezing the life out. That's what Greg Reynolds would have done, she was sure.

Still, though. There was something that didn't add up. He *had* lied to Tessa; she was positive of that.

It was as they were leaving the café that she'd asked him her final question. That locked door at the top of the stairs: what was behind it?

He had hesitated for a split second; he had not been able to meet her eyes when he answered.

He didn't know, he'd said. He'd never been up there.

Tessa didn't believe him. He'd been visiting that house regularly for two years; Linda's bedroom was familiar to him. Surely, in all that time, he would have climbed the stairs to the second floor, if only out of curiosity.

He was lying to her about that, which only made her the more determined to find out for herself what that door concealed.

And if he had lied about that, might he not also have been lying about other things? Maybe he was just a good actor, playing a part. The bereaved, devoted boyfriend.

And if he was so innocent, why hadn't he gone to the police? Even assuming he hadn't killed her, he was possibly the last person apart from the murderer to have seen Linda Nicholls alive, and surely he would realise that the police would want to talk to him, to eliminate him from their enquiries, and to learn from him all of the things he could tell them about the victim. If what Greg Reynolds had said about his relationship with Linda was true, he had probably, over the last two years, known her better than anyone else had done.

But *was* it true? *Could* it be true?

Because if Linda's only lover had been Greg Reynolds, who on earth were all those other men?

Before the afternoon was out, Tessa faced up to another dilemma: what, if anything, was she going to say to Rob about her activities of the day? Could she risk upsetting him by telling him that she had been to Southgate, and about her conversation with Greg Reynolds?

Rob had been outwardly calm, even cheerful, for the past few days, but Tessa remained unconvinced by her husband's placid exterior. Surely he could not, so soon, have put it all behind him – his mother's death, and his complicated feelings about her. Tessa certainly had not been able to do so, and she had not even known Linda Nicholls.

Perhaps, she acknowledged to herself for just a moment, that was part of the problem. She had not known, and now would never know, Rob's mother.

But she had done it for him, Tessa reminded herself. She had gone to the house in Chase View Road in search of the truth behind Linda Nicholls's death, in order that Rob's name might be cleared – not to satisfy any curiosity, morbid or otherwise, that she might have about her mother-in-law.

Would Rob see it that way? Would he understand? What would she say to him if he asked how she had spent her day?

In the event, the subject didn't come up. Rob returned home a bit later than usual and in high spirits, bringing with him a Christmas tree and an assortment of decorations. The evening was spent erecting the tree and adorning it. When it was finished, Rob was exhilarated by their labours, and Tessa had to admit that the results were pleasing.

For James Wooldridge, in his executive home at Milton Keynes, the evening was spent in quite a different way.

Not that the Christmas spirit was absent from the Wooldridge home. Indeed, the room in which he sat – a room which the builders called the 'great room' – was decorated for the holidays in the very best of taste, and with no expense spared. No tacky tinsel garlands hung from the *faux*-beamed ceiling or dangled from the chandelier; instead there were ropes of greenery. The tree had come from Harrods, complete with all of its ornaments. Felicity liked 'themed' trees: last year it had been red fairy lights and tartan bows, but this year it was white fairy lights and golden cherubs. There was no room on one of Felicity's trees for anything outside of the theme, which meant that there were no home-made efforts by the children or carefully collected family heirlooms. The result was exquisitely beautiful but sterile, the sort of thing you would find in a shop rather than a home. Felicity liked it that way.

James Wooldridge was alone in the great room. The children, Emma and Geoffrey, were each in their own rooms, watching different programmes on their individual televisions or videos. And Felicity was out, gone to the theatre with two of her women friends. She wouldn't be back for several hours yet.

Surrounded by a stack of newspapers, James was going through them carefully, looking for some mention – any mention – of the investigation into the murder of Linda Nicholls.

The police hadn't come. That was the most important thing, as far as he was concerned. He didn't know *why* they hadn't come, how they had failed to find him. If not as a suspect, at least to ask him questions.

But they hadn't come. He was safe, at least for now. And

surely if they hadn't come by now, they wouldn't be coming at all.

He was desperate to know what was going on with the investigation, and couldn't very well ring the police and ask them. So each day he bought all of the papers, from the tabloids to the *Telegraph*, and each evening he went through them.

So far there had been next to nothing. No arrests, not even anyone helping the police with their enquiries. Surely, he thought, if they had arrested someone for the murder, it would have been reported in at least one of the papers.

Perhaps he wasn't in the clear yet; perhaps the police were just taking their own sweet time, and would be here one day soon.

James Wooldridge finished the drink he'd poured for himself earlier, then got up and poured himself another. He was drinking more than usual these days; Felicity had noticed the level on the Scotch bottle going down, and had mentioned it, so he'd had to buy another bottle secretly and keep it hidden from her. Not that he was an alcoholic or anything like that, he told himself: he was just anxious.

And no wonder. The anxiety over the police was only part of it. Even worse was the knowledge that, with Linda's death, his life had changed. No more weekends in London.

He hadn't been able to bear the thought that he might actually have to go to his mother's at the weekend, to keep up appearances for Felicity. So he'd told his wife that his mother had gone on a cruise and wouldn't be back till the New Year. That had made Felicity happy, not least because it meant that his mother would not have to be included in the family's plans for Christmas.

After that, he would have to think of something else. Or find somewhere else to go. Could Linda be replaced? He didn't think so. She was one of a kind. His release, his escape.

And, God, he missed her.

*

Later that evening, Father Theo was on his knees at the prayer desk in his study. This, he thought, was his penance: the insecurity, the not knowing.

The police had not come yet. Surely they would, eventually; he wished that they would just do it, and get it over with. Almost two weeks since Linda's death, and still no police.

And no Linda, either.

That was the worst of his penance. He knew that she had not belonged in his life: he was a priest. His life was meant to be exemplary, above reproach. If any of his parishioners had even dreamed . . .

God knows, he had tried to stay away. Time and again he had tried, and sometimes he had succeeded for a week or two. But he had always gone back. The compulsion had been too strong, too irresistible.

And now he couldn't go back. Linda was dead.

Had he been an Evangelical instead of an Anglo-Catholic, Father Theo might have believed that Linda's death was God's judgement upon him, a punishment for his wicked behaviour. But his theology did not follow those lines. He didn't even look upon it as a means of repentance or a chance for amendment of life, knowing full well that if Linda were miraculously restored to life, he would be back in Southgate on Friday, in spite of himself.

What he prayed for was strength. He raised his eyes to the figure on the shelf above the prayer desk and addressed her. 'O Mother of God,' he said aloud, 'I am a weak, fallible man. Help me to live without her.'

It would never have occurred to Harold Dingley that the police, or anyone else, might suspect him of involvement in Linda Nicholls's murder. For Harold it was pure grief, untainted with fear, or any less worthy emotion, that consumed him in the days following the murder and the funeral.

His sister Bunny was quite worried about him. Harold was off his food, and for Harold that was indeed a sign that something was seriously wrong. Even mince pies failed to tempt him, and at this time of year he could usually get through dozens of them. But when she asked him about it, he always made some lame excuse. He'd had a bite to eat at work, at the hospital canteen, he would sometimes tell her. Or he would say, with an attempt at a joky smile, that it was about time he did some serious slimming.

Bunny wasn't fooled. It wasn't just the change in his appetite. Sometimes, late at night, she could hear him sobbing in his bed. That wasn't really something that she could mention to him – after all, he was entitled to his privacy, as she was to hers – but as a loving sister, she couldn't help feeling concerned.

No, it wouldn't have occurred to Harold that the police would be looking for him. And so it was perhaps ironic that he was the first among them to receive a phone call.

The call came during dinner on that Monday evening. Bunny, as was her wont, went to the phone, and came back with a quizzical look which she did her best to suppress. Her brother didn't get that many telephone calls, and the caller had refused to identify himself.

'It's for you, Harold,' she said. 'I don't know who it is.'

Harold didn't recognise the voice either. And it was with total bafflement rather than terror that he heard the man's words. 'Harold Dingley? I believe that you ... um ... knew ... Linda Nicholls.'

Chapter 10

The next day, Tessa was no easier in her mind. If anything, her conversation with Greg Reynolds had thrown up more questions than it answered, and she began to consider what her next step might be. Should she return to the house in Southgate and dig a little deeper? Or was there someone else to whom she could turn for clarification?

Father Theo, she thought. She could talk to Father Theo.

His housekeeper answered the phone, but he was available, and suggested that they might meet later that morning. Wherever, he said, was most convenient for her.

'I'll come to you,' Tessa said. She was curious to see him in his own setting.

Father Theo's church was in Hoxton, to the east and slightly south of Islington. Tessa's only other visit there had been for the funeral, and then she and Rob had gone by car. Without a car, though the distance wasn't great, it was not a straightforward journey; there was no tube station within easy walking distance, so the bus was the only way to get there without taking a taxi. The priest gave her clear instructions on which bus to take and where to get off.

She allowed plenty of time and arrived slightly before the time they had fixed to meet. Reluctant to present herself at the clergy house early, Tessa decided to spend a few minutes in the church. It was unlocked, and she slipped inside.

Immediately she was struck by the silence: here, at last, was an escape from the jangle of synthetic holiday cheer. Here it was not just pre-Christmas, but Advent; the distant altar was hung with purple.

St Nicholas, Hoxton. On her previous visit she had scarcely taken it in, so involved was she in thoughts of another kind.

The only church that she knew well was her father's, the church in which she had grown up: a solid mediaeval stone building with clear-glass windows, whitewashed walls, and the simplest of furnishings. That church smelt of damp stone and dusty kneelers and Brasso. This was something else entirely, something outside her experience.

It was dimly lit, the December sunlight angling in through windows which were filled with stained glass in deep jewel-like tones. Victorian windows, sentimental in subject-matter and not particularly beautiful in design, but the effect the sunlight created was magical, dappling the interior with blotches of colour.

The only other light came not from electric fixtures but from candles, flickering in votive holders. A candle in a red holder burned in the sanctuary, at the very front of the church near the purple-clad altar, but the rest of the candles were in front of two statues: one of St Nicholas himself – a tall plaster figure in a mitre, painted in garish colours – and one of the Virgin.

Tessa moved to the latter figure, fascinated. There had been no statues in her father's church, and indeed she always associated such things with Roman Catholicism. This statue looked, to her unpractised eye, very old. It was smaller than the one of St Nicholas, and somehow invested with more dignity. Carved of stone rather than cast in plaster, the folds of her dress looked almost real. The Virgin was crowned, and she was holding a baby. Involuntarily Tessa smiled at the tiny figure: he was sitting upright in his mother's arms, stretching one hand out, and grinning in a most beatific yet altogether human way. Delighted and captivated, Tessa stood for some time looking at the statue. Then the idea came to her that she should light a candle. A candle for Linda Nicholls.

Awkwardly, for she was unused to such things, she took a candle from the box, set it directly in front of the Virgin, and lit it with a taper. She felt that she ought to say something – a few words, or even a prayer. It had been years since she had prayed, but after a moment the words came to her, and she spoke them aloud. 'Linda Nicholls,' she said to the baby. 'May she rest in peace.'

'And rise in glory,' said a voice behind her.

Tessa turned. She had been so involved in what she was doing that Father Theo had approached without her being aware that she was no longer alone in the church. To her surprise, his silent approach neither startled nor alarmed her, and she found that she wasn't even embarrassed to be discovered saying a prayer. His presence there was natural and unthreatening, and he seemed to read her mind. 'It's beautiful, isn't it?' he said quietly, looking at the statue rather than at her.

'I love it,' she confessed. 'I've never seen anything like it.'

Father Theo smiled. 'I found it in Italy, years ago, and fell in love with it. With *her*, I suppose, and with Him. Look,' he added, pointing. 'Look at her hands, at the way she's holding the baby. The way they're curved, so tenderly, to support Him.'

Tessa looked, and saw. 'Is it old?'

'Oh, yes,' he nodded. 'Very old. Mediaeval. I paid a great deal of money for it,' he admitted with a rueful smile. 'Far more than I could afford at the time. But I've never regretted it.'

Still Tessa gazed at the statue. 'I can understand why you had to have it.'

Father Theo gave a reminiscent chuckle. 'I was spending the summer in Italy, when I was a poor theology student. As I recall, after I bought the statue, I didn't have much to eat for the rest of the summer. But I had *her*, and Him, sitting there in my poky little room with the plaster peeling off the walls, and I knew it was worth it.'

'And you've put it – put *them* – here in your church,' Tessa said. 'Rather than where you live.'

'To share them with other people.'

'But aren't you afraid that they'll be stolen?' she asked. 'The church isn't locked. Anyone could come in here and walk off with them.'

Again Father Theo chuckled. 'They're heavier than they look. Stone. And I should know – I'm the one who had to get them home, at the end of that summer. I don't think anyone could make off with my Virgin and Child without doing themselves some considerable damage.'

'Well, that's a relief.'

'And lest you think I'm being entirely unselfish, putting them here, you'll see when we get to my study that I've had a replica made. So I can keep them close by me always.'

Tessa glanced at her watch. 'I suppose it's time to go there now.'

'No hurry,' he assured her. 'I've plenty of time. Would you like to walk round the church a bit? Or have you already done that?'

'I'd only just come in, really,' she said. 'So I *would* like to walk round.' She wasn't just saying it to be polite, Tessa realised with some surprise; she really did want to spend more time in the church, unfamiliar and beautiful as it was.

'The church isn't nearly as old as my Virgin and Child, obviously,' Father Theo said as they walked up towards the sanctuary. 'A fine example of Victorian High Church piety.'

'It's nothing at all like my father's church,' she said impulsively. 'His church is very . . . plain.'

Father Theo stopped and turned to look at her. 'Your father is a priest? I didn't realise.'

She hadn't told him; she wasn't sure why. 'He wouldn't call himself a priest,' Tessa demurred. 'Just a vicar.'

'If I'd known you had a clergyman in the family, I would never have suggested my taking the funeral,' Father Theo said. 'He could have done it.'

'Oh, no. My father and I are not . . . close,' she blurted.

Father Theo gave her a searching look, but when she didn't say any more, he turned and walked towards the side aisle and pointed to one of the plaques which circled the walls of the church. 'If you're not familiar with Anglo-Catholic churches, then perhaps you don't know about this.'

'No,' she said uncertainly, looking at the plaque. It was painted on wood, stylised and rich with figures. 'What is it?'

'One of the Stations of the Cross. They depict the sufferings of Jesus on the Via Dolorosa, all the way to Golgotha and His death on the Cross.'

Tessa shuddered. 'How gruesome.'

'His death *was* gruesome,' Father Theo reminded her gently. 'And we Anglo-Catholics try to recall His injunction that we should take up our crosses and follow Him. That's why we put the Stations of the Cross in our churches. During Lent, especially, we go round the church and stop at each of the Stations for a meditation on His suffering.'

Tears welled in Tessa's eyes, though she couldn't really say why, and she turned away from the pain, unable to face it. Instead she looked towards the pulpit, and saw that a small stable had been set up nearby. 'Oh – I see that it's Christmas in here as well,' she said, vaguely disappointed that she had not, after all, escaped from its premature pervasiveness.

'Not yet,' said Father Theo. He led her towards the stable. 'See, Tessa? It's empty. Mary and Joseph haven't arrived yet, and the Babe hasn't been born. It's still Advent, and Advent is about waiting. About preparing ourselves, and this is to remind us of what we're preparing ourselves for.'

This she could understand; she, too, was waiting, and preparing herself, Tessa thought, putting her hands on her abdomen and feeling the smooth bulge.

Father Theo saw her gesture, and smiled at her. 'Yes, Tessa. Just like you.' He looked towards the empty stable and mused, 'That's the wonder of the Incarnation. Our Lady was just like you. Great with child, and not sure exactly what lay ahead for her or her family.'

She wasn't sure why, but something in his voice, if not in his words, made her afraid. 'I'd like to go now,' she said.

'Of course,' the priest responded instantly. 'You must be tired, my dear. You've had rather a long journey. Let's go over to the clergy house – Mrs Williams will make us some tea.'

Tessa was content to follow him across the road to the clergy house. 'Why isn't it called a vicarage?' she asked, curious, as they left the church. 'You're the vicar, aren't you?'

'Oh,' he smiled, 'it's an Anglo-Catholic thing. Clergy, plural, rather than vicar, singular. Dating back to Victorian times, when there were slum priests – loads of them. Once this parish would have had a vicar and several curates, and they all would have lived here in the clergy house. Now there's just me.'

'And Mrs Williams,' Tessa added.

'By no means forgetting the worthy Mrs Williams,' he agreed, with only a hint of irony in his voice. 'She takes good care of me, in the time-honoured tradition of clergy house housekeepers.'

'My father has a housekeeper as well,' Tessa said, perhaps revealing more in her voice than she had intended.

Mrs Williams met them at the door, and perceived instantly what was called for. 'Tea,' she pronounced. 'In your study, Father?'

'That would be splendid, thank you. And a few biscuits, perhaps?'

She raised her eyes to him in a reproachful look. 'Of course, Father.'

'Excuse the mess,' the priest apologised to Tessa as he ushered her in to the room nearest the door. 'This is the one room that Mrs Williams isn't allowed to touch.'

It was a very masculine room, Tessa apprehended, with a shabby leather sofa and a threadbare Turkey carpet. And it *was* untidy: papers and books blanketed the desk, more books had colonised the floor, and the bookcases overflowed, with excess volumes stacked on top of the ones that stood upright. An elaborately carved Gothic fireplace surround in dark oak had a mantelpiece topped with an astonishing amount of clutter: a few small statues and religious tat, cheek-by-jowl with photographs in tarnished silver frames, faded postcards, yellowed invitation cards, and even a mummified apple core. Still, the mess was not oppressive or depressing, Tessa found; Father Theo was obviously able to live with it and within it, and seemed comfortable amidst its apparent but perhaps deceptive disorder.

Only one area of the room remained untouched by the clutter, and that was the corner where he had his prayer desk. On a low shelf in front of the desk, just above eye level for someone kneeling, stood the replica of the Virgin and Child. Drawn to it, Tessa went over to look at the statue.

'That means a great deal to me,' said Father Theo.

She regarded it silently for a moment, then at his suggestion took a seat on the leather sofa while he went to the chair behind his desk.

Where to begin? Tessa couldn't remember all of the questions that she wanted to ask him, and while she hesitated, he smiled at her across the untidy desk and asked a question of his own. 'How does your father feel about being a grandfather?'

It wasn't supposed to happen this way. Thrown off guard, Tessa said more than she meant to. 'He doesn't know about the baby. I haven't told him yet. We've never been very close. He's always been too busy with his parish to take much notice of me.'

'And how does that make you feel?' asked Father Theo.

She had never talked to anyone about her father before, not even Rob, but when she opened her mouth, the words came out in a painful rush. 'Terrible. I feel that he doesn't love me. He's never had time for me. And even when I do see him, he's always critical. Nothing I do is ever good enough. I've tried and tried. But I've been a big disappointment to him.'

The priest tented his fingers on top of a pile of papers in front of him and looked at her gravely. 'Are you sure? Have you talked to him about this?'

'Of course I haven't talked to him! When would I? And how could I? But I don't need to. I *know*.' Her voice was passionate, bitter. 'I've lived in London for over ten years, and he hasn't been to see me even *once*. He was too busy even to come to my wedding. He doesn't ring, he hardly ever writes. He hasn't expressed any wish to meet my husband, and he probably wouldn't approve of him anyway.'

'And what about *you*?' Father Theo asked. 'Do you visit him?'

'Sometimes. Once or twice a year. But what is the point?' she demanded. 'Whenever I go to see him, he's always out. Parish business, he says. But the truth is that he just doesn't want to spend time with me!'

Father Theo took off his spectacles to polish them and regarded her with his clear blue eyes. 'Do you have any idea why he might feel that way?'

'Because he doesn't love me,' Tessa stated. Then, after a silence that stretched out into an eternity, without any volition or conscious decision she blurted out something she had never before uttered, had never even articulated to herself. 'Because he blames me.'

'Blames you?'

'That my mother . . . died.' She swallowed, bit her lip, then went on incoherently, 'My fault. He thinks. He *knows*.'

Mrs Williams chose that moment to come in with the tea tray. Without a word she set it down on the desk, on top of a fairly stable-looking stack of papers.

When she'd gone, Father Theo ignored the tea tray and said in a quiet, compelling voice, 'Tell me about your mother.'

Tessa told him: told him how wonderful her mother had been, and how loving; about the unbearable pain of losing her, and the emptiness of her life without her. The words poured out of Tessa; she went on for several minutes, scarcely drawing breath, until finally the words ran out and she stopped.

There was a long silence. 'How did your mother die?' the priest asked at last.

Tessa gulped. 'I don't know. I'm not sure,' she confessed. 'I'm not sure that I *ever* knew. But I think that's how I know it was my fault. Because no one would ever tell me. I was so young then. But even later, when I asked, they wouldn't talk about it.' Her eyes widened at the horror of it, and she stared without seeing at the priest. 'My father. He never mentions my mother. He hates me because he thinks . . . knows . . . that I . . . killed her.' She drew a deep, gasping breath which stuck in her throat and turned into a sob. The sob was followed by another, and then by a flood of tears.

Father Theo moved to her side and sat close to her on the sofa, utilising his considerable priestly skills to comfort her as she wept. He didn't try to stop her, but kept her supplied with tissues from a box on his desk, and made all of the right noises. And when at last the torrent ceased and the flood was reduced to a trickle, he remained beside her while she composed herself.

Before she could begin to apologise for her outburst, he spoke quietly, and there were tears in his own eyes. 'My mother died, as well. When I was very young – younger even than you were. I can scarcely remember her, but I loved her very much, and I've never got over the pain of losing her. And of growing up without her.'

'I'm sorry,' said Tessa, not clear exactly what she was sorry about; for a moment neither of them spoke.

'You just don't get over the loss of a mother.' The priest's head turned and he looked at the Virgin and Child statue. 'And now you've lost Linda as well.'

Tessa opened her mouth, and the words that she spoke came from deep within her subconscious, articulating thoughts that she had suppressed. 'I wanted her to be like a mother to me. I was so happy that I'd found her. And I never had the chance to meet her. Some people – well, Rob, anyway,' she admitted, 'thinks that it means that I don't have a right to grieve for her death. That I don't really have a *reason* to grieve, since I didn't know her. But in some ways that makes it so much worse – that she was taken away from me before I even had the chance to know her. I feel so . . . cheated.' She thought of that locked door in Linda's house, shut blankly in her face.

'I understand,' said Father Theo.

She sensed that he did, and that unstopped her tears again. 'It's just not fair,' she sobbed.

'No, it's not.' The priest handed her a fresh tissue. 'And you have every right to grieve, no matter what Rob or anyone else says. Go ahead and cry, my dear. I don't mind.'

Tessa took the tissue and accepted his permission to cry, allowing herself for the first time to think about her own loss and her grief for Linda Nicholls rather than concentrating on Rob. 'It's like losing my own mother all over again,' she wept.

'I understand exactly what you mean,' Father Theo murmured in a way that was not at all patronising. 'It's only natural, my dear.' He didn't hurry her; he seemed to know that these tears were necessary and long overdue. He didn't try to offer her false comfort, but his presence beside her was itself a comfort, and after a while she reached for another tissue and dabbed ineffectually at her eyes. 'And I'm so worried about Rob,' she went on, more in control of herself. 'At first he was so upset. But now he acts as if it never happened, and he won't talk to me about it.'

'It's commendable of you to worry about him,' the priest said thoughtfully. 'And of course it's important that the two of you should talk. About this and everything else. But if you'll forgive me for saying it, Tessa, I think you need to worry about *yourself* a bit more right now, and Rob a bit less.'

She turned a surprised face to him. 'What do you mean?'

The priest took his time before replying. 'I'm not suggesting that Rob doesn't need your support and your understanding and your love, at this difficult time for both of you,' he said at last, choosing his words with care. 'But Rob seems to me to be quite capable of looking after himself. And you have the baby to think about, my dear, as well as yourself. You owe it to both of you – to *all* of you – to have a healthy, happy baby. You won't do that by worrying yourself sick about your husband.'

Tessa could see the sense in what he was saying, but the priest clearly didn't understand how vulnerable Rob was, or how much he needed her. 'Yes, but . . .' she began.

Father Theo, as if he didn't wish to continue that line of conversation, patted her hand and rose. 'Now I think it's time for some of that tea,' he said lightly. 'Or Mrs Williams will be cross with me.'

The tea was stewed, unsurprisingly, and verging on the tepid, but he poured it out anyway and handed Tessa a cup. 'And she's brought us some rather superior biscuits,' he added, setting down the plate in front of her.

'I'm not hungry,' Tessa demurred. But she took one, for the sake of politeness, and discovered that she was in fact very hungry indeed.

Seeing that she had polished off four biscuits in short order, Father Theo smiled at her across the desk. 'I'll ask her to make us some sandwiches, shall I?'

Sandwiches sounded wonderful. 'I don't want to put her to any trouble,' she objected half-heartedly.

'Nonsense.' Father Theo grinned. 'It's what she lives for. And don't forget about taking care of that baby.'

'All right then,' Tessa capitulated.

Father Theo went to the door; Mrs Williams was evidently lurking not far away, duster in hand. 'Could we have some sandwiches, please, Mrs Williams? And a fresh pot of tea? If it's not too much trouble.'

'Of course, Father,' she said, with a meaningful look. 'Will you have them here in your study, or in the kitchen?'

'In here is fine.'

Eventually the sandwiches arrived and were duly eaten, and Tessa knew that she ought to depart and leave Father Theo to get on with other things. She was loath to go: the priest was so easy to talk to, so empathetic and understanding. She felt as if she had known him all of her life. If only, she thought involuntarily, her own father were like this.

As if reading her thoughts, Father Theo leaned back in his chair and brushed a stray crumb from the sleeve of his black cassock. 'You know that you're welcome to come back here and talk to me at any time, Tessa,' he said. 'But there's one more thing I want to say to you today.'

'Yes?' she waited expectantly.

'Your father.'

Her voice became defensive. 'What about him?' This was where they had begun, and she thought that the subject had been dealt with.

'I want you to promise me that you'll talk to him. Tell him about the baby. And talk to him about how you feel. You may be surprised at what he says.'

'I can't,' she stated flatly, disappointed in Father Theo and not even trying to conceal it. 'You don't know what my father is like, or you'd never say that. I explained it to you. I thought you understood.'

'Oh, but I do,' he said in a soft voice. For a moment he was silent, looking off into the distance, then he returned his attention to her. 'I understand very well, Tessa. Much better than you think.' He picked up his tea cup and swirled the dregs around reflectively. 'You see, I felt the same way about my own father. I thought that he didn't love me, that he didn't approve of me. Didn't approve of the fact that I became a priest, and never married. I never talked to him about it, because I was afraid that he would confirm all of my worst fears – that he would tell me that as far as he was concerned, I was a failure and a total disappointment to him.' He stopped.

'And?' Tessa prompted in the silence that followed, scarcely breathing.

'And I was wrong,' Father Theo said, his face creasing in pain. 'So wrong. He died a few years ago, and left me his diaries. It was all in there, Tessa.' Again he paused, then went on. 'You see, he felt he couldn't talk to me, either, but he wrote it all down. How much he loved me, how proud he was of me. He was delighted that I'd become a priest. *Delighted*. And so proud.'

Tears welled in Tessa's eyes. 'Oh, Father Theo!'

'And about my mother's death. I thought he didn't care, that he was hard-hearted and unfeeling, because he never talked about that either. But he poured it all out in his diaries. He loved her so much, and he was devastated by her death, but he felt that he had to be brave for *my* sake, and not to upset me by talking about it or showing his grief.'

Tessa couldn't help herself. 'That's so sad.'

'And now it's too late,' Father Theo went on. 'He's dead now, and it's too late. Too late for him, too late for me.' He leaned closer to her for emphasis. 'Don't leave it too late, Tessa. Maybe you think that it's too soon for you now, that you're not ready to talk to him. But promise me that you won't leave it till it's too late.'

Tessa had planned to go straight home after she'd talked to Father Theo. But after she got off the bus in the Holloway Road, somehow she found herself heading towards the tube station instead. In twenty minutes she was in Southgate.

Almost in a daze, she walked towards Chase View Road. The keys were still in her coat pocket; Rob hadn't even noticed that they were no longer on the hall table.

She hardly knew what to think after her talk with Father Theo. He had said so many wise things, had unlocked a part of her that she had been so carefully keeping suppressed. And he had done it in such a way that she didn't feel embarrassed about revealing herself to him in all of her vulnerability and pain.

For he had been vulnerable too, and unafraid to show it. She had never met anyone like him. She felt that she could say anything at all to him, and he would understand. It was extraordinary.

She had talked to him about her mother, about her father. About Rob, and even about Linda Nicholls.

But the one thing they hadn't talked about, she realised as she unlocked the front door and climbed the stairs, was the thing that she had gone to see him about: Father Theo's own relationship with Linda. She had not asked him, and he had revealed nothing.

Tessa fumbled with the keys, once again trying each one in the lock on the door at the top of the stairs. Perhaps she just hadn't tried hard enough yesterday, she told herself. Maybe one of these keys really would work. But still the lock refused to yield, and in frustration she banged on the door until the flat of her hand was sore, then collapsed on the floor, sobbing. Crying, this time, for Linda Nicholls, and for herself.

An hour later she made her way home. What *had* Father Theo's relationship been with Linda Nicholls? she asked herself. Was it possible, even remotely, that they had been lovers?

After the time she'd just spent with Father Theo, she couldn't believe that it *was* possible. He was a celibate priest, and he was an honourable man. And there was something else. It was difficult for her to put her finger on it, but Tessa tried to articulate it to herself. Something about the way he had conducted himself with *her*, when she was in an extremity of emotion. He had been comforting, he had made physical contact with her, had even put his arms round her. But there had been nothing the least bit sexual in that contact – not even the slightest undertone of it. Of course he was acting in a professional capacity, as a priest, but there was more to it than that. He just wasn't interested in women – any woman – in that way; Tessa was convinced of it.

Perhaps, then, he had acted as a counsellor to Linda, or a sort of confessor. Maybe, Tessa speculated, Linda had gone to his study, just as she had, to talk about her problems and her doubts. Perhaps she'd sat on that same leather sofa and poured out her heart to him: about her fractured relationship with her son, or problems with the men in her life. That would explain so much – it would even explain the priest's seemingly lukewarm reaction to Rob and her protectiveness towards him. That must be it.

In which case, Tessa realised with a sinking feeling, Father Theo would not be able to tell her anything. Surely he would be bound by confidentiality, if not the seal of the confessional, even though Linda was dead.

She would learn nothing from him, she was sure as she thought about it: nothing about what was on Linda's mind, about the things she had agonised over and cared about. In any case, she couldn't very well go straight back there to Father Theo and start asking questions. Not now.

And now, now that she had finally acknowledged the depth of her own emotions over Linda's death, it seemed more important than ever to her to find some answers; to talk to people who had known Linda, to find out what she was like; to learn what it was in her life that had caused her to be murdered.

For herself this time, Tessa admitted. Not just for Rob, but for herself.

But where could she go now? To whom could she talk?

Tessa tried to think about it logically. She needed answers, but first of all – before she could even begin to think about who could give her the answers – she needed to know what questions to ask.

Like a symbol of all that was eluding her, she saw in her mind that blank, unyielding door. What was behind that door? What secrets did it conceal?

Greg Reynolds hadn't told her. Rob wouldn't tell her, even if he knew – even if she could bring herself to ask him. Where was the key to the door? Who could have it?

The police.

The answer came to her out of some corner of her mind, intuitive yet backed with a clear logic.

The police had had Linda's keys. And the police had searched Linda's house.

Presumably, Tessa reasoned, they had somehow managed to get into that locked room to search it. If they didn't have a key, they would have used other means, but they would have got in somehow.

But if she asked the police – DI Tower, or one of his underlings – there was no reason at all why they should tell her anything. In her dealings with them to date, she had found them courteous but not at all forthcoming.

No, the police, whatever information they had, were not likely to be of any help. If only, thought Tessa, she knew someone on the police force whom she could ask.

It hit her like a cold shower, and she stopped in her tracks in the middle of the pavement on the Holloway Road, causing a chain reaction behind her as various shoppers and other pedestrians tried to avert a collision. Tessa was oblivious. Her stomach clenched, then plummeted.

The answer was so obvious.

Ian.

Chapter 11

Tessa hadn't seen Ian since the day of his wedding. That seemed such a very long time ago, with all that had happened since. She had met Rob for the first time that day, and now . . .

With some trepidation and much nervousness she rang him at work and threw herself on his mercy. Anything he could find out for her would be greatly appreciated, she told him, and explained about the locked room and the empty filing cabinet.

He was surprisingly easy about it. No, it wasn't really his business and yes, he might get in trouble if caught snooping through the files, but no big deal. He wasn't at Southgate now, but he had been stationed there for several years, so he knew where to look and what to look for, and no one would question his presence there. He would see what he could do.

And the next morning, when she was in the midst of making a batch of mince pies, he rang her back. He had a few things to tell her, he said, but he didn't want to do it on the phone. He would call round to see her a bit later, probably in the afternoon, and he checked the address. 'Islington, is it?' he said in the slightly mocking voice that she'd once known so well. 'Gone upmarket from Victoria, have we? Tony Blair country. La de bloody da.'

'It's not *that* part of Islington. Not the trendy part,' she parried defensively. 'And anyway, where are *you* living now?

Seems to me I heard it was one of those posh riverfront developments in Docklands. That sounds pretty upmarket to *me*.'

'*Touché*,' he laughed. 'Tessa, I *have* missed you.'

She hadn't missed him at all. That's what she told herself that morning as she prepared for his visit. No, she hadn't missed him, and why should she? He had treated her badly for years on end, and he had ultimately left her for Amanda.

And she had a new life now, a life without him and without any place for him. She was married to Rob now. She loved him and was carrying his baby. Ian was ancient history.

At least that's what she told herself. But she couldn't help being nervous, and taking great care that everything should show to her advantage at their first meeting after so much water had passed under the bridge.

Conscious that she had neglected the house for the past few days, intent on more important matters, Tessa now looked round and saw that there was dust on the furniture and the carpets needed a good Hoovering. The Christmas tree looked lovely, but already it was beginning to drop its needles. She spent over an hour tidying up and running the Hoover. Then on to the kitchen, where the freshly baked mince pies cooled on a rack. She hadn't put away the baking things, and the breakfast dishes hadn't made it past the sink because the dishwasher was still full of clean dishes from the night before. The dishwasher was one remnant of Amanda's reign in the house for which Tessa was grateful daily, but she acknowledged that it didn't empty itself. She dealt with the clean dishes, rinsed the breakfast things and slotted them into the dishwasher, then she put away the baking equipment, wiped the flour from the work surfaces and gave the floor a quick mopping.

After all that Tessa was ready for a shower. She washed her hair under the shower and, before she got dressed, blew it dry in front of the large bathroom mirror – another Amanda touch – as she observed herself with a dispassionate eye.

There was no doubt that pregnancy suited her, now that she had passed from the lassitude and sickness of the early months into the more energetic middle stages. Her pale hair, usually so fine and flyaway, was glossy and bouncy and full of body. Her skin glowed, her eyes sparkled, and her breasts, which had always been of modest proportions, had swelled and blossomed to something that many women would envy and most men would find worthy of a second look. Ian had always admired large-breasted women, Tessa remembered involuntarily, and that frank preference had fed her insecurity for years. Well, she had nothing to feel insecure about now, she thought with a smile.

And her bump seemed to be growing by the day. The skin of her stomach, stretched to accommodate it, was taut and smooth, and she ran her hands over it as she examined herself in the mirror. Now she was visibly, beautifully pregnant. In a month or two she might begin to look and feel ungainly, but not yet.

For a moment Tessa thought of JoAnn Biddle, so enormous the last time she'd seen her. JoAnn had probably had her baby by now, she realised with a twinge of envy. Much as she was enjoying being pregnant, she longed for her baby.

Her hair dry, Tessa moved to the wardrobe and surveyed her clothes. What should she wear for her meeting with Ian? It was important, somehow, that she achieve just the right look. There were very few of her regular clothes that she could wear any longer, and her maternity clothes were for the most part either too casual – jeans, leggings, loose tops; or too formal – smart dresses. She held a few things up against herself and rejected them as inappropriate or unflattering.

Why should it matter? she asked herself. But it did. She wanted Ian to see her at her best.

At last she settled on a short black skirt which showed her

legs off to good advantage, topped with a new jumper which she hadn't yet worn. The jumper was knitted finely of a thin silk jersey with a bit of Lycra in it, so that it draped beautifully and was a bit clingy and stretchy as well. The colour was a shiny, silvery grey, complementing the grey of her eyes, and the result, she thought as she observed herself in the mirror, was more than satisfactory.

It was well after lunch by the time that Ian arrived. Tessa waited nervously in the front room, in a chair by the window; she tried to read a novel, but at every sound from the street she raised her head and peered out. When his police car finally did pull up in front of the house, she rose and went to meet him at the door.

'Hello, Ian,' she said, deliberately drawing herself up to her full height. That meant that she could look him straight in the eye.

'Tessa!'

She watched his face as he took in the fact of her pregnancy and her altered appearance.

'You look bloody terrific,' he said with what sounded like surprised enthusiasm, giving her a peck on the cheek. 'And I didn't know. About . . . that. I suppose that congratulations are in order.'

Tessa smiled and cupped her abdomen with her hands in an unconscious protective gesture. Some little demon made her say, 'I have you to thank for this, you know.'

His brows drew together, and Tessa could see that he was trying to make rapid calculations. Maths had never been his strong suit; she put him out of his misery. 'I mean,' she laughed, 'that if I hadn't met Rob at your wedding, none of this would have happened.'

He laughed too, sharing the joke. 'Whew! For a second there you had me bloody worried.' As she led him through to the front room, he couldn't take his eyes off her breasts in the clingy jumper. 'Well, I must say that it suits you,' he went on. 'Really. You look . . . beautiful. Fabulous.'

'Thank you,' she said demurely, knowing that it was true.

And he looked just the same, observed Tessa. The same Ian whom she had loved for so many years. Just a bit pudgier, perhaps; a tiny bit fuller in the face. And she was delighted to realise that he meant nothing to her. Nothing at all, or nearly nothing. He was like a favourite character in a book that she had read and loved as a child; there would always, of course, be a lingering affection there, for the sake of old times, but that was all.

That realisation gave her a confidence with him that she'd never felt before. She was his equal now, not some moon struck supplicant who was willing to be satisfied with whatever crumbs that fell from his table. He sensed it too, and eyed her with caution as well as admiration.

'Christmas already,' he said, looking at the tree. He made a face. 'Bloody Christmas. They can stuff it as far as I'm concerned.'

Ian had never been much of a one for Christmas, Tessa remembered. If he wasn't on duty, he usually spent the day at the pub with his mates. Considering her own negative feelings about the holiday, his attitude had suited her just fine. There were no expectations on either side of lavish meals or lavish gifts: she didn't think that Ian had ever given her a Christmas present.

'Though I must say that I wouldn't say no to a snog under the mistletoe, given the right person,' he added with a grin and a wink at Tessa.

Tessa ignored that remark and came straight to the point, not willing to waste any time with flirtatious small talk. 'Were you able to look at the files?' she asked.

Ian pulled a notebook out of his pocket. 'I saw the files, yes.' He grinned. 'It wasn't really a problem. They all know me at Southgate, and I gave them some bullshit story about this murder possibly hooking up with a case I was working on. Pretty bloody clever, if I say it myself. They wouldn't let me take anything away, of course, but I made a few notes.'

She gestured him into a chair and sat down across from him. 'Tell me.'

'Well.' He made a show of consulting his notes. 'Where do you want me to start?'

'The locked room,' she stated.

Ian nodded. 'That's an interesting thing. There is no mention in the files of a locked room.'

'But surely,' she insisted, 'the house must have been searched thoroughly! I mean, it was where the murder took place. Wouldn't they have checked the whole house for fingerprints or other evidence?'

'Yes, of course.' Ian leaned back in the chair. 'And there is a report on the search in the files.'

'And?'

'You say that the locked room is on the second floor?'

Tessa nodded. 'At the top of the stairs. It's like a loft, really, I'd guess.'

'The loft.' He flipped through the notebook. 'The loft was mentioned. Didn't say it was locked, though.'

'Then how . . . ?'

Ian shrugged. 'Skeleton key. Or I suppose they might have had the actual key. We have ways of getting into things, Tessa. You bloody well know that.' He smirked at her.

She ignored the smirk. 'But if the police had the key, where is it now? It certainly wasn't on the key-ring that was returned to us.'

'I can't tell you because I don't know,' he said. 'So do you want to know what was in the room, or not?'

'Tell me.' Tessa found that she was holding her breath, waiting for his answer.

He took his time. 'Equipment,' he said at last.

She looked at him blankly; whatever she had been

expecting, this was not it. 'Equipment?' she echoed. 'What does that mean?'

'I believe it is a fairly common word,' Ian said with an attempt at humour.

'But what *sort* of equipment?'

'It didn't say,' he admitted. 'Just "equipment", full stop. I suppose,' he went on, 'that it might be exercise equipment. Bicycle, Stairmaster, treadmill – that sort of thing.'

That was possible, Tessa conceded to herself, nodding thoughtfully. Linda Nicholls *had* been fit – Greg Reynolds had said so, more than once. But she had belonged to the gym, had worked out there regularly. Why, then, would she need exercise equipment at home? If not exercise equipment, though, what could it possibly be?

'And the other question you asked me,' Ian prompted. 'About *her* files. You wanted to know whether the police had taken things away as evidence, such as the contents of her filing cabinet.'

Tessa tore her mind away from exercise equipment. 'Yes. There's a room in the house that's furnished as an office, but there's hardly anything in it, apart from the furniture. I just thought it was a bit odd that it was so empty, especially the filing cabinet.'

'Well.' Once again Ian flipped through the notebook. 'That's interesting. Because according to the search report, that filing cabinet was empty when the police arrived. No files, no papers. Sod bloody all.'

'So they *didn't* take her papers away as evidence,' she mused aloud. 'But why would she have an empty filing cabinet?'

He shrugged. 'People are strange, Tessa. No one knows that better than a policeman.'

Tessa thought hard. It was just possible, she supposed, that Linda had never used the room as an office. After all, she had once lived in the house with her husband, and he was a doctor. It might have been *his* home office, abandoned when he moved out and never used by her.

In that case, though, there should be records kept elsewhere in the house. Bank statements, bills, tax documents – all that sort of thing. Everyone had them. And if the police hadn't taken them . . .

There was a long silence while Tessa pondered the implications of all that Ian had told her. After a moment he snapped his notebook shut and returned it to his pocket; once again Tessa focused her attention on him.

'I don't suppose . . .' She hesitated. 'I don't suppose you can tell me anything about the investigation? Whether there are any suspects, or if they're close to making an arrest, or even what sort of line they're taking in looking for the murderer?'

His voice was unexpectedly gentle. 'You know that I can't, Tessa. I've stuck my neck out far enough as it is. You bloody owe me one.'

'I know that, Ian, and I wouldn't want you to think that I don't appreciate it.' She gave him a grateful smile.

'But I'll tell you what I *can* do,' he said unexpectedly. 'I can have a little informal chat with the bloke who oversaw the search of the house. Doug Coles – I know him pretty well. We used to work together quite a bit when I was at Southgate, and we still play rugby together. There's a match tomorrow. I'll invite him out for a drink after the match, and see if I can get anything out of him that might help.'

'That's very kind of you.' Tessa had not planned on offering Ian any refreshments, or indeed having him in her house for any longer than was absolutely necessary, but she was overwhelmed by his generous gesture, and said on impulse, 'Would you like a cup of tea? And I have mince pies.'

'Mince pies? You know I could never resist them.' He grinned at her.

'That's a yes, then.' Tessa got up, intending to make the tea and bring it back into the front room, but Ian rose as well and followed her to the kitchen.

She filled the kettle while he leaned against the door jamb and watched her. 'Nice kitchen,' he said. 'All the mod cons. Even a dishwasher.'

There hadn't been a dishwasher in Tessa's old flat. Not that she supposed that Ian had ever noticed whether there had been one or not; he had never been in the habit of washing up. 'I'm very glad to have it,' she remarked. 'Even two people can create a fair bit of washing up, and when the baby comes it will be wonderful.' Her hand went to her bump.

'Amanda isn't much of a one for washing up,' Ian said, raising his eyebrows. 'Our bloody dishwasher is broken right now, and until it gets fixed, if I don't do the washing up, it just doesn't get done.'

Now that the subject of Amanda had been broached, it seemed rude not to enquire about her. 'How is Amanda, then?' Tessa asked, keeping her voice neutral, her back to Ian as she got out a tray.

'Oh, just fine,' he said heartily. 'And Rob?'

'Rob is fine. Apart from having his mother murdered, that is.'

Her tone must have been more tart than she had intended, because Ian apologised straight away. 'I'm sorry, Tessa. That was a bloody stupid question.'

She shrugged. 'Never mind.' Opening a cupboard, she reached for the sugar bowl on the top shelf; Ian always took sugar in his tea.

Automatically he moved forward. 'Need some help reaching that?'

'No, thanks. I have it.'

Ian backed away with a sheepish grin. 'I'd forgotten that you're as tall as I am.'

Amanda was short. Tessa didn't really want to think about Amanda. Presumably Ian didn't have the same problem with Rob: after all, they had both wanted Amanda, and Ian had won her. Rob had lost out; Rob had had to settle for second best.

She fetched a plate and piled it high with mince pies from the cooling rack. 'Not quite hot from the oven, I'm afraid,' she apologised. 'They were warm this morning.'

'Did you bake them yourself, then?' Ian asked, sounding doubtful.

Tessa laughed. 'Oh, I've become quite domestic. Rob said he liked mince pies, so I thought I'd give it a try. I tasted one, and they're not too bad.'

Ian reached for one and bit into it; crumbs cascaded down his chin. 'Not bad? It's bloody delicious!'

'I'm glad. I hope Rob thinks so too,' she added pointedly.

He shoved the rest of it into his mouth, then licked his fingers. 'Rob's a lucky man,' he said, looking not at Tessa but down at his feet.

Tessa lifted the tray and started towards the door, intending to go back into the front room.

'Can't we stay in here?' Ian asked. 'It's cosier.'

She set the tray down on the table. 'All right, then. If you prefer.'

Ian pulled a chair out and sat down, then looked earnestly across the table at her as she poured the tea. 'Listen, Tessa,' he said. 'I wasn't telling the truth a bit earlier.'

'About what, exactly?' She busied herself with the teapot, not meeting his gaze.

'About Amanda. You asked how she was, and I said she was fine.'

Tessa raised her eyes. 'Is there something wrong with her, then?'

'Oh, not exactly with her.' Ian sighed; this time he was the one who turned away. 'With . . . bloody everything.'

Automatically Tessa held out the sugar bowl; Ian had always liked to add his own sugar. She did not, she discovered, want to hear this. She didn't need it; she wasn't really interested. But she couldn't very well say so. 'Do you want to tell me about it, then?' she said with reluctance.

Ian took the sugar bowl from her, and his fingers brushed hers lightly. 'I'd like to. The thing is, you've always been such a good listener, Tessa. So understanding. And I don't really have anyone else to talk to.' He spooned some sugar into his cup and added, 'If you're sure you don't mind.'

She gave a resigned sigh, knowing that it was too late to stop him. 'Go ahead.'

'The marriage. Me and Amanda. It just hasn't . . . worked. Not the way I thought it would.'

Reluctantly at first, but with increasing eloquence, he poured out the tale.

After a rapturous honeymoon, things had gone downhill fast. Amanda was never at home – she worked late into the evenings, and since she had received a long-desired promotion it was even worse. She never cooked; they subsisted on take-away meals. And she was constantly putting pressure on Ian to give up his police work, finish his degree, and become a solicitor so that he could go into partnership with her father and take over his practice one day. 'Can you imagine it, Tessa? Me, a bloody lawyer?' he demanded indignantly.

Worst of all, perhaps, was her nagging. 'She nags me all the time.' Ian put on a high-pitched, precious voice. '"Who do you think I am, your slave? Pick up your *own* dirty clothes, you lazy sod. *Rob* always picked up his dirty clothes." Rob this, Rob that. Bloody perfect Rob.'

Tessa wasn't even tempted to smile, though she couldn't help feeling it was poetic justice. But it was too sad, too painful, for her even to experience a twinge of smugness or vindication.

'*You* never nagged me, Tessa,' he stated, with a plaintive look.

No, she hadn't nagged him. She'd known instinctively that it was one sure way to lose him, and she hadn't wanted to lose him. She had picked up his dirty clothes without complaint; she had endured his absences when he was out with his mates, and even the longer absences when he was off with some other woman, all without a word. And it was when, finally, in spite of herself, she had begun nagging him about marriage and babies that he had cleared off for good.

Ian's gaze shifted to Tessa's middle. 'And she says she doesn't want kids. Not ever.'

At this statement, Tessa stared back at him with astonishment. 'But, Ian! *You* never wanted children! You made that perfectly clear.'

He had the grace to look slightly abashed. 'Not right away, maybe. Not . . . then. Maybe not now. But sometime. Every bloke wants a son, doesn't he? Wants to pass his genes along. I've started to realise that. It's important.' Ian paused. 'And seeing you like this, Tessa. You look . . . so bloody marvellous. Blooming.'

She got up and went to refill the plate of mince pies; in his agitation he had eaten them all. 'We're not talking about me, Ian,' she said evenly. 'We're talking – *you're* talking – about you and Amanda.'

'And the mince pies!' As soon as she'd put the plate back in front of him on the table, he ate another one. 'Amanda would never, in a million bloody years, bake a mince pie.'

'Surely you knew when you married her that she wasn't exactly domestic,' Tessa pointed out. 'It can't have come as that much of a shock.'

'But neither were you, Tessa. Not that much, anyway. And look at you now. You've changed.'

'Yes,' she said. 'I have.'

She was still standing, refilling the tea kettle at the sink. His gaze travelled from her head to her feet, coming back to rest on her breasts. 'You look bloody good to me, Tessa,' he said softly. 'We were always good together, weren't we?'

'Not always, Ian,' she reminded him, her voice calm. 'And you married Amanda. That was your choice.'

Now he looked down at the table rather than at her. 'Maybe I made a mistake.'

'Perhaps you did,' she agreed, marvelling to herself that she could discuss this so dispassionately. 'But it's a bit late.' She supposed that she shouldn't be surprised by his change of heart: after all, he had left her and returned to her so many times in the past. The only thing different this time was the piece of paper which bound him legally to Amanda, and another one which bound her to Rob. She'd been naive to think that would make a difference to Ian.

'Does it have to be too late?' he suggested, glancing up at her face.

Her reply came immediately, and her voice was firm. 'Yes,' she said. 'You left me, remember? You chose Amanda. You married her. And I'm married to Rob now, in case you've forgotten.'

'How could I bloody forget? The perfect Rob,' Ian said with bitterness. He pushed himself back from the table and stood. 'And it's working? You're happy, you and Rob?'

Tessa took a deep breath. 'Yes. Very happy.'

'Then lucky you.' His voice changed, lost its self-pitying edge, and he grinned at her, more like the old Ian. 'But if you should change your mind . . .'

'I think it's time for you to go,' Tessa stated. 'It was good of you to come, Ian. And I do appreciate what you've done for me.' She led him out of the kitchen and towards the front door. By the door she paused. 'Thanks, Ian.'

'I'll be in touch,' he promised. Then, unexpectedly, he moved closer to her, trapping her by the door.

Tessa, sensing danger, tried to draw back. But he cupped her face between his hands and looked earnestly into her eyes, on a level with his own.

'Come on, Tessa – just a kiss,' he coaxed her in the voice that had never before failed to win him his own way with her. 'Just a kiss, for old times' sake. I'm not bloody asking you to go to bed with me. Though I wouldn't say no, if it came to that,' he added jokingly.

She attempted to sound firm. 'I don't think it's a good idea.'

'You owe me one,' he reminded her.

'Ian—'

He kissed her. He had kissed her so many times before, she told herself; there was no harm in it. She could handle it. She no longer loved him – that was something she was sure about.

At first it was all right, and then, for just an instant, her body betrayed her: she kissed him back, her lips parting, and pressed herself against him. A few seconds later, horrified, she pulled away.

Ian looked at her for a long moment, a smile tugging at the corner of his mouth, and as he moved past her to the door, his hand deliberately brushed her breast, lingering there for a few heartbeats. 'I'll be in touch, Tessa,' he repeated softly. 'I'll be back.'

As the sound of his car moved off down the road, Tessa leaned against the front door, trembling.

For the truth was that, apart from that one strange night of passion following his mother's death, Rob had not made love to her in months. Mentally she was dealing with it well; there were, after all, far more important things for her to think about. But her body ached, night and day, for a man's loving touch, and it had betrayed her.

Harold Dingley was in a state. He'd scarcely slept a wink for the past two nights, and today, during his lunch hour, he had to leave the hospital and go to the building society. They had closed the nearest branch, the one he'd always used, so he had to go some little distance, and was afraid that he would be late back to work. Punctuality was important to Harold.

So close to Christmas, it was impossible to make good time. The Underground was jammed, the buses crawled along the streets through massive traffic jams, and the pavements were clogged with pedestrians. Harold chose the latter form of transport: walking might take him just as long, or longer, as the bus or the tube, but at least it didn't cost him anything.

So he pushed his way through the London streets, over-whelmed and on the verge of panic.

It had taken him some time to grasp what it was the man on the phone, the night before last, wanted. 'You wouldn't want your sister to find out what you used to get up to at weekends, would you?' the man had suggested.

Want Bunny to find out? How would Bunny find out? He certainly wasn't going to tell her, and who else would? Harold thought he would die of shame and embarrassment if Bunny were to find out. And how did this man know about it, any-way? How did he know about Bunny? Who was he? Harold had started sweating at that point in the conversation.

And then the man had said something even stranger and more frightening. 'I think that the police might be interested in talking to you. You knew her, and now she's dead. Murdered. You had a good reason for killing her, if you think about it, Buddy.'

'Me?' Harold had squeaked. He was outraged: why would he kill her? How could anyone even think that he could or would?

But his outrage had turned to fear as the reason for the call had become clear: the man wanted money. Money to keep quiet. So that he wouldn't tell Bunny, or the police. Harold was being threatened. And, he thought, there was a word for this: blackmail.

Only two hundred pounds, the man had said. But two hundred pounds was a good deal of money to Harold. He didn't have it just lying about, or even easily accessible. That was why he had to go to the building society, to draw the money out of his savings. He had spent all of yesterday trying to think of another way round it, and had realised at last that this was the only thing he could do.

His nest egg, that little legacy from his mother. He had always thought of that money as sacred, not to be touched for any reason. Not even for his weekends in Southgate; they were always funded with carefully saved cash from his pay packet.

But now he had no choice. The man wanted two hundred pounds by tomorrow, and the alternative was unthinkable. Bunny would find out and he would never be able to look her in the eye again. The police would come round and ask him questions. They might even arrest him and put him in gaol, if he couldn't convince them that he hadn't killed her.

Harold was frightened. For how could he be sure that, once he had drawn out the money, put it in a plain brown envelope, and sent it to a post office box as he'd been instructed, that would be the end of it? What was to stop this unknown man, who knew so much, from asking for more money next week? And the week after? One day the building society account would be empty, bled dry, and then what?

Who *was* this man, anyway? How did he know so much?

Though the December day was a cold one, and already the dark was drawing in, Harold sweated profusely as he battled his way through the crowds towards the building society.

'Mince pies!' said Rob approvingly. 'Home-made, as well. Tessa, you've been busy, you clever girl!'

She'd waited till after dinner to produce them, and was gratified by his response. He'd said once that he was fond of mince pies, especially home-made ones, and she had determined to surprise him with them. The effort had been worth it, judging from the expression on his face.

Thanks to Ian, there weren't as many of them as there had been, but still enough to make Rob happy. She'd arranged them on a plate, and even added a festive sprig of holly from the bush in the back garden.

She wasn't going to tell him about Ian. That had been a foregone conclusion, even before the kiss. She had decided that if he should ask her what she'd been doing that day, she could produce the mince pies as evidence that she had been fruitfully employed.

And she had decided, shocked by her experience with Ian, to take the initiative. It was no good waiting around for Rob to decide that he wanted her – that might not be till after the baby was born, and she certainly couldn't wait that long, even if he could. From the heady days of their honeymoon, and the blissful weeks both before and after, she knew how to excite him, and how to give him pleasure. Tonight she intended to take advantage of that knowledge.

They sat in the front room, lit only by the pinpoint lights of the Christmas tree. Tessa had put on a CD of quiet mood music, the romantic strains of a classical guitar. Rob was on the sofa, and after bringing through the coffee and mince pies, Tessa sat cross-legged on the floor at his feet, leaning against his leg. With one hand he stroked her hair. All, thought Tessa, was going according to plan. A romantic evening, followed by . . .

'I've been thinking,' Rob said. 'What happened to those keys, anyway? The ones for my mother's house?'

Tessa's heart jumped. She swallowed, and tried to keep her voice casual. 'I think I put them away. In a drawer.'

'Well, I need them,' he stated. 'Could you find them for me?'

'What for?' She could have kicked herself as soon as she said it.

Rob didn't seem to notice. 'I've rung someone about having the house cleaned. Some woman that the estate agent recommended.'

'Cleaned?' Tessa echoed. 'Estate agent?'

'To get rid of the bloodstains and everything,' he said calmly. 'No one will want to buy a house with bloodstains on the carpet. We'll just have to hope that no one – like that nosy old cow next door – tells any potential buyers about the murder. People can be funny about that sort of thing, I believe.'

At last Tessa understood what he was talking about, but she couldn't believe it. 'You're planning to sell the house?' she asked.

'Of course. I've already talked to an estate agent in Southgate, and he's agreed to put it on the market as soon as it's been cleaned. He doesn't think he'll have any trouble selling it, as long as it isn't generally known about the murder. It's in a very desirable area, he says. Not many houses in that road come on the market, and people are always on the lookout.'

Tessa twisted round and turned her face up to him. 'But . . . you can't sell the house!' she blurted.

He raised his eyebrows. 'Why ever not? And what else would you do with it?'

Though it was a question she hadn't really thought about, she opened her mouth and the answer came out; as she spoke the words she knew that it was right, and what she wanted. 'We could live there.'

'*Live* there? Tessa, have you lost your mind?' He stared at her as if she'd suddenly sprouted a second head.

His vehemence shook her, but Tessa held her ground, if somewhat falteringly. 'It would make sense, Rob. When the baby comes . . . we'd have more room. We wouldn't have to worry about those steep stairs.' She must not, she realised, say anything to betray the fact that she had been back there this week. 'And it seems . . . right. It was your home, Rob. You grew up there.'

Rob's face looked as though it were carved out of ivory, and his voice was clipped, cold. 'Exactly. And that is why I never want to set foot in the place again. Ever. That's the end of it, Tessa. The house is going to be sold, and the subject is closed.'

She knew, from past experience, that he meant it. There was no point prolonging the discussion; he would only retreat, both emotionally and physically, and make her plans for the rest of the evening impossible.

Taking a few deep breaths, Tessa said in a quiet voice, 'I'll get the keys.' She went out into the hall to the coat tree and retrieved them from the pocket of her coat, then opened and shut the drawer of the hall table, just in case Rob were listening, before going back into the front room. 'Here,' she said, holding them out to him.

He seemed loath to take them. 'The thing is,' he said, 'the cleaner wants to do the job tomorrow morning. I don't know how I'm going to get the keys to her, unless I go out tonight and drop them off.'

The last thing that Tessa wanted was for him to go off anywhere this evening. And, she thought, if she handled this right, it would give her another opportunity to explore the house. 'Maybe I could take her the keys in the morning,' she suggested in a deliberately nonchalant tone. 'Or even meet her at the house and let her in.'

'You wouldn't mind doing that?'

She shook her head. 'I wouldn't mind.'

Rob smiled at her with gratitude. 'Thanks, Tessa. That really would help. I just won't have time tomorrow morning – I have an important meeting first thing.'

'Then you won't mind an early night tonight.' Tessa didn't speak the words aloud, afraid of scaring him off; they echoed in her head as she sat close beside him on the sofa. She felt him tense up at her warm proximity, but she took it slowly. In the glow of the fairy lights and with the classical guitar thrumming delicately in the background, she let him relax in silence, then she moved her hand.

Chapter 12

Tessa woke slowly the next morning, gradually detaching herself from her pleasurable dreams and coming back to a reality which looked a great deal brighter to her than it had only a day before. Suspended between sleep and waking, she was possessed by a delicious languor, every muscle of her body stretched but tingling with life.

It had been wonderful, as good as before. Better, maybe: with her bump in the way, they'd had to be more adventurous, if a bit more gentle than before.

They hadn't slept until the wee hours of the morning.

Sighing happily, her eyes still closed, she reached for Rob. He wasn't there.

'You don't have to get up yet,' came a curt voice from somewhere a few feet away.

Tessa opened her eyes. Rob was standing in front of the mirror, already dressed, knotting his tie. 'I've made my own breakfast,' he went on in the same tone. 'So there's no need for you to get up. But don't forget to ring that woman about the cleaning. I've left the number downstairs by the phone.'

'Yes, I'll ring her.'

Rob turned from the mirror and started for the door. 'I'll see you tonight, then.'

He was going, just like that; Tessa couldn't believe it. She stretched her arms out to him. 'Don't I even get a kiss?'

Returning to the side of the bed, he leaned over and bestowed a chaste peck on her forehead. She twined her arms round his neck, pulling him closer. 'That's not good enough,' she murmured. 'Not after last night.'

Rob recoiled, grabbing her wrists and detaching himself from her embrace. He moved back a step and looked down at her bewildered face with a frown – almost, she thought in shock, of distaste.

'What's the matter?' Tessa faltered.

His voice was as cold as a shower of ice. 'You seduced me. You were quite . . . abandoned. You're no better than . . . well, never mind.'

'But you enjoyed it!' she protested, devastated by his tone of voice and his hurtful words. 'It was wonderful!'

Rob folded his arms across his chest. 'That's not the point, Tessa. But I'm telling you one thing – it won't happen again. If you so much as try to seduce me again, if you lay one finger on me like you did last night, I'll sleep on the sofa.'

Tears stung her eyes. 'I don't understand.'

'No,' he said. 'You wouldn't.' Rob spun on his heel and started for the door again.

Tessa turned her head into the pillow and squeezed her eyes shut; as she did so, there was a strong and unmistakable sensation in her middle. 'Oh!' she cried out, startled.

'What is it?' Rob paused at the door; his voice sounded concerned.

'The baby,' she gasped.

'Is something wrong?' He retraced his steps to the side of the bed and leaned over her. 'Are you in pain? Tessa, are you all right?'

She gave a weak laugh. 'Oh, Rob. She kicked me!' Before now Tessa had felt rumblings and gurglings and faint twinges of movement, but this was the first definite kick, and it had taken her quite by surprise.

Rob perched on the edge of the bed and put his hand on her stomach. 'Right here?'

She nodded, then grimaced. 'She just did it again!'

'I felt it!' He grinned at her. 'I don't know why you go on saying "she". It's obviously a boy, and he's going to be a football player.'

With Rob gone, Tessa made herself a cup of tea and drank it at the kitchen table. She would never figure him out, she decided ruefully. He *had* enjoyed the night before; there was no mistaking it. So why this sudden change of heart?

She didn't want to think about it, Tessa decided. It was too painful, too complicated. And her baby didn't need to be assaulted by any more negative feelings. No doubt she was kicking out in protest.

Tessa had read in one of her books that a baby *in utero* responds to its mother's voice from about twenty weeks; that book recommended talking aloud to the baby. She was now in her twentieth week, so it was time to start. 'Don't worry, Baby,' she said. 'Everything is going to be fine. Your daddy loves me. He really does. Sometimes he's just a bit confused, that's all. And he's still hurting because his mother is dead. But when you're born, everything will be just perfect. I promise.'

She'd almost convinced herself, Tessa reflected wryly, as the phone rang. Ian, she thought, her heart jumping. She was not ready for Ian this morning. They really ought to get one of those caller display phones so that she would know when not to pick up the receiver.

Her hand hovered over the phone as it rang insistently. What if it were something important? Maybe it wasn't Ian after all. She picked it up.

'Tessa?'

It was Andrew, she recognised with relief. The relief was immediately followed by a twinge of guilt: it had been ages since she'd spoken to him, and she never had managed to sort out that invitation to Sunday lunch. 'Oh, hello, Andrew.'

'It's great to hear your voice,' he said. 'I was just wondering how you were getting on.'

'Oh . . . fine,' she said in what she hoped was a convincing way.

'And how is that goddaughter of mine?' he asked. 'You're taking good care of her, I hope?'

Tessa laughed. 'I was just talking to her, in fact.'

'Talking to her?'

'I read in one of my books that babies in the womb can hear, and that they recognise their mother's voice. So I thought I might as well get started.'

'Well, you can tell her that her Uncle Andrew is asking about her,' he chuckled. 'And that he's looking forward to meeting her. He's going to spoil her with lots of presents. But maybe you'd better not tell her that – we don't want to make her greedy.'

How nice Andrew was, Tessa thought with spontaneous warmth. He was a good friend; odd that she hadn't realised it when she worked with him every day. And it was wonderful to have a friend like Andrew, a man who was only interested in her platonically, without the messy complications of sex.

She asked him about work, and for a few minutes he chattered about the latest projects he was working on, and more interestingly about his co-workers and the recent developments in their lives. It all took Tessa back, and she found herself becoming quite nostalgic, in a rather detached way. That place and those people all seemed so very far away, as though she'd known them in a past life, rather than having been in the midst of them until just a few months ago.

'And now it's almost Christmas,' said Andrew. 'We both know that nothing at all will get done for about the next month.'

'What are you doing for Christmas?' she found herself asking. 'Do you have plans?'

'On the day, I always go to my parents'.' He laughed. 'You

ought to understand, Tessa. Since your father is a vicar as well. They can never leave the parish at Christmas. So my sisters and I have to go there. It's the usual family thing, you know. Church, breakfast, presents round the tree, a huge Christmas lunch, crackers, Christmas pudding, the Queen's speech, falling into a coma in front of the telly with some mindless film on, then the Christmas cake with tea, back to church for evensong, and finally turkey sandwiches. Every year the same. My mum complains bitterly, but she loves every minute of it. Sounds dire, doesn't it?' he finished cheerfully.

No, thought Tessa, with a pang of envy. It didn't sound dire at all; it sounded wonderful – cosy and familial. The sort of Christmas, full of shared wonder and joy, that she could only just barely remember, back when her mother was alive. 'You have sisters, then?' she asked with the covetous yearning of an only child.

'Yes, three. All younger. I tease them something rotten,' Andrew confessed. 'One of the little things that makes Christmas so much fun.'

Tessa sighed, then told herself sternly that she *was* looking forward to Christmas with Rob. Just the two of them would be nice. She would *make* it nice, she was determined. But some impulse made her ask, 'What about Boxing Day, then? Do you stay on at your parents' for Boxing Day?'

'Oh, no. One day is quite enough, thank you.' He laughed.

'Then,' she said impetuously, 'maybe you could come to us on Boxing Day. For lunch.'

'I would love that,' he said with sincerity. 'And it's lovely of you to ask me. But do you need to check it with Rob?'

Tessa was confident. 'No, of course not. Rob will be delighted.'

Having arranged with the cleaner to meet her at the house in Southgate at eleven o'clock, Tessa hurried through her shower, dressed quickly in leggings and a warm jumper, pulled her coat on, and walked briskly to the tube station. She arrived at the house just in time; as she unlocked the front door, a car pulled up in the road.

The woman who got out was not at all what Tessa was expecting. In the first place, she was far too young, not even out of her teens if appearances were anything to go by; the woman on the phone had sounded much older and more mature than this girl. And in the second place, the girl looked extraordinary: her hair was dyed a dead black, with short back and sides, and worn in a gelled flat-top like a man; there were multiple rings down the side of one of her ears, a diamond adorned one of her nostrils, and a double-headed stud pierced one of her eyebrows. Under those disfiguring affectations, though, she was one of the most stunningly beautiful girls that Tessa had ever seen.

And she was friendly, Tessa discovered as the girl approached her and explained, in a nearly impenetrable Cockney accent, thick with glottal stops. Her mum, she said, was supposed to come, but her 'li'ul bruvver' had been sent home from school and her mum had asked her to come instead. 'I help me mum out sometimes, like,' she added. 'Wif the cleanin'. It's be'er than bein' on the dole.' Energetically she hauled a Hoover from the boot of her car and carried it into the house, then fetched a carpet-cleaning machine and several carrier bags of assorted equipment.

'It looks as if you know what you're doing,' Tessa remarked, feeling overwhelmed in the presence of so much youthful vitality.

'Oh, yeah,' nodded the girl. Her mum had told her, she explained, that she was to give the whole house a going-over, paying particular attention to the bloodstains in the lounge. 'I'll ge' 'em up, all right,' she promised, seemingly untroubled by curiosity as to their origin.

Then the girl pulled a Walkman from one of her bags,

clamped the earphones on her head, and turned up the volume to such a pitch that Tessa could hear the thump of the bass halfway across the room. She plugged in the Hoover and switched it on, pushing it vigorously over the entrance hall carpet.

'I'll leave you to get on with it, then,' Tessa said as loudly as she could.

'Wha'?' The girl turned, but made no effort to reduce the volume of either the Hoover or the music.

Tessa moved to the door and gestured. 'I'll be back,' she mouthed.

'I'll jus' ge' on wif i',' shouted the girl with a cheerful grin.

Tessa had not intended leaving the house while the cleaning was under way, but it seemed the best course of action in the circumstances. The girl would operate more efficiently without her there watching over her shoulder, and no matter where she went in the house she would feel that she was in the cleaner's way.

The question was, where was she to go for the next few hours? She could walk back into the centre of Southgate, to the shops; she could have a bit of lunch at the café where she'd met Greg Reynolds; she could browse for a bit in the bookshop, and chat with its owner. But the idea didn't really appeal to her. Southgate had been far too crowded for her taste as she'd passed through the shopping district; in the run-up to Christmas, the pavements were overflowing and the shops were impossible.

Tessa hesitated on the pavement, looking right and left, her hands jammed into her coat pockets. From up the road a woman approached on foot, a shopping basket over her arm. She looked vaguely familiar. The woman next door, Tessa realised – Hilda something-or-other. The one whom Rob had referred to only last night as 'that nosy old cow next door'.

She had lived next to Linda Nicholls for years, which

meant that she must have known her quite well. She had been at the funeral. And she had invited Tessa to come round to see her if she ever wanted to talk.

Why not? thought Tessa.

She fixed a smile on her face as the woman approached, wishing that she could remember her name. Steggall – that was it, she recalled at the last moment from somewhere deep within her brain. Hilda Steggall.

'Hello, Mrs Steggall,' she said.

The woman looked at her sharply, as if fearing a Jehovah's Witness or a double-glazing salesman might have learned her name and was waiting to waylay her in the road. Then her face changed as she recognised the young woman in front of her. 'Tessa, isn't it? Robin's wife?'

'Yes, that's right.'

Hilda beamed at her. 'Would you like to come in for a coffee, dear? I'm just back from the shops, as you can see, and it's time for my elevenses.'

'Thank you,' said Tessa. 'I'd like that.'

The house, Tessa observed, as they approached it, was built in an identical style to the one next door, but there the resemblance ended. For this house was stamped, unmistakably, with the personality of Hilda Steggall, even on its exterior, and she was a very different person indeed than Linda Nicholls had been. The entrance hall confirmed that impression, with its gaudy patterned carpet and equally gaudy – though clashing – flowered wallpaper. 'We'll have our coffee in the drawing room,' said Hilda, as if conferring some great honour upon Tessa, and flung open the door of the room corresponding to the one next door in which Linda Nicholls had been murdered. 'You just go in and make yourself comfortable, dear. I'll make the coffee and be along in a tick.'

The carpet in Hilda Steggall's drawing room was not gaudily patterned, but that was about all you could say in its favour, Tessa thought as she followed her hostess's instructions and went into the room. It was a remarkable room: an orgy of bad taste. The wallpaper was flocked, deep claret red on cream in a heavy floral pattern, except for the alcoves on either side of the fireplace, where it changed to red-and-cream stripes. Clashing madly with the deep red of the wallpaper, the curtains – thick velvet – were a magenta colour, and the carpet was a shade of rust. The soft furniture – two bucket chairs and a round sofa – was all very clearly vintage 1960s, the upholstery an astonishing shade of bright orange, patterned with gold daisies. Coordinating with the colour of the furniture was an orange ceramic lamp with a tassled gold satin shade, and an orange shag hearthrug.

The hearth itself was marble, as was the fireplace insert, surrounded by a mantelpiece of vast pretentiousness and guarded by a large pair of china dogs. On a table to one side of the fireplace stood a lavish arrangement of artificial flowers. A chandelier, in the Venetian style – dripping with moulded flowers – hung from an ornate ceiling rose.

But the *pièce de résistance* was the television set in the corner: it was encased in a huge white plastic globe which in turn sat upon a moulded pedestal of the same material, looking like nothing so much as evidence of an alien invasion from outer space.

And the room was, of course, decorated for Christmas, with a tree at the centre of the rounded bay window and gaudy cut-out tinsel decorations hanging from the floral branches of the chandelier.

Overwhelmed by the visual assault, Tessa sank into one of the bucket-shaped chairs. It was not, she rapidly discovered, as comfortable as it looked, and furthermore she now realised that it was going to be extremely difficult to get back out of it. The frightening thing about this room, she thought as she waited for her hostess to return, apart from its egregious ugliness, was the fact that it was so obviously done this way on purpose. It hadn't just happened: it had been planned like this, and lovingly tended, every surface free of dust. Hilda Steggall was house-proud, and the room was her showpiece, not to be defiled by the eyes of casual visitors, but reserved for those who were truly worthy.

This impression was confirmed as Hilda bore the tray into the room a few minutes later. She looked round it with pride, her eyes lingering on every hideous detail. 'I save this room for best,' she said. 'I usually watch the telly in my bedroom.'

'Well, it's certainly . . . impressive,' Tessa managed.

'Isn't it?' Hilda agreed smugly. 'My husband Arthur, God rest his soul, used to say that he'd never seen a room like it anywhere.'

With gratitude, Tessa seized on the opportunity to change the subject. 'You're a widow, then, Mrs Steggall?'

'For almost twenty years now.' Hilda sighed as she handed Tessa a cup of coffee. 'Arthur was taken far too young. The girls were still at school.'

Hilda had two daughters, it transpired, who had duly presented her with several grandchildren. The grandchildren, though they lived at some distance, were the light of her life, and she was easily persuaded to show Tessa their photographs.

'My girls, bless them,' she said with a fond smile, 'are always on at me to come and live with them. Both of them. "That house is too big for you on your own", they say. And they're right about that, of course. But it's been my home for thirty-seven years, and I'm not leaving it now.'

'That's quite a long time,' Tessa remarked.

'Oh, I suppose it seems that way to you.' Hilda smiled indulgently. 'You're young. But the years go by so quickly. It seems like only last week that I came to this house as a young bride. And only yesterday that your husband, young Robin, was in short pants, running about the neighbourhood.'

Tessa was fascinated by the image this conjured up, and longed to know more about Rob's early years. 'What was he like then?' she asked.

Draining her coffee cup, Hilda took her time about answering. 'I suppose he was a typical boy,' she said at last, choosing her words with care. 'I just had girls, of course, so I was used to their more . . . quiet . . . ways.' She paused, then went on, 'I'm not saying that Robin was a nuisance, exactly. But he rode his bike over my front borders on more than one occasion, and I had to have . . . words . . . with his mother. And I had a cat, in those days, who was terrified of him – she hid every time he came out of the house. Of course,' she added quickly, 'it was very difficult for him when his dad upped sticks and left. With another woman, it was – his secretary or practice nurse or some such, no less. I believe young Robin took it very hard. And who can blame him? It was like my girls, when their dad died.' She was trying to be kind, Hilda told herself, and had understated the case considerably: Robin Nicholls had been a right little horror, both before and after his father left. But that wasn't the sort of thing that a new bride wanted to hear about her husband, and to be charitable, perhaps age and maturity had improved him. Though he *had* been rude to her at the funeral . . .

Tessa didn't want to be sidetracked back on to the subject of Hilda's girls, so she asked another question. 'When exactly did his father leave?'

Hilda gave her a speculative look, surprised that she didn't know. 'Well, it was just a few months after my Arthur died. How old is Robin now?'

'Twenty-eight,' Tessa supplied.

'He must have been about ten or eleven at the time,' Hilda calculated. 'I seem to remember that he went off to boarding school a year or so after that.'

How strange, Tessa thought, that she'd never known these details. Rob was so secretive, so unwilling to talk about his past, and up until now there hadn't been anyone else to ask.

And instinctively she knew that he would not be pleased to discover that she had talked to Hilda Steggall – that 'nosy old cow' – about him. She knew, as well, that she wasn't going to tell him.

'I always thought', said Hilda reflectively, 'that it was strange that his mother could bear to send him away like that. My girls were such a comfort to me after Arthur died. I would have thought that Linda would have wanted Robin to stay at home with her.'

There were so many questions that Tessa wanted to ask about her mother-in-law; she scarcely knew where to begin. 'Did you ask her why she sent him away?'

'No.' Hilda busied herself collecting up the empty coffee cups and putting them on the tray. 'Linda and I weren't exactly . . . close,' she temporised.

That surprised Tessa; the impression that Hilda had given up till now was that the two families had known each other well. After all, she thought, they had been neighbours for nearly thirty years. And they had both lost their husbands at about the same time, so that experience should have drawn them together. 'Did you have a row?' she asked bluntly.

Hilda looked away, towards the artificial flowers in the alcove. 'Oh, no. Nothing like that. Not really.' She turned back to face Tessa. 'As I said before, there were times when I had to speak to her a bit sharply, about young Robin and his antics. But it wasn't really that. It wasn't that we didn't get on. We were just . . . two different sorts of people. You can see what *I'm* like, dear – open and friendly. So it wasn't *me*. But Linda was a very . . . private person. Secretive, almost. Kept herself to herself, always. I tried', she admitted, 'to make friends with her. Several times, over the years. But she wasn't interested.'

Tessa was amazed at how disappointed she was: every time she felt that she was getting a bit closer to finding out what Linda Nicholls was like, the essence of the woman slipped away from her. And the people who had known her were no help. Rob wouldn't talk about her at all, Father Theo was little better, and the most she'd gleaned from Greg Reynolds was that Linda had been 'fit', and liked pepperoni on her pizza. Now Hilda was telling her that Linda had been a private person, that she'd scarcely known her at all in the thirty-odd years that they'd been neighbours.

Her disappointment must have shown on her face, for Hilda then turned the tables on her. 'How well did *you* know her? You and Robin haven't been married for very long, have you?' She looked pointedly at Tessa's bulging middle.

'I never met her,' Tessa said bleakly. 'I spoke to her once on the phone. We were coming to have tea with her the day that she . . . died.'

Hilda nodded her head up and down with thoughtful gravity. 'What a tragedy that was. A terrible loss for Robin – and for you, of course, dear. And so sad that Linda will never know her grandchild.'

This so closely echoed her own thoughts that Tessa found herself fighting a sudden threat of tears; she knew that she had to escape, or risk breaking down. 'I suppose I'd better be going, Mrs Steggall. Thank you for the coffee.' With some difficulty she struggled out of the chair and on to her feet. She forced a smile, adding, 'It was very kind of you. And I've enjoyed talking to you.'

'My pleasure.' Hilda escorted her to the door. 'Stop by any time.' She paused on the doorstep. 'You don't happen to know what's going to become of the house, do you?'

'Rob plans to sell it,' Tessa answered truthfully.

'Sell it?' Hilda's eyes widened. 'Well, he'd better hope that no one tells any prospective buyers about what went on in that house. *I* won't mention it to anyone, you can be sure.'

Tessa nodded in grateful acknowledgement. 'The . . . murder, you mean.'

'Oh, that.' Hilda gave a dismissive wave. 'No, I was talking about the men.'

'Men?' Tessa echoed weakly.

Hilda repeated it with relish. 'The men. The ones who visited her. There was the young one with the moustache – he came nearly every day. But the others came mostly at the weekend. "Paying guests", I suppose you might call them.'

Tessa swallowed hard, trying to make sense of Hilda's words. 'Are you saying that my mother-in-law ran a Bed and Breakfast?' she asked.

Hilda's laugh was mirthless. 'You might call it that. But I think it was more of the former and less of the latter, if you know what I mean.'

Tessa was conscious that she was staring at Hilda Steggall. 'You're saying . . .' But she couldn't get the words out.

'A brothel,' Hilda said crisply. 'Don't forget, I lived next door to her for years. I have eyes in my head, and I saw all of those men, week in and week out, and I'm capable of putting two and two together.'

'But . . . that's crazy! It's impossible!' Tessa heard her own voice, shouting, though she wasn't aware of moving her mouth.

'Is it, Tessa?' Hilda narrowed her eyes. 'If you don't believe *me*, ask someone else. That coloured girl who works at the nursing home down at the end of the road – at number two, on the other side. I don't know her name, but she was very friendly with your mother-in-law. She used to come round quite a lot, especially at weekends. If you get my meaning. Though I don't suppose she'll be anxious to admit what was going on in that house.' Her voice softened unexpectedly. 'I'm telling you for your own good, Tessa. You've a right to know what sort of woman Linda Nicholls was. Believe me, she was no saint.' Then she shut the door.

Tessa was numb, in a state of shock. She wasn't quite sure how she'd ended up on the pavement, the monstrous words echoing in her head. A brothel! Hilda Steggall was telling her that Rob's mother had been . . . a prostitute. A hooker. A whore.

Unthinkable. Impossible. Utterly, completely and totally impossible.

And yet . . .

And yet.

She gulped in deep breaths of the icy air, hoping it would help to clear her brain.

If it *were* true, she admitted to herself, it would explain so much. All those men. Not lovers, as she had once believed, but clients. Customers. Men who paid for her body, who paid for sex.

Father Theo, too? asked a voice in her head. No, she couldn't – wouldn't – believe that. Surely he had acted as a counsellor to her. In fact, this would explain his reluctance to discuss Linda Nicholls: he would want to protect her memory, as well as sparing Tessa from the knowledge of what her mother-in-law had been.

And above all, it would explain Rob's disdain for his mother, his unwillingness to talk about her, the years of estrangement. To know that your own mother was a common hooker . . .

By the time Tessa reached the end of the road, she was halfway to believing that it might be true.

After all, what *did* she know about Linda Nicholls? Very little, she admitted to herself, and none of it added up or made sense.

Until now.

Number Two, Chase View Road was a house very much like the others in the road, but it was no longer in use as a single-family dwelling. A discreet sign outside announced the fact that this was Jessop House, a residential care home for the elderly. The rich elderly, if appearances were anything to go by: the place was in immaculate condition.

Tessa went to the door and rang the bell. After a moment it was answered by a woman with glasses and permed salt-and-pepper hair. 'Yes?' the woman said, in a not-unfriendly but rather weary voice.

Glancing at the sign, Tessa made a guess. 'Mrs Jessop?'

'That's right. How can I help you?'

She hadn't had time to formulate an approach, and was in no state for cunning in any case, so she came straight out with it. 'I understand that you have a girl working for you. An . . . um . . . Asian girl, perhaps?'

Mrs Jessop sighed and ran her fingers through her hair. 'That would be Geeta,' she stated. 'And I'm afraid she's not here.' She looked as though she were preparing to shut the door, so Tessa spoke quickly.

'My name is Tessa Nicholls,' she said. 'My mother-in-law, Linda Nicholls, lived down the road at number 27.'

'Ah, yes.' Mrs Jessop nodded in recognition.

'And I was told', Tessa went on, 'that this girl Geeta knew my mother-in-law.'

'That's true enough,' the woman acknowledged. 'She's a good, hard-working girl, is Geeta. Wonderful with the old folks – patient and kind. And when I didn't need her here, she worked extra hours for Mrs Nicholls. There wasn't anything underhand about it – she told me straight off that she was going to do it, because she could use the extra money.'

Tessa summoned up her courage to ask, 'Did she tell you what sort of work it was?'

Mrs Jessop looked a bit surprised at the question. 'Well, I understood that Mrs Nicholls ran a Bed and Breakfast. So Geeta helped out with the housekeeping at weekends. Washing towels and bedlinen, making beds, that sort of thing.' She sighed with feeling. 'You wouldn't believe how much of that needs doing in a place like this. And I need to be getting on with it myself. So if that's all . . .' Once again she made a move to close the door.

'I won't keep you,' Tessa said, taking a step forward, 'but I have just one more question. Will Geeta be here later?'

'That', said Mrs Jessop with another sigh, 'is the problem. Geeta's gone.'

'Gone?' Tessa echoed in dismay. 'For good?'

The woman shook her head. 'No. But I don't know when she'll be back, and I haven't been able to find anyone to replace her on a temporary basis, so I'm absolutely run off my feet at the moment.' She explained, 'Geeta's a conscientious girl – don't get me wrong about that. She didn't just disappear and leave me in the lurch. It was about three weeks ago that the family had a call that the grandmother in India was dying. The whole family went, I believe. I haven't heard anything since, so I don't know when to expect her back. But she'll be back eventually. Soon, I hope,' she added with feeling.

Tessa fumbled in her coat pocket for a scrap of paper. 'If I leave you my phone number, Mrs Jessop, when Geeta comes back, could you ask her to get in touch with me? It's rather important that I talk to her.'

'No problem.' Mrs Jessop watched as Tessa scribbled her name and phone number, then took the paper from her. 'Sorry to be in a rush, Mrs Nicholls,' she said, 'but if you'll excuse me, I really do have work to do.'

Sergeant Doug Coles was in an expansive mood that afternoon. The Metropolitan Police Rugby Football Club had just soundly trounced their rivals, and he had money in his pocket. Two hundred pounds, to be precise, collected just that morning from a post office box.

So he was feeling excessively pleased with himself, and flush with cash.

It had worked, and it had been so easy. So absurdly easy.

He'd tried Harold Dingley first, as an experiment. He knew that Dingley didn't have that much ready cash, so his demands had been modest. And it had worked. Dingley had come up with the readies. Just like that – two hundred pounds.

There was bound to be more where that came from – probably some sort of inheritance from the dead mother, Coles theorised. He would see how far he could push him. It had taken him a while to get the point across; Dingley wasn't the brightest of sparks – at least two sandwiches short of a picnic. But the mere suggestion that his sister might find out the truth about him had scared him shitless. And now that he understood what was at stake – exposure, possible arrest – he would be willing to part with increasing sums of money.

And Dingley was only the first, Coles told himself jubilantly. Only the beginning.

The priest might not have much money himself, but he worked for the Church, for God's sake. Coles had visions of offering bags stuffed with cash, all diverted his way. After all, the priest had more to lose than most – he could be defrocked, disgraced; unable to look his congregation in the eye, let alone his bishop.

And Wooldridge. He owned his own company, as he'd told Coles more than once. Rich, he was. Bloody rolling in it. Who knew how much he'd be willing to hand over to protect his own backside? He had a wife, he had a position in the business community to protect. He would pay up all right, and handsomely.

And that prat Malcolm Hogg. Again, Coles wasn't sure what Hogg's own finances were, though he had a feeling he had inherited rather a tidy sum from his mother. But he was a bank manager, and who had access to more money than a bank manager? Vaults and vaults of the stuff, right at his fingertips. And he was such a self-important pillock that he would do anything to preserve his position.

So with two hundred pounds in his pocket, and his head filled with dreams of untold riches to come, Doug Coles was on top of the world when his mate Ian Spicer invited him to the pub after the match.

'I'll take you up on that invitation,' Coles agreed. 'But *I'm* buying, mate,' he added expansively.

They collected their pints and retired to a quiet booth near the back of the pub. 'Cheers,' said Ian, lifting his glass and clinking it against Coles's.

For a satisfying moment they both drank deeply. Then Ian spoke. 'Sorry to mix business with pleasure like this. But I want to ask you something, mate.'

'Ask away,' Coles invited. He was feeling generous.

'About the Linda Nicholls murder,' Ian said.

'Yes?' Instantly Coles was on his guard, but told himself that it was just a coincidence, and Ian couldn't possibly know anything.

'The thing is, Doug, I'm working on a case that might just overlap with it,' Ian lied smoothly. 'I can't give you the details just now – and it's not really that bloody important. But I've had a look at the Nicholls files, and there's something there that bothers me a bit. I thought I'd ask you about it, since you've signed off the paperwork on the search of the house.'

'What's that?' Coles kept his voice steady and took a gulp of his lager.

'The Nicholls woman's files. Nothing was retained as evidence – no bank statements or tax documents or personal records of any sort. The filing cabinet was empty, it says in the paperwork. Doesn't that strike you as a bit bloody odd?'

Somehow Coles kept his hand from shaking though, just to be sure, he put his glass down on the table, and forced himself to look Ian Spicer in the eye. 'I *did* think it was odd,' he said. 'Maybe she had a premonition that she was going to be murdered, and destroyed all of her papers.' That sounded incredibly stupid, even to his own ears, but he didn't know what else to say. His euphoria had evaporated; in its place was a sudden throbbing headache behind one eye. Bloody hell, said a voice in his head. Bloody, bloody, bloody hell.

Chapter 13

Tessa scarcely slept that night. The baby, having learned to kick, practised that skill repeatedly through the night. And it wasn't just the baby that kept her awake.

While Rob slept soundly beside her, Tessa went over in her mind, obsessively, the end of her conversation with Hilda Steggall: the words themselves, their implications, the ramifications.

She no longer doubted that it was true. Sometime during that long night, imperceptibly, the impossible had become the accepted. Rob's mother had been a prostitute. Possibly even a madam, if she had employed the girl Geeta and maybe others as well.

She thought of Rob's hurtful words of the previous morning: 'You're no better than . . .' 'No better than my mother,' she mentally finished the sentence. No wonder the poor lamb had conflicting feelings about sex, she told herself: to know that your mother sold her body to men would be enough to dampen anyone's libido. As long as Rob was estranged from his mother, as long as she was no part of his life, Tessa analysed, he had been able to lock her away in a compartment of his mind, to forget about her, and to function normally.

And she herself, Tessa realised guiltily, had tampered with that. She had pestered him about his mother, had continually reminded him of her, had not allowed him to shut the destructive memories away.

She had even tried to bring about a meeting, and had nearly succeeded. What damage had she inflicted on her poor husband, all unknowing?

But that was the thing, she told herself: she had not known. She'd done it all from the best motives, even if they were partly selfish ones.

If only he had told her, said a small voice in her head. If he had trusted her, and told her, all of this might have been averted – all of the pain and misunderstanding and grief.

She looked upon her sleeping husband with protective love, and mentally asked him to forgive her.

Other thoughts crowded her mind as well during that long night. She remembered Greg Reynolds, and the earnestness of his expression as he told her that he had loved Linda Nicholls.

What part did he play in all of this? Did he know what business Linda was engaged in? Was he, somehow, involved as well? Her pimp, even?

He had not seemed a calculating person, a deliberate liar. But surely he could not have seen Linda several times a week, sharing her bed, and remained ignorant of the nature of her work. Naivety was one thing, but ignorance on that scale would involve downright stupidity, and Tessa didn't think that Greg was stupid.

The other thing that nagged at her brain, going round and round, involved Linda's murder. Now that she knew what Linda had done for a living, it seemed more than obvious to her that one of her clients had killed her. In a fit of rage over something, one of them had struck her down.

Surely the police would be on to that: would realise, as she had done, that it provided the perfect scenario for murder. Prostitutes got themselves murdered all the time, had done from the days of Jack the Ripper onwards.

Which made the other question all the more fraught: where were her records? She must have kept records – if not of clients, then at least financial records. No matter how she masked her immoral earnings, she would have reported something to the taxman; she would have had bank statements, and kept records for her own information. All that she had seen of the house indicated to her that Linda Nicholls had been an orderly, organised person – almost obsessively so. Where, then, were her records? If they weren't in the office, and the police didn't have them, where were they?

In the morning, Rob seemed refreshed by a good night's sleep, and unaware that Tessa hadn't slept. 'Good morning, my love,' he said in a cheerful voice as he shut off his alarm. 'Sleep well?'

'The baby kicked me all night,' she admitted truthfully. He didn't need to know what else had kept her awake, she decided; she had inflicted enough psychic pain on him already. Sometime she would have to find the words to tell him that she knew what his mother had been. Now was not the time.

Rob was duly sympathetic. 'I hope that doesn't continue for the next few months,' he said, resting his hand on her stomach. 'Settle down in there!' he commanded the baby with a grin.

Tessa covered his hand with her own. 'It will be all right.'

'Maybe you should try to have a nap this morning,' Rob suggested.

'I have my antenatal clinic,' she reminded him. 'And that's likely to take half the day, with all of the sitting around and waiting.'

Rob kissed her forehead. 'Then don't get up just yet. I'll bring you a cup of tea, and you can rest for a bit.'

It was sweet of him to be so concerned, she thought warmly as she lay there waiting for him to make the tea and bring it up to her. She closed her eyes; the baby's kicks had diminished, and she was so tired. Two nights with only a minimal amount of sleep . . .

'Here you are, Tessa, my love,' Rob announced, setting the mug on the bedside table.

Waking from her drowsing state, she opened her eyes and smiled at him. 'Thank you. You're very good to me.'

'And why wouldn't I be?' he said lightly. He perched on the edge of the bed and held her hand.

Tessa left the tea to cool for a few minutes. 'Busy day today?' she asked him.

'Dreadful,' Rob said, making a face. 'The computers have been playing up something rotten this week, and I'm not at all sure that we've got this Millennium Bug thing sorted out. On top of that, we're getting ready to install a new system in the accounts department. It has to be up and running by the end of the year, and I don't know how we're going to manage. And tonight', he added, almost as an afterthought, 'is the office Christmas "do".'

This was the first Tessa had heard of it. 'You didn't tell me!' she protested. 'I don't know what I'll wear! None of my posh frocks fit me any longer.'

Rob looked nonplussed, then squeezed her hand. 'Oh, partners aren't invited,' he said lightly. 'It's not that sort of party. Just a few drinks, some boring speeches, and people wearing silly paper crowns – you know the sort of thing I mean.'

It didn't sound like the type of party that Tessa would enjoy – or Rob either, come to that. 'So you probably won't stay too long,' she said in a hopeful voice.

He shrugged. 'Oh, hard to say. It's usually a useful opportunity to chat to various people, so I can't make any promises. Don't bother with dinner, and don't wait up for me, just in case I'm late.'

Tessa tried not to mind, not to sound too disappointed. 'All right then.'

'You *could* do me one big favour,' Rob went on. 'If you have the time, that is.'

'I'll make the time,' she said simply. 'What is it?'

'Those keys,' Rob said in a matter-of-fact voice. 'They need to be dropped off at the estate agent's. When I spoke to him yesterday, he said that he already had someone who was interested in viewing the property, and the sooner he gets the keys, the better. And', he added, 'he needs to get in himself, to do the measuring up and so forth, so that he can produce the written details. I've left his card downstairs on the kitchen table.'

'Yes, of course I'll do it,' Tessa agreed.

'If you're sure it's not too much trouble.' He released her hand and stood up.

'It's only a few tube stops away,' she said. 'No problem.' She thought about getting up, but couldn't quite summon the energy; as soon as he'd left the room, she closed her eyes again.

Malcolm Hogg packed his holdall with especial care that morning, anticipating the weekend with a keenness sharpened to an exquisite piquancy by the time he had spent away.

For Malcolm Hogg had been on holiday, enjoying his long-anticipated fortnight in sunny Spain.

The holiday had not been quite what he had hoped. Yes, it was good to have the break, and to be away from the bank and the worries of the job for a fortnight. But the food had been . . . well, foreign. And the hotel had been full of foreigners. The joys of the beach and the pool had sounded better in the holiday brochure than they had proved to be in fact, for though Spain was indeed sunny, it wasn't all that hot in December. In practical terms, he might just as well have been freezing at the seaside with Mother.

And, to be honest with himself, he had missed Linda. Three weekends away from her had only made him appreciate her the more. He'd spent a great deal of the holiday shivering on the beach, thinking about her and looking forward to the delights that this weekend would bring.

His return flight had landed at Gatwick on Sunday evening

and he'd been back at the bank on Monday morning. Several times during that week he had thought of ringing Linda, and had longed to do so; sometimes, he knew, she was amenable to making special arrangements on week nights. But Malcolm Hogg was nothing if not self-disciplined. Always he had restrained himself. He would go to Southgate on Friday as he always did, and it would be all the better for the prolonged anticipation.

Now, he thought as he snapped his holdall shut, he had just one day to get through. One day of work – just a few hours – and then he would be in Southgate.

Father Theo was packing as well that morning. But he was going somewhere quite different to Spain or Southgate: he was going to Yorkshire, on retreat.

As the days since Linda's death had passed, Father Theo had found himself more and more distracted, more and more edgy, more and more depressed. He was not, he recognised, coping with it very well. He had, over the years, counselled enough people in similar difficulties to know that he really needed some counselling himself.

Counselling, and confession. Then perhaps he could put it all behind him and begin again.

But where could he go? To whom could he confess the terrible sins which burdened him, without risking condemnation, horror, repugnance?

He had been to Mirfield once, a long time ago, on retreat. He had found the old monks to be terribly wise. Living in community, their experience of the outside world was necessarily limited, but that didn't seem to limit their understanding of human nature and the snares into which that could lead. Their approach was gentle and compassionate, yet rigorous: sin was understandable, it was human, but sin was sin, and the proper response to it was repentance and amendment of life.

That, Father Theo thought, was what he needed. Repentance, forgiveness, absolution. Amendment of life? Perhaps he was strong enough for that as well, or would be after this weekend, with God's help.

The phone rang as he put his worn leather prayer book on top of his clothes and shut the holdall. Father Theo glanced at the clock – he didn't want to miss his train. But there was plenty of time, in case he needed to take the call.

Mrs Williams had answered the phone, and came up to tap on his bedroom door. 'It's Tessa Nicholls,' she said. 'I told her that you might not be available to speak to her.'

'It's all right,' he assured the housekeeper. 'I have a few minutes. I'll take it in my study.'

He carried the holdall down and left it by the front door, then went into his study and picked up the phone. 'Hello, Tessa,' he said warmly. 'How are you?'

'All right,' she responded. 'I was wondering whether I might come and see you again. Not today, perhaps, but maybe tomorrow. You did say . . .'

Father Theo sighed. This was why he hardly ever went on retreat: though he could always get a locum to take the services at St Nicholas's, it was so difficult to go off and leave people who needed him. But this time, he told himself, his need was at least as great as hers. 'I'm really sorry, Tessa,' he said, making sure that he sounded as though he *were* sorry. 'That won't be possible. I'm leaving in a few minutes, going on retreat for the weekend. I won't be back in London until late on Monday. The earliest I can see you is Tuesday morning.'

'Oh,' she said, her voice heavy with disappointment.

'Why don't you plan to come here that morning?' he suggested. 'Say, ten o'clock?'

'All right, then.'

He looked at his watch: still a few minutes to spare. 'Was there anything in particular you wanted to talk to me about, my dear?'

There was a pause on the other end of the phone, then she said in a carefully controlled voice, 'I've found out about Rob's mother. About what she did for a living.'

Oh, dear Lord, thought Father Theo. He had hoped that Tessa would never have to know. Not that she didn't have a right to know, but he'd wanted to spare her the hurt. How had she found out? He supposed that Rob had told her. Now the pause was on his end of the phone. 'And you wanted to talk to me about that,' he said at last, neutrally, playing for time.

'Yes. Unless you didn't feel that it was . . . appropriate.'

He searched for the right words. 'Tessa, my dear. I know that this has been a shock for you. But I do hope that you won't judge Linda too harshly.'

'I'm not judging her,' said Tessa. 'I'm just trying to understand. Trying to understand why . . .'

Father Theo took a deep breath. 'Linda did what she had to do to survive. She was a single mother. Her husband left her for another woman, and she had to support herself.'

'Other single mothers manage without doing . . . that,' Tessa stated. 'And anyway, her husband was a doctor. She wouldn't have starved.'

It was clear that Rob hadn't told her the whole story, but only his slanted version of it. Father Theo felt that he needed to redress the balance, to be the dead woman's advocate. 'Linda was very young when she married,' he said. 'And Rob was born within the year. She wasn't trained to do any proper job, and as long as she was married to a well-off doctor, she didn't need to. But when he left her, he gave her the house, and very little else. She had to find the money to pay the bills, to put food on the table.'

'But Rob says that his father is very generous,' Tessa protested.

'Generous with *him*, undoubtedly,' the priest agreed. 'He paid his school fees, gave him all the spending money he wanted, and even bought him a house when he reached the age of twenty-one. But Linda didn't see a penny of that money. She could have sold the house, of course, and moved into something smaller. But it was her home, and Rob's home. She didn't want to do that.'

'Yes,' said Tessa guardedly. 'I see.'

'I'm not trying to justify what she did. I just want to help you understand why she made some of the choices she did.'

Again Tessa paused, and when she continued, she sounded embarrassed. 'I have one other question to ask you, Father.'

'Yes?' he encouraged her, tense with foreboding.

'I know that you don't have any personal knowledge of this, but would you have said that she was good at what she did?'

At least, he thought with a flood of relief, Tessa didn't know that he was involved. It was cowardly of him, he acknowledged, but he told himself that he could better help her to come to terms with it if she *didn't* know, if she retained her respect for him. He tried not to let his relief show in his voice. 'Very professional, at any rate. Linda was a good businesswoman.'

'A good businesswoman,' Tessa echoed. 'Did she keep records, then?'

Records? he thought. 'Why, yes. I believe that she kept rather thorough records. She had a little office in her house.'

'There's nothing in it,' Tessa stated. 'That's one thing that bothers me.'

Father Theo looked at his watch again. 'Tessa, I've really got to go now,' he apologised. 'We'll talk as soon as I get back. On Tuesday. And', he added, knowing that it was useless, 'try not to think about it too much, my dear.'

Empty words, he told himself as he collected his holdall and walked briskly towards the bus stop. Tessa wouldn't be able to stop thinking about Linda, any more than he would.

But it wasn't until he was on the train, headed north, that the full significance of her words hit him. Linda's records were gone.

Did the police have them? If so, why hadn't they contacted him?

And if not . . . Where were they?

Tessa had slept far longer than she'd intended, and when she'd finally awakened it was with the conviction that she needed to talk to Father Theo; by the time she'd done that, most of the morning was gone and it was almost time for her to go to the antenatal clinic. She had planned to go to Southgate first thing that morning with the keys as she'd promised Rob, getting an early start so she would be back in time for her appointment. But now she knew that was out of the question. Especially, she admitted to herself, since she had a couple of other things to do: she wanted to stop somewhere where she could get some keys cut, so that she could retain a copy of Linda's keys, and she wanted to conduct a more thorough search of the house. There wasn't time for any of that now.

She would, she decided, go to the clinic straight away – a bit earlier than her appointment, and perhaps they would be able to get her through in good time. Then she could go on to Southgate from there, and hope that the estate agent didn't become so impatient that he would ring Rob at work. Rob would be at his party tonight, so it wouldn't matter if she lingered in Southgate and didn't make it back home by the usual time.

She was glad she'd talked to Father Theo. He had given her a great deal to think about. In fact, she realised, he had told her more about Linda Nicholls, and the forces that drove her, than the sum total of Tessa's previous knowledge of her.

A mother, protecting her child. Tessa's hand went to her bump, unconsciously, as she walked towards the clinic. What limits would a mother place on what she would do to protect her child? Was it so incomprehensible, what Linda had done, if it had been done for her child? Never mind that it had gone horribly, disastrously wrong, that her child had hated and despised her for it. The good intentions had been there. Or so Father Theo said.

Clearly Father Theo had liked Linda Nicholls, had understood and respected the choices she had made. That carried some weight with Tessa.

But she couldn't help asking herself a question that had never before occurred to her. She had always assumed, taken it as given, that if afforded the opportunity to get to know her, she would have loved Rob's mother as she had loved her own mother.

Now she asked herself: would I even have *liked* her?

The clinic was busy, but not as busy as it would be a bit later. Tessa checked in at reception and sat down to wait, disappointed to see that Melanie Maybank wasn't there yet. Neither was JoAnn Biddle, but presumably she'd had her baby by now. None of the other expectant mothers looked familiar to her, and she was too shy to start up a conversation with any of them. She flicked through an old, tattered magazine, unable to concentrate on the articles on the relative merits of various models of pushchairs or car seats.

Finally the nurse called her name, and she went through to see the midwife.

The first time she'd been to the midwife, she had been expecting to find a competent-looking middle-aged woman in a uniform, brisk and professional. The reality had surprised her then, but by now she was quite used to Stephanie.

Stephanie was young and not at all brisk; her personality could best be described as bubbly. She had curly red hair and freckles, a merry face, and an infectious laugh which instantly put nervous expectant mothers at ease, and she always wore jeans and T-shirts, even in the middle of winter. Today's T-shirt proclaimed: 'Midwives do it in the bath.'

Tessa laughed at the sight of it. 'Does that mean that I have to have a water birth, then?'

'Only if you want to,' Stephanie grinned. 'I'm just trying to let women know that they have options, and that they're entitled to make their own choices.'

Tessa liked Stephanie and her informality, even if she sometimes found her frankness a bit alarming. Stephanie wasn't one for making soothing noises, and today was no exception. 'How are you feeling, then?' the midwife asked. She was perched on the edge of her desk, her legs swinging free, rather than sitting behind it. 'Are you getting on okay?'

'Not too bad,' said Tessa, then honesty compelled her to add, 'But the baby has started kicking. I didn't get much sleep last night.'

'Vicious little brute,' Stephanie pronounced cheerfully. 'It will only get worse, believe me.'

Tessa felt that she needed to defend her baby. 'She didn't mean to keep me awake, I'm sure.'

'Don't kid yourself,' the midwife stated, not without humour. 'Babies are out for themselves.'

'What do you mean?'

Stephanie was blunt. 'They're parasites, and I mean that quite literally. Think about it. They couldn't survive outside their mothers' bodies until the very end. They fasten on and take everything they need from their mothers – nourishment, and whatever else. If any other foreign body tried to do that, our immune systems would be fighting back like mad, trying to get rid of it. But that's the miracle of it – our immune systems shut down somehow, and let the greedy little beggars take what they need from us.'

'You make it sound pretty grim,' Tessa said.

Stephanie smiled. 'Oh, I didn't mean to,' she assured her. 'That's the way it has to be, or there wouldn't be any babies. But it reminds me a bit of that film *Alien*. Have you seen it?'

'No.' Tessa shook her head dubiously.

'I suppose that's what made me think about it,' the midwife admitted. 'My boyfriend rented the video last weekend. This thing comes popping out of the woman's stomach, all blood and gore and slime – it's pretty horrific stuff. But that's the way babies are – like little aliens.' She laughed. 'The other miracle is that their mums still want them after all that. Most of the time, anyway.'

Tessa didn't think that it was very funny, but she tried to smile. She didn't like the thought of her baby as an alien, as a parasite drawing its nourishment from her against her will. 'But I *do* want my baby,' she protested.

'Of course you do.' Stephanie hopped off her perch on the desk and went into professional mode. 'Now, let's see how you're doing. Take your coat and shoes off and pop on the scale.'

Tessa obeyed, her mind still on the horrible image of the alien.

The midwife checked the scale and wrote the number on Tessa's notes, nodding in approval, then reached into her pocket for a tape measure. 'Pull up your jumper, then, and let's measure the little creature.' With expert ease she ran the tape vertically along Tessa's stomach. 'Spot on schedule,' she pronounced as she wrote down the figure. 'Twenty weeks, is that right?'

'Yes,' Tessa agreed.

'You're halfway there.' Stephanie checked the notes. 'But you haven't had your scan yet. I thought you had an appointment for that.'

'I had to reschedule it,' Tessa explained. 'It was supposed to be last week. But my mother-in-law . . . died. I had to go to the funeral that day. So the scan won't be till next week. That's the earliest the hospital could fit me in.'

'Oh, I'm sorry about your mother-in-law,' Stephanie said sincerely. 'I really am.'

'So am I,' said Tessa.

When she came out of the midwife's examining room, Tessa spotted Melanie Maybank sitting in the waiting room and went over to say hello.

Melanie, now at the beginning of her eighth month, was looking distinctly unwieldy. She smiled delightedly as Tessa approached. 'You're really getting big,' she greeted her.

'I was thinking the same thing about you,' Tessa responded, returning her smile.

Melanie patted her stomach. 'That's the thing about only seeing each other every four weeks. The change is very apparent, rather than gradual.' She indicated the empty seat next to her. 'Have you got a minute to sit and chat? Tell me how you've been.'

Tessa sat down, surprised at how pleased she was to see Melanie. The only contact she'd ever had with her had been at the clinic, but each time she met her there, her liking and admiration for the other woman grew. Now, without planning to, she found herself telling Melanie about her mother-in-law's death. And she added the part that she hadn't told Stephanie: that Linda Nicholls had been murdered.

Melanie listened with a grave expression. 'Oh, Tessa. That's really rough,' she sympathised, touching Tessa's hand. 'Terrible for her, and terrible for you. And your husband too, of course.' After a moment she added, 'I read about it in the paper. But I didn't connect it with you. I'm so sorry. I would have rung you if I'd known.'

Tessa felt her eyes filling with tears at the other woman's sympathy. 'Thanks,' she said inadequately.

'Why didn't you ring me?' Melanie chided her. 'You have my number, don't you?'

She remembered Melanie giving it to her, the first time they'd met. 'I have it somewhere.'

'Well, I'm giving it to you again,' Melanie stated, reaching for her handbag and finding a pen and paper. 'I suppose you probably have plenty of friends to talk to. But if you ever need another ear, don't hesitate to ring me. I may not have any answers, but I'm a good listener.' She scribbled her number and proffered it to Tessa.

'That's very kind,' Tessa said; she took the paper and put it in her coat pocket. 'And you?' she asked. 'Are you doing well?'

Melanie rested both hands on her bump. 'I can't complain. I'm starting to feel a bit tired, but that's to be expected. Especially,' she added, smiling, 'with three helpless daughters and a useless husband at home, all expecting me to carry on as usual, looking after them.'

'But that's not fair,' Tessa protested. 'They should be helping you.'

'I'm joking, really. They're not so bad. In fact they've been wonderful. Clare, especially, has been a great help.' Melanie smiled fondly. 'She's the middle one – ten – and she's always been the practical one.'

'What are the others called?' asked Tessa.

'Helena is the eldest. She's very clever, and a bit shy. Reserved, I suppose, would be a better word,' Melanie amended. 'Quiet. And Poppy, the youngest, is just the opposite of shy. Bags of personality, very much the extrovert. The three of them are all very different from one another.'

'They sound lovely.'

'They are,' Melanie agreed. 'Most of the time.'

'And I like their names,' Tessa added shyly. She was aware that it was time for her to start thinking about a name for her own baby, especially now that she had begun talking aloud to her. Clare, Helena and Poppy were much nicer names than Kayleigh and Kyle, she reflected. That thought led her on to JoAnn Biddle. 'I suppose', she said, 'that JoAnn has had her baby by now. Kyle. Wasn't he due at the beginning of the month?'

'Oh, Tessa!' Melanie turned a stricken face to her. 'You haven't heard!'

'Heard what? Is something wrong with Kyle?'

Melanie didn't answer directly. 'JoAnn had a very difficult labour,' she said, drawing her brows together. 'It went on for nearly three days.'

Tessa recalled her first experience of JoAnn, and the story of her protracted labour with Kayleigh – practically the first words that JoAnn had addressed to her. 'I remember that she said it was the same before.'

'This time it was even worse. Kyle was a bigger baby than Kayleigh, and his head was huge. They wanted to do a Caesarean, but JoAnn wouldn't let them.'

There was something in Melanie's tone of voice – something final, and in the past tense; Tessa felt a tremor of premonition and dread about the end of the story. 'Kyle's dead, isn't he?' she stated flatly. 'He didn't make it.'

'Oh, no, Tessa. That's not it.' Melanie took Tessa's hand and squeezed it between her own. 'Kyle is fine. He's a big, strong, healthy baby. It was JoAnn. She . . . died.'

'Died?' Tessa heard her own voice, as if it were coming from far away.

'It tore her so badly – they couldn't stop the bleeding.'

'No,' said Tessa, as though her disbelief could make it not true. 'No, no.' She pulled her hand away and stood up. 'I have to go now.'

Melanie struggled to her feet. 'Listen, Tessa. I'm sorry I had to be the one to tell you. Why don't you sit here with me for a bit? As soon as I've been in to see Stephanie, you can come home with me. I'll make us some camomile tea, and we can talk about it.'

'No. I have to go.' It wasn't like Tessa to be abrupt and rude, but she felt that she couldn't bear the doctor's waiting room for another second. She needed air.

The next thing she knew, she was out on the crowded pavement, walking towards the tube station. The horrifying image of JoAnn Biddle, dead in a pool of her own blood, obliterated everything else from her mind.

Poor JoAnn. Poor Trevor, poor Kayleigh, poor Kyle. But most of all, poor JoAnn. Tessa hadn't known her very well at all – hadn't even particularly liked her. But now she was dead.

Women didn't die in childbirth any longer, Tessa told herself in disbelief. Once it had been common, but now things had moved on.

Up till now, Tessa had been mildly apprehensive about childbirth, like many first-time mothers, but she had not been afraid. Even JoAnn's stories of her dreadful labour with Kayleigh had not frightened her. She'd trusted in the powers of modern medicine, and she'd trusted Stephanie. Now, though, everything had changed. JoAnn was dead, and Tessa was terrified.

She did the things she needed to do: she found a shoe repair shop with a key-cutting machine and had Linda's keys duplicated, then took them to the estate agent, with an apology for her lateness. All the time she felt that she was drowning for lack of air – in the deep underground tunnels of the Piccadilly Line, on the crowded pavements, in the shoe repair shop with its suffocating smell of rubber and glue, and in the estate agent's office, fuggy with cigarette smoke. It wasn't until she'd left the business district of Southgate, and had turned into the quiet street which led to Chase View Road, that Tessa felt able to breathe. She sucked in great lungfuls of the cold air, and felt better for it.

She had not liked the estate agent. Apart from the fact that he had blown smoke in her face, she had found him smarmy and glib; he was young and self-confident and spoke in cliché-riddled gibberish. Tessa had escaped from his presence as quickly as possible, and hoped not to have to go back again. He had told her that he intended to make it round to Chase View Road that afternoon, to measure up, or if not today, then tomorrow at the latest. Tessa didn't mention that she might be there; she didn't relish the prospect of seeing him again, and with any luck he might not make it today; if he did, she hoped to be gone by the time he arrived.

With a glance at its windows, Tessa hurried past number

25; the last thing she needed right now, she thought, was for Hilda Steggall to see her. She couldn't face Hilda Steggall at the moment; she didn't really want to face anyone.

She let herself into the house, then stood for a moment outside the door of the front room. Up till now she had not dared to open that door. But she sensed that inside that room she would find important clues in her quest to understand Linda Nicholls, and her need was greater than her fear. And, Tessa thought, if she concentrated on Linda, difficult and painful as that might be, at least she wouldn't be thinking about JoAnn. Taking a deep breath, she opened the door and stepped inside.

The cleaner had done a brilliant job. No one, not even Tessa, would have been able to tell that a murder had been committed in that room.

Its décor was as bland as the rest of the house, but somehow it seemed more lived-in. There was a television and video in one corner, a comfortable-looking sofa, and several chairs which could almost be described as well worn. The room, like the rest of the house, lacked what to Tessa was a necessity of life: books. Instead of bookcases, the alcoves on either side of the fireplace contained furniture, on one side a bureau and on the other a large cupboard with double doors.

This, thought Tessa, was promising. She went first to the cupboard and opened the doors, sitting down on the floor, the better to examine its contents.

Inside were shelves holding a quantity of videos and several photograph albums.

Tessa pulled out one of the photo albums at random and opened it. It contained snapshots, most of them of a boy who could only be Rob, seemingly at about age five.

Her first thought was that her husband had been an exceptionally beautiful child, with his startlingly blue eyes and his very black hair. If their baby looked like Rob, she would be very lucky indeed.

She went back to the beginning and flipped through the pages of the album, following Rob's progress as he blew out the candles on his birthday cake, modelled his school uniform, played in the back garden, and opened presents beneath the Christmas tree. Quickly she discovered that the young Rob had two characteristic facial expressions, both of which, in their grown-up versions, were familiar to her: one was a charming smile, straight into the camera, and the other was a look of sullen boredom, brows drawn together and the mouth set in an unsmiling line.

His mother, she was sure, had taken the photos, lovingly chronicling his young life. It was a reminder to Tessa that Rob's mother had loved him. No matter what she was, or what she did, she had loved her son.

Tessa decided to go through the albums systematically, and started with the first one on the shelf. It contained wedding pictures.

She drew in her breath. Here, at last, were Rob's parents: the people who had give him life, brought him up, and shaped him.

Tessa pored over the photos, avid for what they might reveal. The newlywed Mr and Mrs Nicholls seemed an oddly-matched couple. Rob's father was tall and well-built and handsome, like Rob; his mother was very much smaller and seemed several years younger than her new husband. From her, it was clear, Rob had inherited his colouring: the black hair – worn long and straight – and the blue eyes. She was attractive, but in a way that would be described as pretty rather than beautiful, and that owed much to the freshness of youth.

The wedding, it seemed, had been a fairly low-key affair, held at a register office. And, Tessa noticed with a faint shock, though the new Mrs Nicholls's gown had been cut to conceal the fact, it was pretty apparent, in one or two of the photos, that she was already pregnant.

Tessa wasn't sure why this shocked her; she herself had by
no means gone as a spotless virgin to her own marriage, and
she was not labouring under the common delusion that her
generation had invented sex. Rob's parents had been married
well after the sexual revolution of the early sixties had made
'free love' an accepted lifestyle, so why should she be surprised that they had pursued it? Perhaps, she analysed, it was
because of her own parents: though she was living evidence
that he had done so, she could not imagine her strait-laced
father laying a finger on her mother even within the bonds of
holy matrimony, let alone before.

The next album focused on the new house, the expanding
pregnancy, and eventually on the new baby. Linda Nicholls
held tiny Rob gingerly, self-consciously smiling at the camera,
and in a later photo fed him with a bottle. A somewhat out-
of-focus shot showed his father giving the baby a bath,
looking proud yet embarrassed. Pages and pages of baby Rob
followed, as he grew incrementally into a toddler.

Fascinated and enchanted, Tessa lost track of the time.

Malcolm Hogg watched the clock impatiently that afternoon.
It seemed to him to be crawling; it was almost like during his
old school- days, with those endless hours of sitting in the
classroom waiting for the lessons to end.

He had several appointments, as he usually did on a Friday
afternoon, and he was not disposed this week to treat his
customers kindly. In fact he took pleasure in turning down an
application for a car loan, his heart warmed and the sense of
his own power fed by the look of intense disappointment on
the face of the young supplicant.

At last – at long last – it was five o'clock. His mood ele-
vated rapidly as he left his office; he even found it in him to
smile at his secretary and wish her a good weekend.

But traffic was bad, this close to Christmas – even worse
than on an ordinary Friday – and soon he was enmeshed in a

jam-up of monumental proportions, crawling along with the speedometer barely registering above nought. He frowned, drummed his fingers on the steering wheel, and cursed every driver who tried to pull out in front of him from a side street.

Finally, though, he made it to Southgate, and pulled the car into the long-term car park where he customarily left it. Taking his holdall from the boot, and feeling in his pocket for the key to Linda's front door, he hurried on his way with rapid, mincing steps, out of the car park and towards Chase View Road.

Tessa had reached the last photo album, the one that took Rob into adolescence. He'd sported long hair then; rebelliously it brushed his collar, as he glowered into the camera. Then, without any warning, in mid-album, the photos stopped. There were none of Rob in later years; there was no recent photo of Linda Nicholls.

Tessa realised that she didn't possess a picture of Rob. None had been taken at their wedding; she didn't even own a camera. 'I should get a camera,' Tessa said to the baby. 'We'll need one when you're born, won't we?' Christmas, she thought, would be a good time to buy one. She and Rob could take photos of each other enjoying their first Christmas together, and start filling an album. These days you didn't have to know anything about photography to use a camera; modern cameras were so sophisticated that they did all the work for you.

As she thought about this, she heard the key in the front door lock. 'Oh, bother,' she said aloud; it would be that obnoxious estate agent, with his unctuous know-it-all demeanour and his smelly cigarettes. He didn't know she was here; if she sat quietly for a few minutes, perhaps she would be lucky and he wouldn't come into this room straight away.

Good fortune seemed to be with her. Straining her ears, she heard his footsteps going up the stairs. He was going to start measuring the bedrooms first, then.

She returned the photo album to the cupboard, closed the doors, then got up from the floor and went to the bureau. Just a quick look through, she promised herself, and then she'd be off before the estate agent came back downstairs.

As soon as she'd lowered the flap, Tessa realised that here, at last, was at least some of what she had been looking for. In a tidy array were packets of bank statements, a cheque-book, and a few bills.

She didn't have time to go through them now. Another day, she told herself. She would come back on Monday and examine them thoroughly.

Above the writing surface of the bureau was a row of small drawers. One, Tessa discovered, held stamps, while another was full of paper- clips. She pulled out the third one: it contained a single key. Tessa took it out of the drawer and held it in the palm of her hand; she knew instinctively that it would open the door at the top of the stairs. She wasn't sure why she was so positive of that fact, but she had no doubt that it was so.

By now she had forgotten about the estate agent, or at any rate she was so driven that she counted him as irrelevant. Still, Tessa moved quietly as she went up the stairs, along the landing, and up the next flight to the second floor.

The key fitted into the lock, as she had known that it would. The handle turned, and as the door swung open at last into a spacious room, Tessa stared in amazement at its contents.

It could, she supposed, be described as 'equipment', but it was unlike any equipment that Tessa had ever seen before, in scale if not in function. For the room held half a dozen enormous cots, an equal number of gigantic high chairs, a vast play-pen, a huge wooden rocking horse, and various toys which suggested by their size that a race of giants had abandoned their nursery. In one corner was an oversized rocking chair, and in it sat a very large teddy bear, missing one eye.

Tessa wasn't sure how long she stood there, trying to make sense of it all. What was certain was that in her bemused state she didn't hear the footsteps on the stairs. The first awareness she had of someone behind her was the single querulous word: 'Mummy?'

Startled more than frightened, she spun round, expecting to see the estate agent.

It was not the estate agent. She had never seen this man before.

He had a heavy five o'clock shadow, and very hairy legs. In between, starting well above his knees, he was wearing a frilly pink frock with little puffed sleeves, trimmed with lace and smocking. His greasy dark hair was tucked inside a matching frilly bonnet which tied under his chin, and on his feet he wore white bootees fastened with pink bows. '*You're* not Mummy,' he accused her. 'Where is Mummy?'

Tessa clutched at the doorknob for support as her knees buckled under her, and she lost consciousness.

Chapter 14

When Tessa came to a few minutes later, the man was bending over her, so close that she could smell his baby powder. Her eyes fluttered open, and she recoiled involuntarily.

'Are you all right?' he said, then: 'Where's Mummy? Who are you?'

Tessa was badly shaken, and terrified. Her heart thudded in her chest; she gasped for breath. She wanted to scream, but her throat felt paralysed.

'Who *are* you?' the man repeated, but not in a threatening way, his brows drawn together in puzzlement. After a moment Tessa realised that he didn't mean her any harm, and she took courage from that; her panic subsided a bit, and her breathing slowed. She closed her eyes again; it was easier to speak to this grotesque creature if she didn't have to look at him. 'I might ask you the same thing,' she said, striving for self-control. 'Who are *you*? What are you doing here? And how did you get in?'

'I have my own key,' he answered self-importantly. 'Mummy gave it to me.'

Mummy. What on earth was he talking about?

'Where *is* Mummy?' he repeated.

'What do you mean?' Tessa's eyes opened.

'I want *Mummy*. Mummy Linda – where is she?' His thin lips quivered; he looked as if he might cry. 'I *need* Mummy.'

Tessa stared at him. 'I don't understand.'

'What have you done with Mummy?' He raised his voice then, calling out in an infantile wail, 'Mummy! Mummy Linda! Where are you?'

'Linda?' Tessa echoed with horror. 'Are you looking for Linda Nicholls?'

He nodded, lowering his voice. 'That's right. Mummy Linda.'

'She's dead,' Tessa blurted.

'Dead?' The man's small eyes widened and he stared at her. 'Mummy can't be dead!'

Tessa struggled to her feet. 'But she is. Over a fortnight ago. She was murdered,' she added, backing away from him.

He threw himself on the floor just inside the room and screamed at the top of his lungs. First he lay on his stomach, pounding the floor with his fists, then he rolled over on to his back and drummed his heels, his legs flailing in the air. He was, Tessa could see, wearing a nappy.

She had to escape, had to get away from this hideous grotesquerie, this incomprehensible monstrosity. This was her chance. Tessa backed down the landing, then fled down two flights of stairs, through the entrance hall, grabbing her coat from the newel post where she'd left it; she slammed the front door behind her.

It was cold, bitterly cold. There was an icy rim round the moon, and Tessa's ragged breath froze into white clouds. She took no notice. Almost as soon as she was outside the house, her mind was blank, as if it too were frozen.

Tessa walked. She propelled herself without thinking, wherever her feet happened to take her. Initially this was into an area where there were other people, bundled up in coats and rushing to get to wherever they were going and in out of the cold. After a while, though, there were no other people, and she walked down streets of houses in which Christmas trees twinkled out through windows and lights spoke of warmth and cosiness within.

Still she walked, until her feet were so cold that she could no longer feel them. As she passed a bus stop, a red double-decker approached, and she climbed on board.

Tessa didn't care where it was going. She huddled next to the window, where a feeble stream of heat issued from the floor, warming her feet. After a while she realised, dimly, that they were passing beneath the gaudy Christmas lights which spanned Regent Street, turning into Piccadilly Circus with its neon glare.

Her feet were warmer now. She got off the bus and walked some more, through the crowds of merrymakers who always flocked to this part of London on a Friday night, heedless of the weather. There were young girls in short, skin-tight dresses, their exposed legs blue with the cold, and young lads more sensibly dressed but behaving as if they had no sense at all, larking about and showing off for the girls and each other.

Tessa ignored them, and walked. Leicester Square, with its vast Christmas tree, then Covent Garden.

Covent Garden tube station. Outside the station, on the pavement, sat a homeless woman; crowds of young people streamed past her without a glance. The woman was swathed in a filthy blanket, inside which, against her chest to share her meagre warmth, was the face of a young child. The child screamed, its unattractive face blotchy with cold and misery; its mother made no effort to stop its screaming, but watched the passers-by with hopeless resignation, her head drooping to one side.

Tessa stopped. She wasn't carrying a handbag, but had a purse in her coat pocket. Her cold fingers closed around it and she pulled it out. Keeping back just enough change for her fare, she emptied all of her money – notes and coins alike – into the woman's blanketed lap.

Their eyes met for an instant. 'God bless you,' said the woman softly, then called after Tessa as she turned and went into the tube station, 'Happy Christmas!'

*

She was home. Somehow her instinct had guided her there, on the tube and through the streets from Caledonian Road.

No lights greeted her as she approached, no twinkling Christmas tree in the front window. Rob wasn't back from his party yet, then, Tessa thought vaguely. She let herself in with her key, turned on a light, and only then, as the heat of the house surrounded her, realised how very cold she was.

She was frozen, and she was hungry – she hadn't had anything to eat since breakfast. But more than anything, she was tired. Tessa climbed the stairs, and without bothering to undress or even to remove her coat and shoes, she crawled into bed and wrapped herself in the duvet. For the first few minutes she was too cold to sleep, but she warmed up quickly and her exhaustion overcame her. Tessa slept soundly.

Malcolm Hogg screamed until he was hoarse, tears streaming down his face, and kicked the floor till his bootees came off. His pink frock – quite his favourite, worn especially today – was crumpled and soiled from his squirmings on the floor.

Gradually his screams became sobs; he dragged himself up off the floor. In the ordinary course of things Malcolm quite enjoyed a good temper tantrum – it was one of the pleasures of his weekends at Mummy Linda's, to throw a few toys about and scream until Mummy came upstairs to the nursery, took him on her lap, and soothed him into placidity.

But this tantrum was different. Mummy wouldn't be coming upstairs, if that woman were to be believed. Not today, and not ever again. Mummy was dead, and Malcolm's grief was extravagant.

Still crying, he climbed into the rocking chair where he had so often sat on Mummy's lap, and hugged the worn old teddy for comfort. 'Mummy,' he whispered tearfully. 'I want Mummy.'

Teddy didn't answer. So after a time Malcolm clambered

over the side of one of the cots, pulled the blankets over his head, curled up in a ball, and cried himself to sleep.

Friday evening. James Wooldridge tried to read the papers, tried to watch television. But the papers couldn't hold his interest, and the television was dominated by frothy American sitcoms to which he couldn't relate in the least.

He was alone in the house, apart from the dog. Felicity had gone out with her chums, to a ladies' night at the health club, and the children were sleeping over with their respective best friends. This, apparently, was their normal pattern on Friday evenings when he was away; though his routine had changed, they carried on as usual.

The house seemed so empty. On weekday evenings, even though the children were quiet and well behaved, they made their presence felt. And Felicity was usually around and about, chatting to him about various things.

This was not where he wanted to be. James Wooldridge admitted to himself that he missed Mummy Linda desperately, that he would give anything to have her restored to life.

In the New Year he would have to start making discreet enquiries about a replacement. Surely there were other women out there who would provide the same services that Mummy Linda had done, if not perhaps on such an organised scale, and in such a convenient location. He would wait until he was absolutely sure that he was free of suspicion of causing her death, and then he would see what he could find. A new mummy . . .

But for tonight, that wasn't good enough. Tonight he needed more than just hope.

Impatiently he punched the button on the remote control and the television screen faded to black.

He had tried to control himself. But it was Friday night, with all the connotations that had in his mind, and he was alone in the house. He could resist no longer.

James Wooldridge went upstairs to the bedroom and retrieved, from the bottom drawer of his elegant antique mahogany chest of drawers, a parcel which he had concealed there earlier. He had stopped at the Central Milton Keynes shopping centre on his way home from work, nipped into Boots, and bought a packet of Depends, muttering something to the sales assistant about an incontinent grandfather.

Now he took one out of the packet. Not really very satisfactory – stiff and papery and uncomfortable-feeling. No substitute at all for the fluffy cotton nappies which Mummy Linda had supplied. But he had no choice, and it would be better than nothing.

Office Christmas parties were not exactly Amanda Spicer's idea of a good time; she would much rather be working than wasting time watching her colleagues drink too much and make fools of themselves. But these parties were, she recognised, a necessary evil. Sometimes, if one kept a level head oneself, one could take the opportunity for an informal chat with someone important, and hope to make a good impression. In the past these events had worked to her advantage; a few years ago she had chatted up the assistant managing director of the company over a drink, and the next month she had been promoted. There might have been no connection between the two, but one never knew, and it didn't hurt to keep an eye to the main chance.

So Amanda took one glass of wine at the beginning of the party and nursed it for quite some time, standing off to one side and looking round for a likely target. The financial controller? Rumour had it that he was on the way out, whether he knew it or not, so she wouldn't bother. And anyway, he already had a glazed look in his eye, and was leaning very close to one of the secretaries, staring at her chest as though trying to read an invisible name badge. Perhaps, Amanda smiled to herself, that was why he was on the way out.

A better prospect was the up-and-coming young head of

marketing, who was – not coincidentally – the son-in-law of the chairman of the board of directors. The trouble with him was that she found him physically repellent, but she decided that it would be worth the temporary discomfort of spending a few minutes with him.

It was easy to lure him to her side, with a sidelong glance and a half smile. In short order he made his excuses to the person with whom he was carrying on a conversation, and approached Amanda, offering to get her another drink.

She declined the offer, looking up at him through her lashes. He moved closer and addressed her in a confidential whisper. She had to steel herself not to step backwards from the pong of his stale-fag breath; a smile fixed on her face, she focused her attention dispassionately on the dandruff that littered his shoulders and lapels, and the texture of his skin, pitted with ancient acne scars. His hand was inclined to stray from his side, touching her arm with an intimate gesture and even brushing her breast. Amanda gritted her teeth and tried to keep their conversation on a professional level. 'I'm a married woman now, you know,' she said at last, her voice light, when his crude fumblings began to verge on groping.

'Since when did that stop anyone from having a good time?' he leered. 'I'm a married man myself.'

Amanda came back quickly. 'Yes, but my husband is a police-man,' she reminded him with a smile. 'And he's very big and strong. And jealous.'

'Details, details.' The man leaned even closer, looking into her eyes, and Amanda wished she hadn't started this. The 'married woman' line often worked, bringing the gropers and the flirts up short, but this one wasn't buying it.

It was, she knew, just a line. She *was* a married woman now, but the change in legal status hadn't really altered anything in the way Amanda approached life. And, to be honest, marriage had been a disappointment. More to the point, *Ian* had been a disappointment.

She hadn't known him well enough when they married, she now admitted to herself. Yes, he had a great body. But that was about all you could say in his favour. Though he fancied himself a great lover, he was no ball of fire in bed, and far too selfish about it for her liking. He was bone idle, he was a filthy slob, he had no ambition in life. A lazy drifter, with no desire to better himself. And after all she'd done for him, too – encouraging him to finish his degree, getting Daddy to agree to take him on in his firm if he could get his qualifications as a solicitor. He had made it quite clear that he didn't want any of it. He wanted to spend the rest of his life coasting along, wasting himself on the police. And he wanted *her*, the woman with a brilliant career ahead of her, to stay at home and have his babies, to become his drudge and domestic slave.

She'd thought of him as a diamond-in-the-rough, waiting for her to come along, take him in hand, and bring out his potential. She had thought she could change him; she had been wrong.

Marrying Ian had been a mistake. She'd rushed into it foolishly, impetuously, without thinking of the consequences, without considering how much of value she was throwing away.

Rob. He might not have been perfect – he was inclined to be moody, she admitted to herself – but he had in so many ways been the ideal companion: considerate, tidy, and a marvellous lover.

Amanda was thinking these thoughts, trying hard to ignore her companion's assaults upon her person, when Rob walked into the room.

She had scarcely seen Rob since their respective marriages; they worked in different departments in the company, and their paths rarely crossed. Now she was struck afresh by how handsome he was. Tall, slender, elegant – to continue her metaphor, he stood out from this crowd of losers like a brilliant-cut diamond on a tray of cheap rhinestones. Next to him, she concluded disloyally, Ian was a muscle-bound dolt. How could she ever have thought otherwise?

She remembered what it felt like to be kissed by those lips; she remembered what it felt like to be held by those arms. Inside she began to tremble, though she concealed it from her revolting companion. 'Excuse me,' she said to him politely but abruptly. 'I have to go now.'

Amanda crossed the room, her attention fixed on Rob as though he were the only person in it. She had the advantage of him; he didn't see her coming.

'Hello, Rob,' she said softly.

Rob turned and smiled down at her: that enigmatic smile which she had once found so infuriating, and which she now found breath-stoppingly charming. He took his time in replying. 'Hello, Amanda,' he said at last, quirking an eyebrow at her. 'Fancy seeing you here.'

Tessa did not have a restful sleep. She dreamed of JoAnn Biddle.

JoAnn was lying in her coffin, still and quiet as Tessa had never seen her in life. Tessa approached the coffin, her heart pounding. She leaned over and looked at the dead woman, whose hands were folded over her now-flat stomach.

'Poor JoAnn,' Tessa said.

At that moment JoAnn's eyes flew open, and she sat up in her coffin. 'Oh, Tessa, I'm glad to see you,' she said. 'I wanted to tell you all about it. It was awful. You know I told you I was in labour for fifty-three hours with Kayleigh? Well, this was much worse. That little rascal Kyle just wouldn't come out! I say little, but the problem was that he wasn't little at all! Ha ha. His head was huge. I showed you the scan photos, didn't I? Stephanie said it was the biggest head she'd ever seen. They wanted to do a Caesarean, but I wasn't having that! Not me. I've always been terrified of knives, and I could never have worn a bikini again! Ha ha. It went on for sixty-four and a half hours! Can you believe it? I couldn't, and neither could

Trevor. He finally came out, the blighter. Kyle, I mean, not Trevor. Ha ha. By that time I thought I was going to die. And you know something funny? I *did*. Ha ha,' she laughed. Then she laid back down and closed her eyes.

After that, the nightmares really started.

Tessa was on a roller-coaster. She hated roller-coasters – she had only ever been on one once, goaded into it by Ian, who had relished the experience. For Tessa it had been every bit as bad as she had anticipated, and possibly worse. Shaky and sick, she had crawled off at the end and sworn that she would never ride one again.

In the dream she was aware that she hated roller-coasters, and found the very thought of them terrifying. But Rob had wanted her to go with him, so she had embarked on it to please him.

As the car chugged to the top of the first peak, she turned to Rob to say, 'I really hate this, you know.' Rob wasn't there; she was alone in the car. For an instant it teetered at the brink, then plunged over and down, down and down into a dark pit. Tessa held on to the bar and screamed until she thought her lungs would burst. Still the car hurtled down.

With a neck-snapping jerk it reached the bottom and began to rise again. Round it went, curving sickeningly, and up, higher than before. And then down, down, faster and faster, with Tessa's screams echoing in her own ears.

The dream seemed to go on for hours: the rising and the plunging and the screams. The pace never let up; the terror never subsided. But just before the dream ended, Tessa became aware that she was not, after all, alone on the roller-coaster. Going round a curve, she could see another car ahead of hers, with someone in it. The figure in the other car laughed, and, just as Ian had done, flung daredevil arms in the air at the instant that the car was about to hurtle over the brink of the next precipice. But the other rider wasn't Ian, nor was it Rob: it was JoAnn Biddle.

In her next dream, Tessa was the Virgin Mary. She wasn't sure how she knew this, but she did; she was also aware that the baby she was carrying was something very special: the angel had told her that he would be called Jesus, the Son of the Highest. She was riding on a donkey towards Bethlehem, and the trip was endless. Joseph walked at her side, saying nothing, but leading the donkey along. She couldn't see Joseph's face, as he was wearing a sort of hood; she was sure, though, that he looked like Rob.

As she rode, her stomach grew visibly and rapidly. Starting from about the way it was now, it puffed up as if someone were inflating it with a bicycle tyre pump. Eventually it got so big that she could no longer sit on the donkey. 'I have to get off now, Joseph,' she said. 'It's time.' But Joseph was no longer there; somehow, while she was involved in watching her stomach grow, he had disappeared.

Terrified by the size she had now achieved, she got off the donkey and walked. Still she grew larger and larger, bigger by far than any pregnant woman she had ever seen, till she spotted the stable ahead of her, the empty manger waiting to receive her baby. With a cry of relief she staggered towards it.

Then a huge fist smashed out through her stomach, followed by another fist. The pain was searing; she was being ripped apart. Still some distance from the stable, she fell to the ground. A head emerged, followed by a giant body, bigger than her own, wearing a frilly pink dress. 'It's a girl, then,' she said aloud, surprised.

But when the creature turned towards her, she could see that he needed a shave. 'You're not my mother,' he accused her. 'What have you done with my mother?'

Tessa's pillow was wet with tears when she awoke in the morning. She couldn't remember all of the details of her nightmares, but the terror was still with her; her heart thudded uncomfortably, and she felt as if she were burning up, sweating and clammy. Inside her the baby wriggled like a fish on a hook.

Instinctively she reached out for comfort: for Rob. But he wasn't there, and what's more, it was evident that his side of the bed had not been slept in.

Tessa was still wrapped in the duvet; no wonder, she thought, she was hot. She unwound herself from it, and discovered that she was wearing her coat and shoes. Her memories of the night before were vague at best; she had no recollection of arriving at home or getting into bed.

She *did* remember that Rob had been going to the office Christmas party. Had something happened to him? Had he, perhaps, drunk too much and had an accident with the car on his way home? Should she ring the hospitals, the police?

Maybe, she thought, striving to calm her panicked fantasies, he had left her a message on the answering service, last night before she got home. And, given the condition she'd been in, it wasn't even impossible that he had rung later and she had slept right through it. She ought to check that before she jumped to any alarming conclusions.

She dialled the access number, waiting impatiently as the digital voice proclaimed that she had one new message.

'Tessa, it's me,' said the next voice she heard. But it wasn't Rob: it was Ian. Very circumspect, not identifying himself by name, in case it was Rob who picked up the message. 'I've got a thing or two to tell you. Sorry I didn't get back to you sooner, but I've been busy. Give me a ring, will you?'

Talking to Ian was the last thing she needed at this moment. She didn't even want to think about Ian, or what it was he might have to tell her. Frowning, she pressed the button to delete the message, then put the receiver down. Almost instantly the phone rang.

Chapter 15

Tessa snatched the phone from its cradle and spoke into it anxiously. 'Hello?'

'Hello, Tessa,' said Rob's voice. 'I hope I didn't wake you.'

'Rob! Where are you?' she blurted. 'Is something the matter? I was so worried!'

'I'm sorry if I worried you,' he said soothingly, apologetically. 'But I was longer than I thought I'd be at the party last night. And I had rather more to drink than I'd planned.' He gave a half-embarrassed laugh. 'So I didn't want to risk driving home. One of my colleagues offered me a bed for the night, and it seemed the best thing to do.'

She tried not to sound accusing. 'But why didn't you ring?'

'It was late,' he explained. 'I didn't want to disturb you – I thought you needed your sleep. And I *did* tell you not to wait up for me.'

Tessa admitted to herself the sense of that. 'Where are you now? When are you coming home?'

'Well, that's the thing.' Again his voice was apologetic. 'I've got to work today.'

'Work? On a Saturday?' He'd never done that before, not since they'd been married.

'I told you how busy we've been,' Rob said. 'I'm going to have to work flat out to get this new system installed by the end of the year. I'm really sorry, Tessa. Tomorrow I'll be at home, and we'll do something special.'

The thought of being at home all day on her own was insupportable. Tessa knew that she needed to do some Christmas shopping – at the very minimum, she needed to buy a present for Rob and a present for her father – but she couldn't face the thought of going into town on a Saturday so close to Christmas.

Tea, she thought. She needed tea. As she went downstairs, she realised that she was ravenously hungry. When had she last eaten? She couldn't remember. In fact she couldn't remember much at all about yesterday, and she shied away from trying to do so.

Tessa went into the kitchen and switched on the kettle, then surveyed the contents of the fridge for inspiration. She hadn't been shopping for days; there wasn't much to choose from. Closing the fridge door with regret, she moved on. In the bread bin she found half a loaf of rather stale wholemeal bread: that would have to do. While the kettle came to a boil and the tea brewed, she popped slice after slice of the bread into the toaster, piling it high on a plate, then found a jar of strawberry jam in a cupboard and a bit of Flora in the fridge.

She sat for a long while at the kitchen table, sipping tea and eating vast quantities of toast. No matter what else she did that day, Tessa told herself, she would have to go to the shops and stock up on food.

That was good: it was a decision made for her, in a way, without the necessity to think. She finished up her tea and toast, put the dishes into the dishwasher, and went upstairs to shower.

After her night sweats, and still dressed in yesterday's clothes, Tessa felt that she really needed that shower. She turned the water up as hot as she could bear it, then scrubbed herself almost raw with a loofah. Feeling better after that, she dressed and retrieved her coat.

Tessa rarely carried a handbag, preferring to use her pockets for the necessities of life. So she delved into her coat pocket for her purse: she had better check to see whether she had enough money, she thought; she might need to stop at the cash machine on the way to the shops.

The purse was completely empty of both notes and change. Tessa stared at it, baffled; she had no recollection of having spent all of her money, but if someone had picked her pocket, they wouldn't have returned her empty purse to it.

There was something else in her hand as well: a scrap of paper with a phone number on it. Melanie Maybank, it said. And Tessa's mind resonated with a faint memory of yesterday: JoAnn.

Tessa knew what she wanted to do, and didn't allow herself time to stop and think about it. She went to the phone and punched in the number from the paper.

'Hello?' said a young, clear voice.

Not Melanie, then. Tessa almost apologised and hung up, but forced herself to persevere. 'Is . . . is your mother available?' she ventured.

'Just a moment, please. May I tell her who is calling?'

Tessa gave her name, then held the receiver for a moment, trying to remember the last time she'd spoken to such a polite child.

'Tessa!' came Melanie's voice. 'I'm so glad you've rung! I've been thinking about you, wishing that I knew how to get in touch with you. I felt so bad about yesterday, and wanted to make sure that you were all right.'

Yesterday. Still the memory was indistinct. Tessa closed her eyes, and it came flooding back over her. JoAnn was dead. Melanie had told her so. And Tessa had run away. To . . . what? She couldn't remember; she didn't really want to remember. 'I . . . I'd like to talk to you,' Tessa said.

'Come round,' was Melanie's instant reply. 'Are you free? I can't come to you just now, I'm afraid, but if your husband doesn't mind, you can come round here.'

'He's not at home,' Tessa said. 'He's working today. I'm on my own.'

'That's perfect, then. Do you have something to write on? I'll give you the address.'

It wasn't far, Tessa realised. In the posher, trendier part of Islington, but well within walking distance.

She set off straight away, walking quickly because of the bitter cold, and within a quarter of an hour she had found the house. It was on a quiet tree-lined street of graciously-proportioned houses, most of them detached. Tessa stood for a moment on the pavement, suddenly shy, then cold overcame her and she went to the door and pressed the bell.

Melanie opened the door. 'Tessa!' In spite of her protruding bump, and Tessa's smaller one, Melanie managed to embrace her, drawing her into the warmth of the house. 'I'm sorry if I've managed to get flour all over you. Clare and I are in the middle of baking.'

'It's a bad time for you, then,' Tessa apologised. 'I shouldn't have come.'

'Don't be silly!' Melanie's voice was robust. 'Saturdays are a bit chaotic here, but as long as you don't mind taking us as you find us, you're more than welcome. Come on through to the kitchen,' she added.

It was, Tessa observed as she followed her hostess, an unusual house: almost open plan on the ground floor. Several rooms appeared to have been knocked into one huge one, with areas for various activities. There was a piano, a computer, a television, and an enormous quantity of books. Books everywhere, filling the high wooden bookcases which circled the room and spilling over on to the floor. Inviting, intriguing.

The kitchen, at the back, seemed almost as large as the enormous front room, but managed to be cosy nonetheless, with a red Aga warming it, the lovely homely smell of baking in the air, and the clutter of children's belongings giving it a comfortingly domestic feel. The presence of several arm-chairs indicated that the room was used for more than just cooking and eating. A vast length of scrubbed-pine table stretched down its centre; a young girl leaned over the table, deploying a rolling pin on some pastry.

Melanie made the introductions. 'This is Clare, my middle daughter. Clare, my friend Tessa.'

'Nice to meet you,' said the girl, smiling. 'I won't shake hands – I'm a bit of a mess.'

Clare wasn't a great beauty, Tessa observed, but her face, with its pointed chin and large eyes, had character and determination, and she possessed a lovely smile, inherited from her mother. She was thin, her legs almost spindly in jeans; her hair was straight and as fine as Tessa's own, but light brown like her mother's, pulled back from her face into a short, wispy pony-tail to keep it out of her face while she laboured over her pastry.

Melanie explained what they were doing. 'Making mince pies. I should have done them weeks ago, of course, but I just never got round to it. Clare offered to help with them, or I might have ended up buying some at Marks and Spencer instead.'

'They're not difficult, really,' Clare added. 'Not if you buy the mince in jars. Just a bit fiddly.'

'Can I help?' Tessa offered.

Melanie shook her head and gestured towards a shabby but comfortable armchair. 'Thanks for the offer, but we've got it down to a system here. You just sit there and watch. As soon as we've finished this batch and popped them in the oven, I'll put the kettle on.'

Tessa sat as directed; warmed by the Aga and the welcome she had received, she relaxed into the chair and tucked her legs up under her. Strangely, she felt at home here already, as if she were a member of the family who had been away for a few years but was now back where she belonged. It was a good feeling. And there was something soothing about watching other people engaged in domestic tasks, she mused, almost tempted to close her eyes and doze.

In a few minutes the last of the mince pies were in the oven, and the old-fashioned kettle on top of the Aga had boiled. 'Camomile, or ordinary?' Melanie asked.

'Camomile, please.' That sounded therapeutic.

Melanie made the tea, handed Tessa a cup of the yellowish liquid, then sank into a chair herself. Clare remained at the table. 'I'm going to make a sausage plait, for lunch,' the girl explained. 'We learned to do it in Domestic Science this week.'

'You'll stay for lunch, of course,' Melanie stated in a voice that brooked no arguments; Tessa nodded meekly.

'Where are the rest of your family?' Tessa asked, feeling less shy.

'As I said, Saturdays are chaotic.' Melanie stretched her legs out in front of her and gave a luxurious sigh. 'Poppy's at her ballet class. Ned – my husband – dropped her off, then took Helena on to the library. They'll all be home for lunch.' She grinned at Tessa. 'Clare and I took advantage of the momentary lull to do the mince pies.'

'This afternoon I've got my cello lesson,' Clare reminded her mother, competently rolling out the puff pastry for the sausage plait.

'Yes, of course.' Melanie sighed again and sipped at her tea. 'Daddy will take you. You've been practising, haven't you?'

Clare nodded. 'Every day. And when I've finished this, I'll do a bit more practise, before everyone gets back.'

'I'd like to hear you play,' said Tessa, and she meant it.

The girl smiled, delighted; a few minutes later she put the completed sausage plait on the counter top, ready to be baked at the appropriate time, took the fragrant mince pies from the oven, washed her hands, and went off to get her cello.

'I saw the piano,' Tessa said. 'You must be a musical family.'

Melanie laughed. 'All except me, that is. I wish I could claim some credit for it, but the girls get all of their musical talent from their father.' Ned, she explained, was a mathematician, and everyone knew that there was a very real link between mathematical skills and musical aptitude. The girls had all inherited that, in varying degrees. Before Clare returned, she elaborated: Helena's instrument was the piano. She was, her teacher insisted, greatly talented, with a natural gift for the instrument. But she was also lazy, and practised only sporadically, when the mood struck her or she was nagged into it. Poppy might, it was thought, be even more gifted, but she was a great one for fads. She had started taking piano lessons with great enthusiasm, and had made swift and brilliant progress on the instrument. Soon, though, she'd got bored with it, and had taken up the flute instead. Her skills on the flute were astonishing for a child of eight, but now she was keen on ballet; her flute playing had suffered. Clare was perhaps not as musically gifted as the others, but she was determined to learn the cello, and practised it with dogged persistence, achieving a certain level of competence. 'And Ned plays a mean violin,' Melanie concluded as Clare dragged her cello into the kitchen. 'I'm madly jealous of them all – I would love to be musical, but it's my curse that I can only appreciate music, not produce it.'

Tessa nodded her agreement. 'I wish I could play the piano.' She was silent for a moment, remembering her own mother, and found herself saying, quietly, 'My mother played the piano. She used to play for me, when I was small, and sing songs. I wanted to play the piano too. But then my mother . . . she died. And my father sold her piano.' She closed her eyes; it had been years since she'd thought about that piano. Suddenly the memory was fresh, as real to her as this child and her cello: her mother's laugh; her fingers on the keys; her voice as she sang, untrained but sweet.

'Oh, Tessa. I'm so sorry.' Melanie's sympathy was genuine. She gave Tessa a meaningful look before focusing her attention on her daughter.

Clare set up her music stand, then pulled out a straight-backed kitchen chair and arranged herself carefully, her cello between her knees. She drew the bow across the strings; an amazing deep note resonated through the kitchen. Her hair, freed from the scrunchie which had held it back, fell forward to frame her earnest face as she played, leaning into the music, grave yet exalted with the joy of it. She played for several minutes; her playing was by no means perfect, but it was deeply felt, and each missed note brought a little frown.

The music moved Tessa: it was so sad, so melancholy, but so beautiful, seeming to resonate inside her. When the music stopped, she clapped spontaneously. 'Oh, that was lovely!'

Clare flushed with pleasure, sensing that the compliment had been sincere. 'Thank you,' she said.

She put her cello away, and preparations for lunch resumed; Clare put the sausage plait in the oven and began making a salad while Melanie poured some squash concentrate in a glass jug and diluted it with tap water. 'You're sure I can't help?' Tessa offered, feeling useless. 'I could lay the table.'

Clare looked at her mother. 'It's Helena's turn to lay the table. We take it in turns,' she added for Tessa's benefit.

'We'll leave it for Helena,' Melanie decided. 'She should be home soon. But thanks for offering, Tessa. You just sit there and relax. You look as if you could use a bit of a rest.' She turned her head. 'That sounds like them now.'

She was proved right a minute later, as Ned and Helena came through into the kitchen. 'Something smells good!' Ned declared, rubbing his hands together. 'I hope that means that lunch is almost ready.' Then he spotted Tessa and stopped. 'Hello.'

Melanie made the introductions as Tessa observed the newcomers.

Ned didn't look like a mathematician, she decided – whatever that meant. He had a very jolly face, a slight gap between his two front teeth, round spectacles, and a halo of lovely dark blond curls, cropped short. In stature he was on the small side, but slim; he wore a wild multicoloured baggy jumper and a pair of jeans. He didn't stand on ceremony, greeting Tessa with a welcoming kiss on the cheek. 'It's splendid to meet you, Tessa. Mel has told me about you.'

Helena hung back, though she smiled at Tessa nicely enough, shy but not unfriendly. She wasn't much like her sister in looks: she had inherited her father's blond hair, which she wore long and wavy, held back with an Alice band. Her coat hung open to reveal, beneath her jersey, tiny buds of nascent breasts. On the brink of adolescence, she was at an awkward stage, still growing into her face: her mouth and nose seemed out of proportion to the rest, waiting for the other parts to catch up. In her bone structure, Tessa perceived, there was a promise of beauty, but that promise was a very long way from being fulfilled, and at the moment she could almost be described as plain. And her shyness was evident in the way she carried herself, head down and shoulders rounded, face closed. She reminded Tessa, painfully, of her own adolescent self, and her heart went out to the girl.

'You've been to the library, I hear,' Tessa said.

The girl nodded, raising her satchel of books in confirmation. 'I love to read.'

'So do I,' Tessa confessed. 'Perhaps after lunch you could show me your books.'

That brought a smile, which was immediately followed by a frown as Melanie suggested, 'Why don't you put those books down, take off your coat, wash your hands, and lay the table?'

'I thought it was Poppy's turn,' Helena protested.

Melanie's voice was calm and reasonable. 'No, it's your turn. Poppy did it last night. And anyway, Poppy isn't back yet.' She turned to explain to Tessa, 'Ned takes Poppy and her friend Sophie to ballet class, and Sophie's mother collects them and brings Poppy home afterwards.'

Sulkily and silently Helena complied with her mother's instructions. As she did so, a banging on the front door heralded Poppy's arrival. 'I'll let her in,' offered Clare, who had just finished the salad.

A moment later Poppy pirouetted into the room, with Clare trailing behind. Tessa could see from the first that Poppy was the extrovert of the family, an irrepressible sprite, a pixie: tiny, with a small heart-shaped face – merry, mobile and vivacious, as open as Helena's was closed – and a mop of short brown curls.

'I suppose I don't need to tell you that this is Poppy,' Melanie said dryly. 'Poppy, this is my friend Tessa.'

Tessa rose from her chair and Poppy stopped in front of her, staring upwards. 'You're tall!' she declared with a mixture of frank admiration and envy. 'I wish I were as tall as you. My teacher says I'll never be tall enough to be a proper ballet dancer. And that's what I want to be more than anything else in the world.' For good measure she added, 'And I wish that my hair was as yellow as Helena's and as straight as Clare's. Then I'd look like a real ballerina.'

'Lunch is almost on the table, Poppy,' her mother reminded her.

Poppy ignored her, continuing her conversation with Tessa, looking her up and down. 'You're having a baby, like Mummy, aren't you?'

Self-consciously Tessa rubbed her bump. 'That's right.'

'Do you know if it's a girl or a boy?'

'No,' said Tessa. 'I haven't had my scan yet, and they can't always tell anyway.'

The girl nodded knowledgeably. 'Mummy doesn't know,

either. She told them that she didn't want to know. I hope,' she added, 'that it's a boy. I'd like a baby brother.'

'Boys are gross,' said Helena with pre-adolescent certainty, wrinkling her nose.

'She only wants it to be a boy because Sophie has a baby brother,' Clare stated.

'I don't!'

'You do too.'

Melanie interrupted. 'Poppy, wash your hands. All of you, sit down.'

'I want to sit by Tessa,' Poppy announced.

They arranged themselves round the table; Tessa found herself between Poppy and Ned, who sat at one end. Directly across from her was Clare, with Melanie and Helena beyond.

Melanie served up the sausage plait and passed the plates round. 'We have Clare to thank for this,' she announced, giving her middle daughter a proud smile. 'Help yourselves to salad.'

'What is it?' Helena glared at the plate in front of her suspiciously.

'Sausage plait,' Clare explained. 'I learned to make it in Domestic Science.'

'Sausage?' Helena made a face. 'Meat is gross.'

'Are you going vegetarian on us, sweetie?' Ned asked with a tolerant smile.

Helena's mouth set into a self-righteous line. 'Eating dead animals is gross.'

'She's only saying that because her best friend Charlotte is vegetarian,' Poppy confided to Tessa in a loud whisper.

'I am not!'

'You are, too. And I wasn't talking to you.'

Clare looked troubled. 'But, Helena. Animals are reared for meat. If we didn't eat them, what would happen to them?'

'I'm not eating it,' Helena announced.

'Then have a bit more salad,' her mother suggested, passing her the bowl. 'If there's not enough, I can make more.'

'I'd be interested to hear your reasons for not wanting to eat meat,' Ned said as he took a bite of the sausage plait. 'Umm – Clare, this is delicious.'

Through most of lunch they good-humouredly debated the issue: whether it was healthy to eat meat, vegetarianism as a moral choice, alternatives to meat-eating. Tessa listened in amazement to the free give-and-take of opinions, noting the respect with which both parents treated their children's views. Her memories of her own childhood meals were so completely at odds with this: her father had been very much of the 'children should be seen and not heard' school. And he hadn't exactly been full of dinner-table conversation himself. 'Tessa, sit up straight' and 'Tessa, chew your food more slowly – no one is going to take it away from you' – that was about the extent of it, at least as far as she could remember. If she had ever dared to refuse to eat anything, as Helena had – and she knew that she *wouldn't* have dared – she was sure that her father's response would have been very different from that of Helena's parents. Such nonsense would not have been tolerated. 'You'll eat what's put in front of you, and like it,' he would have said. Possibly even that old chestnut, 'People are starving in China. You should be thankful that we have good wholesome food on the table.'

Clare cleared the plates in preparation for the next course. 'Mince pies!' declared Ned. 'I thought I smelled mince pies when we came in. Clare, you *have* been busy.'

The girl basked in the recognition of her labours, but wanted to be fair. 'I only helped. Mummy did most of it.'

'Never mind.' Ned bit one in half. 'And very superior mince pies they are, too.'

There was a short silence round the table as the others followed suit. Tessa, who felt that she'd scarcely had a chance to speak to Ned, addressed him. 'Melanie tells me that you're a mathematician.'

'An academic hack, really,' he said with a self-deprecating grin. 'I teach at the University of London.'

'Ned is one of the world's greatest experts on complexity theory,' Melanie amplified loyally, then undermined it by adding, 'whatever that is when it's at home. I don't even pretend to understand what it's all about.'

'You may mock,' Ned grinned. 'But when I win the Nobel Prize one day, I'll remind you that you didn't take me seriously.'

'Oh, I take you *very* seriously,' his wife assured him. 'I just don't understand your work.'

'Neither does anyone else,' he said equably. ' Not even my students. That's the trouble.' He turned to Tessa. 'But I've got a guilty secret. My fortune is founded on something else. All of this –' and he waved his arms round to indicate the house, 'was made possible by something of which I'm not all that proud.' He paused provocatively, giving her time to speculate.

Inherited money? guessed Tessa, though she didn't dare to speak her thoughts aloud. Gambling? Something even worse?

'Daddy wrote a textbook,' Clare stated. 'He's made bundles of money from it.'

'Prostitution of my talents,' he confessed with a cheerful smile. 'I wrote an entry-level algebra textbook, years ago. O-level as was then, now GCSE. Absolutely basic stuff – *anyone* could have written it. But I was just lucky, I suppose. It became part of the syllabus, and has never been out of print. Still sells in the tens of thousands of copies. And', he said, grinning round the table, 'it allows my family to live in the style to which they have become accustomed. Music lessons, ballet classes, the lot. So sneer not.' He reached for another mince pie.

'Daddy! Don't eat them all!' Poppy protested. 'They'll be gone before Christmas.'

'Then Clare will just have to make some more,' he stated, conveying it to his mouth. 'Or at a pinch, St Michael can do it for her.'

Tessa spoke her thoughts aloud. 'I can imagine that Christmas in this house will be very jolly.'

Poppy, who had taken quite a shine to Tessa, turned to her new friend. 'Tessa, you'll come here for Christmas, won't you?' she coaxed.

'I can't,' said Tessa automatically. Her first Christmas with Rob. She was looking forward to that very much, she told herself.

'Are you going to your Mummy and Daddy's house, then?' Poppy probed.

'No, but I'll have to make lunch for my husband,' she temporised.

'Well, then.' Poppy slapped both hands on the table triumphantly. 'He can come here, too. Can't he, Mummy? You can *both* come for lunch.'

Melanie's affirmation was prompt. 'Yes, of course. We'd be delighted to have you, Tessa. You and Rob.' She looked across the table at her, smiling her sincerity. 'Really. You'd be most welcome.'

'We can't. But thank you for asking.'

'The offer stands,' Melanie said easily. 'If you should change your mind.'

After lunch, the family scattered again: Ned drove Clare to her cello lesson, Helena retreated to her room with a book, and a reluctant Poppy was persuaded to practise her flute. 'But I want to talk to Tessa,' she protested.

'Tessa has had quite enough of your conversation,' her mother laughed. 'Now it's *my* turn to talk to Tessa.' She made a pot of tea, got out a tray, and said to Tessa, 'Let's go upstairs to my study. We can shut the door and have a good private natter.'

Her study, at the top of the stairs, was small and cosy, the walls lined with books; it was furnished with a desk, a comfortable chair, and a sofa. Melanie directed Tessa towards the sofa, then poured the tea. 'There,' she sighed, sinking in the chair. 'That's better. Peace and quiet and tea.' She smiled at

Tessa. 'I'm afraid you got more than you bargained for when you came here this morning – here you were, thinking you could come and have a nice quiet chat, and you end up having my family inflicted upon you. I do apologise.'

'Not at all,' protested Tessa. 'In the first place, I practically invited myself, so I'm the one who should be apologising. And in the second place, I've really enjoyed it. They're lovely.'

Melanie put her head to one side, considering the matter dispassionately. 'They're not so bad, most of the time. Of course they were on their good behaviour for you. But they're quite capable of being little horrors – there are times when I'd like to throttle the lot of them. Poppy can be such a cheeky little monkey, and as for Helena . . .' She sighed. 'I fear that Helena is going to get a whole lot worse before she gets better, with the dreaded teenage years just over the horizon. The poor lamb. And,' she added, shaking her head, 'her poor parents.'

'But you're such *good* parents,' Tessa stated impulsively. 'I was so impressed with the way you and Ned treated the girls at lunch – treating them like human beings, listening to their opinions, encouraging them to discuss things rather than just telling them to shut up and accept *your* view of the world.'

Melanie looked surprised. 'But how else would they grow up into intelligent adults, able to think for themselves?' She stretched her legs out. 'Or is that just the psychologist in me?'

It was Tessa's turn for surprise. 'You're a psychologist?' She looked at the sofa on which she was sitting, feeling that perhaps she ought to be stretched out on it instead.

'Oh, didn't you know?' Melanie waved her arm to indicate the books on the shelves. 'Not in the sense you probably think,' she added. 'I'm not a *clinical* psychologist, not a shrink. I'm an academic, really. Psychology is my field.'

'You teach psychology, then?'

'I used to.' Melanie blew on her tea, then took a sip. 'I was at the University of London, like Ned. Until the girls came along. When it was just Helena, and she was a baby, we managed to juggle our schedules so that I could still do some teaching. But it got too complicated after that. Since then I've stayed at home and done other things.'

Tessa was curious. 'What sort of things?'

'Oh, I do some freelance work for the examiners – marking exams, even setting a few questions,' Melanie explained. 'I still supervise one or two graduate students. And I do some writing.'

'Scholarly journals?' Tessa surmised, looking at the rows and rows of thin spines on the book shelves.

Melanie smiled. 'Sometimes. But Ned isn't the only one with a guilty secret.' She paused and sipped her tea, then made her confession. 'I'm afraid, Tessa, that most of my writing is done for women's magazines. You know the sort of thing: "How to tell if your husband is cheating on you", "Talking to your children about sex", "What do you say when your son tells you he's gay?". Or the less sensational ones: "What to do when your child is being bullied", or "Ten steps to feeling better about yourself". Watered-down pop psychology of the worst sort. All based on sound psychological principles, of course,' she added, one side of her mouth twisting self-mockingly. 'I must admit that it pays rather better than scholarly journals. And its shelf-life can be nearly as long – these magazines seem to live on forever in doctors' waiting rooms and hairdressers' salons.'

'But that's fascinating,' Tessa said, impressed. 'Where do you get your ideas?'

'Many of them are commissioned. Once you get a reputation for being able to produce this sort of thing on demand, the editors start coming to you. And some of them are inspired by my own experiences – not the ones on cheating husbands or gay sons, of course. But I'm working on one at the moment called "Pregnancy and mental health: how you feel *does* affect your baby". And I have a horrible feeling,' she added, smiling ruefully, 'that in the years to come, I'll be writing any number of articles with titles like "Every parent's nightmare: surviving your child's teenage years". Not something I'm looking forward to, really.'

Tessa had liked Melanie from their first meeting, and had instinctively trusted her; now her liking was enhanced by an enormous respect for her. She managed to combine raising a family with a rich professional life, and she made it sound so easy and natural.

'But you didn't come here today to hear me wittering on,' Melanie said, leaning over to refill Tessa's teacup. 'Any more than you came to hear my children wittering on. How are *you* doing, Tessa? You were obviously very upset by the news about JoAnn. Tell me how you feel about it.'

Tessa hesitated. Perhaps she *had* come here with the idea of talking to Melanie about JoAnn's death. Her motivation hadn't been as well formulated in her mind as that, but something of the sort must have impelled her to pick up the phone and ring Melanie. An impulse towards friendship? She wanted Melanie to be a friend, with an intensity of longing that was almost painful. But she was a professional as well, Tessa now knew – a person who had been trained in these things. Did that make it easier to talk to her, or did it make it more difficult?

Melanie was smiling at her in encouragement. Then she leaned across the gap between them and squeezed Tessa's hand.

She was a friend. Tessa opened her mouth to tell her how much that gesture meant to her, and found that she was crying.

Chapter 16

'I'm . . . so . . . frightened,' Tessa gulped, struggling for control.

'Tell me,' said Melanie. She didn't loose her grip on Tessa's hand.

In fits and starts, Tessa told her how her anticipatory joy in her baby had suddenly turned to terror: the incessant, sleep-denying kicking, followed by Stephanie's flippant remarks about parasites and aliens. And then JoAnn.

'Her baby killed her,' Tessa stated tearfully. 'Kyle killed her. He was out for himself, just like Stephanie said. He's strong and healthy and alive, and she's dead.'

'And you're afraid that your baby will kill you as well. That you'll die.'

Tessa nodded, gasping, as a fragmentary memory of the nightmare about the roller-coaster flashed through her mind. 'I'm not ready to die. But it's too late. I can't stop it.'

'Tessa, look at me.' Melanie leaned closer and fixed her eyes on Tessa's, then spoke in a calm and earnest voice. 'You are *not* going to die. Your baby isn't an alien who's out to kill you – she's part of the most natural process in the world. The most wonderful, miraculous process. Hundreds of thousands of women give birth every day. Yes, a few of them *do* die, but these days, in the Western world, it's very rare.'

'JoAnn died,' stated Tessa unarguably.

'JoAnn was unlucky. And a bit foolish, to be honest.' Melanie went on, 'If she'd had a Caesarean like the doctors wanted her to, she would still be alive. I'm telling you, Tessa: you're *not* going to die.'

Tessa wanted to believe her friend, but still her tears flowed. There was something else buried in her memory, something monstrous: it seemed to be pressing down on her, stifling her, even as it remained hidden from her conscious mind.

As if sensing that, Melanie said in a gentle voice, 'That's not all, is it? It's not just JoAnn. Something else is bothering you. Tell me, Tessa. Does it', she added intuitively, 'have anything to do with your mother-in-law?'

Tessa wanted to tell her. At the mention of her mother-in-law, suddenly the memory surfaced, hideous and complete, like a bloated corpse emerging from its watery grave. Tessa gasped with the horror of it. 'A baby,' she whimpered. 'A monstrous baby.'

Melanie drew the story out of her, disordered, fragmentary. How she had gone to her mother-in-law's house on various occasions. The locked room, tantalising her for so long. The enigma of Linda's life; the suggestion – the certainty – of her unorthodox lifestyle. And then the final chapter: the key to the locked room, her brief glimpse of the room's contents, the overgrown infant in pink frock and nappy, screaming for his mother, for Mummy Linda. 'I don't understand,' Tessa admitted. 'It was just . . . so . . . awful. And I don't understand it at all.'

Throughout the story, Melanie had made all of the right encouraging noises. But when Tessa reached the end, Melanie sat still for a moment, looking not at Tessa but off into space. 'Oh, my,' she said softly, almost to herself. 'Infantilism.'

Tessa was startled out of her tearfulness. 'What?'

'Infantilism.' Melanie struggled out of her chair and plucked a book from the shelves. 'I've read about it, though I've never come across it myself.' She flipped through the book. 'Yes, here it is. The posh name for it, the scientific name, is "autonepiophilia", but it's usually called "infantilism". It's a recognised condition.'

'But what is it?'

'To put it in simple terms, it involves adults dressing up and behaving like babies,' Melanie explained. 'That's what you saw – I'm sure of it.'

Tessa stared at her blankly, uncomprehending. 'But why? Why would anyone do that?'

'Oh, various reasons.' Melanie settled back down with the book on her lap. 'Usually it's because they didn't receive enough love and affection from their mothers when they were babies – maybe their mothers *didn't* love them, or didn't cuddle them enough, or weren't there, and then when they're grown up they need to make up for the lack. Or sometimes, I suppose, it's because they had such a wonderful time when they were babies that they want to recapture that feeling and relive it.'

'So they . . .' Tessa's voice trailed off as her imagination failed her.

'They dress up in baby clothes. They wear nappies. And if they're lucky,' Melanie added, 'they find someone to act the part of their mummy. To change their nappies and give them bottles and play with them.'

Tessa took a deep, ragged breath. 'And you think . . .'

'I think', Melanie said carefully, 'that it's possible – probable, even – that your mother-in-law acted as a mummy to this . . . baby.'

'But he was wearing a *dress*,' Tessa blurted, unable to confront Melanie's conjecture head-on. 'He was a man, I'm sure of it. With hairy legs and . . . he needed a shave. But he was wearing a dress. A pink dress. And a frilly bonnet.'

'That's an interesting thing about adult babies,' Melanie said. 'From what I've read, almost all of them are men, and most of them dres as girls. They even have their own baby-names. And they'll be girls' names.'

'I don't understand,' Tessa repeated. 'Why?'

Melanie shrugged. 'Why are they men, or why do they dress as girls?' She spent a moment scanning the book on her lap. 'Most people who have studied this condition seem to feel that women have socially acceptable ways available to them to express these needs. Women can pamper themselves, wear cuddly clothes, sleep with stuffed animals. They can hug their friends,' she added, raising her head to smile at Tessa. 'But men don't have those outlets. The need to be nurtured can build up in them until it becomes a compulsion that can only be satisfied by this extreme form of behaviour. And somehow taking on the persona of a girl makes it more acceptable to them. It has something to do with control, as well. It's difficult to make generalisations, but often men who have this particular hang-up are in positions of authority in their real lives, jobs where they have to make decisions, or where people look up to them. Relinquishing control to someone else, in a controlled situation, can be very attractive.'

Tessa closed her eyes, feeling sick. It was absurd; it was crazy. If anyone but Melanie had told her this, she would have felt sure that they were making it up, having her on, pulling her leg, taking the mickey.

And yet, she had seen . . . him. Or her. What other explanation could there be for that hideous apparition?

It couldn't be true. It must be true.

And Linda? *Had* Linda fed this creature, changed its nappies, been its mummy? Why would she do such an unnatural, disgusting thing? For money?

'Do you think that she did it for money?' Tessa blurted.

'The mummy, you mean?' Melanie considered the question. 'Well, that's possible. Or perhaps she had a relationship with this . . . man, and did it to please him. I believe that happens sometimes.'

'No,' Tessa asserted with certainty. 'I saw him. She couldn't have done.' She'd seen something else, she remembered suddenly: a row of cots, not just the one. A quantity of high chairs.

All of those men. She'd seen them, too. And Hilda Steggall had confirmed it.

'Linda was a good businesswoman,' Father Theo had said.

'He wasn't the only one,' Tessa stated, convinced of the truth of it even as she said it.

Melanie raised her eyebrows. 'Not the only one?'

'There were several cots in the . . . nursery, and several high chairs. Not just one.'

Melanie was quick to grasp the implication of Tessa's words. 'You think that your mother-in-law ran a nursery for adult babies?'

Tessa nodded as her conversation with Father Theo came back to her; she echoed his words. 'She did what she had to do to survive.' That big house to run, with no money from her ex-husband to help her, and a child to bring up.

Rob, she thought, catching her breath with a painful gasp. Rob must have known. How could he not know?

Once again Melanie seemed to read her thoughts, or perhaps they were reflected clearly on her face. 'Your husband,' Melanie said. 'Rob. Have you talked to him about this at all? Have you told him what you saw last night?'

'No.' Tessa shook her head and averted her eyes. 'He wasn't home last night. I . . . was in shock. I didn't even remember what had happened until I told you just now. And Rob . . .' She searched for the right words, trying not to be disloyal to her husband. 'His mother's death was a great shock to him. Very painful. He doesn't like to talk about her.'

'But, Tessa,' Melanie looked at her earnestly, 'this is something you *must* talk about.'

Tessa wasn't at all sure about that. Rob's reluctance to talk about his mother was all too understandable in the light of this new knowledge. He hadn't wanted Tessa to know what his mother did, and who could blame him? He was trying to protect her, she told herself. To bring the subject up now would only distress him even further. 'I don't think so,' she stated. 'Rob wouldn't like it.'

'You *must*,' Melanie insisted. 'For the sake of your relationship. It's not the sort of thing that can remain a secret between husband and wife. Get it out in the open. Tell him that you know, and it will bring you closer together.'

Still Tessa resisted. 'You don't know Rob.'

'Of course he's upset about his mother's death. And of course he's ... embarrassed ... about her life, if all this is true,' Melanie went on. 'But I'm sure he'll be much happier when he can share these feelings with you. When he doesn't feel he has to keep it a secret. Promise me that you'll talk to him about it.'

Melanie was the professional, Tessa acknowledged to herself. Reluctantly, miserably, she nodded. Painful and difficult as it would be, she would have to find a way to talk to Rob about his mother.

Doug Coles had had two days to consider his position. Two days of agony, wondering what the hell Ian Spicer knew about Linda Nicholls's murder. And why, in God's name, was he poking his nose into it anyway?

In his more sanguine moments, Coles told himself that it was as innocent as it seemed, a mere coincidence. Ian *was* working on an overlapping case, and had looked at the Nicholls files in all innocence.

He didn't really believe that, though. If there was an overlapping case, why hadn't *he* heard about it? Why hadn't Ian told him what it was?

But if it wasn't true, then why was Ian interested? Why was he sniffing about the Nicholls files?

No, Ian knew something, and he was trying to find out more.

After his shift ended on Saturday afternoon, Coles went

straight home, foregoing his usual stop at the pub on the way. He still hadn't made up his mind about the best course of action, but he knew that he would have to make a decision soon, before Ian got any closer.

Before he ended up in the deepest shit of his life.

He hadn't really bothered to hide the papers very well; he'd just stuffed them under his bed, knowing that no one would be looking for them there.

Now he pulled them out. Piles of them: financial records, files on each of her clients. It made interesting reading, some of it. He'd been looking forward to perusing the stuff at his leisure.

But time had run out; he knew that now.

Doug Coles went into the lounge and carefully laid a fire in the grate. He didn't often bother with a fire, but he did have enough coal and kindling on hand to make a proper job of it.

And as he carried a pile of Linda Nicholls's papers to the lounge, his mind made the connection that had been eluding him up till now.

He'd always had the feeling that he'd seen Tessa Nicholls before – before the day of Linda Nicholls's murder. But he couldn't remember where or in what context, and it hadn't really troubled him or caused him to lose any sleep. It wasn't that important.

Now he remembered. And it *was* important. He had seen her with Ian Spicer. Years ago, at some post-rugby bash. Hanging on Ian's arm. His woman.

'Bloody hell,' he said aloud.

The fire had caught well. Coles scattered papers over the burning embers and watched as they flamed, curled, and blackened.

It took a surprising length of time to burn the lot. He shoved each batch in with the poker – fitting, that – until they were all reduced to ash.

All except for one sheet of paper. One sheet only, with the names and addresses of Linda's clients.

That one sheet was his insurance policy. Just in case. He folded it up, then thought carefully where he might hide it.

Late that afternoon, Tessa went home. Melanie pressed her to stay longer, to join them for dinner, but much as she would have liked to accept the invitation, she felt awkward at having taken up so much of Melanie's day already. 'Rob's probably at home by now,' she said. 'He'll be wanting something to eat.'

Ned insisted on driving her home, in spite of her protests that she would be fine on foot. It was cold, Ned said, and dark – no fit conditions for her to be out. He pulled up in front of the house, which, she was dismayed to see, showed no signs of Rob's return, and he even escorted her to the front door to make sure that she got in safely. 'Don't be a stranger, Tessa,' he said with a grin. 'Come back to see us soon. We've all enjoyed having you.'

It had been, Tessa reflected as she shut the door behind him with repeated expressions of her thanks, a most extra-ordinary day. In a way it was a relief that Rob wasn't there; it gave her time to digest the events of the day, and it spared her the necessity for immediate explanations of where she'd been. And, she admitted to herself, she could put off the con-versation about his mother just a bit longer.

She checked the answering service: no message from Rob. Wondering how much later he might be, she went into the front room, switched on the lights of the Christmas tree, and collapsed on to the sofa. Their little tree, with its shop-bought decorations, seemed so sterile compared to the one at the Maybanks's house. That tree, towering tall in the high-ceilinged room which took up most of the ground floor, was covered with ornaments which the girls had made over the years. A tree of happy memories.

Tessa tried to imagine their own home, a few Christmases hence. Would *they* have a tree like that, with home-made paper chains and glittery decorations fashioned lovingly by childish hands? She cast her mind forward ten years into the future: two children, or three, gathered round the Christmas tree; Rob, with perhaps a tiny touch of distinguished grey appearing at his temples, smiling benignly at his family, as Ned had smiled at his girls.

Perhaps it would be like that. But even in her vision, Rob refused to conform to her wishes; in her mind's eye, Rob was frowning.

Disturbed by her inability to control her own fantasy, she squeezed her eyes shut and switched her mind over to a more gratifying line of thought: the Maybank girls. What a delight they were, and how she had enjoyed her time with them. Solemn Clare, ebullient Poppy. Even Helena had warmed to her, according her the supreme privilege of an invitation to her room to look at her books, and they had forged a real bond over their common interest.

Gratifyingly, the girls had all seemed reluctant to see her go. Poppy was the most demonstrative, hugging Tessa and making her promise to come back. 'Come for Christmas,' she had begged.

That invitation, backed up by Melanie, was most alluring. But it would never do, Tessa realised. Rob would be uncomfortable, and it wouldn't be fair to him.

When *was* Rob going to come home? Tessa looked at her watch: it was nearly seven o'clock. Even on weekdays he would be home by this time, and this was Saturday. When he did arrive, she reminded herself, he would be wanting his dinner.

On her way to the kitchen, Tessa remembered that she had not, after all, been to the shops that day. There would be no more food in the kitchen now than there had been in the morning.

She also realised that she was hungry.

There were still two slices of the stale bread left, she discovered, and she also found one solitary egg. It ought to be reasonably fresh, Tessa thought, and decided to feed herself now and worry about Rob later.

She boiled the egg and made toast soldiers from the bread, then wolfed the lot down. Craving a cup of tea, she checked the milk: it had gone off. She would have to settle for black coffee instead.

Tessa made the coffee and sat down with it at the kitchen table, applying her mind to the problem of what to feed Rob. They could always order a pizza to be delivered tonight, she supposed. Tomorrow would be a thornier problem: Rob quite liked a roast on a Sunday. From the beginning of their marriage she had always given him a proper Sunday lunch, and he'd come to enjoy and expect that custom. The supermarkets didn't open till noon; the corner shop would be open earlier, but she wouldn't be able to get a joint there. A tinned ham, perhaps – that might have to do.

The coffee was scalding hot and tasted bitter, almost metallic in her mouth. It would, she thought, probably give her indigestion, and keep her awake all night into the bargain.

The phone rang. Rob, she thought, abandoning her coffee and hurrying to the phone.

'Tessa?'

She caught her breath in disappointment: it was Ian. 'Hello, Ian,' she said, swallowing hard.

'Tessa! Where have you bloody been? I've been trying to get you for a couple of days!'

'I've been . . . out.' She didn't, Tessa told herself firmly, owe him any explanations or apologies.

'I left one message,' he said. 'But I didn't want to leave any more. Just in case.'

Just in case Rob retrieved the messages, Tessa realised. 'Well, I'm here now,' she pointed out.

'Are you . . . alone?' Ian probed.

She closed her eyes. The last thing she needed or wanted right now was to have Ian descending on her. 'I'm expecting Rob home at any minute,' she said in a firm voice.

'Oh, lucky you,' Ian digressed bitterly. 'It seems like I haven't seen Amanda in days. At least that means she isn't bloody nagging me.'

Tessa didn't intend to get on to the subject of Amanda again. 'What is it that you wanted to tell me?' she asked.

'I don't want to tell you over the phone,' Ian stated. 'When can I see you?'

Did he really have something important to share, Tessa wondered, or was this all just an excuse to see her again? She couldn't cope with him just now. 'One day next week,' she said vaguely. 'I'll ring you.' She put the phone down and ignored it when it rang again and again.

The coffee really was undrinkable. Tessa poured it down the sink and rinsed the cup, slotting it into the dishwasher. What she really wanted, she now realised with certainty, was sleep. She was exhausted: emotionally drained and physically weary.

When *was* Rob coming home? She went back into the front room and settled on the sofa to wait for him; after a few minutes, she closed her eyes.

Dim daylight filtered through the curtains when Tessa woke, with the disorienting certainty of being somewhere other than her own bed. The bitter tang of coffee filled her mouth, and her neck ached from its unnatural position against the arm of the sofa. She stretched her cramped muscles as she tried to remember where she was and how she had got there.

The front room, she perceived as she opened her eyes. There was the Christmas tree. She didn't recall turning its lights off, but they were off now. And she was covered with a blanket.

Rob, she remembered guiltily, struggling to sit up. She'd been waiting for Rob to come home.

'Good morning, Tessa, my love.' Rob sounded supremely cheerful as he pulled the curtains open. 'Did you sleep well, then?'

Weak winter sunlight slanted into the room and it became clear to Tessa what had happened. 'I must have fallen asleep. Waiting for you to come home,' she explained.

'Yes, I know.' He leaned over her and kissed her forehead. 'You were sleeping so peacefully when I got home that I decided not to disturb you. I tucked you in with a blanket, turned the lights out, and went to bed.'

'But . . . your dinner,' she recalled. 'I'm really sorry, Rob.'

'Not to worry, my love,' he assured her. 'I grabbed a bite to eat before I came home. I tried to ring you to let you know that I'd been delayed, but there was no reply. I was a bit worried, but I suppose you must have fallen asleep and didn't hear the phone.'

Those calls that she had ignored, thinking it was Ian, Tessa recalled, feeling more guilty than ever. Her guilt drove her to further apology. 'There's nothing to eat,' she said. 'Not even any milk for tea. I'm so sorry.'

'Yes, I've discovered that.' Rob was smiling, not frowning. 'I was going to make you a cup of tea a few minutes ago, to wake you up gently. But it doesn't matter,' he added breezily. 'We can stop on the way and get something to eat. And pots of tea, if that's what you'd like. I fancy a good breakfast, don't you?'

'On the way?' Tessa echoed, utterly baffled. 'On the way to *where*?'

'Ah,' Rob grinned. 'That's a surprise. I told you we'd do something special today, and that's exactly what we're going to do.' He reached for Tessa's hands and pulled her to her feet. 'So come along, my love. It's time to get moving, tea or no tea. Why don't you run upstairs and have a shower?'

She hardly knew what to say. 'But . . . what should I wear?' Rob, she saw, had already showered; his hair was still damp, which gave him an appealingly boyish air. He was looking fresh and handsome in khaki-coloured trousers, an open-necked shirt, and his navy blue blazer.

'Oh, something comfortable but smart,' he suggested. 'You'll look beautiful no matter what you wear.'

Tessa felt rooted to the spot in amazement at his unexpected high spirits. Rob put his arms round her and gave her a squeeze. 'I do love you, you know,' he said into her hair. Just as she relaxed into his embrace, half hoping that it might lead to something else, he released her. 'Now hurry up,' he added, with a playful pat on her bottom.

What, Tessa wondered as she followed his orders and went upstairs, had happened to put him in such a good mood? But she wasn't about to question her luck. Nor was she about to do, just yet, what she had promised Melanie that she would do at the earliest opportunity. Now was not the time to mention his mother.

'Bring your passport,' Rob said, tantalisingly, just before they went out of the door. But it wasn't until they were some way out of London, eating a cooked breakfast in a motorway café, that he divulged the plan.

'We're going to France,' he said with barely suppressed excitement. 'Just for the day. We'll drive into the country for lunch, then we'll have time to do some Christmas shopping at one of the hypermarkets, and stock up on wine and drink for the holidays as well.'

Tessa had never done such a thing before – indeed, it had never even occurred to her to do so, but the idea of it intrigued her, even as it made her a bit apprehensive. 'But the ferry,' she said dubiously. 'I don't much like the idea of bobbing round in the water for two hours.' Hungry as she had been when she ordered it, and appealing as it sounded, the breakfast had arrived swimming in grease; the little she had managed to eat of it had made her feel a bit queasy. She wished, now, that she'd settled for cereal and toast instead.

Rob, who had polished off his breakfast with evident enjoyment and no ill effects, laughed. 'Oh, we're not taking the ferry. We're going on the train – on the Shuttle.' He looked at his watch and put down his cutlery. 'In fact, we'd better be pressing on. I've booked a crossing, and we don't have much time to spare.'

It was remarkably easy, and remarkably quick: at the Shuttle port near Folkestone, Rob drove the car on to the train, and just over thirty minutes after departure he drove it off again at Calais. There he turned on to a motorway, heading away from the coast.

'Do you know where we're going, then?' Tessa asked. 'Or do you need me to look at a map or something?'

'I know where we're going.' Rob turned his head briefly to smile at her, steering with one hand while with the other he slotted a tape into the tape player. The music filled the car and he sang along with it at the top of his voice.

Now, thought Tessa, was not the time. Perhaps over lunch she might broach the subject. With Rob's jubilant voice filling her ears, she looked out of the window at the French country-side as they whizzed through it. It didn't look anything like England: flat and almost featureless, except for occasional rows of bare poplar trees, punctuated with small run-down farm-houses and boxy, ugly retail parks on a monumental scale.

They were on the motorway for nearly an hour before Rob took a slip road on to a lesser highway, which in turn led them to a series of narrow country lanes. Still he drove with assurance, neither asking for nor needing any navigational help.

At last he pulled up in front of a modest-looking inn, deep in the country. Tessa stated the obvious. 'You've been here before.'

Rob nodded, smiling. 'Several times, on holiday. You'll love it, I promise. The food is wonderful.' He went round the car and opened her door for her, then took her hand and led her into the inn.

A short, saturnine waiter beamed in recognition as they came through the door. 'Monsieur Rob!' he exclaimed.

'*Bonjour, Georges! Comment allez-vous?*' Rob's accent was impeccable.

'*Très bien, monsieur. Et vous?*'

'*Moi, je vais bien aussi.*'

The waiter looked at Tessa and said in a lower voice, '*Je vois que vous amenez une autre femme!*'

'*Oui, c'est mon épouse,*' Rob stated with a proud grin. '*Nous sommes mariés, il y a six ou sept moins. Elle est très belle, n'est-ce pas?*'

'*Ben oui, monsieur. Très belle, très jolie.*' He leered appreciatively at Tessa, then led them to a table. '*Voici votre table, Monsieur Rob.*'

Rob pulled Tessa's chair out for her, then took his seat on the other side of the table. 'Champagne, my love?' he suggested merrily as Georges hovered nearby, awaiting instruction.

She was sorely tempted, but managed to resist. 'Oh, Rob, I mustn't.'

The tiniest shadow of a frown crossed his face, the merest flicker of displeasure. Tessa observed this with dismay, but it was gone as soon as it appeared, and he turned, smiling, to the waiter. '*Pour moi, le champagne, Georges. Un seul verre. Et pour ma femme, l'eau gazeuse, s'il vous plaît.*'

'*Oui, monsieur.*' He was back in just a moment with the drinks and the menu, providing a verbal run-down of the daily specials. Rob ordered for both of them, without consulting Tessa, then settled back to enjoy his champagne.

Tessa's French was rudimentary; she'd studied it for a year or two at school, many years ago, and hadn't had occasion to use it since. She had only just managed to follow most of

Rob's conversation with the waiter, and was greatly impressed by his fluency and accent. 'You were marvellous,' she said with an admiring smile. 'I had no idea you spoke French so well.'

Rob grinned. 'There are a few things you don't know about me, Tessa.'

That was a painful reminder of the conversation they needed to have. But not now, Tessa said to herself. Definitely not now.

Rob reached across the table and took her hand, entwining his fingers with hers and stroking her palm with his thumb. 'You *are* looking lovely today,' he said softly. 'I like showing off my beautiful wife.'

Life couldn't get much better than this, Tessa thought in a rapture of delight, smiling into her husband's eyes. If only time could stand still and things could stay just like this . . .

Then the baby kicked her, as if to remind her that soon her life was going to change, whether she wanted it to or not.

The lunch was leisurely and delicious. Pleasantly sated, they relaxed during the drive back towards the coast.

They had almost reached Calais when Rob pulled into the vast car park of one of the hypermarkets, then checked his watch. 'We've got two hours,' he stated. 'Why don't we go our separate ways? I'll take care of the wine and the drink, and you do whatever you need to do, and we'll just meet back here at the car at six o'clock.'

Two hours, thought Tessa, amazed at the enormity of the hypermarket. There, under one roof, was virtually anything that one might want to buy.

Christmas shopping, she told herself firmly: that was the first priority. But she was attracted to the food section and, after all, she *did* need to buy some food. She pushed a trolley up and down the aisles, filling it with intriguing-looking jars and bottles, with tubs of pâté and lumps of sweet butter and beautiful crusty cheeses.

Then she moved reluctantly towards the men's department. Rob and her father were the two names on her Christmas list, but as she passed through the children's department, she found herself thinking instead about the Maybanks, and what fun it would be to buy presents for the girls. She *would* buy them gifts, she decided impulsively. But not until she'd found something for her father and Rob.

Tessa had always found her father very difficult to buy for. He lived a simple, solitary lifestyle; he wasn't interested in fine wines or gourmet foods. His clothing was a function of his profession, and he always wore a dog-collar, so even the old perennial favourite gift of stumped women for difficult-to-please men – a tie – was a non-starter.

A tie for Rob, then, perhaps. Tessa stopped at the display of colourful silk ties, but didn't see anything remotely like the sedate, businesslike ties that Rob favoured. She didn't think he would wear any of these, with their blotches of wild colour or their cartoon characters. Rob in a Bugs Bunny tie? She couldn't even picture it. Funnily enough, the ties made her think of Andrew, who had always liked to wear outrageous ties to work. Impetuously she chose one which she thought he would like: an abstract design in acid tones of orange and yellow and lime green. He was coming for lunch on Boxing Day, she recalled, and she would wrap it up and give it to him then.

Beyond the ties, her eye was caught by a display of braces. They weren't ordinary braces, but were printed with designs not unlike those on the ties. Rob would hate them, she was sure. But they *were* good fun. Looking at a pair adorned all over with musical notes, she was reminded of Ned Maybank – Ned would have a good laugh when he opened them, and he would wear them. She added them to her shopping trolley. It was settled, then: she was buying gifts for all of the Maybanks. Suddenly her mind overflowed with ideas and possibilities.

There was no doubt at all about Helena, she knew: she

would buy a book for Helena, so that was something to be accomplished in England rather than here in France. What's more, she knew exactly what book: *A Long Way from Verona* by Jane Gardam, with its plucky and eccentric almost-thirteen-year-old narrator. It had gripped her when she was Helena's age, and she was sure it would grip Helena as well.

For Poppy, it had to be something to do with ballet. That wasn't too difficult; she found, in an area of the hypermarket devoted to decorative art, a small framed print of a Degas painting of ballet dancers.

Clare was a bit more difficult. Nothing too frivolous for Clare, Tessa judged. Again, music provided her with an inspiration, and she chose a compact disc of Jacqueline du Pré playing the Dvořák cello concerto.

That left only Melanie, and she was perhaps the most difficult of all. It should be, Tessa decided, something for her alone – not to be shared with the family. Something luxurious, self-indulgent, the sort of thing she would never buy for herself.

Perfume, then. Expensive French perfume, in a tiny crystal bottle. She hoped that Melanie would like it.

Her trolley was filling up, time was getting on, and still she had done nothing about the two people on her original list. Discouraged, Tessa pushed her trolley along the jewellery counter, then stopped. A watch for Rob? Lately he had been complaining that his watch was unreliable, and it wasn't a particularly good one to begin with.

She pored over cases of costly Swiss watches, bewildered by the various features on offer. At last she chose one which looked elegant without being over-the-top, pointed to it, and waited while the sales assistant put it in a box.

While she was waiting, she spotted a display of pens, and felt that once again inspiration had struck. Her father always wrote with a fountain pen, and these were beautiful as well as useful. Quite expensive, some of them, but there were several which she felt were within her price range, so she selected one.

Tessa checked her own watch: she had a few minutes before she had to think about going through the check-out and finding the car. She raised her head and scanned the huge expanse of the hypermarket, remembering that she had intended buying a camera in time for Christmas.

One more stop, then, before hitting the tills with her full shopping trolley and her credit card.

After their filling lunch, Tessa hadn't thought she would want to eat again that day. But the sight of so much wonderful food on offer at the hypermarket had piqued her appetite, and by the time they reached home, she was hungry again.

She cut a fresh baguette into chunks and put it on the kitchen table with some sweet butter and two sorts of cheese. Perhaps, she told herself as she got out plates and cutlery, this would be the time to talk to Rob about his mother, to tell him what she had discovered.

'I don't know how you can even think about eating again,' Rob stated cheerfully as he joined her at the table. 'I thought I'd given you a good lunch.'

'Oh, it was wonderful!' she assured him. 'But the baguette will be stale by tomorrow, and I just couldn't resist buying it – it smelled so divine.'

He relaxed in his chair and smiled at her. 'We had a good day, didn't we?'

'The best,' she assured him. 'Thank you so much for thinking of it and planning it.'

Rob reached for a chunk of baguette and applied some butter. 'Nothing is too good for my wife.'

Tessa smiled and, in the spirit of the moment, teased him gently. 'Perhaps you could remember that next week when you decide to stay at work all night. Indispensable Rob – they can't run the company without you.' She gave a little laugh.

His brows drew together. 'Are you laughing at me?' he demanded in a quiet yet serious voice.

She had been lulled into a sense of security by his high spirits of the day, and, feeling closer to him than she had since their honeymoon, laughed again. 'Not really. Or maybe just a little bit. You *do* take yourself so seriously sometimes.'

Rob's hand tightened on the bread and the skin round his mouth grew white as he pressed his lips together. 'I will *not* be laughed at,' he said through clenched teeth.

Still Tessa was oblivious; she gave another laugh. 'Oh, Rob. Lighten up. I'm just teasing you.'

'Don't you *ever* laugh at me again!' He didn't shout, but the concentrated venom in his voice got through to Tessa, too late, as he pushed himself up from the table. Deliberately he hurled the piece of bread, aiming not at her but at the wall over her shoulder, then turned and stalked out of the kitchen.

Chapter 17

She had not talked to Rob about his mother. Tessa's sense of failure pressed heavily upon her on Monday morning as she tidied up the kitchen.

He hadn't apologised for last night's outburst, but he had been perfectly amiable by morning, and she hadn't wanted to do anything to disturb that fragile equilibrium. If he had been so upset over a little joke, what would his reaction be to the reminder that his mother had . . .

Tessa shuddered; she didn't even want to think about it.

The phone rang and she went to answer it. 'Detective Inspector Tower, Mrs Nicholls,' the caller identified himself. 'Is your husband available?'

'He's gone to work.' Tessa bit off the next part of her retort, which was that it *was* Monday morning, and contented herself with adding, 'Do you have some news, then? Have you made an arrest?'

'We're still pursuing our enquiries.' His words came out sounding like pat police-speak, and it infuriated Tessa.

'Then what do you want Rob for?' she demanded. 'If you have anything to tell him, you can tell *me* and I'll pass it on to him.'

The policeman's voice was patient. 'We just have a few more questions for your husband, Mrs Nicholls. What time do you expect him home tonight?'

'Oh, why can't you just leave him alone?' Tessa fought down panic; if she were too defensive, too hysterical, the policeman would think that she had something to hide. 'My husband did *not* kill his mother,' she stated, rather more calmly. 'Please stop treating him as if he did, and go out and find the murderer.' She put down the phone, and discovered that she was shaking.

Ian, she thought. She needed to talk to Ian, to find out what he knew, and what the police were now on about.

She found Ian's number and reached for the phone, but before she could pick up the receiver it rang.

That policeman again. Tessa snatched up the phone angrily. 'I don't know what time he'll be home,' she announced without preliminaries.

There was a pause at the other end, followed by a tentative female voice. 'Mrs Nicholls?'

Confused, Tessa confirmed her identity. 'Yes, I'm Mrs Nicholls. Sorry – I thought you were someone else.'

'This is Geeta Patel. You wanted to speak to me?'

Geeta Patel? Tessa's brain wasn't working quickly enough. She didn't know a Geeta Patel. 'Did I?' she said.

'Mrs Jessop said that you wanted to speak to me,' the woman repeated patiently. Her voice had a musical foreign lilt.

Mrs Jessop. Geeta. It all came back to her now: the nursing home in Chase View Road. The girl who had worked for Linda Nicholls. 'Oh, yes, of course.'

'I'm back from India now, obviously. And Mrs Jessop told me about . . . well, about the Mrs Nicholls down the road. That she was . . . dead. Are you some relation of hers, then?'

'Her daughter-in-law,' Tessa verified.

'And you'd like to talk to me? About . . . Mrs Nicholls?'

Tessa hesitated. *Did* she want to talk to Geeta Patel? Could she bear it? Her curiosity reared up and got the better of her: of course she wanted to talk to her. 'Yes,' she said. 'But not over the phone.'

'I understand,' Geeta replied. 'And not here, either. I could see you today, on my lunch hour. Shall I meet you at Mrs Nicholls's house?'

She couldn't face it, Tessa discovered. Not now. Not after the last time. 'No, not there. How about the café – the one across from the tube station?'

'Yes, I know it. All right.' They arranged to meet at one o'clock, and Tessa put the phone down.

She went back into the kitchen and made herself a fresh cup of tea, then sat at the kitchen table to drink it. She needed to think.

One thing was suddenly, blindingly clear to her: Linda Nicholls had been murdered by one of her . . . clients. She admitted to herself that she wasn't sure why one of them had murdered her, but it was the only scenario that made sense to her. One of them had killed her: if not the one she had seen – and his surprise and distress at the news of her death had seemed genuine – then one of the others. How many others were there? Who were they?

Geeta Patel was the one with the answers. Perhaps the only one, Tessa said to herself.

That wasn't strictly true, of course, she realised. There was Father Theo, who must know something about it all. Father Theo, who had defended Linda's lifestyle. Yes – he knew all about it, all right. She thought back to their last telephone conversation: she'd told him that she knew about Linda, and he had taken that statement at face value, unaware that at that point she had the wrong end of the stick.

She needed to talk to Father Theo, now that she *did* know the truth. He would be honest with her, give her the answers. But Father Theo was away; he wouldn't be back till tomorrow.

There was, she recalled suddenly, one other person who knew something of the truth about Linda. Someone who had been evasive with her, and no wonder: Greg Reynolds. She thought of tiny Linda and those huge high chairs, not where they belonged in the kitchen but all the way up on the second floor, jumbled into a corner. Linda couldn't possibly have wangled those chairs up two flights of stairs by herself. Who better to help her than muscular Greg, who loved her? Greg, who had lied when he said he knew nothing about what was behind that locked door.

Tessa didn't have Greg's home telephone number – it had been on Linda's speed-dial button. But she did, she recalled, have the number of the gym. On impulse she went and retrieved Linda's keys from her coat pocket and rang the number on the plastic tab.

'Southgate Gym and Fitness Centre. Can I help you?'

'Is Greg Reynolds available?' Tessa queried.

'He's with a client,' the receptionist told her. 'In the middle of a fitness assessment. Can I give him a message? Have him ring you when it's more convenient? Or were you wanting to book an appointment with him for a trial session?'

Perhaps, judged Tessa, it would be better to catch him unawares, with his defences down. She had an inspiration. 'I'd like to book an appointment,' she stated. 'This morning?'

'Certainly.' There was a pause while the receptionist checked the diary. 'Would eleven o'clock suit you? The session will take about an hour.'

'Yes, that's perfect.'

'Wear loose clothing,' the woman advised. 'Something like track suit bottoms and a T-shirt would be suitable. And trainers. What is the name, please?'

Not Nicholls – not if she wanted to catch him unawares. Smoothly Tessa reverted to her maiden name. 'Rowan,' she said. 'Initial, T.'

'Is that Miss or Mrs?'

'Ms,' said Tessa, hand on her bulging abdomen.

She followed the instructions to the letter, dressing in a pair of track suit bottoms which belonged to Rob. It was fortunate, she reflected, that she and her husband were much of a height, as his trousers had just that bit of extra room at the waist to accommodate her bump without restriction. She found a loose, roomy T-shirt in one of her drawers; it bore the logo of a well-known brand of soap powder, one of the accounts she'd worked on during her advertising agency days. Those days seemed a very long time ago, she thought as she pulled it on. And though she wasn't really one to wear trainers, she had a new pair, bought a few weeks earlier when her ankles felt swollen and in need of comfortable support.

The weather was still cold – colder even than it had been at the weekend. Tessa pulled her coat round her and warmed her hands in her pockets as she walked to the tube station, stopping at a cash machine on the way. She had forgotten, she realised, to bring her *A–Z*, and wasn't at all sure she could find the gym without it. Once in Southgate, she decided to splurge on a taxi.

She was glad that she had; though the gym wasn't far from Southgate station, it was off the main road and not immediately visible. And the pre-Christmas crowds were, if anything, worse than the week before.

The fitness centre was a bewildering complex, encompassing a swimming pool, changing rooms, rooms for exercise classes, and – tucked towards the back – the gym. Tessa got directions at the front desk, from the receptionist whose voice she now recognised, and made her way past the pool to the gym. 'Greg will be waiting for you,' she'd been told.

Greg *was* waiting for her, dressed in a sweat suit with the gym's logo emblazoned on his left breast; his brows inched up towards his cropped ginger hair as he saw her, and his eyes dropped to the clipboard in his hand to check the name that was written there. '*You*,' he said. 'But you're not . . .'

'Tessa Rowan was my maiden name,' she told him. 'I needed to talk to you.'

He swallowed hard, his Adam's apple bobbing. 'But I'm

working.' Behind him was an array of exercise bikes and other instruments of torture on which scantily clad and sweaty people laboured away.

'And I'm here for a trial session,' Tessa said firmly. 'We can talk while you show me round.'

Greg hesitated for a few seconds, then thrust the clipboard at her. 'You'll have to fill this form out first. About your medical history, state of health, and so forth, Mrs . . .'

'I told you to call me Tessa,' she reminded him, taking the clipboard. Quickly she went through the form, ticking off various boxes – non-smoker, no known heart conditions – and then scribbled her signature.

'But you *are* pregnant, Mrs . . . Tessa,' Greg pointed out.

'What difference does that make? My midwife says that exercise is good for me.'

'In moderation,' he cautioned. 'And if you're used to it. We don't advise pregnant women to take up a vigorous new exercise programme.'

Tessa wasn't sure whether he was being professionally con-scientious or was just reluctant to talk to her. 'Just show me round,' she repeated. 'I won't do anything too vigorous. I promise.'

He led her across to an unoccupied exercise bike. It was a state-of-the-art model, with a digital control panel which looked as if it would be more at home in the cockpit of a 747. 'Try this for a few minutes,' he suggested, pushing several buttons to set it up to run with the lightest possible resistance.

Tessa climbed up on the seat and began pedalling. 'Now,' she said, in a loud voice to make herself heard over the insistent thump of the rock music which blared through an amplifier. 'I have a few things I need to ask you about.'

Nervously Greg looked over his shoulder at the other in-habitants of the gym. None of them was paying a blind bit of notice to the tall young woman on the bike, each one locked in a private world of straining muscles and glistening sweat. 'All right.'

'You lied to me,' she stated flatly.

'Did I?' His voice was defensive; he wouldn't meet her eyes.

'You said that you'd never been into the room at the top of the stairs,' Tessa reminded him. 'That was a lie. You know perfectly well what's in that room.'

Still he didn't look at her. His tongue worked along the bottom edge of his thick auburn moustache. 'And what if I do?'

'Listen, Greg.' Something in Tessa's voice forced him to turn his head and meet her eyes. 'I've been in that room. I've seen . . . everything. The cots, the high chairs. I know that Linda was fit – you've said so. But she was a small woman. She could never have moved all that stuff on her own. The high chairs weren't there normally, were they? You moved them up from the kitchen.'

Again he swallowed, but Tessa could see the relief on his face, mingled with defensiveness. Greg Reynolds was not a man who enjoyed lying. 'Before you and your husband came for tea. The night before. I *did* tell you that I helped her to get ready before you came,' he reminded her. 'She didn't want you to see them, of course. So I carried them up to the . . . the room upstairs. That was a job, I can tell you,' he added with a heartfelt sigh. 'They're jolly heavy.'

'To the nursery,' Tessa stated baldly, continuing to pedal. She looked down at the gauge which showed how far she'd gone, no longer able to bear the expression in those sad eyes. 'Greg,' she went on, 'I know what Linda did. You don't have to pretend. I know about . . . those men. The . . . babies.'

Greg was silent for a moment, as if deciding how to reply. 'She only did it for the money,' he said at last. 'She didn't enjoy it. But she needed to make a living.' He paused, chewing on his moustache. 'I know that makes her sound like some sort of tart. But it wasn't like that at all. There was nothing . . . like that. You know. It was just a job, like any other job.'

'Not exactly like any other job,' Tessa shot back acidly. 'It's not something you usually see in the "Sits. Vac." adverts: "Mummy wanted – must be good at changing nappies".'

Greg flinched. 'Okay. So it was a bit . . . weird. I'll admit that.'

'*You* weren't one of the babies, were you?'

He stared at her in horror. 'Me? No way! I told you before – I was her boyfriend. Her *only* boyfriend. And nothing else.'

'But you knew about it.'

'Linda told me, yes,' he admitted. 'She trusted me.'

'And she found you useful.' Tessa's words came out raggedly; she was beginning to feel tired already. Was she *that* out of shape? With wonder she looked round at the other inhabitants of the gym. A skinny woman in a brief Lycra top and shorts had been pumping madly away on the Stairmaster since Tessa's arrival; she seemed almost in a trance, her eyes glazed over, not even breaking her rhythm as she wiped the sweat from her face with a limp towel. Nearby an overweight man walked on a treadmill, his arms swinging at his sides, his grey T-shirt damp with perspiration. Someone else whizzed back and forth on a rowing machine, eyes intent on a display screen, grunting with the effort at each stroke.

Greg leaned over the bike's digital display and pushed the stop button. 'I think you've had enough of this.'

'I'm not finished talking to you.' Winded, Tessa climbed off the bike. She didn't really fancy having a go on the other cardiovascular equipment, but she certainly wasn't going to let Greg fob her off at this point.

'Let's go into the weight training room,' he suggested. The volume of the music in the back room was not quite so loud, but the machines looked, if anything, more sinister and for-bidding – more like updated, state-of-the-art versions of mediaeval instruments of torture. A muscle-bound giant of a man worked his biceps on one machine; a fat woman exercised her thighs on another. 'Here,' said Greg, indicating a vinyl seat, flanked by two widespread white wings, like some giant bird. 'Sit here.'

Tessa sat and followed Greg's instructions, grasping the handles on the white wings and pulling them together till they met in front of her. She picked up the conversation where she'd left it. 'Linda found you useful.'

He didn't deny it. 'I helped her when I could. With the equipment, mostly.'

'Did you help her with the . . . babies?'

Again he looked horrified. 'Not me. I kept well away from there at weekends.'

She believed him; his horror was genuine. Disappointed, Tessa tried to think of what else she might ask him. But it was difficult to concentrate on anything but the torture she was now inflicting on herself: her arms felt, after just a few strokes, as if they were going to fall off. Abruptly she let go of the handles and the machine's wings flew back with a clang. 'Sorry,' she said. 'I suppose you're right – this isn't the time for me to be taking up an exercise programme.'

Greg sighed, relieved. 'Perhaps later, after you've had your baby,' he said perfunctorily, and started for the door.

Tessa remained seated, forcing him to come back to her. 'Can't you tell me anything else, then?' she appealed to him. 'She must have talked to you about them – about those men. Who were they?'

Reluctantly he nodded. 'She talked about them sometimes. Laughed about them, really. About how ridiculous they were, and how much they were willing to pay for . . .' He stopped, as if embarrassed, then went on, 'But she only ever talked about them by their baby names. So I don't know who they were. Baby Mimi, Baby Dulcie. That sort of thing – that's all I know.'

Again, Tessa believed that he was telling her the truth. Carefully she framed her next question. 'Has it ever occurred to you that one of them might have killed her?'

Greg's eyes slewed away from hers. 'No,' he said. 'Why would they want to do that? And what difference does it make?' he added. 'She's dead. That's all that matters.'

For the first time that morning, Tessa had the feeling that Greg was not being entirely truthful, that he was trying to evade her prying questions, that he knew more than he was saying. Why, though, would he lie to protect one of them? 'Don't you *want* to know who killed Linda?' she demanded with some asperity.

As if secure in his own innocence, he shook his head, lifting his muscular shoulders in a shrug. 'Not really,' he said. 'Knowing who killed her won't bring her back.' He paused, then added deliberately, 'I'd leave well alone, if I were you.'

Tessa had plenty of time in hand before she had to meet Geeta for lunch, so she walked back towards the town centre, too wrapped up in her own thoughts to be aware of the cold. Leave well alone, indeed. How could she? Whether she wanted to be or not, she was involved.

Was Greg hiding something? Protecting someone? Tessa still didn't believe that he'd had anything to do with Linda's death, but that didn't mean he was being completely truthful about what he knew. And something that he'd said – she couldn't remember what it was – nagged at the edge of her mind like a sore tooth. Something that might have been important, if only she could remember . . .

Reaching the town centre, she called into the bookshop and found the book she wanted for Helena's Christmas gift. She would have liked to have spent a few minutes chatting with the shop's owner, but he was busy; several people were clamouring for his attention, requiring recommendations for their child's teacher or their mother-in-law who only read Catherine Cookson but had read them all.

Perhaps, Tessa decided, she would just go on to the café and wait for Geeta there with a warming cup of coffee.

On the way, though, she passed the estate agent's office, and a memory of Friday afternoon assailed her like a blow to the stomach. The estate agent had been planning to go to the house to measure up. She had thought, indeed, that he was in the house doing just that, when she had made her horrifying discovery.

She had, she remembered now, rushed from the house without a thought to the consequences. *Had* he visited the house, armed with the key she'd given him? If so, what – dear God, *what*? – had he found there?

Tessa took a deep, bracing breath and pushed the door open, stepping into a fug of smoke.

Looking up from his desk and putting down his cigarette, the estate agent pasted on his patented smile. 'Mrs Nicholls,' he greeted her, his pride at remembering her name evident. 'What can I do for you today? Looking for a property for yourself and your husband, perhaps?'

She tried to keep her voice neutral. 'I wondered whether you'd been round to the house in Chase View Road to measure up.'

His smile didn't falter. 'Not yet, Mrs Nicholls. Bit of a rush on Friday afternoon. And the couple who had said that they wanted to look at your property found something else. Not to worry, though,' he added heartily. 'We'll soon sell your property for yourselves. It's in a highly desirable area of the town. Properties in Chase View Road rarely come on the market, and they don't last long.'

'Oh, there's no hurry,' Tessa said, edging back towards the door.

'I'll go round there this afternoon, or tomorrow at the latest,' he promised. 'As soon as the details are ready, I'll pop a copy in the post to yourselves. Did I understand from Mr Nicholls,' he added, 'that carpets and curtains are to be included in the sale?'

Tessa didn't know what Rob had told this man, but that seemed to make sense. 'Yes, I suppose so.'

'And he mentioned that the property was furnished, and that you might be willing to sell the contents as well, if the buyer was interested.'

A bubble of laughter, almost of hysteria, rose in Tessa's throat at the ludicrous thought of someone – knowingly or unknowingly – buying the contents of Linda's nursery; she bit her lip and covered her mouth with her hand. Perhaps, she thought, it ought to go on the details: a business opportunity. 'I'm . . . not sure about that,' she said, controlling her voice with some difficulty.

The estate agent didn't seem to notice. He took a puff of his cigarette and blew the smoke in Tessa's direction with a reassuring smile. 'That can all be sorted out later.'

Tessa had managed to reach the door. 'Thank you,' she said, making her escape.

He hadn't been in the house yet: that was the important thing. She stood on the pavement for a moment, debating what she should do.

She had not intended going back to the house in Chase View Road. Not today, not ever. But unless she wanted the estate agent to find the evidence of Linda's source of income, she had little choice.

Taking a deep breath, she headed in the direction of Chase View Road. She *could* do it, she told herself bracingly. She had to do it. She had to lock that door.

Tessa wasn't even sure what had happened to the key. Her last coherent memory was of opening the door. What had she done with the key? It wasn't in her pocket with the rest of Linda's keys; she could only hope that she had left it in the lock, and that no one else had taken it.

That awful man in the pink frock. Surely he wouldn't have taken the key.

She'd left the house in such a rush – she had left him there on his own.

Steeling herself, Tessa let herself in the front door and

went straight up the stairs to the second floor. The door of the nursery stood open; the key was indeed in the lock where she'd left it. Firmly she pulled the door closed and turned the key, dropping it in her pocket.

In spite of the detour, Tessa arrived at the café before the appointed time. Rather than wait outside for Geeta, she hurried in, thankful for the warmth. The windows were steamed up on the inside, the café crowded with shoppers lingering over their elevenses and workers getting an early start on their lunch hours. Tessa ordered a coffee at the counter, then waited a moment until a pair of shoppers gathered up their bags desultorily and abandoned their table She claimed it straight away and settled down to wait.

The hot coffee revived her; she cupped her hands round the mug to warm them, watching the door.

Geeta was prompt, arriving just at the time she had promised; Tessa spotted her straight away as she came through the door, looking round uncertainly. Afraid of losing her table, she stood to beckon the girl over.

'You must be Geeta,' she said.

'Mrs Nicholls?'

Tessa nodded. 'Please, sit down. And you can call me Tessa,' she added.

'Thank you,' Geeta said, smiling. Her smile was friendly, not at all shy, but she seemed possessed of a sort of dignity which set her apart from the other young women, not far from her age, who clustered around tables in groups, joking and chatting.

And, Tessa observed, Geeta was beautiful: not just attractive, but beautiful, in a very natural and unselfconscious way. Her heavy black hair was long, pulled back and secured to the back of her head with a large butterfly clip, and her eyes were huge, fringed with lashes as dark as the eyes themselves. She had a wonderful complexion, which, due to the colour of her skin, could not be described as porcelain or peaches̶ it was more, thought Tessa enviously, like sunbak̶ terracotta, rich and warm and fresh.

After she'd sat down, the girl pulled off her gloves and rubbed the palms of her hands together. 'I'm freezing,' she said. 'I've just got back from India, and I'm not used to the cold.' Her voice was charmingly accented, with a pleasing deep timbre.

'Would you like to order some lunch?' Tessa suggested. 'Some soup, perhaps?'

A waitress appeared to take their order, announcing that the soup of the day was split pea with ham. 'That sounds marvellous,' Tessa said. 'I'll have a bowl. How about you?'

'I'm vegetarian,' Geeta said, not apologising but stating a fact. 'I think I'll have a toasted cheese sandwich. And a pot of tea straight away, please.'

The waitress departed, and Geeta leaned back in her chair, smiling across the table at Tessa. 'Now. You wanted to see me?'

Faced with this self-possessed and astonishingly beautiful young woman, Tessa found herself at a loss to know how to begin. 'I understand that you ... knew ... my mother-in-law,' she said cautiously.

'Mrs Nicholls? Yes, of course.' That was all; she waited for the next question.

This wasn't going to be easy, Tessa realised, reminded of her first conversation with Greg Reynolds in this same café. 'I was told that you worked for her.'

Geeta nodded. 'Just part-time, the odd few hours each week. When I wasn't working at Jessop House.'

How could she ask the next question? Tessa plunged ahead. 'First of all, I want you to know that I am aware of what my mother-in-law's business was. I know about ... those men. The ... babies. But I was hoping that you could shed a bit of light on it all for me.'

'What do you want to know?' Geeta asked calmly.

What, exactly, *did* she want to know? How much could she bear to hear? She would start with the peripheral details – the ones that might have a bearing on the matter of who had murdered Linda Nicholls. 'Were they the same men all of the time? Or different ones? How many of them were there altogether?'

'Mostly the same ones,' Geeta said. 'One or two of them have been – *had* been, I suppose I should say – coming for years. Or at least so I understand – I'd only been working there for about two years myself. Most weekends there were four or five of them. They came on Friday, always. Sometimes they would leave on the Saturday, and sometimes on the Sunday. They never came during the week.' Her pot of tea arrived; she thanked the waitress, then she expanded a bit. 'I would go in at weekends and give Mrs Nicholls a hand. And sometimes, when I could, I would put in a few hours earlier in the week – helping out with the laundry and things like that. There were always plenty of linens to be washed.' Geeta smiled. 'Sheets, mostly. And nappies, of course.'

Nappies. 'They didn't bring their own, then?' Tessa asked weakly, half in jest.

Geeta gave her a serious answer. 'Some of them did. But others couldn't, because someone would find out – wives and things like that. Nappies were an optional extra, Mrs Nicholls said. She could provide them if required.'

'The men had *wives*? They were *married*?'

'Not all of them. But one or two were.' Geeta poured her tea. 'They talked to me, the men did. One of them, Baby Mimi, was always going on about his wife. Felicity, she was called. And he had kids, as well.'

Tessa massaged her forehead. It was all so difficult to take in, to visualise. 'So apart from helping with the laundry,' she blurted, 'what exactly did you *do*?' That sounded awful, she realised as soon as she'd said it. 'I'm sorry,' she apologised. 'You don't have to answer that.'

'It doesn't matter. I don't mind talking about it.' Geeta took a sip of her tea and smiled wryly. 'It wasn't all that different from working at the nursing home, in fact. Changing nappies, feeding people. And talking to them, listening to them talk. That's what I do all day at Jessop House. And that's what I did at weekends for Mrs Nicholls. The only difference, really, was that the babies were there voluntarily, that they *wanted* to be looked after. That,' she added, 'and the fact that they liked to drink everything, even their tea, out of baby bottles.'

'So what did *they* do all weekend?' Tessa blurted. 'The babies, I mean? How did they spend their time?'

Geeta shrugged. 'About how you would expect. They played in the play-pen, with the toys. Rode on the rocking horse. Sometimes Mrs Nicholls – the other Mrs Nicholls, Mummy Linda – would read them stories. They had their meals in the kitchen, in the high chairs. And believe me,' she added, 'feeding them all at one go was a real challenge. They slept in the nursery, in their cots.' She drank a bit more tea and went on, 'But they didn't just do baby things all of the time. Sometimes they would read the papers, or watch the telly. One or two of them really liked to watch sport on telly – *Grandstand* on a Saturday afternoon was very popular. And they'd have beer in their baby bottles for that.'

It was all so matter-of-fact. Tessa felt her gorge rising, and regretted that she had ordered the soup. Just now she didn't feel like eating anything.

As if sensing Tessa's revulsion, Geeta went on, 'I didn't mind it at all. I wasn't being exploited or anything. Mrs Nicholls paid me quite well. And the babies . . . well, they're really quite sweet, when you get to know them.'

The one she'd encountered had *not* been sweet: he'd been terrifying. 'I saw one of them,' Tessa told her, swallowing hard. 'He needed a shave. Thin lips, greasy hair. A pink frock.'

'Oh,' Geeta nodded in recognition, 'that would be Baby Priscilla.'

'Baby Priscilla!'

'Most of them have girls' names,' Geeta explained. 'And they dress like girls as well. All except for Baby Buddy – he's a boy.'

Tessa couldn't understand how Geeta could treat the whole matter so calmly. 'Don't you find them . . . well, frightening?'

Geeta shook her head. 'They're absolutely harmless,' she assured her. 'And they're not hurting anyone. So why should I be frightened of them?'

The waitress brought their food. Geeta attacked her sandwich with enthusiasm, and Tessa discovered that she had an appetite after all. The soup was good; they ate in silence for a few minutes.

All the while, though, Tessa was thinking. Harmless? she asked herself. If they were so harmless, why was she so positive that one of them had killed Linda?

There were no records in Linda's office; whichever one had killed her, he had taken them, had made sure that he couldn't be traced. The police didn't even know that these men existed.

Suddenly she knew that there was only one way to approach this. 'How can I find them?' she asked Geeta with urgency. 'I need to talk to them.'

But Geeta shook her head and shrugged. 'I can't help you, I'm afraid,' she said. 'I only know them by their baby names: Baby Priscilla, Baby Dulcie, Baby Mimi, Baby Sharon, Baby Buddy. That's not going to get you very far, is it?'

Chapter 18

Father Theo travelled back from Yorkshire very early on Tuesday morning, long before it was light. He'd been meant to leave on Monday, but when Monday came he'd found that he wasn't yet ready to go: he couldn't bear to tear himself away from the soothing rhythms of the monastic day before it was absolutely necessary. So on Monday night he had packed his bag, and after the first Office on Tuesday had made his way to catch the early train from Wakefield to King's Cross.

The train was surprisingly crowded. Were there really, he wondered, people who lived in Yorkshire and worked in London? But he didn't spend much time pondering that question; he found himself a window seat, slung his holdall on to the overhead rack, and settled down, looking out of the window.

No matter what he wore in private, Father Theo always wore his clericals in public, believing that his identity as a priest was the most important thing – the defining thing – about him. He had found, over the years, that wearing a clerical collar had one of two effects on other people: either they avoided him as though he had some rampant communicable disease, or they were drawn to him, in search of a sympathetic ear. On the train up to Yorkshire on Friday he had encountered the latter: a young man who had approached him with a tentative, 'Vicar? Is this seat taken?', and had sat next to him for the entire journey, pouring out his heart. Father Theo had always found such random encounters to be meaningful; he felt privileged to be in a position where he could help other people, and saw in such meetings the evidence of the grace of God at work. He would never, as some of his fellow clergy did, travel 'incognito', hoping for a bit of peace and quiet. That would be cheating, denying his identity, thwarting the work of God.

Still, though, he was selfishly relieved when his seat-mate on this journey turned out to be someone who didn't want to talk to him. The woman had, in fact, after one dubious look at him, fallen asleep as soon as the train pulled out of the station, and snored gently beside him as he watched the dark shapes and occasional lights flash past the window.

Father Theo had much to think about. His weekend had been wonderful: all he had hoped for, and more.

He had been fortunate in the man who had served as his counsellor and confessor. Father Bernard represented the best that Mirfield had to offer: theologically rigorous, intellectually gifted, and thoroughly human. The old monk had listened to Father Theo for hours, and had told him exactly what he'd needed to hear.

It had, of course, taken quite a few of those hours for Father Theo to get to the point, to be able to verbalise the exact nature of his problem. He was so embarrassed, so ashamed; even with the old monk's wise eyes encouraging him, he'd been unable to bring himself to spell it out.

When he had finally done so, sweating and on the verge of tears, Father Bernard hadn't even raised his eyebrows.

'Tell me,' said Father Bernard. 'Who are you hurting when you do this thing?'

Startled, Father Theo had shaken his head. 'I don't know.'

'This woman – this Linda. She did this voluntarily? No coercion was involved?'

Father Theo had agreed that this was so.

'And you never neglected your parish duties? Let down your parishioners?'

Again, Father Theo had affirmed this. 'It was only ever on my day off.'

'Then you've been hurting no one. No one but yourself, and that only because you've inflicted so much pain and guilt on yourself. Let go of it – the pain and the guilt. Give it all over to God.'

That was when Father Theo had cried: he had wept for what seemed like hours. Healing, cleansing tears, scouring him out. Leaving him drained, but free.

Now he felt wonderful. He had gone to Yorkshire hoping to be 'cured' of his compulsion, only to have received an even better gift than that. It was as if a boil which had been festering for years had been lanced at last: the lancing was painful for a moment, and unpleasant as the poison came out, but only with that lancing could the healing come. The healing, and with it the realisation of just how debilitating – and unnecessary – the boil had been. He could have got rid of it years ago; it had always been within his power – with God's help – to do so. That, now, was his only sorrow: that he had carried this burden for so long when he need not have done so.

There was nothing wrong with him. The words echoed in his brain, over and over, in time with the clacking of the wheels on the track. *There is nothing wrong with me*. He was not horrible, sick, depraved. He was only a man who had found a way – albeit a way that most people would find unacceptable – to meet his psychological needs. No worse than people who got their kicks from chasing a little ball round a golf course or sticking stamps in an album in their leisure time. And better than people whose needs drove them to over-eat or take drugs or gamble or drink themselves into an alcoholic stupor: better, because he was hurting no one.

Father Theo believed in sin – he was aware that it was

unfashionable to do so, but he did. Now he knew that the sin was not in what he had done, but in the extent to which he had allowed it to come between him and God.

The important thing – the huge hurdle – was in realising this, and shedding the guilt. The guilt was gone, and in some miraculous, mysterious way, Father Theo felt that the compulsion itself had disappeared with it.

There was only one tiny thing that was worrying him, and his consciousness of it grew as the train drew nearer to London.

Tessa. Little Tessa was coming to see him this morning. Though he wasn't at all sure, he thought, smiling to himself, why he thought of her as 'little' Tessa, when she was at least half a head taller than he. Nor was she, he realised, as fragile as he tended to picture her: no, she'd had to be pretty tough, with a strong core that could bend and not break, to have survived the things that had happened to her in the past few months. Her mother-in-law's murder – finding the body herself, even; making all of the funeral plans without any help from her husband; coming to terms with the death of a woman whom she'd been prepared to regard as a second mother, and dealing with that complicated double bereavement. So much for a young woman to bear. And from what he'd heard in the past from Linda about her son – moody, difficult, unpredictable Robin Nicholls – he didn't imagine that being married to that young man was exactly a bed of roses, even for a woman in love.

And now yet another blow: discovering what Linda's line of work had been. Father Theo couldn't help feeling that Rob could have spared her that knowledge, that it was cruel of him to have told her, that it was unnecessary now that Linda was dead.

Now it was going to be up to him to try to help Tessa to make sense of it. He had already tried to explain, in their phone conversation, what had motivated Linda and driven her to make the choices she'd made. And he wasn't just making excuses for Linda, either: even when he'd hated himself for going to Linda's, he hadn't blamed her. She was just doing her job, and doing it well. Making people happy, bringing some sort of pleasure into their lives.

He could understand why Tessa might feel differently about it: in the abstract, it sounded disgusting, inexplicable. He had to convince her, somehow, that it wasn't really like that.

And still, though he had now come to accept and forgive his own involvement in it, he didn't want Tessa to know about that. He was very fond of Tessa; he felt they had developed a real rapport, and that she trusted and liked him. But that relationship was too new, too tenuous, for him to risk ruining it by confessing to her what part Linda had played in his life. She wouldn't understand; he wouldn't be able to explain it to her as Father Bernard had explained it to him. After all, it had taken him years to understand, to come to terms with it. She would be disgusted; she would recoil from him. The knowledge would destroy her trust, their friendship. He was sure of this. Much as he would have liked to be honest with her, as he had enjoined her to be honest with him, he just didn't feel that he could take the risk.

As the first blush of pink sunrise began to glow on the eastern horizon, throwing the bare trees into stark black relief and heralding the arrival of the shortest day of the year, he remembered something which had been thrust to the back of his mind since Friday morning: Tessa had told him that no records had been found in Linda's house. No list of her clients, no names and addresses: nothing. He had been disbelieving when Tessa had told him, but with the earnest young man on the train, and all that had happened at the weekend, he hadn't had time to examine this discrepancy, or its implications. Father Theo wasn't sure why it made him so uneasy, but it did.

The train arrived at King's Cross a few minutes late; Father Theo realised, looking at his watch, that by taking the bus he would be cutting it close to get home in time for Tessa's visit.

He decided to be extravagant and took a taxi, arriving with a comfortable margin of ten minutes. That gave him time to stop off at the church to offer up his prayers of thanks, to light a candle in front of his beloved Virgin and Child statue.

Tessa was already there, in the church, gazing at the statue. She turned at the sound of his footsteps. 'Oh! Father Theo. I got here a few minutes early, and decided to come in the church.'

'Hello, my dear.' They stood together for a moment, contemplating the Virgin and Child, neither feeling the necessity to speak. It was bitterly cold in the church; the heating hadn't been on for two days, and in any case the antiquated radiators did little to remove the chill from that brick barn of a building, warming only those fortunate enough to be within a few feet of them.

Tessa stamped her feet to warm them, and Father Theo, realising that they were both freezing, suggested that they should retreat to the comparative warmth of the clergy house.

She was reluctant to leave. 'Can't we stay here just a bit longer? Walk about, perhaps?'

'All right,' he acquiesced. They moved round the perimeter of the church, looking at the Stations of the Cross without seeing them, as they talked.

Tessa scarcely knew where to begin: there were so many unanswered questions to which only Father Theo could provide the answers. 'You've known all along about Linda's . . . work,' she stated, trying not to sound accusing. 'Why didn't you tell me?'

His reply came out in an icy cloud. 'I didn't think that you needed to know. Linda was dead. What good could it do for you to rake all that up?' But who, he asked himself with painful honesty, was he trying to protect: Tessa, or himself? 'You didn't know her,' he went on. 'I didn't think that you would be able to understand the . . . context. It all sounds pretty strange in the abstract.' .

She didn't disagree. 'Tell me about the context, then. Make me understand it. You've already given me some explanation for Linda's behaviour – she needed the money, she had a house to keep up and a child to look after. I can just about accept that.' Could she? she wondered as she said it. 'But those *men*. The babies. Why?'

Father Theo had been afraid that she would ask him something like this. He thought back to the wise words of Father Bernard, and tried to explain. 'All of us have certain . . . needs, Tessa. We need food and water and shelter and air to breathe. Most people think we need sex,' he added with a wry smile, 'though some of us manage to do without it, through our own choice or through circumstance.' He searched for the right words. 'But our needs don't end with the physical. We have psychological needs as well. Most importantly of all, we need love and affection. And that is our earliest, most basic need.'

They had come all the way round the nave; he stopped again by the statue of the Virgin and Child. 'Our mothers,' he said simply. 'From the time of our birth, they satisfy our needs. They feed us, they keep us warm. If they didn't do those things, we would die. And in an ideal world, they fulfil our psychological needs as well: they cuddle us, rock us to sleep. They give us our first and most unselfish experience of love.'

Tessa's cold hands went to her abdomen, unconsciously cradling her baby. 'Yes,' she nodded. 'I see that.'

'Sometimes, though, something goes wrong,' Father Theo went on. 'Sometimes a mother *doesn't* love her baby. Perhaps she didn't want it to begin with. Maybe there is another more favoured child, before or after. Or too many children already for her to be able to lavish attention on the newcomer. Or,' he added, swallowing painfully, 'she might die. And when this happens, the child grows up with something missing. With a basic, essential need unfulfilled. Are you following me, Tessa?'

She looked at the statue rather than at him. 'Yes.'

'Some people never really recover from this. They spend their lives searching for what they missed out on. Some of them are lucky – they find nurturing relationships later on, spouses or partners who will give them that unconditional love. But others don't have that. Sometimes, in fact,' he added, 'because they never received enough love from their mothers, they are unable to give it to anyone else. It cripples their adult relationships.'

'Go on,' Tessa said.

'So the men who found Linda were, in a way, some of the lucky ones. What Linda was doing was providing a way to fulfil those needs. Belatedly, and perhaps in a way that most people would find unacceptable, but the important thing was that she wasn't just making them happy. It wasn't just a game, Tessa. On a very deep level, she was meeting their needs.'

Tessa was silent, staring at the statue. He wondered whether he'd said too much; whether he had, in fact, betrayed himself by his intimate knowledge.

But she was just trying to take it all in, to fit it into her picture of the world. 'It just seems . . . *wrong*,' she said at last. 'Weird. Kinky, even. I'm surprised that you can defend it.'

He took a deep breath and went a step further. 'Wrong for whom? For Linda, or for the men?'

'Both, I suppose.'

'As I said, she was meeting their needs. Even if it was a rather unconventional way of doing it. And,' he added, echoing Father Bernard's words, 'who were they hurting? No one.'

It was, Tessa recalled, exactly what Geeta had said. They weren't hurting anyone. But Linda? 'Wouldn't you say that Linda was exploiting them?'

Father Theo winced; that was a bit close to the bone. 'She was meeting their needs,' he repeated. 'And she had to make a living.' He stamped his frozen feet. 'Let's go to the clergy house and have some tea,' he said abruptly, hoping that he had answered all of Tessa's questions to her satisfaction and the subject could now be dropped.

They had their tea in the snugness of his study, a cosy fire burning in the grate, but Tessa was not ready to abandon the subject. Though she felt that she was beginning to have some understanding of the set-up in Chase View Road, that still left so many questions unanswered. She was more than ever convinced that the absence of records was significant, and had a direct bearing on Linda's murder. When they had warmed up a bit, and Father Theo had relaxed, she pressed on. 'I mentioned to you the other day that there were no records in Linda's house,' she said. 'Don't you think that's strange?'

The priest tensed. 'What do you make of it?' he asked guardedly.

They were both sitting on the sofa, a little distance apart. Alerted by the change in his tone of voice, Tessa turned to look at him. 'Someone murdered Linda,' she said baldly. 'I think it was one of . . . them. One of the babies. And I think that whoever it was, after he killed her, he took her records, cleaned out her files, to cover his tracks. So the police wouldn't know about the babies, and wouldn't be able to trace him. Why else would someone have taken her files?'

Father Theo gasped; the colour drained from his face.

Tessa could see the effect that her words had on him, and she pressed on. 'What I *don't* understand is *why*. Why one of them would have killed her, when she was, as you put it, meeting their needs. There must be a reason, a motive. And I think you can help me to find out.'

Involuntarily he closed his eyes. *Did* she suspect his involvement? He played for time. 'But why is it so important for you to . . . well, to get involved? Wouldn't it be better to leave well alone, to let the police get on with doing their job?'

Tired of having people telling her to leave well alone, Tessa spoke with passion. 'The police don't know about the babies.

Someone – the murderer – has made sure of that. I'm positive
that they think that Rob had something to do with it, and they
won't leave him alone as long as they don't have any other suspects. I can't allow that to happen – I can't just stand by and
see my husband hounded. I have to do something about it.'

Father Theo nodded in acknowledgement. He knew that
he should tell her to inform the police about the babies, to
allow things to take their course, but he couldn't quite bring
himself to say those words. If the police knew . . . And there
was, he acknowledged to himself, truth in what she'd said. If,
indeed, those records were missing, it strongly suggested that
one of them was involved. Just as, he admitted, he had always
suspected. With trepidation he asked, 'Why do you think that
I can help you?'

'Because you knew Linda,' Tessa stated. 'She trusted you,
obviously. She talked to you, confided in you.' She reached
out and touched his hand. 'Think about it, please. For me.
Can you remember anything at all that would have a bearing
on this? Did she ever tell you that she'd had a row with one of
them for some reason? Or do you have any idea who any
of them were? Baby Priscilla, Baby Dulcie, Baby Buddy –
whatever the rest of them were called? Would it be possible
to track them down, even without her records? Then I would
have something to take the police. Something concrete that I
could give them.'

Profoundly and unexpectedly moved by the light touch
of her fingers as well as by her words, the priest got up and
walked behind his desk. He needed time to think.

There was no way that he could help her without revealing
the truth about himself. That was the one thing he had vowed
not to do, the one final piece of knowledge that he wanted to
spare her.

But her logic was impeccable. It seemed obvious to him, as
it had from the beginning, that one of them had killed her;
the disappearance of the records confirmed that.

There was another reason, though, why he didn't want to confront the truth of that head-on. He knew of a very good motive for the murder – a motive that all of them had in common. But to acknowledge it would be to face some facts about Linda which he had heretofore managed to suppress in his subconscious. In his grief over her death, and in his love for her, he had submerged the negative aspects of the hold that she had over all of them.

And if he shared all this with Tessa, confessed all that was unspoken and unthought . . . what then? Where would she go – *they* go – from there?

She was watching him with her clear grey eyes. She trusted him. How could he tell her these things which would, perhaps for ever, destroy her respect for him?

He couldn't tell her. It was impossible. Father Theo paced behind his desk, trying not to think about those trusting grey eyes fixed on him. But when he looked at her again, involuntarily, he saw that she was gazing now at the statue: at his Virgin and Child.

That did it. He had to tell her, no matter what the consequences. 'Tessa,' he said softly. 'My dear . . .'

Something in his voice warned her; with a shiver of premonition she turned to him. 'What is it?'

Father Theo couldn't bear to look at her. He turned his back and looked out of the window towards the church. 'I hoped I wouldn't have to tell you this,' he said. 'But there is something else. I'm one of them.'

Tessa could feel herself go rigid with shock. 'You mean . . .'

'I'm one of the babies. I'm Baby Dulcie. That's how I knew Linda. You thought, I'm sure, that it had something to do with the church, but that wasn't it at all.'

Still not looking at her, Father Theo crossed the room and knelt at his prayer desk, raising his eyes to the Virgin and Child. Taking his time, he told her the whole story, in detail. How his mother had died when he was very young, leaving

him in the care of an undemonstrative and apparently un-
loving father. How he had always felt the lack of a mother,
had always felt that something was missing from his life, felt
that he wasn't like other children in some way. How, as an
adult, he had developed a fascination with nappies, keeping
one in his bottom drawer to be fondled with guilty pleasure,
though he had never got as far as wearing it. How one day
he had, in a newsagent's shop in Soho, stumbled upon
a magazine which catered for people with his particular
fixation; how he had bought the magazine, amazed to
discover that he was not the only person in the world who felt
as he did. How, in the classified section in the back of that
very magazine he had found the advert that had changed
his life: 'Do you need to be babied? Mummy Linda, North
London'. How, after weeks of agonised turmoil, he had rung
the number, gone for his first visit. How from the start he
had known that Mummy Linda was exactly what he had been
looking for. How with the pleasure and the satisfaction had
come the guilt, the shame. How he had striven with himself
to stop, had promised himself each time that it would be the
last time, but all in vain. How he had hidden his compulsion
from everyone, keeping his baby things locked in the bottom
drawer away from the prying eyes of Mrs Williams. How he
had learned, with shock and sorrow, of Linda's death. How
he had brought himself to phone her, Tessa, and how glad he
was that he had done so. Finally, how he had gone to Yorkshire
in search of some sort of resolution, and how he felt that he
had found it.

Tessa listened to it all numbly, her eyes closed and her
hands folded over her abdomen. Now that the truth was out,
she discovered that on one level she wasn't entirely surprised.
He had told her before about his mother's death; he had
explained the psychological compulsion behind the babies'
activities with compassion and understanding. She knew that
she should be feeling revulsion towards Father Theo, as she

had towards Baby Priscilla, but it was too late for that: she cared too much about him.

When he had finished his recital, there was a long moment of silence, punctuated only by the traffic noise from outside and the gentle crackle of the fire. Tessa spoke first. 'It doesn't matter,' she said quietly. 'Thank you for telling me. I suppose you thought that I'd hate you if I knew. But it doesn't matter. I'm glad that I know the truth.'

'Oh, my dear!' At last Father Theo turned to look at her, and his eyes were filled with tears. The telling of the tale, for the second time in just a few days, had exhausted him emotionally, especially since, as with the first time, he had been unsure of what the listener's response would be. Now his sense of relief and release was as great as it had been with Father Bernard: perhaps even greater, as he had more at stake in personal terms. Tessa's generous response overwhelmed him. He went and sat beside her on the sofa, taking her hand. 'Thank you,' he said simply.

After a moment he roused himself to go on. 'But that's not all, I'm afraid. I haven't told you everything.'

'There's still the question of *why* one of them . . . one of you . . . would want to kill her,' Tessa said. 'You know something about that, don't you?'

Father Theo bowed his head. 'Yes. And this is just as difficult to tell you.' He paused, then went on in a different tone of voice, affirmative rather than apologetic. 'I *loved* Linda, you know. And what she did . . . well, it didn't make me love her any less. You need to understand that. She was human, like any of the rest of us. She had her faults, she wasn't perfect. I'm not trying to excuse her. But I loved her.'

'What did she *do*?' Tessa demanded impatiently, sure that she was on the verge of a breakthrough in her understanding of her mother-in-law and the circumstances that had led to her murder.

'It had to do with money,' the priest said at last. 'We all

paid very well for our weekends, and that was fair enough –
there was all of the food, and the lodging and so forth. And
the extras like nappies, for people like me who couldn't bring
their own. But a few months ago . . .' he paused, gathering
strength to go on. 'A few months ago there started to be more
extra charges. Substantial ones. Crippling, even, for people
like me who aren't on a large income. And when we asked
Linda about it, she would say things about how important it
was for all of us that no one should find out about what we did
at weekends.'

'Blackmail!' Tessa gasped.

'That is a crude word for it,' he said painfully. 'But yes. It
was blackmail, in a sense. There was always the implied threat
that if we didn't pay, we might be found out. None of us could
risk it, of course. Our careers were at stake, and in some cases
there were families involved as well – Baby Mimi has a wife
and children, Baby Buddy has a sister. So we paid up, one way
and another. We all found the money somehow.'

Tessa took a deep breath as the implications of this sank in.
'So you think that was the motive.'

'As soon as I heard that she'd been murdered,' he admitted,
'I was convinced of it. I knew that one of us had done it –
someone she'd pushed too far. And,' he added with a pained
grimace, 'in case you were wondering, it wasn't me. I didn't
kill her.'

The possibility hadn't crossed Tessa's mind. 'Of course not.'

'So,' Father Theo said carefully after another pause. 'Do
you want to go to the police? Tell them what I've told you?
Tell them about the missing records?'

'Tell them about the babies and that you were involved?
That you had a motive for killing her?' Tessa gave a shaky
laugh. 'That wouldn't make much sense, would it? It might
get them off Rob's case, but it would destroy your life. I don't
think I can do that.'

'Then what shall you do?'

'Not *me*,' Tessa reminded him. '*We*. We're in this together now.' She rubbed her temples and tried to think. 'Couldn't we talk to the other babies? Try to get some feeling for which one it might have been? Don't you have any idea of how to contact them?'

'It's possible,' he said slowly. 'We only used our baby names when we were at Mummy's – at Linda's. But I'm used to listening to people – it's my job. And enough things were said . . .' He stood up, smiling at her. 'Leave it with me, Tessa. I'm sure I'll be able to come up with something.'

In the end it wasn't as difficult as Father Theo had anticipated. He sat at his desk that afternoon, trying to remember all of the relevant snippets of conversation which had been addressed to him or overheard. Most of the babies, he now realised, were far from discreet in the security of Mummy's house. They talked about themselves, about their jobs, about their families.

He looked at the notes he had jotted down as things had occurred to him. Baby Priscilla, for instance: he knew that Baby Priscilla was a bank manager, and he even knew at which branch of which bank he worked. Baby Priscilla had been going to Mummy's for a long time, a number of years – longer than any of the others, he was always proud to remind them, so he was in effect Mummy Linda's oldest baby. His own mother had died not all that long ago – within the year. But though he had lived with her and looked after her, he had not felt close to her. There had been an older brother, the favourite, but he had also died.

Surely this would be enough to go on: all he had to do was to ring the bank and ask for the manager. He didn't even need to know his name.

Baby Buddy was even easier. Buddy talked a lot. His real name was Harold Dingley; he had let that fact slip in an unguarded, thoughtless moment. He worked as a hospital porter. He lived with a sister called Bunny, about whom he spoke constantly. Buddy – Harold – should be easy to find. He was almost certainly in the telephone directory.

Baby Mimi, likewise, wasn't too difficult. Father Theo knew that he lived in Milton Keynes with his wife Felicity and their two children, Geoffrey and Emma. His real mother lived near St Albans; he had several times boasted of the subterfuge that allowed him to spend his weekends at Mummy Linda's while his wife believed him to be at his mother's. He ran his own company, Wooldridge Enterprises Ltd, in Milton Keynes, and drove a very posh company car, a BMW which he occasionally left parked in Chase View Road. All that would be required to find him would be a call to directory enquiries to obtain the number of Wooldridge Enterprises Ltd, and a further call to the company, asking for Mr Wooldridge.

The most problematical was Baby Sharon. Although he was not shy in telling his fellow babies about his successes with women, or in discussing his sporting interests, he tended to be close-mouthed about his personal circumstances. He had never mentioned his job, except in the vaguest of terms, and Father Theo didn't have any clues as to his real name.

He would, he decided, begin with the easiest. Father Theo reached for the telephone directory and located, straight away, the phone number for H. Dingley.

Harold was at home when the phone rang. He regarded the ringing instrument with trepidation; ever since that man had rung last week, asking for money, he had been chary of answering the phone for fear that the demand would be repeated. But in the end his curiosity overcame his reluctance and he picked up the receiver. 'Hello?'

'Hello, Buddy,' said a familiar voice on the other end. Familiar, but not the same as before. 'This is Baby Dulcie.'

'Oh, hello.' Harold was pleased; he had always liked Baby Dulcie, who was never too busy for a nice chat, and it didn't occur to him to wonder how Baby Dulcie had obtained his number.

A few minutes later, after a short conversation, he put the phone down, feeling more elated than he had done since Mummy Linda had died. He was going to see Baby Dulcie, and maybe the other babies as well. It would be almost like old times – they were going to get together at Mummy's house.

Oh, it would be lovely. He would wear his favourite outfit. And Baby Dulcie had mentioned that, apart from the other babies, someone else would be there as well: Mummy Linda's daughter-in-law, who was called Tessa.

There was only one reason for that, Harold told himself, jubilant: she was going to be their new mummy. Baby Dulcie hadn't said that, exactly, but Harold could figure it out for himself. Soon, he was sure, everything would be just like it used to be.

Chapter 19

With so many other things to occupy her mind, Tessa had almost forgotten about her ultrasound scan. She might have missed it altogether if she hadn't glanced at the calendar on the kitchen wall while she was making Rob's breakfast on Wednesday morning. When the appointment had been changed, around the time of Linda's death, she had noted the new date on the calendar, and it was this morning.

She had hoped, of course, that Rob would accompany her to hospital for the scan; it would, she was sure, make him more enthusiastic about the baby if he could see it.

Not that she was all that enthusiastic herself at the moment, she admitted, with the business of JoAnn still painfully fresh in her mind. But perhaps the scan would change that. When she'd been given her first scan date she had been excited, had longed for the day to arrive so that she could see her baby. Maybe the scan would help her to recapture that feeling of anticipation.

She was almost afraid to mention the subject to Rob, and feared that, busy as he was at work just now, he wouldn't be able to make it. But she summoned up her courage as she brought his boiled egg to the table. 'I'm having my ultrasound scan today,' she began neutrally.

'Yes.' Rob smiled at her. 'I have it in my diary. Eleven o'clock, isn't it?'

Relief and delight washed over her. 'You're planning to come, then?'

'Yes, of course.' He lopped the top off his egg with practised neatness, adding, 'If I can possibly manage it, that is. You know how busy I am just now, so I might be delayed at the last minute. The best thing would be to meet at the hospital, if you don't mind making your own way there. Then you wouldn't be dependent on me to be right on time.'

Tessa agreed, and even accepted his suggestion that she might take a taxi rather than trying to get there by public transport. Arriving at the hospital early, she checked in at the desk and went to the waiting room.

The waiting room was full of people; she could see that she would be there for a while. So even if Rob were late, she told herself, it would be all right.

She had brought a novel along to help her pass the time. But she found it difficult to concentrate: she was feeling uncomfortably bloated, having followed instructions and drunk a large quantity of fluids before coming. A full bladder, Stephanie had explained, would help them to see the baby better; it was, though, a persistent distraction, especially with no relief in sight.

And no Rob in sight, even as eleven o'clock approached. Watching the clock, suddenly Tessa was reminded of that other time when she had waited for Rob: outside Linda's house on that fatal day. That day she had feared that he wasn't coming, but he had made it.

Tessa didn't want to think about that day. She tried again with the novel; the words blurred on the page, so she tucked it back in her bag and picked up a glossy magazine from the table. It was months old but that didn't really matter. She flicked through its tattered pages, glancing at the photos of willowy models in brief bathing costumes and the recipes for barbecued food.

Quarter past eleven. He wasn't coming, then, she told

herself, fighting her disappointment. But it wasn't his fault; this new system he was installing was proving a real problem, and he hadn't been home till quite late for the past couple of evenings. He had wanted to come, intended to come. That was the important thing.

Half past. One by one the women who had been there when she arrived were called into the treatment room, accompanied by their solicitous partners. It would be her turn soon, she calculated. Not long to wait now.

Several of the other women's heads turned, as they did each time the nurse called out a name. But it wasn't the nurse they were looking at, she realised with a surge of pure joy: it was her husband, crossing the waiting room in her direction. And it was no wonder that they were staring at Rob: he was so handsome, tall and slim in his well-cut suit, his tasteful silk tie. Tessa could sense the other women's envy, and smiled at him as he came up to her, reflecting how lucky she was to have such a husband. How could she ever have doubted that he would come?

'Sorry I'm late,' he said. 'I left on time, but the traffic was a real bugger. And I couldn't find a parking space to save my life. But I was counting on the fact that they wouldn't take you on time, and apparently I was right.'

He was cool and collected, not agitated as he had been that other time. And he was *here*. Tessa's delight and her pride showed on her face as he sat beside her, holding her hand.

The scan was much as Stephanie had described to her: not at all painful but a bit uncomfortable, with her full bladder and the freezing cold gel – and even colder ultrasound device – on her abdomen. Nothing, though, had prepared Tessa for the joy and wonder of seeing her baby appear on the monitor. A tiny perfect hand, splayed like a starfish; the fluttering heart. She'd looked at lots of photos in books, but this was different: this was *her* baby. Hers and Rob's.

'Rob, look,' she said softly. 'Look at her heart beating.' She turned to smile at him, to share the moment, and saw that his face was averted from the screen.

Rob stood. 'I don't feel very well,' he stated, and headed towards the door. 'I'll wait for you outside.'

The technician chuckled. 'Never mind, dear,' she said to Tessa. 'Some men just can't cope with seeing their wives' insides. He won't be any good at the birth, either,' she predicted.

Swallowing her disappointment, Tessa tried to put him out of her mind and focused on the shifting image on the screen. 'Is the baby all right?' she asked the technician.

'Absolutely fine, Mrs Nicholls,' the woman assured her. 'Perfect, in fact, from what I can tell. And right on schedule, as well.'

An unbidden memory of JoAnn surfaced. 'The head looks awfully big,' Tessa said. 'Is it normal?'

The woman's voice was matter-of-fact. 'Absolutely normal. Their heads *are* big at this stage, in comparison to the rest of them. But everything else soon catches up, I can promise you.'

'Can you tell whether it's a girl or a boy?'

The technician shook her head. 'Nothing definite. Not that I've seen yet, anyway. Are you sure you want me to tell you if I do?'

Tessa nodded. 'I'd like to know.'

'Let's see, then.' Expertly the woman moved the wand to the other side of Tessa's abdomen. 'Well, at a guess I'd say it's a girl. But that's just a guess, mind you. It's not so easy to tell for sure with girls, and I may just be getting the wrong angle on things. Don't hold me to that.' She added, 'If you have another scan later on, closer to the birth, it might be a bit more clear-cut.'

A girl, thought Tessa. Just as she had imagined and dreamed of. A little girl.

*

True to his word, Rob was waiting for her outside the scan room, smiling as though nothing had happened. 'Lunch?' he suggested. 'Could I talk you into an early lunch?'

He took her to a dim Italian trattoria where they'd been just once before, during the first week they'd known each other. The place was replete with romantic associations for them, especially as the waiter showed them to the same private table at the back of the restaurant. Tessa remembered that night so well: they had held hands across the checked tablecloth, gazed into each other's eyes by candlelight, drunk lots of Chianti, eaten spaghetti sloppily, laughed a great deal about very little, then gone back to Rob's house – rather than Tessa's flat – and made love for hours. That night he had said that he loved her; that night he had asked her to be his wife. Of course she had said yes: even on such short acquaintance, she'd known that she wanted to spend the rest of her life with him.

The fact that he had brought her here again seemed a good sign. They ordered the same spaghetti dish as before, though this time Tessa passed on the Chianti in favour of mineral water, and while they waited for their food they again held hands across the table.

It was really the first time that she'd seen Rob for any period of time since their day together in France, with him working late in the evenings. She hadn't abandoned her plan to talk to him about his mother, but there just hadn't been the opportunity to do so. Now, she thought. Now she should do it. As soon as the food arrived, she would do it.

'Remember that silly thing we did with the spaghetti?' Rob said as the plates of pasta were put in front of them.

Tessa remembered. They had taken a single strand of spaghetti, each at one end, and had worked their way towards the centre till, leaning over the table, their lips had met. At the time it had seemed terribly romantic; maybe now, with the hindsight of an 'old married couple', it was merely silly.

She had placed the scan photos on the table in front of her, unwilling to put them away yet, so she moved them out of the way of the pasta plate. The photos fascinated her. But she shouldn't allow herself to be distracted by them. 'Your mother . . .' she began, watching Rob's face.

By now she knew that face so well: knew the tiny changes in it which signalled his displeasure. The infinitesimal drawing together of brows and narrowing of eyes, the subtle shift in the planes of his handsome face. As soon as the words were out of her mouth, she observed these changes, and lost her nerve. 'I wish she could have seen the first photos of her grandchild,' she said lamely, touching the scan photos.

Rob had declined to look at the photos; now he turned his face away. 'Send them to your father instead.'

Her father. Tessa hadn't spoken to him in weeks; she hadn't contacted him, as she had promised Father Theo that she would do. In fact she hadn't even told him she was pregnant. It wasn't, she felt, something she wanted to tell him over the phone, perhaps fearing his disapproval. She'd planned to write instead, but she'd never got round to writing the letter. It was high time that she told him, high time that he knew he was going to be a grandfather. Assuming, she thought bitterly, that he would be interested. She would write to him tonight, send him his Christmas present and a card, and enclose copies of the scan photos. Happy Christmas, Daddy.

Rob didn't seem in a great rush to finish lunch, and he drove Tessa home before heading back to work. 'But this means I'll have to work late tonight,' he warned her. 'Very late, probably. Don't wait up for me.'

This wouldn't last for much longer, she told herself. These long extra hours – surely things would settle back down to normal after Christmas, and she could look forward to enjoying her husband's company in the evenings once again.

The phone was ringing as she came in the door; she moved quickly and managed to get to it before it stopped. 'Hello?'

'Tessa!' said Father Theo. 'I've been trying to reach you.'

The dash for the phone had left her a bit short of breath; her words came out in choppy sentences, interrupted by gulps of air. 'I've been out. My scan. The hospital.'

'Oh! I hope it went well.'

'Wonderful.' She smiled to herself and her free hand touched her bump.

'I'll talk,' suggested Father Theo, 'while you catch your breath. I told you I'd see what I could do about the . . . babies, and I wanted to let you know where I've got to.'

'Yes?' Her voice was eager.

'I've managed to track down all but one – Baby Sharon is proving elusive.'

'But that's brilliant!'

'I've told the three of them – Baby Buddy, Baby Mimi, Baby Priscilla – that you would like to meet them. They've all agreed, and they could all make it this evening. Early evening, after work.' He paused. 'I know that timing is a bit awkward for you, with Rob coming home about that time, but they can't manage the afternoon. And this close to Christmas, if we don't do it today, it might be a fortnight before we're able to find another time when they can all come.'

By this time Tessa had recovered. 'Don't worry about Rob,' she said promptly. 'He's working late. So that's no problem.'

'Good. I've tentatively set it up,' he told her. 'I've said we'll meet at Linda's house, at half past six. Is that all right?'

Linda's house. Tessa stood for a moment, holding the receiver to her ear, at a loss for words, panic making her once again short of breath. She had sworn to herself that she would never go there again. Not after the hideous shock she'd had there, running into Baby Priscilla. But, she told herself firmly, she *had* gone again, to lock the nursery, and it hadn't been so bad. She could do it. It was important. 'Yes, all right,' she said at last.

'I thought that would be the easiest thing, since they all

know how to get there, and they . . . we . . . all have keys,' the priest explained.

'Half six it is, then,' Tessa confirmed, sounding braver and more confident than she felt.

Tessa allowed plenty of time to get there, as it was during rush hour, and arrived a few minutes early, just about the same time as Father Theo. 'Let's go into the front room,' he suggested as he unlocked the front door. 'That will be the most comfortable place to meet.'

'Oh, it's cold in here,' said Tessa.

Father Theo switched the heating on at the hall thermostat. 'Maybe we could get a fire going in the front room.' There was a half-full coal scuttle by the fireplace; he went about the job of laying and starting the fire with practised efficiency.

Tessa's eyes were drawn to the set of fireplace irons at the side: one was missing, of course. The murder weapon – evidence. With visions of television detective programmes running through her head, she said, 'We'll be able to observe them in here. See if any of them are nervous about being here, or if they can't stop looking at the fireplace irons. I'll try to watch out for that.'

'Yes, Sherlock. Or is it Inspector Morse?' Father Theo, still on his knees, smiled at her fondly.

She grinned back at him. 'That depends on whether you would rather be Dr Watson or Sergeant Lewis.'

The fire was taking hold slowly; a curl of flame licked up towards the chimney. 'It should be reasonably warm in this room – by about nine o'clock tonight,' said Father Theo with a grimace.

'I'll make some tea,' Tessa offered.

The priest lumbered to his feet. 'No, my dear. You sit down and have a bit of a rest, and I'll do it. I know where everything is.'

But a moment later he was back, looking sheepish. 'No

milk,' he said. 'That is to say, there *is* some milk, but it's curdled solid. I'll pop down to the shop and get a pint.'

Terrified at the thought of being on her own in the house when the others arrived, Tessa got up. 'No, let me go instead,' she insisted. 'You know . . . them. You can talk to them if I'm not back yet.'

He acknowledged the sense of that. 'All right, then. But I'll make the tea when you get back.'

Tessa's excursion took longer than she'd expected: the nearest corner shop was out of milk, so she had to go to Asda in the town centre and fight the heavy pre-Christmas grocery shoppers, all of whom seemed to be buying enough food for a protracted siege. It was nearly seven by the time she got back.

The front room lights were on, though the curtains in the bay window were drawn. From the road, as she approached, this gave the house an appearance of lived-in cosiness for the first time in her experience of it. This was how she had expected the house to look on her teatime visit, the day that Linda was killed. That day, though, the windows had been dark. Tessa shivered as she let herself into the house.

Father Theo was waiting for her at the door of the front room. 'They're all here,' he said quietly. 'Prepare yourself – I'm afraid this isn't quite what you had in mind. It's my fault, I'm afraid. I probably wasn't specific enough with them.' He opened the door and said, 'This is Tessa.'

The house was still cold; the three of them stood close to the fire to warm themselves. She stepped into the room as the men turned. They were wearing baby clothes. There was Baby Priscilla, in a yellow frock which emphasised his sallowness even more than the pink one had done, and another man, tall and fair, wearing an expensive-looking creation of white lace and broderie anglaise. The third, a pudgy, youngish man, was dressed in a little blue sailor suit with the trousers ending above the knees. He was the man, Tessa recognised, who had been crying at the funeral.

'Baby Mimi. Baby Priscilla. Baby Buddy,' Father Theo introduced awkwardly.

Tessa saw the look of recognition in Baby Priscilla's eyes. Her stomach lurched with nausea; she wanted to be sick. She wanted to turn, to run as she had run from him the first time. But with a superhuman effort, and a few deep breaths, she controlled herself. She was here for a reason, and she would not allow her gut reaction to hamper her search for the truth. 'Hello,' she said, her voice surprising her with its firmness.

After hovering in the door for a moment to make sure she was going to be all right, Father Theo took the milk from Tessa. 'I'll make the tea now,' he said, and disappeared.

Baby Priscilla, perhaps feeling uncomfortable about the circumstances of their last meeting, turned away from her and began to talk to Baby Mimi. That left Baby Buddy, who approached Tessa eagerly.

'You're having a baby,' he said, reaching out to touch her bump.

He was not the first person to have done this; Tessa had found that, as soon as her pregnancy had become obvious, she was somehow considered public property. People touched her all of the time – strangers, people in shops, on the tube – in a way that would have been unthinkable in any other circumstances. It had startled her at first; now she was used to it, though she still didn't like it. 'Yes,' she confirmed. 'In May.' She tried to keep her voice and her expression neutral.

'Do you know if it's a boy or a girl?'

'I'm not sure,' Tessa admitted. 'When I had my scan they couldn't tell for sure. They think it might be a girl, but they're not positive.'

His face fell. 'But what if it's a boy?'

'Oh, that would be all right as well,' she said.

'You like baby boys, then?' Baby Buddy smiled at her hopefully.

'I like *all* babies.'

It was the right answer. Baby Buddy beamed, then leaned closer to her and said in a confidential voice, 'Mummy Linda liked boys best. She didn't say it to the others, because she didn't want to hurt their feelings. But she told *me*. She liked boys better than girls. My own mother – she thought girls were best. But Mummy Linda liked boys.'

For some reason – perhaps because in his little sailor suit he looked ludicrous rather than terrifying – Tessa found Baby Buddy less frightening than the other two. And there was something touching about his naivety, something that aroused her protective instinct. This man, she was sure, had not killed Linda Nicholls. He didn't have it in him to plan a cold-blooded murder, or to commit a hot-blooded one. And besides, it was evident that he had loved her; his eyes, as he spoke her name, were filled with tears. 'You miss Mummy Linda, don't you?' Tessa said impulsively.

'Oh, yes. Every day. I think about her all of the time.' He swallowed hard and bit his lip. 'I wish she wasn't dead.'

Baby Mimi turned and joined their conversation. 'It's a shame that Baby Sharon couldn't be with us today. This is almost like old times, isn't it, Buddy?' He had an educated voice, a posh accent.

'But no Baby Sharon. And no Mummy Linda.' Buddy seemed to be getting more and more agitated; he clasped his hands together in front of him, and his pale face had turned very pink.

'And Baby Dulcie in that ridiculous dog-collar,' added Baby Priscilla scornfully, not wanting to be left out. 'Doesn't he know how silly he looks?'

'I never knew that Baby Dulcie was a priest.' Baby Mimi looked thoughtful. 'Or not until the funeral, anyway. I scarcely recognised him, I must say. He was wearing a long black cape sort of thing with gold embroidery.'

At the mention of the funeral, Baby Buddy's face crumpled and his tears spilled over. 'Oh, don't!' he pleaded. 'It was so sad.'

Baby Priscilla ignored him. 'I missed the funeral, of course. I was on holiday. Spain,' he added, as if that would impress them. His lipless mouth curved into a self-satisfied smile.

Buddy blubbered on. 'Mummy is dead! Who cares about your stupid holiday, anyway?'

In an effort to make peace and to soothe the crying baby, Tessa said the first thing that came into her head. 'Perhaps you'll find another mummy.'

Baby Buddy's tears stopped abruptly; this was the opening he'd been waiting for. He turned to her, stretching out his hands in supplication. 'Oh, Tessa,' he said, pleading. 'Won't *you* be our mummy?'

'Please, do,' Baby Mimi added.

Baby Priscilla, clearly, did not want to be left out. 'Yes, be our mother. That's why you've come, isn't it?'

The hairs rose on the back of Tessa's neck; her skin tingled. 'No,' she said in a breathless voice. 'No, no.' Her resolution to see this through had evaporated, and she took a step backwards, retreating from the circle they had formed round her. 'I have to go now,' she added faintly. 'Tell Father Theo . . .'

Before the babies knew what had happened, she was gone.

Father Theo came back a few minutes later with a tray containing five steaming mugs. 'This will warm us up,' he said cheerfully, then looked round. 'Tessa?'

'She's gone,' Baby Priscilla announced nonchalantly. 'She said to tell you she had to go.' He was sitting on the sofa and had switched on the television to catch the seven o'clock news.

The priest frowned, puzzled. 'She never mentioned anything to me about needing to leave at a certain time,' he said.

'Never mind,' pronounced Baby Mimi. 'Let's have our tea.'

Baby Buddy, still upset by Tessa's abrupt departure, snuffled in a chair. 'I don't want a mug. I want my bottle,' he whimpered.

'Yes, bottles,' Baby Priscilla agreed in a whiny voice. 'Where are our bottles?'

Father Theo was apologetic but firm. 'Mugs today. I couldn't find the bottles.'

'Oh, never mind.' Baby Mimi took a mug, and the others followed suit reluctantly.

They drank their tea, Father Theo still puzzling over Tessa's disappearance as he looked at the mug left on the tray. 'You're sure that Tessa didn't say anything else?'

'She just said to tell you she had to go,' Baby Priscilla repeated with a shrug.

The priest swirled the tea round in his mug thoughtfully. 'It seems very strange.'

'She was such a pretty lady,' Baby Buddy interjected, disconsolate. 'And she's going to have a baby.'

Baby Priscilla, bored with the news, switched off the television with the remote control. 'Seems impossible, doesn't it?' he remarked. 'Robbie Nicholls being married, I mean. And expecting a baby. Fancy that.' He shook his head. 'It seems like no time at all since he was a schoolboy. Have I ever told you about that time, years ago, when we—?'

'Yes, you've told us,' Baby Mimi replied firmly.

'Lots of times,' added Baby Buddy. 'Millions of times.'

'Oh, it was funny.' Baby Priscilla chuckled to himself in reminiscence. 'Mummy Linda laughed so hard . . .'

Baby Mimi put down his tea mug. 'I could do with something stronger,' he announced. 'Anyone else for some whisky?'

'I wouldn't say no,' nodded Baby Priscilla.

Baby Buddy made a face. 'Whisky tastes nasty, like medicine. I don't know how you can drink it.' He quite liked a thimbleful of Bailey's – they always had a bottle at Christmas – or failing that, a bit of sweet sherry.

They all knew where the whisky was kept: in a decanter on the sideboard in the dining room. Baby Mimi went off to get it, returning a minute later with an almost-empty decanter. Ruefully he poured the last few drops into his tea mug. 'That's not like Mummy Linda, to let the whisky run out,' he said.

At the mention of Mummy Linda, Baby Buddy's face puckered dangerously, so Father Theo intervened. 'There's some beer in the fridge, if you're desperate.'

Baby Mimi tossed back the whisky. 'Baby Sharon's beer, I suppose.'

'Where *is* Baby Sharon?' Buddy looked round, uneasy that their group was incomplete.

'I didn't know how to find him,' Father Theo admitted. 'I knew enough about the rest of you to track you down, but he's never said that much about himself. I didn't really know where to begin.'

'He's a policeman,' Baby Mimi contributed. 'Right here in Southgate, I believe.'

'A *policeman*!' Father Theo stared at him. 'In Southgate? But how do you know that?'

Shrugging, Baby Mimi explained. 'One day we were watching a rugby match on the television. He let it slip that he was a keen player himself – said that he played for the MPRFC, the Metropolitan Police Rugby Football Club. And another time he said something about how convenient it was for him to come here to Mummy Linda's, since he worked only five minutes away.'

Father Theo nodded to himself, trying to contain his excitement in front of the others. That, he reflected, could explain a great deal.

The huge crowds at Asda had reminded Tessa that there were only two full days left before Christmas. Not really inclined to spend the rest of the evening at home alone, brooding on the events which had just taken place, she decided that it would be a good time to shop for the food they would need to get them through the holidays.

The shops were open late on the evenings running up to Christmas. She stopped at the Marks and Spencer in the Holloway Road, loading her trolley with a small turkey, a ham, a luxury Christmas pudding, and everything else she could think of that they might need, including a box of crackers. It was more than she could carry home, so she rang for a taxi to convey her and her shopping the short distance.

While Tessa was waiting for her taxi to arrive, Father Theo was trying to ring her. Her abrupt departure had taken him by surprise and he wanted to make sure that she was all right. More importantly, though, he wanted to tell her about what he had learned.

Baby Sharon was a policeman. A policeman! The implications of that fact were staggering.

And he worked at Southgate.

Father Theo didn't know his real name, but he could describe him quite accurately. It was possible that, in the course of the police investigation of Linda's death, Tessa had encountered him and would recognise the description.

But there was no reply on Tessa's phone. The answering service kicked in; Father Theo decided against leaving a message. It could wait till morning, he told himself. He would talk to Tessa in the morning.

Chapter 20

Tessa was ashamed of herself. She had wimped out, more than once. She had still not talked to Rob about his mother, and she had run away from the babies. After all she'd put herself through to get some answers to the riddles surrounding Linda's death, she had fled.

Her dreams that night were not pleasant: doughy-faced Buddy, no longer a harmless character, reaching out with a sinister leer to touch her bump. 'Will you be our mummy?' In one of her dreams – a nightmare – she gave birth to triplets, a boy and two girls. 'Oh, good,' said Rob, at her bedside. 'I wanted a boy, and now I've got one. Let's call him Buddy, and the girls can be called Mimi and Priscilla.'

It was the phone that woke her. Startled and disorientated, she reached for the extension on the bedside table. The bedroom was dark; Tessa was unsure whether it was morning or the middle of the night. Rob, she thought. He hadn't been home when she went to bed.

'Hello?' she gasped sleepily into the phone.

She heard Rob's voice; it took her a moment to work out that he wasn't talking to her, but was speaking to someone else on the downstairs phone. 'Tessa is still asleep,' he was saying. 'Can I give her a message and have her ring you later?'

'This is Father Theo,' said a second voice. 'If you could tell her—'

'I'm here,' Tessa announced. 'I'm awake.'

'All right, then,' Rob said.

In the dark, Tessa could just make out a cup of steaming tea on the bedside table. Morning, then, she realised muzzily. Rob was up; he'd brought her a cup of tea. Still, though, something wasn't right. 'Father Theo!' she said.

'Tessa, my dear. I'm so sorry to wake you.' His voice was concerned. 'How are you? What happened last night? Was something the matter?'

Tessa closed her eyes, remembering. She couldn't tell him. 'Oh, I just felt sick,' she said. That was true enough.

'I was a bit worried.'

'Thank you,' Tessa said. 'And thanks for ringing.'

'That wasn't the only reason I've rung,' he went on quickly. 'There's something I really need to talk to you about. To do with . . . well, the reason we had the get-together last night.'

'Linda's murder, you mean?' Tessa asked, now quite awake and not afraid to be blunt. 'You've found something out, then?'

Father Theo hesitated, choosing his words with care. 'Let's say I have a little idea. Something that one of them said, after you left, made me start thinking. I think I'm a step nearer to knowing who killed her.'

'Tell me, then!' Tessa demanded.

There was another pause. 'Not now,' he said. 'Not on the phone. I don't think that's a good idea.'

She was already out of bed, her bare feet freezing on the cold floor. 'When? Where? Tell me where to meet you.'

'The church,' he said. 'St Nicholas. This morning. Nine o'clock?'

'Yes. All right,' she agreed. 'If I can get there by then.'

'I'll wait for you in church. Don't worry if you're a few minutes late.'

'See you soon,' said Tessa. She tried to think what was wrong as she put the phone down. But she could come up with no good reason for her unease, and she tried to banish it by telling herself that Father Theo was on the way to knowing the identity of Linda's murderer. Surely that was good news.

She wrapped herself in her dressing gown, realising that what she needed to clear her brain was a nice hot shower, as hot as she could stand it. 'I'll be down in a minute,' she called to Rob. 'As soon as I've showered.'

Indeed, the shower warmed her up and made her feel much better. But when she went downstairs, Rob had gone.

As Tessa approached the bus stop, she saw the red double-decker pulling away. That would mean a wait for the next one, she knew, almost crying out in frustration. It was still dark, though the clouds which had lowered over the skies had gone, promising a clear day. But the lack of cloud cover meant that it was even colder than the day before; the warmth engendered by her shower dissipated quickly and she stamped her feet to keep them from freezing.

Others formed a queue behind her, and when the bus finally arrived it was full to overflowing. Tessa squeezed on and stood until, with bad grace, a spotty young man gave up his seat for her. 'Thank you,' she said, smiling her gratitude.

' 'Sa'right,' he mumbled, his head down.

The bus crawled through the London traffic. Was it always this bad on a weekday morning, Tessa wondered, or was it because it was so close to Christmas? Tomorrow would be Christmas Eve.

By now she knew exactly where to get off the bus, and was glad that she didn't have far to walk. She was more than a few minutes late already, and Hoxton was not a salubrious neighbourhood; in the first light of morning, even the cheer of the occasional Christmas decorations couldn't disguise the grime, the boarded-up shopfronts and the graffiti, the rubbish that strewed the pavements. Why, she wondered, had Father Theo chosen to work here? Surely a man of his gifts could have done better than this. If not in the country, like her father, then a nice suburban London parish, full of comfortable middle-class people?

But that, she recognised, was not Father Theo's style. Part of what made him so attractive, so admirable, was his refusal to accept the easy option. He was, she felt sure, a wonderful priest. Hoxton was lucky to have him.

A faint source of light within the church illuminated the stained-glass windows. The heavy wooden door, though closed, yielded to Tessa's tentative push, and she stepped inside.

For a moment she stood at the back of the church, her eyes adjusting. The only light came from candles, flickering on the candle stand in front of the Virgin and Child statue. Or at least where the statue *had* been: it was no longer there. And Father Theo was nowhere to be seen.

Had someone moved the statue? Or stolen it, even? It was old; it must be valuable. In this sort of neighbourhood, it wasn't safe to leave the church unlocked with something like that inside and available for the taking. The statue was heavy, Father Theo had told her, but it would be worth a bit of effort to steal it. Tessa went towards its empty stand to investigate, her sense that something was wrong growing with every step she took.

By the light of the candles she saw. Something was indeed very wrong. Father Theo lay next to the candle stand, and on top of him was the statue.

He wasn't moving.

He was dead. Surely he was dead.

Tessa wasn't aware that she had opened her mouth, but screams echoed from the high wooden roof, and they weren't coming from Father Theo.

The next few minutes were a blur – pounding on the door of the clergy house; standing by, shaking, as Mrs Williams rang 999; the ambulances, the paramedics.

The paramedics, not the medical examiner. Father Theo was alive, if critically injured.

They allowed Tessa to accompany them in the ambulance as it rushed the priest to hospital. He was hooked to monitors and drips, barely breathing, unconscious. But he was alive.

Then, for Tessa, the endless hours of waiting in the impersonal sterility of the hospital; staring at the wall, at the glittery Christmas decorations which bedecked the waiting room, at the flickering images on the television screen, trying not to think, waiting for news of any sort.

She wasn't his next of kin, but at the moment she was all that he had, so they took pity on her and treated her as if she had a right to know. Eventually a doctor came into the waiting room and called her aside. He sat next to her, with his most concerned bedside manner, and told her that Father Theo would probably live. Probably, almost certainly. He was, of course, badly injured. The statue had toppled on him, with all the weight of solid stone. He had sustained severe head injuries, and it could be some days before he regained consciousness. *If* he regained consciousness. There was a possibility, the doctor admitted, that he might end up in a vegetative state. It was too soon to tell.

When the doctor had left her, patting her hand, Tessa remained in her chair and tried to absorb what he had said, repeating the phrases over and over in her mind. Severe head injuries. Vegetative state.

Absurdly, all she could think of was Christmas. Tomorrow was Christmas Eve, and the next day would be Christmas. Who would take the services at St Nicholas? What would happen without Father Theo there to make sure that the empty crib received the baby it was waiting for?

Her own baby kicked her, and Tessa cradled her abdomen with both hands, thinking of that empty crib.

Eventually, when they had done all that they could for him in the operating theatre, they settled Father Theo in the intensive care unit and allowed Tessa in to see him.

Even against the whiteness of the sheets and the whiteness of the bandages, he was very pale, and so still. An oxygen mask covered the lower part of his face; machines monitored his vital signs. An almost obscene splash of colour was provided by the bag of deep red blood which was suspended above his head and connected to his pale white arm by a tube: a thin tube, showing red against his skin like an external artery.

Something else was jarring, as well: Tessa realised that it was the first time she had seen him without his dog-collar and black clerical shirt.

'Can I touch him?' she asked the nurse.

The nurse nodded. 'But be careful.'

One of his hands had a drip going into it; Tessa touched the other one as it lay limp on top of the sheet. 'I'm here,' she said to him. 'I'm going to stay with you, if they'll let me.'

'You can stay,' the nurse told her. 'Since there's no family present. But he can't hear you,' she added. 'He's not conscious.'

Tessa didn't care whether he could hear her or not. 'I'm staying,' she stated. 'And I shall talk to him anyway.' She talked to her baby, so why not talk to an unconscious man?

She pulled the single visitor's chair up next to the bed and sat down. 'Don't worry about Christmas,' she told him. 'I'm sure that someone will put the baby in the crib for you. It will all get sorted.'

For the next hour or so she talked to him, as if he could hear her and respond to her. At first her words were general: about the weather, about getting her Christmas shopping done. 'But I forgot to buy wrapping paper,' she said. 'Isn't that silly? I had to make another trip out to the shops to get some.' Then she talked about her baby, and started listing names which appealed to her. 'Maybe Alys for a girl,' she said, spelling it for him. 'That sounds pretty and old-fashioned, like something out of a book. I haven't thought too much about boys' names.' Later, though, she moved on to telling him about JoAnn Biddle and her fears about her own baby. 'That's one reason it was such a relief to have the scan. The technician assured me that my baby is perfectly normal, and that her head isn't abnormally large. I wish I'd shown you the scan photos yesterday, but I didn't even think about it.' She found the photos in her coat pocket and held them up in front of the inert figure in the bed.

'And I wish', she went on, 'that you could tell me about your accident. How did it happen?' She tried to visualise it: Father Theo kneeling at the little prayer desk before the statue, his head bowed. The statue toppling . . .

But statues, she realised with a sudden, horrible certainty, didn't just topple over by themselves. There had been no earth-quake, no shifting of the church's foundations.

Someone had pushed that statue on to the priest's bowed head. Deliberately, and with intent to kill.

Tessa's breathing was rapid as her mind leapt from one certainty to the next. Someone had tried to kill Father Theo, had left him for dead.

But why?

He knew too much.

He knew who had murdered Linda Nicholls – he had as good as told her so, on the phone. One of the babies had let something slip, just as she had hoped that they would. But she hadn't been there to hear it. Father Theo had, and the murderer had decided not to take the chance that he could pass the crucial information on to anyone else – to her, or to the police. He – the murderer – had crept into the church with the intent to surprise Father Theo and kill him before he could tell anyone what he had discovered.

After all, Linda Nicholls's murderer had killed once already; why should he stop at that?

Linda's murder had been, it would seem, a spur-of-the-moment act, but this was different: this was premeditated, with the intent to silence Father Theo and protect himself.

What, Tessa asked herself, would have happened if she'd been a few minutes earlier? If the bus had not been bogged down in so much traffic, pausing to load and unload passengers at every single bus stop? Would she have been in time to prevent what had happened? Would the murderer have missed his opportunity, have slunk away, too late to do what he'd come to do? Or would she have caught him in the act, and forced him to add one more death to his tally? She shivered: two more deaths, if you counted her baby. Her arms went round her stomach and she hugged her baby to herself.

But Father Theo wasn't dead. He was alive, and with luck he would survive and recover. He would be able to tell them what he knew, who had done this to him. Even if he hadn't seen him, he would know who he was. The murderer had failed.

Tessa hadn't prayed properly in years. But now she bowed her head and squeezed her eyes shut. 'Please, dear God,' she whispered. 'Please let Father Theo live. Let him get better. Please let it not be too late.'

One thing was clear to Tessa: she needed to talk to the police. Unwilling to leave the priest's side for more than a few minutes, she found a pay phone down the corridor and rang 999, asking to be put through to the police.

'It's important,' she told them. 'Someone has killed one person, and they've just tried to murder someone else.'

She must have been sufficiently convincing, for within an hour a pair of plain-clothes officers from CID arrived at the hospital and found her where she'd said she would be, at Father Theo's bedside in the intensive care unit.

'Let's talk in the waiting room,' suggested the senior policeman, who introduced himself as DS Kendall.

They found a corner away from the television and thus away from most of the people.

'Now,' said DS Kendall, 'what is this about an attempted murder?'

Tessa explained how she had been summoned to the church by Father Theo, had found him lying beneath the statue. How she had come to the conclusion that it had not been an accident. 'Don't you see? Statues don't just fall over like that. Someone pushed it on to him, and left him for dead.'

The policeman glanced at his silent fellow, the one who was taking notes. 'But he's a vicar, didn't you say? Why would anyone want to kill a vicar? They don't generally go about making enemies – at least not ones who hate them enough to kill them.'

'It was to keep him quiet,' she said. 'He knew too much about . . . another murder. And the murderer wanted to prevent him from telling anyone.'

'And what other murder would this be?'

Tessa took a deep breath; it was fairly evident to her that the policeman didn't believe her, that he had already dismissed her as an hysterical pregnant woman, hormonally imbalanced and paranoid. 'My mother-in-law,' she said firmly. 'Linda Nicholls. She was killed several weeks ago, at her home in Southgate.'

'Oh, yes.' DS Kendall nodded. 'No one has been charged with that, have they?'

'That's just my point,' said Tessa. 'The police don't seem to have any real suspects – at least as far as I can tell. But Father Theo found out who killed her.'

'And do you happen to know who it was, then?' Again DS Kendall looked at his colleague, with a lift of his eyebrows.

'He didn't have a chance to tell me, did he?' she snapped, exasperated. They didn't believe her. And what would they think, how would they treat her, if she were to inform them that when last seen, the three candidates for the role of murderer were wearing baby clothes?

She still didn't know their names, Tessa realised with a

sinking feeling. Baby Priscilla, Baby Mimi, Baby Buddy: that was all she knew. Father Theo was the one who had tracked them down, and at the moment that was no help.

'Do you have any idea at all, Mrs Nicholls?' The policeman spoke patiently, as if talking to a child or someone with diminished responsibility. 'Any names you can give me?'

Tessa bowed her head, defeated. There was no way that they would believe her if she told them what she knew. Three men, three suspects: Baby Priscilla, Baby Mimi, Baby Buddy. But how would she ever find them? 'I've told you all that I know,' she said.

DS Kendall nodded at his colleague, who snapped his notebook shut. 'Well, thank you for the information, Mrs Nicholls,' he said with perfunctory politeness, handing her a card. 'If you should think of anything else, please give us a call.'

When the police had gone, Tessa looked at the clock in the waiting room. It was almost teatime. She really ought to ring Rob, to let him know that she wouldn't be home for a while.

She hadn't, she realised, seen Rob since he'd dropped her off at home after their lunch yesterday. She'd gone to bed before he got home last night, and this morning he'd left while she was in the shower. He would probably be late again tonight, but she ought to let him know just in case he came home to an empty house and got worried about her.

Ringing Rob at work was something she didn't often do, hesitating to bother him. But she knew the number. She went to the pay phone in the corridor.

'Where have you been?' he said at once, as soon as he'd heard her voice. 'I've tried ringing several times.'

Startled, she blurted an answer. 'I'm at the hospital.'

'Oh, God, Tessa! What's happened?'

'It's not me,' she assured him quickly. 'And it's not the baby. It's Father Theo. He's been . . . injured.'

There was a sharp intake of breath. 'Injured? How badly?'

'Quite seriously. He's unconscious. In a coma.' She swallow-ed hard as her voice caught, then went on. 'The doctor says he'll probably survive. But it's possible that he'll remain in a vegetative state – that he'll never regain consciousness.'

'I see.'

'So I'll be here for the rest of the day,' she told him. 'Until they throw me out.'

'Why *you*?' Rob asked. 'Doesn't he have any family? Any-one else to stay with him? And if he's unconscious, what differ-ence does it make anyway? He doesn't know whether you're there or not.'

'I'm staying,' Tessa stated. 'He needs someone to be with him, and as far as I know, there isn't any family.' Then she remembered how he'd started the conversation. 'Why were you ringing me, then?'

'To say that things are *really* crazy at work today, and to tell you not to expect me home this evening – not till nine or ten at the earliest. This is really the last day to get things sorted,' he added. 'Nothing gets done on Christmas Eve, so if I don't finish today . . .'

'Then it won't matter if I'm at the hospital,' Tessa pointed out. 'I'll see you later, then.'

She went back to the intensive care unit. 'No change,' said the nurse. Still Father Theo was immobile and pale, the oxygen mask whooshing with each breath.

Tessa regarded him with a complex mixture of sadness and frustration. He was the only person who could help her to find the man who had killed Linda; he alone knew the names of those three men, one of whom had surely tried to kill him as well. Baby Priscilla, Baby Mimi, Baby Buddy. Why hadn't she asked him for their real names when she'd had the chance? Now it might be too late.

'Don't leave it too late,' Father Theo had told her once. He'd been talking about her father, of course.

The thought hit Tessa like a hammer-blow to the heart, and she gasped. What if it had been her father lying in that hospital bed, poised between life and death? How would she feel then, knowing that she had waited too long – as Father Theo had done with *his* father – to put things right between them?

She *must* write to her father. She hadn't done it last night, as she'd promised herself, though she had slipped his present in an envelope, with no message, and posted it so that he would be sure to get it by Christmas. She would, she determined, write to him right now, before another day had passed.

Tessa looked at her watch. If she wrote that letter immediately, she could probably catch the last post tonight. Then he would get her letter tomorrow, on Christmas Eve. Otherwise it would be days before he received it, with Christmas and Boxing Day coming at the weekend and two compensatory Bank Holidays at the beginning of the week.

'Where can I get some writing paper?' she asked the nurse, and was directed to the hospital shop. She accomplished that errand quickly, buying a stamp and managing to have the scan photos photocopied as well. Then she settled down in her chair next to Father Theo's recumbent form and put pen to paper.

At first she hardly knew what to say. The habit of reticence between Tessa and her father was deeply ingrained, not easily broken. But this was something she had to do; she looked at Father Theo, imagining that he was her father, remembering his words to her. 'Don't leave it too late, Tessa.'

She would start with the baby, she decided. She told him that he was going to be a grandfather in a few months' time, and about how happy she was in her pregnancy, how much she was looking forward to the baby's arrival. She explained about the scan photos which she was enclosing.

'It's only when you're about to become a parent yourself

that you realise what an awesome job it is,' she wrote. 'Thinking about my baby has made me think about you and Mummy as well. I know that I've been a disappointment to you in so many ways.' She hesitated, her pen hovering over the paper, then she went on to write the words that she'd thought she would never be able to say to him: that she knew she was somehow responsible for her mother's death, that she knew he blamed her for that, and that she hoped he might forgive her one day.

Her pen raced on, trying to get the thoughts down on paper as they tumbled from her troubled mind. 'I know that we've never been close, that you've found it difficult to love me for so many reasons. But I do love you, Daddy. I want you to know that. And I want you to love your grandchild. Give her a chance. Don't blame her for my failings.' Her tears fell on the paper, blurring the ink. At last she finished, signed the letter, and addressed the envelope.

As she stuck down the flap, she hesitated. Was this really the right thing to do? Then she looked at Father Theo in the bed, and his words echoed in her head. 'Don't leave it too late.' Boldly she wrote 'SWALK' on the back flap, as she had done when she was a child. What, after all, did she have to lose? Her relationship with her father was already a shambles: could this possibly make it any worse?

Doug Coles was at his desk when the call came through. It might have been put through to DI Tower instead, but he was out.

The voice on the phone identified itself as DS Kendall. 'Sid Kendall,' he said. 'Hoxton CID. It's a courtesy call, really.'

Kendall explained that he had just interviewed a Tessa Nicholls, regarding an injury to a man called Theo Frost. The *Reverend* Theo Frost, a vicar. Mrs Nicholls claimed, Kendall said, that Frost's injuries had not been the result of an accident but had been deliberately inflicted – attempted murder, in fact. And what's more, she insisted that it was connected to the murder of her mother-in-law, Linda Nicholls.

He outlined what he knew about the circumstances of the accident that had rendered Theo Frost unconscious and seriously injured in hospital. 'I know there's nothing in it,' he said. 'But I just thought you ought to be told what the woman said. In case you think it's worth following up.'

'Thanks,' said Doug Coles. He drummed his fingers on his desk. Shit, he thought, and tried to keep his voice offhand and nonchalant. 'I shouldn't think it is, really. Tessa Nicholls is a bit . . . well, hysterical is the word that springs to mind. You know. Hormones and all that crap.'

'That's what I thought,' Kendall affirmed. 'Just thought I'd pass it on.'

'Thanks, mate,' said Coles. 'Thanks a lot.' He put the phone down.

'Shit,' he said aloud.

Returning to the intensive care unit from her foray to the pillar-box outside the hospital doors, where she had caught the postman just as he was emptying the box, Tessa felt her stomach rumble and realised how long it had been since she'd eaten. The nurse, kindly and efficient, had brought her a cup of tea at one point, but she hadn't actually eaten anything since breakfast.

Reluctant as she was to leave Father Theo on his own, she knew that she ought to have something to eat, not just for herself but for the baby's sake as well.

A passing nurse directed her to the hospital canteen. They were serving traditional Christmas fare, and it looked surprisingly good: sliced turkey, dressing, roast potatoes and parsnips, Brussels sprouts. Then there were mince pies and even Christmas pudding. Tessa filled her tray, her mouth watering in anticipation.

She pushed the tray to the till, paid for her food, then looked round for an empty table.

Her eyes passed over the man without seeing him, focusing on him only as he rushed up to her, his face beaming with delighted recognition. He was dressed in the uniform of a hospital porter. 'Tessa!' he cried, and it was then, when she heard his voice, that she knew him.

Baby Buddy.

She dropped her tray. Crockery broke, gravy spattered her shoes, and Brussels sprouts rolled across the floor.

'Oh, dear, dear,' he tutted, squatting down to tidy the mess.

Tessa's first impulse was to turn and run from him. But that, she told herself firmly, would be ridiculous, given the fact that she'd just been wishing she knew how to find him.

'Could we talk?' she asked him.

Together they cleared up the ruins of her dinner, then they went to a remote table, away from eavesdropping ears. Tessa had lost her appetite, but she watched as the man across from her tucked into a large portion of Christmas pudding, smothered in custard. 'This is good,' he said. 'You should have some.'

'I'm not hungry.'

Tessa used the time while he was shovelling food into his mouth to think about what she wanted to say to him, to ask him. Buddy was not the murderer, she reminded herself. He couldn't possibly be. But he had been there last night, and had presumably heard whatever it was that had started Father Theo thinking, had led to the priest's own near-miss.

A clump of lank hair had detached itself from its fellows and dangled across his forehead; Tessa resisted the temptation to reach across the table and brush it back from his face. Instead she said, 'Well, Buddy . . .'

He gasped in panic and looked over his shoulder. 'You shouldn't call me that,' he whispered nervously. 'Not here.'

'All right, then.' Tessa nodded, trying not to display her satisfaction. 'What shall I call you?'

His hesitation was only momentary. 'Harold,' he said. 'That's my real name. Harold Dingley.'

'Harold, then.' It was a start, she thought. 'I need to ask you a few questions, Harold.'

He put down his spoon. 'Questions? What about?'

'About last night,' she said, deciding not to beat about the bush. 'After I left. What happened?'

'Baby Dulcie came in with our tea. In mugs, not in our bottles. I wanted my bottle, but he said he couldn't find them.'

Tessa swallowed back her nausea at the image but managed to maintain eye contact. 'And what did you talk about, Harold? All of you, I mean.'

'About . . . you.' He was the one who looked down, suddenly shy. 'I said how pretty you were, and about your baby.'

'And what else?'

He shrugged. 'I can't remember. Nothing, really.'

Tessa stifled a sigh. That was, she realised, probably all she would get out of him. But there was one other important matter. 'Do you know the names of the other . . . the others?' she finished, as the panicky look returned to his face. 'Priscilla, Mimi? Sharon? What are they really called?'

Harold shook his head. 'I don't know. We only ever use those names. But', he added, smiling at the sudden inspiration, 'Baby Dulcie knows. He's the one who found us. So he knows. You can ask *him*.'

'I can't ask him.' Now was the time to deliver the shock, to watch his reaction to the news. 'He's been hurt. Badly hurt, Harold. He might even die. That's why I'm here at the hospital.'

If she'd had even a tiny doubt about Harold's innocence, that was dispelled by the look of sheer horror and surprise on his face. 'But he can't be! Just last night he was fine!'

'Someone hurt him, Harold. On purpose,' she added bluntly. 'I need to know who it was.'

He stared at her, baffled by her words, as tears welled in his eyes and trickled down his cheeks. 'How should I know?' he whispered.

Tessa clenched her hands in frustration, then reached into her pocket for a scrap of paper and a pen. 'Here,' she said, scribbling. 'Here is my phone number. If you should think of anything at all that might help . . .' But she wasn't very hopeful.

When she got back to the intensive care unit, Tessa was surprised to see that her chair at Father Theo's bedside was occupied by another woman: Mrs Williams.

'Hello,' said Tessa, feeling awkward.

The housekeeper looked up. 'Hello. The nurse tells me that you've been here with him all day.' She smiled, not unkindly, but the very attitude of her body as she leaned towards the priest was proprietary in the extreme. 'I've been on the phone all day, notifying people. Now I've finished. It was good of you to stay, but you can go now.'

It was clear to Tessa that she was being dismissed. 'If you're sure . . .'

Mrs Williams nodded. 'I'll stay with him this evening. And I've rung his family. They should be here tomorrow.'

'His family?' Tessa echoed, frowning in bafflement. 'I didn't know that he had any family. His parents are dead.'

'He has a brother who lives in Belfast,' stated Mrs Williams. 'He and his wife are coming.'

Tessa knew that she'd been defeated, and wasn't sure why that made her so sad. 'All right, then,' she acquiesced. 'I'll be going.'

As if recognising the other woman's disappointment, the housekeeper added, 'I'll make sure that someone rings you if his condition should change.' She patted the priest's hand. 'It really was very kind of you to stay, Mrs Nicholls. Very kind indeed.'

Chapter 21

Harold Dingley never suffered from insomnia. Working shifts, going to bed at odd hours, he had always fallen asleep as soon as his head hit the pillow.

At least that had been the case until the past few weeks. Mummy Linda's death had given him a few sleepless nights of grief, and then there had been that man wanting money. Now it was his conversation with Tessa that was keeping him awake while nearby church bells tolled one and then two.

And all of those things – Mummy Linda, the man, Tessa – were linked together somehow.

He had told Tessa – pretty Tessa, who was going to have a baby – that the babies only knew each other by their baby names, that Baby Dulcie was the only one who knew their other, their real, names.

But that wasn't true, he now realised. Someone else knew as well: the man who had asked him for money.

And that man was one of them. One of the babies. His voice had sounded familiar, and Harold was sure that was why. And he had called him Buddy, he remembered. He was one of them.

Not Baby Dulcie, though. The voice just wasn't right. Baby Dulcie had a cultured, educated sort of voice. Not quite posh, but not far from it. And Baby Dulcie was a priest – priests didn't do things like that.

One of the others. Harold tried to hear their voices in his head, to remember what each of them sounded like.

Definitely not Baby Mimi. Not Baby Priscilla. Baby Sharon, then.

Yes, Baby Sharon. That was it. A common sort of voice, very London.

That was when Harold remembered a part of the conversation at Mummy Linda's the night before, the conversation that pretty Tessa had asked him about.

Baby Sharon was a policeman.

He must tell Tessa.

First thing in the morning, he took the little scrap of paper she'd given him – so carefully placed on the top of his chest of drawers – and went to the phone. He rang the number.

A man answered, brusquely.

Startled and dismayed, Harold put the phone down.

Tessa rang the hospital first thing. Father Theo's condition was stable, she was informed.

Through the first part of the morning she forced herself to stay at home. She wasn't needed at the hospital, she told herself. His family would be there; they would resent her interference, her presumption.

She wrapped her Christmas presents and put them under the tree. She took the turkey out of the freezer to thaw, and began making other preparations for Christmas lunch: this would be her first time, and she wanted it to be just right for Rob. She even laid the table in the dining room so she wouldn't have to do it at the last minute. Two places, two crackers. The table looked bare; she went out into the back garden and cut a few sprigs of holly to add a bit of festivity.

Then she did something out of the ordinary: she rang Melanie Maybank.

'I'm sure that you're busy, on Christmas Eve,' Tessa apologised. But Melanie insisted that a chat with a friend was just what she needed to take her mind off all that needed doing. They talked for a long time. Melanie told her that the girls were all playing up, full of pre-Christmas high spirits, that Ned was almost as bad, and that it was driving her mad. Tessa found herself telling Melanie about Father Theo, and about her meeting with the babies. In spite of the habits of a largely lonely lifetime, it seemed so natural to be confiding these things, sharing her thoughts and listening to the other woman's reactions.

By the time she put the phone down, smiling to herself at how good it was to have a friend to talk to, most of the morning had gone.

Again she rang the hospital; again she was informed that the priest's condition was stable. He had, in fact, been moved out of intensive care and into a private room. They must, Tessa deduced with relief, think that he was going to live.

How she regretted that she didn't have a Christmas present for Father Theo, something to take to him in hospital that could sit in its pretty wrapping paper on the table by the bed until he was able to open it. Then he would *have* to get better, to regain consciousness.

She had an idea, then, sparked by something in her conversation with Melanie. Getting her coat, she set off for Hoxton and the clergy house.

Mrs Williams opened the door to her, looking surprised. 'What can I do for you, Mrs Nicholls?'

Tessa explained her idea. Mrs Williams was dubious at first, but with a bit of persuasion she agreed. 'How will you get it there, though?' she queried.

'I'll take a taxi,' said Tessa. 'And I don't think it's that heavy.'

Mrs Williams found her a blanket to wrap it in and rang for a taxi. The taxi was prompt; cradling her precious burden in her arms, Tessa arrived at the hospital a few minutes later, and at reception was given directions to Father Theo's new room.

She had second thoughts only as she approached the room. Mrs Williams had told her that Father Theo's brother and sister-in-law were with him: what if they thought that she had no business being there, barging in on them like this? It was too late now, she reminded herself sternly. She would just have to be brave. She was doing it for Father Theo.

Tessa pushed open the door, her eyes going first to the man in the bed; perhaps it was her imagination, but he seemed to have a bit more colour, though he was as immobile as before, and the oxygen still whooshed. Then she noticed the flowers, bunches of them in vases and baskets, covering the window-sill and the table in the corner of the room, and the aggressively red poinsettia plant which claimed pride of place on the bedside table. Only then did she take in the man standing beside the bed, garbed in a suit and tie; he looked up enquiringly as she came in.

There was an obvious family resemblance, mostly in the shape of the face, the eyes, and the prominent bald spot on top of the head. But this man was taller than Father Theo, thinner, a bit older, with a worried expression. That this worry was habitual rather than specific to the situation was evident in the deeply etched line down the centre of his forehead, the downward turn of his mouth.

'I'm Tessa Nicholls,' she explained, trying to sound as if she belonged there. 'A friend of Father Theo's.'

The man nodded in recognition. 'Ah, yes,' he said in a voice rather like his brother's but with the overlay of a slight Ulster accent. 'Mrs Williams told us that you . . . found him.'

'Yes.'

'I'm Russell Frost, Theo's brother,' he introduced himself. 'I'm glad you've come,' he added. 'I'd like to hear your account of what happened. It was a terrible accident, wasn't it?'

Tessa went through the brief story; there wasn't all that

much to tell. There was no point, she decided, in challenging his assumption that it was an accident, even though she was certain that it had been nothing of the sort. She couldn't prove it; the police didn't believe her. Why add unnecessary worry to the load that Father Theo's brother already had to bear?

She shifted her blanket-shrouded burden, and the man seemed to notice it for the first time. 'What do you have there?' he asked.

'Something to put on the table by the bed,' Tessa said. She unwrapped the blanket to reveal the plaster copy of the Virgin and Child statue from Father Theo's study. Scooting the poinsettia out of the way, she placed the statue carefully on the table, turning it towards the man in the bed. 'He loves it,' she explained. 'I think he would want it to be the first thing he sees when he wakes up.' Melanie had told her that when she'd had an emergency appendectomy, a few years back, the first thing she'd seen when she came round from the anaesthetic was Poppy's favourite doll, placed as an offering of love on her bedside table.

'The doctor says that he might not . . . wake up,' Russell Frost said sadly, shaking his head.

'Oh, but he will,' Tessa stated with more confidence than she felt. 'Especially with *her* watching over him. The Virgin.'

The man continued to shake his head. 'My wife won't like it,' he predicted. 'She's fiercely Protestant. Doesn't go in for graven images, you know.' His glance shifted to the man in the bed. 'I never did understand why my brother wanted to be a priest,' he mused softly, in a different tone of voice. 'And a celibate one, at that. I was against it, and I told him so. But it was his choice, and I've come to respect him for that, even if I don't understand it. My wife has never accepted it, and never will.'

The door swung open as if on cue, and a stout, square-faced woman in late middle age marched in. 'Who are *you*?' she demanded of Tessa, in a voice as strongly Ulster as Ian

Paisley's. 'And what is *that*?' She pointed an accusing finger at the statue.

Tessa knew that if she backed down now, she would always feel that she had failed Father Theo. 'I'm Tessa Nicholls,' she stated firmly. 'A friend of Father Theo's. And this is Father Theo's statue. I've brought it here for him.'

'Popish nonsense!' Mrs Frost pronounced, sounding more like Ian Paisley than ever. '*Father* Theo, indeed. He's just plain Theo as far as I'm concerned. And that statue isn't staying. You can take it back where it came from, and be good enough to put my poinsettia back where you found it.'

The two women stared at each other for a moment, Tessa forcing herself to maintain eye contact. She had the advantage in height, by nearly a foot, while the other woman had the advantage in bulk. It seemed to be a stand-off, with the potential of continuing for a very long time.

It was Russell Frost who broke the silent deadlock. He sighed, and said unexpectedly, 'Oh, just leave it, Lois. She's right – Theo would want it there, whether we approve of it or not.' Then, before his wife could protest, he changed the subject. 'Someone has been here looking for you, Mrs Nicholls. Several times already. A man – one of the porters. He wouldn't give his name.'

Tessa's heart missed a beat. Buddy. Harold. Perhaps he'd remembered something! 'I'll be going, then,' she said, trying to keep her voice calm. She smiled at Russell Frost, who was not, after all, such a bad fellow, and nodded at Mrs Frost, then made a dignified exit. If Father Theo had had much contact with his sister-in-law, she reflected grimly, it was no wonder that celibacy had seemed an attractive option.

Locating Harold Dingley was more difficult than Tessa had anticipated. She asked several unhelpful people before being directed to Harold's supervisor, who in turn told her in which ward he was working.

She found Harold, finally, pushing a wheelchair into the ward, bringing a patient back from x-ray. His face lit up at the sight of her. 'Tessa! I've been looking for you!'

'So I've heard.' She waited while he settled the patient back into bed, tucking the covers round the frail old woman and patting her claw-like hand while he murmured encouragingly. Tessa marvelled at his gentle manner with the woman. That was something she hadn't expected; he was evidently very good at his job.

'Bless you,' rasped the old woman.

'Happy Christmas,' Harold responded, smiling. Then he turned to Tessa. 'Can we talk? I have to tell you something.'

She suggested the canteen, but he demurred. 'I don't want anyone to hear us,' he said, leading her down a back stairway and outside into a small private courtyard where one determined smoker in a nurse's uniform braved the cold for the sake of a nicotine hit.

Harold waited until the nurse disappeared back inside; when he spoke, his voice was so quiet that Tessa leaned forward to hear. 'I tried to ring you at the number you gave me, but a man answered. Then later it was engaged, for a long time. I thought you might come back here today. So I found out from the desk where they'd put Baby Dulcie, and looked for you there.' After this protracted explanation, he paused. 'You told me to ring you if I remembered anything. And I've remembered something.'

'Yes?' she encouraged him.

His first words didn't make any sense to her; they didn't seem to have any bearing on the matter uppermost in her mind. 'Some man rang me up,' he said. 'He wanted me to give him some money. Two hundred pounds.'

Tessa frowned. 'Last night?'

'Oh, no. Last week, I think. I can't remember exactly.'

She didn't want to rush him, but she was anxious to get on with it. 'Why did he want two hundred pounds?'

'He called me Buddy. He knew about Mummy Linda. He said that if I didn't give him the money, people would find out. The police, my sister. I had to give it to him.'

'Blackmail!' Tessa gasped, horrified. 'But who was he? How did he know?'

'Don't you see? He was one of *us*,' Harold blurted. 'I should have known that, but I didn't think about it until last night. After you said that Baby Dulcie knew our real names.'

She recoiled. 'You're not suggesting that Father Theo—'

'No, not him,' Harold said quickly. 'Not Baby Dulcie. It was Baby Sharon. I know it was. I remember his voice. It was Baby Sharon.'

'Baby Sharon.' The missing baby, the one that Father Theo couldn't track down. 'But who *is* Baby Sharon?' she thought aloud, not expecting an answer.

'Baby Mimi knows something about him. He said so the other night. I remember now.'

'Tell me!'

Harold wasn't wearing a coat; his pasty face was beginning to go blue with cold. Nevertheless he launched into a complicated account of the conversation which yesterday he'd said he couldn't remember. 'Baby Priscilla started to tell us some boring story about Robbie – your husband, but it happened a long time ago. About when Mummy laughed. We've all heard it a million times.'

'Yes, yes.' Tessa, too, was cold, even with her coat wrapped round her, and was impatient for him to get to the point. 'Then what?'

'Then Baby Mimi asked where Baby Sharon was. And Baby Dulcie said that he hadn't been able to find him, that he didn't know his name or anything. So then Baby Mimi said that he knew something about Baby Sharon – that he's a policeman.'

'A policeman!' Whatever she'd been expecting, it wasn't this. Tessa stared at him.

'A policeman,' Harold confirmed. 'And he works in Southgate. Baby Sharon told him so.'

For a moment Tessa stood immobile, her mind working at a furious pace. She could see that Harold was regarding her with an anxious expression, hoping he'd said the right thing. 'Oh, Harold – Buddy – whatever you're called,' she said impulsively. 'Thank you. Thank you! I could kiss you!' Matching her action to her words, she cupped his cold face in her hands, leaned over and planted a quick kiss on his forehead.

He ducked his head, as a bright red blush replaced the blue in his cheeks.

A policeman. Baby Sharon was a policeman. And at Southgate, as well. That explained so much, if it were carried to its logical conclusion.

It explained not just the empty files, but also the odd discrepancies in the paperwork on the search of the house – 'equipment', indeed. It explained why the babies had not been questioned.

It might even explain why the police seemed less than anxious to catch Linda's killer, and somewhat dilatory in making an arrest.

No wonder Father Theo had wanted to talk to her; no wonder he thought he knew who the murderer was.

Not that it necessarily followed that Baby Sharon was the murderer, Tessa told herself, trying to be fair. There was enough at stake – his career, his reputation, perhaps a family as well – if his involvement with Linda were to become public. That was reason enough for him to take her files, to do all that he could to conceal the true nature of her business from his colleagues.

And if he'd stopped at that, she reasoned, if he'd destroyed Linda's records and fiddled the paperwork and called it a day, he would have got away with it. The only other people who knew the truth about the house in Chase View Road were the other babies, and they weren't likely to draw attention to themselves by going to the police. They had, in fact, probably thanked their lucky stars that the police hadn't come looking for them, treating them as suspects; Father Theo had said as much.

But he hadn't stopped at that: he'd got greedy. He hadn't been able to resist the temptation to use the information in the files to benefit himself, knowing full well how much the babies had at stake, how far they would go to protect themselves. And he'd picked on poor Harold Dingley – Baby Buddy, the easy target, the one least able to fend for himself. The one least likely to put two and two together.

It all made sense; it all held together.

Baby Sharon was a thief, a blackmailer. Was he also a murderer?

If he wasn't the murderer, then who was?

The traffic in front of the hospital was at a standstill: buses, cars, taxis, spewing clouds of dirty exhaust. Christmas Eve: everyone rushing to get where they were going, to do that last-minute shopping, to be on time for a party, to go home.

Tessa stood at the kerb, trying to flag down a taxi. But every taxi was occupied, and they weren't moving anyway. Her eyes stung with tears of frustration; the tears froze on her cheeks.

She was a long walk away from the nearest tube stop, and the tube wouldn't be any less crowded than the roads; the very thought of being crushed in a packed tube train, deep under ground, was enough to make Tessa feel faint and claustrophobic.

It was too far to walk home: several miles – in this weather, not an option. The bus would be the best bet; at least it would be warm, and would get her home eventually. A number forty-three bus, if she could find one, would take her up the Holloway Road, within a few streets of home.

Eventually.

Tessa walked along the road until she overtook a number forty-three, engulfed in traffic. She climbed aboard and prepared for a long journey.

It took the better part of two hours, inch by inch. By the time she climbed off the bus in the Holloway Road, the sky was quite dark. Her bladder felt uncomfortably full and she badly needed a cup of tea. First things first, she thought. She hurried home, let herself into the dark house, and took care of her bladder straightaway, then put the kettle on.

The long bus journey had given her plenty of time to think about what to do with the information she now possessed.

Ian. She needed to talk to Ian. He had, as promised, spoken to the officer who had signed the paperwork on the search, over a week ago, but she'd never managed to get back to him to hear what the man had said about it. Tessa tried to remember the name that Ian had mentioned: Doug Coles, she thought. And unless she was very much mistaken, Doug Coles must be known in other circles as Baby Sharon.

While the kettle boiled, she rang Ian's number at work, surprised to discover that she still knew it by heart, and crossing her fingers that he would be there.

He was; in just a moment his voice came on the line, heavy with accusation.

'Tessa!' he said. 'You said you'd ring me. I thought you'd bloody forgotten.'

Why did he always put her on the defensive? 'I haven't forgotten. I've just been busy,' she explained. 'But I need to talk to you now. Urgently.'

'Go ahead, then.'

Tessa hesitated. 'Not on the phone,' she said at last. 'It's a bit . . . delicate.'

'Then what did you have in mind?'

'Couldn't you come here?' she suggested. 'It won't take long.'

'Bloody hell, Tessa!' Ian exploded. 'It's bloody Christmas Eve! Have you seen the traffic out there? Do you know how bloody busy we are here, gearing up for all of the bloody drunks who will be out tonight? Do you really expect me to bloody drop everything and come running, just because you've chosen this moment to bloody talk to me?'

Tessa winced. 'I'm sorry, Ian. I wasn't thinking. When do you think it might be convenient for you?'

'Next week. After bloody Christmas. Wednesday, at the earliest,' Ian said promptly, then paused; when he spoke again, his voice had changed. 'Unless,' he said in an almost caressing tone, 'you're prepared to make it worth my while. A poor lonely man, practically abandoned by my bloody wife . . .'

His meaning could not have been more clear. 'Shall we spend the evening together, then, Tessa?' he asked her softly. 'Like old times? Keep each other company? Your husband isn't likely to be home any sooner than my wife, is he? I could come round right now.'

She closed her eyes, drew in her breath sharply. Nothing, she told herself, was worth that price. 'No, Ian,' she said. 'It's out of the question.'

Now his voice was curt. 'Then I'm afraid you'll have to wait until next week. Give me a ring on Wednesday. I might have some time then.'

'All right,' she sighed. 'Happy Christmas, Ian,' she added.

Ian snorted cynically. 'And a happy bloody Christmas to you, sweetheart,' he replied.

There was nothing for it, nothing she could do. It would have to wait until Wednesday. After all, she tried to convince herself, what difference would a few more days make? Difficult as it was, she would have to try to put it out of her mind till then, and try to enjoy her first Christmas with Rob.

All day, as she concentrated on Father Theo and the

babies, Tessa had been putting something else out of her mind, quite deliberately: her father. By now he should have received her letter. How had he reacted to it? Had he tried to ring her? She'd been there all morning, but as Harold had pointed out to her, she *had* been on the phone for quite some time with Melanie. And this afternoon she'd been out.

Summoning her courage, she picked up the phone and rang their answering service.

There was only one message; it was from Rob. He would, he told her, try to be home in time for dinner, though he couldn't really make promises. If he were going to be too late, he would ring.

Swallowing her disappointment, Tessa went back into the kitchen and re-boiled the kettle, making herself the much-needed cup of tea. She switched on the tree lights in the darkened front room and took her tea in there to enjoy it.

Christmas *was* going to be good, she told herself with determination. The tree looked lovely, with the presents beneath it, and it filled the room with the clean fragrance of pine.

The phone rang. Rob was going to be late, she thought with a sigh as she went into the hall to answer it.

But it was her father. 'Happy Christmas, Tessa,' he said.

'Daddy! Happy Christmas!' She smiled to herself, picturing him on the other end of the phone, seated in his study at the vicarage.

'I thought I'd ring now, between the crib service and the Midnight Mass,' he explained. Her Low Church father, who would have been horrified at his communion services bearing the name of 'mass' at any other time, bowed to tradition just this once in a year. 'Tomorrow will be a busy day.'

'Yes. It always is.' She tried to say it without bitterness.

'Thank you for the gift,' he said. 'It arrived in this morning's post. I haven't opened it yet, of course.'

Of course not; her father was a most disciplined man. 'Well, I hope you like it,' Tessa said lamely.

'I'm sure I shall. Have you had the cheque I sent?' he enquired.

'Yes. Thanks, Daddy.'

There was a long pause; Tessa waited, breathless, for him to bring up the subject of her letter, or at least some of the issues she had raised in it. 'What are your plans for Christmas?' he said at last.

'Oh, I'll be cooking lunch. It will be just the two of us. This year.' Tessa emphasised the last words, giving him an opening to mention the baby.

'Well, I hope you enjoy it.' He added, vaguely, 'Perhaps next year we can all be together.'

Tessa gulped. 'Perhaps.'

'My best wishes to your husband,' her father said in a formal voice. 'And have a happy Christmas.'

'You too, Daddy.' Hearing a click on the other end, she put the phone down. This year he hadn't even bothered to ask the question he had put to her on most other Christmases: 'Are you going to church?' He must have suspected that the answer would, as always, be no.

Maybe she *would* go to church, Tessa thought defiantly. That would show him.

Rob rang a few minutes later. 'I'm just about to leave,' he said. 'I'm sure the traffic is bad, but I should be home within the hour.'

Tessa was delighted; it would be their first evening together all week. And her delight increased when he made his next suggestion. 'You're probably already hard at work on the food for tomorrow. So why don't I stop on the way home and pick up a Chinese take-away?'

'That would be lovely,' she assured him. 'Be sure not to forget the fortune cookies!'

He was as good as his word, arriving home about fifty minutes later, burdened with two carrier bags full of steaming hot Chinese food. He hurried upstairs to change into casual clothes, then they sat cross-legged on the floor in the front room, eating with chopsticks straight from the foil trays, while Christmas music played on the stereo. It was the sort of evening – full of fun and laughter – that they had enjoyed on a regular basis in the first months of their marriage. Tessa hadn't realised how much she had missed such times together. Even the contents of the fortune cookies brought a lump to her throat: hers said: 'The months ahead will bring many changes. Be happy!', and Rob's read: 'When looking for treasure, do not overlook the treasure that is already yours.'

But as the clock crept towards eleven o'clock, and they sprawled, sated, amongst the wreckage of their meal, Tessa looked at Rob shyly. 'How would you feel about going to church? To Midnight Mass?' she asked.

'Tonight?' he said, surprised.

'Yes, tonight.'

Rob shrugged. 'I don't see why not. If that's what you want to do.'

If Father Theo had been conducting the service at St Nicholas's tonight, she might have suggested going there. Instead she was happy to settle for the local parish church.

Neither of them had ever been in their parish church, though Tessa walked past it regularly on her shopping expeditions. It wasn't far, but they decided, in view of the cold weather, to go by car, and were fortunate enough to find a parking spot just round the corner from the church.

They were early; hand in hand they went in and found seats near the back.

Sitting there, waiting for the service to begin, Tessa was obscurely disappointed. She wasn't sure what she'd expected, but if her expectation had been of something similar to St Nicholas's, her disappointment was virtually guaranteed.

This church had nothing of the dark mystery of Father Theo's church: no candle stands, no statues, no Stations of the Cross. It was plain, pre-Victorian, with classical columns and a gallery, brightly lit by brass chandeliers, decorated with swags of greenery.

But she forgot all of that when the lights dimmed and the single treble voice sang the first verse of 'Once in Royal David's City'. She held her breath at the beauty of it; she had not known how wonderful it could be.

The rest of the service was the same. The words and tunes of the old familiar carols came bubbling up from some forgotten corner of her brain and she sang along: 'O Little Town of Bethlehem', 'While Shepherds Watched Their Flocks by Night', 'The First Nowell', 'It Came Upon the Midnight Clear', 'O Come, All Ye Faithful'. She had a fleeting memory of her mother at the piano, her clear voice raised in song, tiny Tessa joining in.

And when the time came to pray, Tessa went down on her knees and prayed silently: first for Father Theo, then for her father, and finally for her baby.

Coming out into the frosty night, the sky spangled with stars even in the midst of the city, Tessa felt elated. Things were going to be different from now on, she was determined. Better than ever. Tonight would be a new beginning for her and Rob.

He reached for her hand, enfolding her cold fingers in his. 'Happy Christmas, Tessa,' he said.

'Happy Christmas,' she echoed happily.

Doug Coles had left his hospital visit until late, reasoning that the later he went, the less likely he would be to run into anyone who would stop him.

He'd found out the location of Theo Frost's room earlier that afternoon, by the simple expedient of ringing the hospital desk and asking. So now he could go straight to the room without having to make any enquiries, arouse any suspicions. They'd told him on the phone that Frost was still unconscious, still in a comatose state. He needed to see for himself.

Late night on Christmas Eve. Most staff were at home with their families, and only emergency patients were being admitted.

He had a brief scare when he encountered, in the corridor, one such emergency patient being wheeled to his room. The man pushing the wheelchair was none other than Harold Dingley.

But it was evident that Dingley didn't recognise him, out of context and dressed in such an unfamiliar way. Coles shook his head, bemused by the man's stupidity, and moved on.

He found the ward without any problem. The nursing desk was unstaffed; so much the better.

Frost's room. Doug Coles pushed the door open and stepped inside, moving quickly and silently to the bed.

The man in the bed was inert. So was the unexpected person in the chair beside the bed, but as Coles drew near, she started and jumped from her chair. 'Who are you?' she demanded in a strong Ulster accent.

Coles took a step backwards. 'A friend of Reverend Frost's,' he said, attempting an unconvincing smile. 'I thought I'd see how he was doing.'

The woman, short and broad, didn't return his smile. 'It's an odd time to drop in,' she observed. 'What did you say your name was?' Her eyes narrowed, looking at him with suspicion.

His nerve failed him. 'Perhaps I'll come back in a day or two,' he temporised, backing towards the door.

'I'll be here,' the woman said. It was a threat, not a promise.

Doug Coles had met his match.

Chapter 22

On Christmas morning, Rob and Tessa had a rare lie-in, sleeping until nearly nine o'clock. Rob was up first; as a surprise, he brought Tessa breakfast in bed, then they went downstairs to exchange their gifts under the tree.

First she gave him his present, looking on eagerly as he unwrapped the watch. He professed himself delighted with it, strapped it on his wrist, then handed her a small jeweller's box.

Tessa lifted the hinged lid; inside was a stunning diamond solitaire ring, the stone at least a carat in weight. 'Oh, Rob!' she breathed.

It was, he explained, to make up for the lack of an engagement ring; they'd married so quickly that he'd never bought her one.

She smiled at him with tears in her eyes. 'Put it on,' she requested softly, holding out her hand, almost too moved to speak.

Rob slipped it on her finger, next to her wedding ring. 'A perfect fit,' he observed.

'Thank you. Thank you.' She held up her hand and admired it for a moment, then gave him a huge hug.

His arms went round her; she savoured the moment, not wanting to let go. Fleetingly she wondered whether she might lure him to bed, but decided against it; she hadn't forgotten how badly that had backfired the last time she'd tried it. She should be satisfied with what she had, she told herself. When the baby was born, things would be different; everything would return to normal. Till then, she should be happy that she had a husband who loved her, whether he wanted to make love to her or not.

Rob released her and smiled. 'Now. What can I do to help you with lunch?'

'Let me see.' Tessa ticked off the stages of meal preparation on her fingers. 'The turkey won't take long to cook – it's not a whole bird, only a little breast roast, so it won't need to go in for a while. The ham is already baked. The Christmas pudding has kindly been made by St Michael on our behalf, and can be bunged in the microwave to heat it up. That leaves the vegetables, mainly. How do you feel about peeling potatoes?'

'Lead me to them,' he said stoutly.

He was wearing a smart new jumper, so Tessa pulled an apron over his head and tied the strings behind his back. 'Very fetching,' she pronounced, handing him a bowl of potatoes and a paring knife.

She cleaned the Brussels sprouts, thinking how nice it was to be sharing such a homely domestic task with her husband. She didn't even envy Andrew or the Maybanks their cosy family holiday gatherings, as long as she had Rob.

Rob was peeling the potatoes with practised ease, the skins snaking off like brown Christmas ribbons; the naked potatoes he dropped into cold water.

'If I'd known how good you were at peeling potatoes, I would have made it your regular job a long time ago,' Tessa laughed.

'It's just as well that I'm good at something,' he said, making a face.

Tessa wished that she could remember this moment for ever, could capture it and hold on to it: Rob in the flowered apron, waving a paring knife in the air. Suddenly she thought about the camera she had bought at the French hypermarket. This would be a perfect opportunity to inaugurate it; after all, she had bought it with Christmas in mind.

'Just a second,' said Tessa. 'I'll be right back.' She found the camera where she'd put it, and discovered that the film had only to be dropped in before it was ready for use. Holding the camera behind her back, she came back into the kitchen. 'Carry on peeling,' she ordered, then whipped out the camera and took his photo. 'Brilliant! That will be one to save for our grandchildren,' she laughed.

Rob blinked at her, blinded by the flash. Then his face changed: he paled, his eyes widened in shock. His hands fell to his sides; a potato skittered across the floor.

Tessa watched him with consternation growing into alarm. 'What is it, Rob, darling? Are you all right?' She started towards him.

'Of course I'm not bloody all right!' he snarled, his face transformed yet again, this time into an ugly mask of anger. 'You took my photo!'

'Yes . . .'

'Don't you *ever* take my photo,' Rob shouted. '*No one* takes my photo! Not ever. I won't have it!'

Stunned and uncomprehending, she just stood there. 'But Rob – I don't understand.'

Rob narrowed his eyes, looking at her with something more akin to hatred than anger. 'You don't understand? That's the trouble with you, Tessa – you don't bloody understand *anything*!' He reached for the camera; automatically Tessa stepped away from him and put it behind her back.

The paring knife was still in his other hand. For an instant he looked at it, and for that same instant – little more than a heartbeat – Tessa felt fear. But a second later he threw the knife down on the worktop, then tore at the apron. Tessa heard the fabric rip; through the tears that sprang to her eyes she saw him fling the remnants of the apron on the floor, snatch the camera from her now-flaccid hand, smash it down on the worktop with enough force to shatter it, and stalk out of the room. A moment later the door of his computer room slammed shut with a crash that could clearly be heard all the way to the kitchen.

She dared not follow him. And she still didn't know what she'd done wrong.

Tessa went on cleaning the Brussels sprouts, tears streaming down her face. A few minutes later the phone rang; by the time she got to it, the ringing had stopped, and she assumed that Rob had answered it upstairs.

Not long after, Rob appeared again in the kitchen. He was wearing a suit and tie. 'I've got to go in to work,' he said in a reasonable voice, with no reference at all to the last words he'd spoken to her. 'The whole computer system has crashed.'

'But it's Christmas!' Tessa protested. As soon as the words were out of her mouth, she regretted them: would they bring on another display of anger?

Rob smiled at her and raised a hand to her cheek. She flinched, but he merely wiped away a tear with a gentle finger. 'You know that, Tessa, and I know that. But the computer doesn't know it. I'm afraid I have to go in. And from what the chap said on the phone, it's going to take me hours to get it sorted.'

'But . . . lunch.' She waved her arm in the general direction of the food preparation. 'Christmas lunch.'

'It can't be helped.' He shrugged. 'Won't it keep till tomorrow?'

There was only one possible answer. 'I suppose so.'

'Well, then. Christmas lunch becomes Boxing Day lunch.' Rob leaned towards her and kissed her damp cheek. 'Sorry, Tessa. As I said, it can't be helped.'

'But you'll need something to eat,' she protested in concern. 'You won't be able to grab a bite anywhere – nothing will be open today.'

'True,' he acknowledged, opening the fridge. While Tessa stood by, watching helplessly, he made himself a ham sandwich and popped it in his briefcase. Then he was gone, taking Tessa's dreams of their first Christmas together with him.

'Happy Christmas,' she said to herself as his car pulled away from the front of the house.

It didn't take Tessa long to determine that she was not going to sit about waiting for him and feeling sorry for herself. She went to the phone.

Melanie answered after several rings. 'Sorry,' she said over a non-specific but distinct din. 'It's a bit noisy here.'

'Is it too late to change my mind about coming?' asked Tessa.

Melanie's reply was prompt and sincere. 'Absolutely not. I told you that the offer would remain open. There's always room for two more.'

Tessa gulped and tried not to sound forlorn. 'Just one. Rob was just called away to an emergency at work.'

'Well, then. You *must* come – if you can stand us, that is,' Melanie chuckled. 'I'll send Ned to fetch you in the car.'

About to demur, Tessa remembered the presents. None of them was heavy or bulky, but they added up to a substantial little pile. 'All right, then.'

Ned was there in a few minutes, grinning cheerfully; he came to the door and rang the bell. 'Happy Christmas, Tessa,' he greeted her with a peck on both cheeks.

His face was icy. 'Happy Christmas,' she returned, her spirits lifting already. She'd changed into a warm red chenille jumper, long and loose over her leggings, and had put the presents into a carrier bag emblazoned with Christmas designs. She slipped into her coat and picked up the bag of presents.

'You look like one of Father Christmas's elves, at the very least,' Ned teased, taking the bag from her and leading her to the car.

'Look who's talking,' she came back, indicating his jumper, knitted in scarlet wool with a huge green tree in the centre of his chest.

She *was* going to have a good Christmas, Tessa told herself as Ned helped her with her seat-belt. She was not going to allow it to be spoilt. Not by Rob, not by anyone or anything.

Ned pulled the car into the drive of the Maybanks's house. The lights blazed on the massive Christmas tree in the front window, beckoning Tessa inside. 'Come in, come in,' he said. 'The girls will be so pleased to see you.' The fragrance of roasting turkey hit them as the door swung open.

Poppy was waiting just inside the door. 'I *knew* you'd come,' she announced triumphantly, throwing her arms around Tessa's middle.

Tessa knelt down and hugged her, resting her cheek on the springy curls. 'Happy Christmas, Poppy.'

Eventually Tessa released her; the girl drew back and eyed the bag which her father carried. 'Did you bring us presents, then?'

'Yes.'

'Then you must have known all along that you'd come,' Poppy said shrewdly. She took Tessa's hand and led her into the large room. 'We've already opened our presents,' she added.

That was evident from the shambles under the tree: wrapping paper was strewn everywhere, and bits of ribbon decorated the floor. Ned pushed some of it aside and deposited Tessa's carrier bag amidst the chaos.

Tessa looked round. 'Where are your sisters?'

'Clare is helping Mummy with lunch,' Poppy detailed. 'And Helena is in her room. Reading, I suppose.' She wrinkled her nose in eloquent testimony to her opinion of that activity.

'And what were *you* doing, before I got here?'

'Playing games with Uncle Miles.' Poppy pointed towards a corner of the room where, unnoticed by Tessa till now, a man sat at a table, poring over a board game. The girl lowered her voice. 'He's not really our uncle, you know. He's a friend of Daddy's, from the university. But we've known him forever, and we call him Uncle Miles. He's nice. He comes to us every Christmas.'

'I see.'

Poppy pulled her in his direction. 'Uncle Miles, this is Tessa,' she announced. 'I knew she'd come, and she *has* come.'

The man rose and nodded to Tessa. Though his unlined face proclaimed him to be under forty, he was dressed, she observed, like a stereotype of an ancient academic: a shabby tweed jacket with leather patches on the elbows, worn corduroy trousers, a tattersall checked shirt and clashing striped tie, greasy with age. He wore thick horn-rimmed glasses, and his hair, receding at the front but with unfashionably long and curling side whiskers in compensation, was untidy, sticking out from his head, thought Tessa, as though he'd been dragged through a hedge backwards. But he had a nice smile, with unexpectedly even and well-cared-for teeth. 'Greetings, Tessa,' he said, bowing from the waist in a courtly way.

'You'll play with us, won't you?' Poppy wheedled. 'It's better with three. The game isn't over so quickly that way.'

Tessa shook her head reluctantly. 'I think I'd better check with your mother in the kitchen. She might need some help with lunch.'

'But I *told* you. Clare is helping.' Thwarted, Poppy frowned.

'I'll play after lunch,' promised Tessa.

In the kitchen, though, Melanie seemed to have things well under control. She gave Tessa a hug and a glass of warm non-alcoholic punch, in that order, and invited her to sit down while she and Clare took care of the last-minute touches.

'I made the punch,' Clare said proudly. 'Cranberry juice, apple juice, orange juice, a bit of lemon, and some spices, all simmered together.'

'Good for children and pregnant women,' Melanie added with a wry smile.

The spicy fragrance wafted tantalisingly from the glass, mingling with the other mouth-watering smells which signalled that Christmas lunch was nearly ready. Tessa took a sip. 'It's delicious. Just right.'

'Uncle Miles said it would be better with rum in it,' Clare said, scrupulously honest. 'I think he and Daddy added some to theirs.'

'Sit down and enjoy it,' urged Melanie.

'But I feel useless, watching the two of you working so hard.'

'If you really want to do something,' Melanie capitulated, 'you can put the crackers on the table.' She handed Tessa a box. 'Miles always brings them – his contribution to the festivities. You've met Miles, haven't you?'

'Poppy introduced us.' They were, Tessa observed, a very superior sort of cracker, large and covered with shiny silver foil. She moved round the table, putting one at each place.

'Uncle Miles always brings posh crackers,' Clare told her. 'They have better prizes in them than you usually get – things like little screwdriver sets, and lace handkerchiefs. But', she added with candour, 'the same stupid jokes and silly hats.'

'But Christmas wouldn't be Christmas without stupid jokes and silly hats,' Melanie pointed out cheerfully. She crossed her arms above her prominent bump and surveyed the table. 'It looks great. I think we're just about ready, if you want to summon the troops.'

Clare had to go upstairs to find Helena, but within a few minutes they were all assembled around the long table in the kitchen. Tessa found herself between Poppy and Miles as they stood for a moment of ritual solemnity: the Loyal Toast. 'Ladies and gentlemen, the Queen,' said their host in a voice which might have been ironic; they all raised their glasses.

'The Queen,' they echoed.

Helena added fervently and with no irony whatsoever, 'God bless her.'

Ned gave his daughter a fond smile. 'Our little Royalist.'

'To absent friends,' said Melanie, catching Tessa's eye. Again they raised their glasses, though Tessa found it difficult to swallow with the lump in her throat. Father Theo, she thought. And Rob.

But she had little time to brood; things quickly descended into hilarity, as they all crossed hands to pull the crackers to an almost simultaneous series of loud bangs. 'I got a necklace,' shrieked Poppy as her prize tumbled out. 'And a purple crown!' For a moment everyone scrambled for their prizes, some of which had flown on to the floor, then they donned their paper hats. 'Listen to my joke,' Poppy ordered, unfolding the bit of paper. 'What is black and white and red all over?'

'A newspaper,' her father answered straight away. 'That has to be one of the oldest jokes in the book.'

'Wrong!' she crowed. 'It's a zebra with sunburn!' Everyone groaned obediently.

Melanie brought the turkey to the table while, at Poppy's insistence, they took turns reading out their jokes. Ned carved, and soon they each had a plate heaped with food in front of them. That put an end to jokes for the duration, as they all applied themselves to the succulent bird and its accompaniments.

Helena had been given a tiny nut-roast instead of turkey, Tessa observed. She was still refusing to eat meat, then. The girl poked at it with her fork and cast glances of secret envy at the juicy slices of white breast meat on everyone else's plates.

'Have some wine,' Miles urged Tessa as he refilled his own glass from the bottle which he had positioned in front of his place at the table. 'Our host has provided us with a jolly good claret.' He waved the bottle at Ned and smiled his appreciation.

'Thanks, but I'm not drinking right now,' Tessa demurred. 'The baby.'

Miles gave a philosophic shrug. 'Well, that leaves more for me, then.' Before they had emptied their plates, he had finished the bottle and started on a second, with a bit of help from Ned.

The wine seemed to be loosening his tongue, observed Tessa. Soon his voice could be heard ringing out over the table, drowning out even Poppy's most strident tones.

But Poppy played up to him; the two of them bantered merrily over and around Tessa. She found it amusing, and was content to listen without joining in. When Miles addressed Tessa directly, it was with a sort of laboured flirtatiousness, harmless and flattering, though once or twice when, under the table, his hand grazed her knee or her leg, she suspected that it was perhaps not by accident. But his touch was tentative, falling far short of a grope; Tessa chose to ignore it.

It was Clare who, with due solemnity, brought the Christmas pudding to the table. Blue flames leapt up, licking the rich brown sphere. 'What a waste of good brandy,' declared Miles, winking at Tessa, but he was mollified by an extra-large dollop of brandy butter on his portion, melting immediately into an alcoholic puddle.

'I don't think I can eat more than a bite of this,' Tessa protested at the huge serving she'd been given. The pudding looked so moist and delicious, though, and tasted even better than it looked; one bite led to another and soon it was gone.

Helena, who hadn't had much to say during the meal, struggling as she'd been with the nut-roast, now glanced at the clock as the spoons began scraping the bottoms of the bowls to signal everyone's approval of the pudding. 'There's not much time until the Queen,' she announced.

'Oh, crikey.' Ned got up and began clearing the table. 'Not enough time to finish the washing up, but if we get on with it, we can probably just about get everything rinsed and stacked.'

'Daddy and Uncle Miles always do the washing up,' Poppy informed Tessa. 'It's a tradition.'

A tradition that Melanie no doubt appreciated, thought Tessa: perhaps this year more than ever. She smiled down the table at her friend as a grimace of discomfort flickered across Melanie's face. 'Are you all right?' Tessa asked quietly.

Melanie nodded. 'It's just the baby. Objecting to all that rich food, I suppose.' She struggled to her feet, her hands at the small of her back. 'Only seven more weeks to go,' she sighed. 'I'll be glad when it's all over.'

'Hang in there, Mel.' Ned, reaching past her for the brandy butter bowl, touched his wife's arm with easy intimacy, and gave her a look of such pure love that Tessa's heart contracted in an unexpected twinge of envy. Unworthy, she told herself sternly. She was *glad* that Melanie's husband adored her; Melanie deserved it. Besides, Rob loved *her*, though she had to admit to herself that he sometimes had an odd way of demonstrating it.

'Let's go and turn on the telly,' Helena urged. 'We don't want to miss any of it.'

They were all still wearing their paper hats. Tessa took hers off and laid it on the table along with her napkin. 'No,' objected Poppy. 'You've got to keep it on all day. That's the rule.'

Obediently Tessa put the green crown back on and followed Helena to the television, with Poppy at her side and Clare trailing behind with Melanie. The two women sat on the sofa, Poppy snuggled between them, and Helena made a big show of turning on the set and tuning it to BBC1. The credits were rolling at the end of the umpteenth special Christmas episode of a tired old sitcom which had passed its sell-by date years before.

'Helena has a crush on Prince William,' Poppy announced. 'That's why she's so keen on watching the Queen all of a sudden.'

Helena looked daggers at her sister. 'She is our monarch,' she stated with as much dignity as she could muster.

'But I thought you said that boys were gross?' Clare, with the unerring memory of sisters, chipped in from her position on the floor.

'Prince William isn't a *boy*,' Helena stated scornfully. 'He's our future king.'

Poppy giggled. 'See, I told you that she had a crush on him!'

'It's not a crush!' She folded her arms across her chest. 'I'm in love with him. I think he's dreamy. And I want to marry him one day.'

Melanie raised her eyebrows. 'That's the first I've heard of it,' she said. 'Just imagine, Tessa – visiting the in-laws at Buckingham Palace!'

'It's not funny!' stormed Helena.

'Prince William isn't the ideal husband for a vegetarian,' Clare pointed out. 'He doesn't just *eat* meat – he shoots it himself. And hunts foxes, too.'

'Little baby foxes,' Poppy added gleefully.

Helena scowled. 'Oh, shut up.' But as the first strains of the National Anthem were heard, and the royal standard flapped on the screen, she stood to attention and turned towards the television.

'Daddy!' Poppy called. 'Uncle Miles! She's on! The Queen is on!'

The men came through, Miles carrying a glass and what remained of the second bottle of wine. 'A toast to the Queen,' he said in a jovial voice.

'I thought you were a republican,' Ned teased him.

'I am.' Miles filled his glass and took a gulp. 'But I'm also a believer in any excuse for a toast.'

Helena frowned. 'Shhh,' she whispered. 'The Queen is talking!'

For a moment they all obeyed her and watched the screen,

then Miles refilled his glass. 'Just listen to all that rubbish about the Millennium,' he said. 'Doesn't the silly old bag know that the Millennium starts in 2001, not 2000?'

Helena glowered, restraining herself from telling him to shut up.

'Oh, Miles. You're such a pedant,' Melanie said with tolerant affection.

'But that's exactly what I am, dear Melanie,' he proclaimed, patting her shoulder. 'An old pedant. Not to be confused, I might add, with a paederast. Or even a paediatrician.'

Tessa wasn't really listening to any of it: not to the Queen, nor to the banter in the room. She was thinking how strange it was that at this very moment, people all across the country – all across the world, even – were united in watching this rather ordinary-looking white-haired woman saying pretty much what everyone had expected her to say. There was something almost surreal about it. Andrew and his family would be watching. Probably Stephanie and her boyfriend, Greg Reynolds, Geeta Patel, Mrs Williams, Baby Priscilla and the other babies would all be in front of a television set somewhere. Even her father would take time out from his busy day to watch the Queen. Only Father Theo, insensate in his hospital bed, and Ian, who hated Christmas and despised the Queen, would be missing this collective moment. And Rob, of course, she added to herself with a little spasm of pain, her eyes stinging with tears.

Harold Dingley sat in his favourite chair in front of the telly, feeling comfortably stuffed after the delicious lunch that Bunny had cooked. Last year he'd had to work on Christmas Day – after all, hospitals didn't cease functioning just because it was a holiday. But this year he had the day off, and he was enjoying it to the full.

He and Bunny had exchanged gifts in the morning: she had given him a box of thick linen handkerchiefs and a bottle of after-shave; he had reciprocated with some perfume and a pot plant. Then lunch, and now it was time for the Queen. Bunny got out the bottle of Bailey's and poured a healthy tot for each of them. Harold sipped it contentedly.

Harold always enjoyed watching the Queen. She was such a nice, motherly-looking sort of woman, with those glasses and that hair. Like someone's granny, even. Funny that she was in charge of the whole country, but he liked thinking of the country in those safe hands. Come to that, he liked to think of *himself* in those safe hands, and wondered how it would feel to have the Queen change his nappies for him.

Lost in these pleasant fantasies, he went on sipping his Bailey's long after the royal standard had faded from the screen and the credits started to roll for the blockbuster movie which followed.

'Harold?' said Bunny. She stood in front of his chair, clasping her hands together, a slight tremor in her voice.

He looked up. 'Is it time for tea, then?'

'Not quite yet, Harold. Are you hungry?'

'Oh, no,' he assured her. 'I'm still full from lunch. But I thought maybe you were getting ready to cut the Christmas cake.'

'In a little while.' She paused, chewing on her lip, then said in a rush, 'Harold, someone is coming for tea.'

Harold noticed, then, that Bunny had changed her clothes; she was no longer wearing the baggy old trousers and the ancient pinny – once their mother's – in which she had cooked lunch. She was, in fact, wearing a smart new dress that he'd never seen before. Earrings, too, and make-up, just as if she were going to work. No, even smarter than work. He sniffed and realised that she had splashed herself with the perfume he'd given her. 'Who is it?' he asked. 'Who is coming?'

'Someone I've met at work. He's called Colin, and he's very nice.'

An ominous rumbling began in Harold's stomach; suddenly he felt as if he were going to be sick. 'I've never heard you mention him before,' he said, trying to stay calm.

'No, I . . . well,' she stumbled. 'It was early days. But now he's coming for tea. You'll like him, Harold.' Her voice was pleading and her eyes were huge with entreaty. 'Please, Harold. Please be nice to him. It's important to me.'

Harold closed his eyes but the nausea didn't go away. Blindly he reached out towards the little table next to his chair, putting the glass of Bailey's down, slopping a bit of the sticky brown liquid on his hand. With a howl like a wounded animal he got up and blundered in the direction of the bathroom.

There was a television set mounted on a wall bracket in Father Theo's private hospital room. Russell Frost, who was paying for the room, felt that he was also paying for the right to watch the television, so after an indifferent lunch in the hospital canteen, and a re-run of his favourite Christmas sit-com, he prepared to enjoy the Queen's speech with his wife.

'Her Majesty,' said Lois Frost with feeling. 'God bless her.'

'She's bound to talk about the Millennium,' her husband predicted.

'She can talk about anything she likes,' declared Mrs Frost. 'She's our Queen, head of the United Kingdom of Great Britain and Northern Ireland. Long may she reign over us.'

Intent on the television screen, neither one of them noticed when the man in the bed moved his hand.

Tessa became aware that the Queen's speech was over, though the badinage so characteristic of this household continued unabated.

'Charades are for babies,' Helena stated scornfully.

'But we *always* play charades,' insisted Poppy.

Melanie sighed. 'That's enough, you two. When Daddy and Uncle Miles have finished the washing up, we *will* play charades.'

'Oh, Mum!' Helena's brow was creased in exasperation.

'But you don't have to play if you don't want to,' her mother added.

Helena was already on her way back to her room. 'Good,' she said over her shoulder. 'I *don't* want to. Call me when it's time to cut the Christmas cake.'

The absence of Helena meant that the two teams were evenly matched, with two adults and one child each. Poppy declared, in a voice that brooked no argument, that she and Tessa and Uncle Miles would play against her parents and Clare.

'Is there any more of that claret?' Miles asked before they began. His face was noticeably redder than before – almost as red as the paper crown which now tipped rakishly on his head – but the wine didn't seem to impair his abilities. To Tessa's surprise, he was a good charades player, with a comprehensive grasp of film, television, and book titles. Their team had a decisive and hilarious win, then the Christmas cake was served with tea.

'Tessa brought us some presents,' Poppy recalled, her mouth full of cake. 'We haven't opened them yet!'

Embarrassed, Tessa produced the carrier bag. 'Just a few little things,' she said.

They all opened their gifts; all professed themselves delighted. 'Nothing for *me*, then?' joked Miles with a mock pout. 'I suppose I'll have to settle for a kiss under the mistletoe instead.'

In a sudden tongue-tied panic, Tessa looked for the mistletoe and tried to think of something to say that would be off-putting without being insulting. Melanie sensed her discomfort and did it for her. 'Oh, Miles, you old reprobate! Don't you ever give up? Come on – kiss me instead. At least my husband is here to supervise.'

Miles gave Melanie a chaste peck on the cheek, but looked significantly at Tessa and winked. 'Later,' he mouthed at her.

'Well, I love my picture,' Poppy proclaimed with fervour,

hugging Tessa. 'Thank you, thank you, thank you. I'll hang it on the wall by my bed where I can look at it every day. And now I have something for *you*.' She ran upstairs and returned with a small package, clumsily wrapped.

Tessa tore off the paper to reveal a thin woven strip of coloured threads.

'It's a friendship bracelet,' Poppy explained. 'I made it myself – Sophie gave me the kit for my birthday. I made it for you, specially. I *knew* that you'd come.' She tied it round Tessa's wrist. 'There! When you wear it, you're supposed to be reminded of me.'

Tessa tried to speak, but was choked with emotion at the girl's loving generosity. Instead she hugged her.

'I think it's time for some music,' said Ned, who had already put on his musical braces over the top of his Christmas-tree jumper. 'Miles, are you going to do the honours?'

'Just try to stop me!' He went to the piano and pulled out the bench with a flourish, then sat and brought his fingers down on the keys in a resonant chord.

They all gathered round the piano and sang along as he played through the repertoire of familiar Christmas carols. As she had done at Midnight Mass, Tessa lost herself in the words and melodies and forgot to be self-conscious, singing out with feeling. During a pause, while Ned went to fetch his violin, Melanie turned to Tessa. 'I thought that you told me you weren't musical!'

'I'm not.'

'But, Tessa, you can sing! You have a beautiful voice,' she declared. 'I think you've been hiding your light under a bushel.'

Tessa blushed as Miles reached for his wine glass, deposited on top of the piano for safekeeping. 'I'll drink to that!' he said, suiting his actions to his words.

'Let's do "White Christmas" next,' Poppy suggested. 'I wish it *were* a white Christmas. I wish it would snow and snow and snow. Then we could build a snowman and have a big snow-ball fight. Wouldn't that be fun?'

'It makes me cold just thinking about it,' shuddered Melanie. 'It doesn't sound like much fun to *me*.'

Ned came back with his violin. 'It's the warming up after-wards that's the fun part, Mel, my love,' he said, grinning at his wife and draping an arm around her shoulders. 'Don't you agree?'

'Drinking coffee, you mean?' She patted her bulging abdomen ruefully. 'That's about all the warming-up activity I could manage at the moment, I'm sorry to say.'

The mention of coffee made Tessa aware, suddenly, of her full bladder; and she slipped off upstairs to use the lavatory. On her way back, feeling better, she was startled to find Miles waiting for her on the landing. 'Oh!'

'Helena decided that she wanted to take over the piano for a bit,' he said. 'She and Ned are playing a duet. So I thought I'd grab the chance to catch up with you and have that kiss.' He grinned at Tessa with an owlish leer and took a step towards her.

She was flustered more than repelled or frightened: he looked so ridiculous with that wild hair sticking out beneath his rakish paper crown, with his bibulous complexion and magnified eyes behind his spectacles.

'Oh, it's very kind of you, but no thank you,' she said firmly.

'But Tessa . . .' He took another step in her direction.

Counting on the quantity of his alcohol consumption to slow his reaction time, she walked straight past him and down the stairs. Her coat was draped over the bannister at the bottom; she put it on and let herself out of the front door, closing it behind her with a click. He wouldn't follow her out here, she was confident.

For a moment she stood on the front step, unsure what to do next. It was time to be getting home; Rob might be home already, wondering what had happened to her.

She knew that she should go back in and make her fare-wells, but she couldn't face it – couldn't face the explanations, or the embarrassment of trying to convey her gratitude to these kind friends for absorbing her into their family Christmas and making her feel such a part of it all. Melanie would insist that Ned should drive her home; it would all become very complicated. It was easier to slip off now, rude as it would seem to them. Later she would ring Melanie and apologise for her unceremonious departure, she told herself.

And deep down inside, Tessa knew that if she didn't leave now, she might not want to leave at all.

But Rob would be waiting for her at home. If he wasn't there now, he would be quite soon. She was sure of it.

Tessa put her hands in her pockets and started off towards home. There was no traffic; the streets were dark and still. 'Silent night, holy night, all is calm, all is bright,' she hummed.

It seemed, somehow, to be not quite so cold as it had been. She lifted her face to the sky: no stars tonight. It smelled like snow. Perhaps, she told herself, Poppy would get her wish before Christmas was over. Snow, cleansing snow, making all things fresh and new. An omen.

And before she reached home, the first white flakes fell on her upraised face like an icy benison.

Chapter 23

The snow produced scarcely enough for a snowball, let alone a snowman: there was just enough of it to cover the ground and slick the roads. Tessa, returning home, was relieved to see Rob's car in front of the house; she would have hated to think of him driving home in such conditions.

He was waiting for her at the front door, his face as white as the flakes which filled the air. 'Where have you been?' were his first words, in a voice fraught with tension.

'I went to Melanie's,' she said.

'You didn't leave a note or anything! What am I supposed to think when I come home to an empty house, with no indication of where you are?'

Tessa might have retorted a good many things: she might have said that it was unreasonable of him to expect her to spend Christmas Day on her own, waiting for him to come home. She might have said that he was not always scrupulous about letting her know where *he* was at any given moment. But she sensed that this was not the time for that. 'I'm sorry,' she said contritely. 'I should have left a note.'

In her eagerness to appease him and make it up to him, she forgot about ringing Melanie until the next morning. Then, once again, she found herself apologising. 'I'm *so* sorry,' she said. 'It was really rude of me to leave like that, without a word.'

'It did seem a bit strange,' admitted Melanie. 'You just sort of disappeared into thin air. It wasn't', she added intuitively, 'by any chance because of Miles, was it?'

'I suppose it was,' Tessa confessed. 'I met him on the landing. He said he wanted to kiss me. I managed to escape from him, but after that I just couldn't face everyone.'

Melanie laughed richly. 'You didn't believe him, did you?'

'Well . . . yes.'

'Oh, Tessa.' Still Melanie chuckled. 'Surely you could see that Miles was safe. He's the biggest closet queen I've ever met.'

'You mean . . .'

'Yes, of course that's what I mean. He's no danger to any woman. Not to me, not to you.'

'But he tried to kiss me,' Tessa insisted.

'I don't imagine he tried very hard,' Melanie pointed out. 'If he'd really wanted to, I'm sure he would have done it, wouldn't have let you escape.'

Tessa was baffled. 'Then why did he say he wanted to?'

'Because he's in denial, of course,' expounded the psychologist. 'He's trying very hard to convince everyone. Especially himself, and especially when he's had too much to drink. That's when he gets really outrageous. I suppose I should have warned you,' she added. 'There just wasn't an opportunity.'

Remembering how heavy-handed his flirtation had been, how half-hearted his groping under the table, Tessa felt both deflated and embarrassed: perhaps she *should* have realised. Now that it had been explained to her, it seemed rather obvious.

'It's Ned he really fancies,' Melanie went on. 'Has done for years. So when he's around Ned, his need to convince himself and everyone else can get a bit out of hand.'

'But don't you mind?' Tessa blurted.

Melanie laughed. 'Why should I mind? Miles is too

closeted ever to lay a finger on Ned, or even to say a word to him about how he feels, and even if he did, Ned certainly wouldn't be interested. No, I think it's rather sweet.'

'Well, anyway,' Tessa changed the subject, 'I do apologise for disappearing like that. I really did have a wonderful time.'

'And we enjoyed having you. You've made such a big hit with the girls.'

Tessa smiled to herself at the thought of the girls.

'Now they're pestering me about when you're coming back,' Melanie continued. 'Helena and Clare were very put out that Poppy had a present to give you and they didn't. So they've each come up with something for you.'

'How sweet. I suppose I could come round one day this week.'

'Oh, they don't want to wait that long,' chuckled Melanie. 'They're insisting that Ned bring the presents round to you today. Will you be in this afternoon?'

'Yes,' said Tessa. This afternoon she would be entertaining Andrew at lunch, she remembered. The thought of that, the anticipation of seeing him again, brought her more pleasure than she had expected.

This time Rob didn't offer to help her with the lunch. 'I have things to do,' he told her, disappearing upstairs to his computer room.

Tessa added another place setting at the dining room table, removing the crackers. Then she disposed of the potatoes that Rob had peeled the day before and started on a fresh batch. She hoped that Andrew wouldn't mind a repeat of what he had undoubtedly had for lunch the day before; at least it wouldn't be leftovers.

She had just finished the potatoes and put them on to boil when the phone rang. It might well be Andrew, she thought, asking for directions to the house. Drying her hands on a tea towel, she went out to the hall to answer it.

As she put the receiver to her ear, she heard Rob's voice saying hello, and realised that he had picked up the extension in his computer room. She might as well hold on, she decided, and see who it was: if it were Andrew, Rob would shout down the stairs for her to take the call.

'Hello, darling,' came a throaty female voice. 'Happy Boxing Day.'

Though she'd only heard that voice a few times before, Tessa recognised it immediately as Amanda's. In shock she gripped the receiver.

Rob's next words sounded annoyed. 'I thought I told you not to ring me at home. What if Tessa had answered?'

'Then I would have hung up without saying a word.' Amanda chuckled. 'Lighten up, darling. She's not going to find out.'

'But I . . .'

'You weren't worried about Tessa yesterday, if I recall correctly. You were magnificent, by the way,' she added.

Tessa knew that she should hang up the phone, should try to forget what she had just heard and carry on as if this had never happened. But it was too late: she was afraid that if she put the phone down now, the click would betray her. Rob would know that she had overheard.

A tiny alarm bell sounded at the back of her mind, unfocused and vague.

'Why are you ringing?' asked Rob.

'I miss you,' Amanda purred. 'Yesterday just whetted my appetite. Can't we get together this afternoon? Carry on where we left off?'

'We agreed not to meet today.'

'But Ian's gone off to work,' Amanda said. 'I'm lying here all alone in this big bed, thinking about you. Wishing you were here. Come on, darling,' she wheedled. 'You can get away for a few hours. You have the perfect excuse, with this Millennium Bug thing – Tessa won't suspect. And I have a few ideas for how we can improve on yesterday.' Her chuckle was ripe with sensuous promise.

'But Tessa has someone coming for lunch,' Rob explained. 'Some chap she used to work with.'

Amanda laughed. 'You're not afraid she's going to have it off with him if you're not there, are you? Timid little Tessa? And preggers, to boot?'

Rob gave a snort, almost of contempt. 'No, that doesn't worry me in the least. I think he's a poofter, anyhow.'

'And you would rather spend the afternoon with some fairy than with *me*?' she said in a provocative voice. 'Me, and a bottle of champagne? I read one time about some interesting things you can do with champagne. And that's just for starters.'

'If you put it *that* way,' Rob drawled, 'it doesn't sound like much of a choice.'

'Just tell Tessa what you told her yesterday,' Amanda instructed. 'Emergency at work, blah de blah. She bought it once, she'll buy it again.'

'All right, then,' he capitulated. 'I'll be there as soon as I can.'

'You won't be sorry,' Amanda said huskily. 'I promise you – I'll make it worth your while.' Then her voice changed. 'But be careful darling. The roads are really slick. That's why Ian had to go out to work today, when he hadn't expected to be on duty – there have been so many prangs that they needed to pull in extra people to cope with it.'

'I'll be careful,' Rob promised, putting down the phone with a click.

For a moment Tessa stood, receiver clenched in a hand that seemed so unconnected to her that she had to will herself to take it away from her ear and replace the phone in its cradle.

That done, with the same sense of disconnectedness from her own body, Tessa found herself going up the stairs; she met Rob coming out of his computer room.

'Oh, hello,' he said. 'I was just coming to look for you. I'm afraid that—'

'You're having an affair,' she blurted. 'With Amanda. You've been sleeping with her. You're going there now.'

Rob pressed his lips together, then said curtly, 'You've been eavesdropping. People who eavesdrop sometimes hear things they don't want to know.'

'But, Rob!' Her voice seemed ripped out of her, raw with anguish. 'How could you do this to me?'

'Do this to *you*?' He took a step backwards and looked at her, his eyes moving from head to toe and back up again. 'It's *your* fault. All your fault. Everything that has happened is your fault.'

'*My* fault? And what do you mean, everything?' Her voice was bewildered rather than angry.

'Amanda, for starters,' he said. 'It wouldn't have happened if you hadn't—'

'Hadn't *what*?'

Rob narrowed his eyes and spoke with chilly calm. 'I keep telling you, Tessa. You just never know when to leave well alone. We were happy. We had everything. You should have been satisfied. But then you went and got pregnant.'

'I know I was wrong not to tell you before I went off the Pill,' she admitted painfully. 'But I wanted a baby. I thought—'

'*You* wanted. *You* thought,' he said. 'That's just my point. You don't ever think about *me*, about what *I* want.'

'Oh, Rob, that's not fair.'

'Fair? Getting pregnant without telling me was *fair*?'

Her throat was tight, her mouth dry. 'All right, I should have told you. I admit that. But what does that have to do with Amanda?'

'I'm not made of stone,' he stated, his face looking very much as though it were. 'I have needs. When I can't sleep with my wife, what do you expect me to do? Amanda wanted me. She wants me. She gives me what I need.'

'*I* want you,' Tessa cried. 'And who says that you can't sleep with me? I told you what the doctor said – making love won't hurt the baby, and it won't hurt *me*. It's perfectly safe. I don't understand!'

'You don't understand. You don't understand,' Rob sneered. 'I've told you before, Tessa – you don't bloody understand *anything*.'

'Then tell me.' Her hands stretched out to him in supplication. 'Explain it. Tell me what I don't understand.'

He took another step away from her. 'You're going to be a *mother*,' he said, the final word expelled as though he were spitting out poison.

A mother. It had to do with his mother, then. He had brought up the subject. Now, thought Tessa, was the time to get it all out in the open, to be honest with him, to clear the air. 'Listen, Rob,' she said, dropping her arms to her sides, trying to be calm. 'I know about your mother.'

'Oh, God, Tessa! You don't know a *thing* about her. Not a bloody thing!'

She took a deep breath. 'I know about the babies.'

Rob stared at her for a moment. 'Do you?'

'I know. And I know that she started doing it for your sake, Rob. Because she needed the money. Because she had to survive.'

'Well, then, you don't know a bloody thing. Like I said.' He closed his eyes, as if in pain. 'She didn't do *anything* for me. Can you imagine what it was like for me, coming home during the school holidays before she built that bloody nursery and finding my room occupied? Finding one of those . . . those freaks, sleeping in my bed?'

Tessa suddenly felt aggrieved on Linda's behalf. 'Your father left her for another woman! She had a child to bring up!'

His eyes flew open. 'Leave my father out of this!'

'But he abandoned her, abandoned *you*!'

'My father has nothing to do with this! How dare you mention him in the same breath as that bitch?' he challenged her in a voice that was still furiously controlled. 'He should never have married her – and he wouldn't have done, if she hadn't trapped him by getting pregnant. Just like you,' he added with venom.

'I didn't trap you!'

'No.' Rob folded his arms across his chest. 'You were worse than that. You knew I wouldn't marry you if you tried that little trick. You knew I would have made you get rid of it, or would have left you. So you waited till after we were married to get yourself up the spout.'

'I didn't get myself pregnant,' she pointed out tartly. 'You had something to do with it.'

'Did I?' he sneered. 'Maybe it isn't even mine.'

'Don't be ridiculous!' Tessa cried. '*You're* the one that's having the affair, not me.' She clenched her fists so tightly that her nails dug into her palms, trying not to burst into tears. Tears, she knew intuitively, would only make things worse.

Rob must have known he was on shaky ground; he changed the subject. 'How did you find out about her, anyway?' he demanded. 'I suppose it was that meddlesome priest who told you.'

There was no point going into the story about Baby Priscilla; it would only anger him if she admitted that she'd been to his mother's house. 'We talked about it, yes,' she temporised.

'He's as bad as you are. Sticking his nose in where it doesn't belong, minding other people's business, getting himself into trouble.' A small smile, almost of triumph, flickered across his face.

Tessa gasped. Her ribs felt so tight that she couldn't breathe as several things juxtaposed themselves in her mind and fell into place. The horrifying vision of Father Theo on the floor of the church, crushed beneath the statue. Rob's smug smile just now. And the click of the telephone. No, that wasn't quite right. It was the non-click – the click that hadn't been there, that morning when Father Theo had rung her to say that he had an idea about who had murdered Linda. Rob hadn't put the phone down; he had heard their conversation. That was what had bothered her at the time, what had started the little subconscious alarm bell this morning. Rob had heard the conversation with Father Theo.

All of these thoughts flashed through her mind in the space of a heartbeat, followed closely by others. She tried to recall what Rob had said when she'd rung him from the hospital to tell him about the accident. He'd seemed surprised that Father Theo was injured, had asked how badly he was hurt.

He hadn't asked how it had happened, or how she happened to be involved – none of the questions that he should have asked.

Was his surprise caused not by the fact that the priest was injured, but that he wasn't dead?

'How badly?' he had asked. Not 'How?'

But why?

There was an obvious answer, but she wasn't yet ready to take that step. 'His accident . . .' she faltered.

Her horror must have shown on her face; Rob gave a contemptuous laugh. 'Accident? I suppose you could call it that. Millions wouldn't. He only got what he deserved for meddling in other people's affairs. For not leaving well alone.'

She covered her face with her hands, unable to look at him, as the enormity of it all struck her like a hammer blow. 'You . . .' she whispered through her fingers.

'Yes, I did it,' he said in a careless voice. 'I pushed that . . . that stone thing on top of him. Pity it didn't kill him. But with any luck he'll be a cabbage for the rest of his life.'

Enough, said Tessa's brain. But her mouth opened and the word came out without volition. 'Why?'

'Why do you think?' He put his hand in his pocket and

began jiggling the change, as if they were discussing what to have for dinner. 'Oh, Tessa. If you don't know the answer to that, you *are* bloody stupid. Stupider than I thought.'

She lowered her hands from her face and stared at him for a long moment. 'No,' she choked.

'It was your fault. I told you to leave bloody well alone,' he stated. 'From the beginning I told you that.'

'No . . .'

'But you wouldn't listen to me,' he went on. 'You *had* to meet my mother. I told you I never wanted to see the bitch again, but you wouldn't have it. You wouldn't leave it alone. My mother would be alive today, living happily in Southgate with her freaks and perverts, if it weren't for you and your bloody meddling.'

'No . . .'

'I suppose you want to know why I killed her,' he said dispassionately.

'No,' Tessa moaned, putting her hands over her ears. 'No, no, no.'

He went on as though she hadn't made a sound. 'Since it's your fault, you deserve to know.'

'No.'

'She – laughed – at – me.' He spoke in a deliberate way, spacing the words out for emphasis.

Tessa stared, startled out of her denial mode. '*Laughed* at you?'

'I told you, Tessa. No one laughs at me. Not ever.'

'She *laughed* at you?' Still she didn't quite believe what she was hearing.

Rob was looking at her, but Tessa could tell that he didn't see her; rather, he saw through her to some horror that she couldn't share. 'I went to talk to her that afternoon,' he said. 'Before we were meant to be there. I wanted to prepare her for our visit. I wanted to make sure that she wouldn't tell you about those perverts.'

Numb, Tessa held her breath.

'She took me into the front room. She started talking as though nothing had happened – as though it hadn't been eight years since I'd bloody seen her.' Rob flexed his hands convulsively. 'Then she said you'd told her about the baby. She said that she couldn't believe I was going to be a father. She said how could I have a baby of my own, when I was nothing more than a baby myself? A big baby. Then . . . she laughed.'

His words were coming in ragged gasps. 'She turned her back on me. Turned away, laughing. The fireplace irons were there. I picked up the poker. I didn't really mean to kill her. But she wouldn't stop laughing. Till I hit her. Then she stopped. But *I* didn't stop until she was dead.'

'Oh, God,' breathed Tessa, taking a step away from him towards the stairs.

'I tried to ring you, tried to stop you from coming. But you weren't there. I drove home. Changed my clothes. Threw the bloody ones in a skip somewhere. I didn't want you to go in there. I didn't want you to be the one to find her. But you wouldn't listen to me. You had to go in. It was your fault. All your fault.'

'But you killed her!'

'She shouldn't have laughed at me,' he stated, then shook his head, as if coming out of a trance.

'What are you going to do now?'

'Me? What am I going to do?' Rob smiled. 'I'm going to see my mistress and spend the rest of the day in bed with her. *She* doesn't ask me stupid questions. *She* doesn't laugh at me. Amanda knows when to keep her mouth shut.'

'I meant, what are you going to do about the police . . .' gasped Tessa, with another backward step, her arms round her abdomen.

'The police?' Now he looked at her, seeming to register her retreat. 'This has nothing to do with the police.'

Tessa had almost reached the stairs. With a few long strides he caught up with her and grabbed her wrist. 'You're not going to tell them, are you?'

'Please,' she whispered. 'Let go of me.'

It happened quickly. Rob twisted her wrist as he released it, and that unbalanced her. She grabbed for the handrail, but he gave her a shove.

Tessa fell down the whole steep flight of stairs, landing heavily at the bottom.

Rob walked down slowly. 'I'm sorry, Tessa,' he said, standing over her, looking down at her.

She was drowning in pain, mental and physical. Everything hurt. 'Rob,' she whispered. He was sorry. It was all a bad joke. First he was going to ring for an ambulance, and then he was going to tell her that it was all a joke, that he'd made the whole story up to teach her a lesson.

He aimed a half-hearted kick at her head, then another one – quite deliberate – at her abdomen. 'I'm sorry, Tessa,' he repeated. 'Sorry that you couldn't have left well alone. We could have been happy together, you know.'

The door slammed.

I'm going to die, thought Tessa, welcoming it. It was too bad that her baby would die with her, but perhaps it was all for the best. What sort of life would it be, growing up with not just a dead mother but a murderer for a father?

Tessa closed her eyes and gave in to the pain.

Chapter 24

The first thing that Tessa saw when she opened her eyes was the plaster statue of the Virgin and Child. The unlikeliness of that convinced her, even through the fuzziness of her mental processes, that she was still asleep and dreaming. Then she saw, next to the Virgin, in a bizarre juxtaposition, a long-legged plastic doll with shiny blonde hair and a pink tutu. 'Poppy,' she said aloud, and though her voice was faint, the sound of it made her think that perhaps, after all, she was awake.

She had no idea where she was or how long she had been there. A series of faint mental images teased her, flitting round the edges of her brain. Dreams, half recalled, or things that had really happened?

Melanie's kind face, and Ned's as well. Poppy's voice. A man in a dog-collar. Father Theo? No, Father Theo was injured and unconscious. Could it have been her father, then? And Andrew, with his puppy-dog eyes.

Not Rob.

That was when she remembered, with sickening clarity, and gasped in pain. Rob.

She closed her eyes as the memories washed over her, then opened them again quickly to check her abdomen. Yes, there was still a bulge under the smooth white sheet; she ran her hands over it in confirmation.

A white sheet. She must be in hospital, then. Four white

walls, a square of a window with several vases of flowers on the deep sill.

She raised her hands off the sheet so that she could see them; there was a drip going into the back of one of them, just like Father Theo's. With the other hand she touched her head. There seemed to be a bandage on her forehead, though not a huge one.

'Hello?' she said aloud. There was no reply, no one else in the room. A private room, then: Rob's health insurance must have provided it. Her fingers fumbled for the call button which she knew must be there, attached with a clip to the bed. Father Theo had one; she must have one too.

She found it and pressed down. A moment later a young nurse appeared. 'Mrs Nicholls!' she said. 'You're awake, then.'

There were so many questions Tessa wanted to ask, so many things she needed to know. Where to start? 'My husband,' she said. 'Rob.'

The nurse busied herself with Tessa's pillows, evading her eyes. 'There, now,' she said. 'Let's get you nice and comfy. Is that better?'

Tessa tried again, this time with a more direct question. 'Where is my husband?'

'Your friend Mrs Maybank is here,' the nurse told her. 'She's hardly left your side all the time you've been here. But a few minutes ago she popped down to the canteen for a bite to eat. She ought to be back soon.'

Giving up, Tessa attempted another line of questioning. 'How long have I been here, then?'

The nurse seemed more amenable to this. 'Let me see. I think it must be about a week, or nearly that. Today is the thirty-first.' She looked at Tessa's notes. 'You came in on the twenty-sixth. Boxing Day.'

'New Year's Eve,' said Tessa.

'That's right,' the nurse confirmed brightly. 'Lots of parties tonight.'

Once again Tessa's hands went to her abdomen. 'My baby,' she said. 'Is she all right?'

The nurse went to the window and began rearranging the flowers in one of the vases, plucking out a blossom that was beginning to droop. 'Oh, I should think so.' She glanced towards the door. 'Here's your friend now,' she announced with what sounded like relief. 'Look, Mrs Maybank! Our patient is awake!'

Melanie came into the room swiftly and crossed to the bed, leaning down to look full into Tessa's face. 'Tessa!' she said happily, smiling. 'Welcome back!'

'I'll leave you to it, then,' said the nurse. 'Unless there's something you need?'

'I'd like a drink of water,' requested Tessa. The effort of speaking had made her realise how dry her throat was.

'Just a sip, then.' There was a jug on the bedside table. The nurse half-filled a cup and brought a straw to Tessa's lips. 'We don't want to overdo it straight away,' she cautioned.

'We'll be fine,' Melanie assured her as she departed. 'I can look after her.'

She took Tessa's unencumbered hand and held it between her own. For a moment neither of them said anything, scarcely knowing where to begin.

'How did I get here?' asked Tessa at last.

Melanie seemed to be weighing up her answer, trying to gauge how much Tessa remembered of what had happened. Then she recounted how Andrew, arriving for lunch, had been concerned when he'd had no reply to the bell, and was beginning to wonder whether he had the wrong house – or the wrong day – when Ned turned up to deliver Helena and Clare's presents.

'I didn't know that you knew Andrew,' Tessa interposed.

Melanie laughed. 'We didn't then. We do now. He and Ned have become great mates. They've got a similar sense of humour.' She continued her story, telling how the two men, strangers until that moment, had consulted on the doorstep, both sure that Tessa was meant to be there. Finally they'd gone round to the alley which ran behind the road. After some trial and error in determining exactly which was the right house, Andrew – with a boost from Ned – had scaled the wall into the back garden and had found the back door unlocked.

'Thank goodness I'd been out to the rubbish bin earlier and hadn't locked the door,' said Tessa.

'Oh, they would have got in one way or another,' Melanie assured her. 'They were both very determined. And very worried.'

The rest of the story Tessa could imagine without being told: the frantic phone call to the emergency services, the ambulance, casualty, the long wait for news. She had been through all of that herself with Father Theo, only days before.

The memory of Father Theo brought with it the recollection that she now knew what had happened to him, and at whose hands. She closed her eyes and swallowed, then said, 'Rob. Where is Rob?'

Melanie was silent for so long that Tessa opened her eyes and looked at her troubled face. 'Where is Rob?' she repeated.

'The doctor insists that it's very important for you to remain calm,' Melanie said in a soothing voice.

'Is he . . . in gaol?' Tessa caught a flicker of surprise on Melanie's face before her friend averted her eyes, shaking her head.

'No.'

The alternative was even worse, yet somehow inevitable. 'He's dead, isn't he?' Tessa whispered. 'Rob is dead.'

Melanie hesitated, then nodded reluctantly. 'The doctor didn't want you to be told.'

'Did the doctor think I wouldn't notice that my husband wasn't here?' she said with uncharacteristic sarcasm, then insisted, 'Tell me what happened. I need to know. I deserve to know. How can you keep it from me?'

'All right then.' Melanie sighed. 'I hate dishonesty, but I didn't want to be the one to tell you.'

'What happened?'

'It was an accident – a traffic accident.' Melanie squeezed her hand. 'The roads were slippery from the snow. He was apparently driving too fast for conditions, and went head-on into another car. The other man was well over the limit for blood alcohol, so there's still some dispute about who was at fault.'

'But they're both dead,' Tessa stated in a soft, flat voice.

'He wouldn't have felt anything,' Melanie reassured her. 'It was instantaneous.'

Again Tessa closed her eyes. It was over, then. A death for a death. There was something fitting about that, she told herself.

He had murdered his mother. He had tried to kill Father Theo, and he had – arguably – tried to kill her and their baby as well. She should feel relieved that it had ended like this, without the pain and humiliation of public exposure, a trial, prison.

But he had been her husband. She had loved him; he had loved her. They had known much joy in each other's arms. They had built a home together, and together they had created a new human life. Now their baby would come into the world without a father. Half an orphan already, before she was even born.

Tessa's throat closed, stifling a sob, but tears oozed from her eyes. Rob was dead. Her husband, her love. A murderer, and dead.

Though the pain of it would not depart so quickly, Tessa's tears had dried by the time the doctor stopped by on his rounds. 'She's awake, then?' he addressed Melanie.

'She woke about an hour ago.'

He flipped through her notes. 'Well, I don't see any reason why she can't go home in a few days, as soon as we have her stabilised on solid foods. Strict bed-rest, of course. That's essential. That's what she really needs, and she can get it at home as well as here, provided there is someone to look after her.'

He was talking about her as though she weren't even there, Tessa fumed. Who did he think he was, anyway? 'I can't go home,' she said, loud and deliberate. 'My husband is dead.'

The doctor turned accusing eyes on Melanie. 'You told her. I gave strict orders that she wasn't to be told.'

'Don't blame her,' said Tessa. 'I guessed. I made her tell me. I had a right to know.'

He looked at her for the first time, assuming a bedside manner like a cloak. 'Mrs Nicholls,' he said soothingly, 'it is very important that you remain calm. Your friend was only following my orders. Try to put it out of your mind, now, and concentrate on getting better.'

'But why?' demanded Tessa. 'Why is it so important to remain calm?'

Again he ignored her and spoke to Melanie. 'Will there be a place for her to go when she's released from hospital?'

'She'll be coming to us,' Melanie said in a firm voice, before Tessa could interrupt. 'We'll look after her. My husband and I.'

'That's all right, then.' The doctor returned her notes to their slot at the end of her bed.

'But you can't look after me,' Tessa protested, struggling to raise her head from the pillows. 'You have Ned and the girls to look after. And yourself, and your baby. I couldn't possibly impose on you like that.'

'It's all settled,' said Melanie in a voice that brooked no argument. 'You're coming to us, for as long as necessary. We shall *all* look after you: Ned and I and the girls. And stop being so stroppy,' she added with a smile, 'or I shall change my mind.'

Tears of gratitude stung Tessa's eyes as the doctor retreated towards the door. 'There's one other thing,' Melanie said to him so quietly that Tessa knew she was not meant to hear. 'The police. They'd like to talk to her. They've been waiting for days. Would it be all right for them to have a word with her? They say it's important.'

He made a gesture, as if washing his hands of the matter. 'For a few minutes, as long as they don't upset her too much. You stay with her and keep an eye on her, and if she gets too agitated, you can call a halt to it. You seem to know best,' he added tartly, departing.

The police. It was inevitable, Tessa knew. She might as well get it over with.

Melanie explained it to her: that they needed to talk to her, had a few questions to ask. 'Are you up to it?'

'Yes,' said Tessa, her face set.

It was DI Tower who arrived a few minutes later, as Tessa had expected. The sergeant with him, equipped with a note-book, was not Doug Coles. 'Mrs Nicholls,' said Tower awkwardly, sitting down at the side of her bed, opposite Melanie. 'I'm sorry about your accident. It's very good of you to have a word with me.'

'It wasn't an accident,' Tessa stated calmly. 'My husband pushed me down the stairs.' She could hear Melanie's sharp intake of breath, even as the policeman nodded.

'I wondered,' he said.

Tessa didn't look at Melanie. 'And he killed his mother. And tried to kill Father Theo.' It was the only way she could tell him – factually, unemotionally, trying to pretend that it didn't matter. That it didn't hurt like no pain she'd ever felt before.

He made little comment, allowing her to tell the story in

her own way, only occasionally prompting her with a question. 'And you really didn't suspect anything, Mrs Nicholls?' he said when she'd finished.

'I loved him,' Tessa said simply. 'I believed in his innocence. I thought I knew him, and I didn't think he was capable of murdering anyone, let alone his own mother.'

'Dear God,' said Melanie under her breath, squeezing Tessa's hand.

'And there's something else,' Tessa went on. 'I thought I'd figured out who the murderer was.' Without any pleasure she watched the dawning astonishment on the face of DI Tower as she explained her suspicions of his colleague Doug Coles, and the reasons for those suspicions.

'You're sure about this?' Tower demanded. 'These are serious charges you're making. Obstruction of justice, at the very least.'

Tessa nodded. 'Ask Ian Spicer,' she said. 'DI Spicer.'

'Right.' Tower's voice was brisk, but he was unable to keep his mouth from twitching with amusement as he made a note of Ian's name. 'I'll leave you then, Mrs Nicholls. Thanks for your help.'

Tessa put out a hand to stop him. 'You knew all along, didn't you?' she asked. 'That's why you kept coming back. And why you wouldn't tell me anything about the investigation. Because you knew.'

'We suspected,' the policeman admitted. 'We didn't have any proof, but, yes, we did have a very strong suspicion that your husband was implicated. I never believed that he picked up that murder weapon by accident. And his alibi was pretty vague – we were never able to find anyone at his office who could confirm that he was where he said he was at the relevant time.'

'And I made life difficult for you by trying so hard to protect him,' mused Tessa. 'If I hadn't been so stupid about it, none of the rest of it might have happened. Father Theo . . .'

'The Reverend Frost confirms your story, by the way,' DI

Tower said. 'He saw who pushed that statue over, just before it hit him. It was your husband.'

It took Tessa a few seconds to grasp the implications of his words. 'Father Theo told you that? Then he's conscious? He can talk?'

'He regained consciousness a few days ago,' the policeman told her.

'He's making good progress,' added Melanie. 'I've been keeping an eye on him.' She smiled at Tessa. 'How did you think the Virgin and Child got here? He asked me to bring it to you – he said that you needed it more than he did.'

Tessa squeezed her eyes shut, her emotions close to the surface, but this time her tears were tears of joy.

Exhausted, Tessa slept for a time. When she woke, Melanie was still at her side. 'You don't have to stay with me all day,' Tessa protested. 'You've done enough. I'll be quite all right on my own. Why don't you go home?'

'What makes you think you'd be on your own? There *are* other people waiting to see you,' said Melanie. 'But the doctor thought it was better that they come one at a time, strictly rationed, so you don't get over-stimulated.' She gave a crooked, self-deprecating smile. 'I suppose he thinks I'm a calming presence.'

'You *are*. But what other people?'

'Well, there's Ned, of course. He's at home with the girls, waiting to be summoned for his turn. Andrew, as well. And there's your father.'

'My father?' Astonished, Tessa struggled to sit up. It hadn't been a dream, then.

Firmly Melanie pushed her back down. 'Bed-rest, remember? No getting up. He's in the waiting room right now. Would you like to see him?'

'Oh, yes!' she cried, without stopping to think about it. Then, as Melanie went to fetch him, she was assailed with second thoughts. *Did* she want to see him? Everyone kept telling her to be calm. Would she be able to remain so, confronting her father?

He came in quietly, standing for a moment at the end of the bed and smiling at her, then he moved to her side and took her hand, bending over to kiss her cheek.

'Daddy,' she said. He looked older than the last time she'd seen him – nearly a year it had been, she realised with a twinge of guilt. There were new lines in his face, and his hair was now nearly as grey as his clerical shirt.

'Tessa, my dear.' His voice cracked. 'Oh, Tessa.'

She felt the need to reassure him. 'I'm going to be all right, Daddy.'

'Yes, of course you are.'

For nearly a minute they just looked at each other; the habit of silence between them was deep-seated.

'Tessa,' he said at last. 'I've had your letter.'

'Yes.' She tried to smile, but her face wouldn't co-operate. 'You didn't mention it when you rang. On Christmas Eve.'

'But I hadn't received it at that point!'

'I posted it the day before,' she said. 'First Class. In time for the last post.'

'At Christmas time? Surely you would know that it takes longer at Christmas. The letter didn't arrive until the middle of the week.'

'But I thought you would get it on Christmas Eve,' she reiterated.

'Tessa, you are the most disputatious child!' he frowned, barely containing his vexation.

'I *am*?' she gasped, astonished. Tessa had always thought of herself as something of a stoic, passively enduring her father's fault-finding and his fraught silences.

'You always have been, but never mind.' He patted her hand. 'I didn't come here to quarrel with you. Far from it, my dear. We need to talk about that letter.'

'Yes, all right, Daddy.' Tessa swallowed hard and prepared herself for the worst.

'I've never been more amazed by anything in my entire life,' he said. 'I thought at first that you must have meant it as a joke.'

'It was no joke.'

Her father looked towards the window, as if he couldn't trust himself to meet her eyes. 'How could you ever have thought that I found it difficult to love you? That you were a disappointment to me? You've been the joy of my life, always. And you're all that I have, since your mother died.'

Tessa gulped. 'You never said.'

His head drooped. 'I'm not good at talking about feelings,' he admitted, the words wrenched out of him. 'I loved your mother so much, and it has been one of the great sorrows of my life that I didn't have a chance to tell her so, before she died. And when she was gone . . .'

'How did my mother die?' Tessa asked, sensing that this moment of weakness on the part of her father was her opportunity to learn the truth at last.

Now he looked at her. 'But you know very well,' he said. 'I never made a secret of it. She was hit by a car. A hit-and-run driver. She had just popped out to the corner shop to buy a pint of milk, and she never came home.' One side of his face twitched, an incipient tic held barely under control. 'I didn't understand what you were going on about in your letter – saying that I wouldn't talk to you about her death, and that I blamed you. That's ridiculous, Tessa. There was no one to blame but that driver. You've always known that.'

'Oh, God.' Tessa thought the words, but didn't say them aloud, knowing how her father felt about blasphemy. She remembered. It was all there, as if it had happened yesterday. Her mother, standing in front of the fridge, wondering what to make for pudding. Not enough milk for rice pudding, her mother said, suggesting tinned fruit instead. 'Rice pudding,' insisted young Tessa. 'I want rice pudding. You promised.' So her mother had gone off to the shop, saying that she would be back in a minute. She hadn't come back.

Her fault. She had wanted the rice pudding. She had sent her mother to her death.

All of those years she had suppressed that memory. *She* had been the one, not her father, who couldn't talk about it.

'And your letter was the first I knew about the baby. I was so happy, so excited at the thought of being a grandfather. And then . . . when I thought it was too late . . .' His voice broke.

'Oh, Daddy,' she whispered, clinging to his hand.

Chapter 25

Her next visitor was in fact not alone: Ned came in, with Poppy beside him. Poppy must have been given strict instructions to behave herself; in contrast to her usual ebullience, she was almost subdued. 'Hello, Tessa,' she whispered. 'Mummy says you're awake now, but that I mustn't get you too excited.'

Tessa smiled at her, then at Ned, who bent down to kiss her. 'I worked my charms on that nurse,' he grinned. 'She said one visitor only. But I managed to persuade her that Poppy hardly counts as a *whole* visitor. Half, maybe. And if she was prepared to accept my word that I'm no more than three-quarters of a visitor myself, then we're scarcely more than one put together.'

'And she bought that?'

'Well, I pointed out that I *am* a mathematician,' he said with a wink. 'I think that tipped the balance in my favour. In short, she turned a blind eye. Do you reckon it was my mathematical prowess, or just my incredible good looks?'

Poppy giggled, and Tessa laughed out loud. Ned seemed to have that effect on her; she felt better just for being in his company.

'Daddy brought grapes,' Poppy announced. 'He said that you're always supposed to bring grapes to people in hospital, but I'm not sure why.'

'It's so the visitors will have something to eat, silly.' Ned pulled a bunch of grapes out of his bag and popped one in his mouth. 'I do love grapes. It makes visiting people in hospital a positive pleasure. Not that visiting Tessa wouldn't be that, in any case. Have a grape, Tessa. See how generous I am?'

'I don't think I'm allowed to eat anything yet,' she said with regret; the grapes looked delicious. 'Not till the nurse says I can.'

'Mummy told us that they feed you through that tube,' Poppy said, pointing to the drip. 'That sounds horrible. And Helena wanted to know if it was vegetarian!'

'Where are your sisters?' Tessa asked Poppy.

'Helena's gone to a party. And Daddy said that only one of us could come with him this time, so Clare and I flipped a coin. I won,' Poppy crowed. 'So Clare will come tomorrow.'

'Clare is already getting your room ready,' Ned said. 'And Helena's looking for suitable books to put on the bedside table.'

Poppy was beginning to forget that she was meant to be calm; the top half of her squirmed on to the edge of Tessa's bed. 'We're so excited that you're coming to stay with us!'

'But only if you can be good,' her father reminded her. 'Tessa's going to need a great deal of peace and quiet.'

Tessa's eyes filled with tears. 'It's so kind of you. I just couldn't face going back home after ... after what's happened.'

'That's out of the question,' Ned stated.

Poppy touched Tessa's hand and put on a sympathetic expression. 'I'm sorry that your husband died.'

So Melanie had told them. Tessa wondered how much of the truth they knew.

'But now', said Poppy, brightening, 'you can marry Andrew. I thought for a while that you should marry Uncle Miles, but now I've decided that you should marry Andrew instead.'

'Marry Andrew!' Tessa stared at the girl, then laughed. 'Andrew is just a friend, Poppy. I'm not going to marry him.'

'Oh, but you must!'

'Andrew has made quite a hit with Poppy,' explained Ned. 'He said that she reminds him of one of his sisters, when she was small.'

'He plays games with me,' Poppy said, then added, with a look of cunning, 'He would be such a good daddy for your baby. Every baby should have a daddy.'

'Poppy, you're incorrigible,' laughed her father. 'Why don't you play with your Barbie, or something? Give us grown-ups a rest?'

'Thank you for sharing her with me,' Tessa said as Poppy took her doll from the bedside table. 'It was such a sweet thing for you to do.'

Poppy grinned in acknowledgement, then danced her Barbie down to the end of the bed and over to the window-sill.

Tessa turned to Ned, remembering what Melanie had told her. 'And I must thank you for what you did. Finding me, and all of that. I would still be lying there if you hadn't come along.'

'I doubt that,' he said. 'And it was Andrew, more than me. He was brilliant.' Ned looked round to make sure that Poppy was occupied, then leaned closer and said quietly, 'Joking aside, Tessa, Andrew is crazy about you.'

'But that's ridiculous!'

'No it isn't,' Ned insisted with an uncharacteristic seriousness of expression which did more than anything else to convince Tessa that he wasn't just teasing her. 'Take my word for it. He loves you, Tessa. Treat him gently.'

She felt weak with shock. 'But . . .'

'We've spent a lot of time together over the past few days. And he's been in such a state about you that he's said things to me he probably wouldn't have said in other circumstances. Maybe I shouldn't be telling you this – Mel would probably kill me for putting my oar in. I know it's not the right time, but I think you ought to know.' He dropped his voice yet further. 'He's loved you for years. But you had Ian, and then when you and Ian split up, Andrew thought you needed some time to get over it and decided to wait a while to make a move. He couldn't know that you would meet Rob, and that he'd miss his chance.'

Those were details of her life that Ned couldn't have learned from anyone but Andrew. He wasn't making it up, then. Andrew in love with her? Tessa didn't know what to think. 'He never said . . .' she faltered.

'It was too late,' Ned pointed out. 'By the time you met Rob, it was already too late for Andrew.'

Tessa's voice was a mere whisper. 'I didn't know.'

Ned took her hand. 'Listen, Tessa. I'm not telling you what to do. And I know that the time isn't right – it's way too soon for you even to be thinking about things like this. You've got to concentrate on getting better, on having a healthy baby. But don't shut him out. Give him a chance. He's waited a long time for you, and I know that he'll be willing to wait for as long as it takes.'

After Ned and Poppy took their leave, Tessa fell into a dreamless sleep, as if her brain had taken in too much information, had seen too many entrenched preconceptions turned on their heads, to be able to process any of it.

It was the nurse with the tea-wagon who woke her. 'Are you ready for a cuppa, dear?'

A cup of tea: it sounded wonderful. 'Yes, please,' said Tessa before the nurse could change her mind.

'Do you have an extra cup for a visitor?' came a familiar voice from just outside her door.

Tessa started. 'Father Theo!' she cried.

A wheelchair cleared the door skilfully, manoeuvred from behind by a porter. Harold Dingley. 'Hello, Tessa,' said Harold with a bashful smile. 'I've brought someone to see you.'

'Hello,' Tessa returned. But her attention was on Father Theo, still bandaged prodigiously and looking less than robust, but sitting upright in the wheelchair. She struggled to lift her head so that she could see him better.

'Hold on a mo', dear,' ordered the nurse, pushing a button to raise the head of the bed. 'You're meant to be taking it easy, you know.'

She supplied them both with cups of tea, then departed with Harold, leaving Tessa alone with Father Theo.

'You look better than the last time I saw you,' she said to him.

'And you look worse.'

They both laughed. 'We *are* a pair, aren't we?' the priest added.

'Thanks for coming,' said Tessa. 'It's so good to see you.'

Father Theo made a face. 'I escaped just as my sister-in-law descended for tea. But I was already in the wheelchair, so it was too late for her to do anything but squawk.'

'Lois,' Tessa recalled. 'She's still about, is she?'

'You've met her, then? I suppose you must have done.' He raised his eyebrows. 'The dreaded Lois. Yes, she's still about. She sent my brother back to Belfast, but insisted on staying here to nurse me back to health. "Blood is thicker than water", she's fond of saying, though she's no blood relation herself. She's installed herself at the clergy house and is driving Mrs Williams mad – when she's not here doing the same to me.'

'I suppose she means well,' Tessa said neutrally.

Father Theo looked sceptical. 'I suppose so. Just between the two of us, I can't abide the woman. Never could. I can't understand what Russell ever saw in her. I suppose that having to put up with her now is my penance.'

Penance. 'My father is here,' Tessa told the priest. 'He came in to see me this afternoon.'

'I know.' Father Theo grinned at her surprised expression. 'Your father and I have spent a bit of time together this week. That is to say, he passed some of the time, while you were out of things, sitting in my room and talking.'

'But you don't *know* my father!'

'Oh, yes I do,' the priest chuckled. 'We were at school together. I recognised him as soon as Melanie brought him in and introduced him.'

'I don't believe it!' Yet another surprise, reflected Tessa, readjusting her thinking once more.

'We weren't close friends or anything like that, but we knew one another, and have various acquaintances in common. So we had quite a lot to talk about,' said Father Theo. 'We disagree about churchmanship, of course, but he's not such a bad old stick, you know.'

'Yes, I know,' acknowledged Tessa softly.

The priest paused, then went on, choosing his words with care. 'We talked about *you*, Tessa. You were wrong about him when you told me that he didn't love you, didn't approve of you. He loves you so much, my dear.'

'Yes,' said Tessa. 'Yes, I was wrong.'

She'd been wrong about so many things.

Tessa licked her lips and wondered how to say the next difficult thing. 'About Rob,' she said at last, managing to bring his name out without stumbling. 'I was wrong about him as well. He wasn't the person I thought he was. And I'm so sorry that you had to suffer for that – I feel responsible for what happened to you. If I'd been less dense . . .'

'You loved him,' stated Father Theo. 'Don't feel guilty about that.'

'But he killed his mother!' Tessa blurted painfully, afraid to look at him. She hadn't meant to tell him quite like that.

The priest's voice was gentle. 'Yes, I know.'

Still another surprise. 'But how did you know?'

Father Theo tented his fingers together. 'Remember that morning when I rang you? When I said that someone had said something to give me an idea of who had killed Linda?'

Tessa nodded. 'Baby Buddy – Harold – told me about Baby

Sharon being a policeman. I was sure that was what you were going to tell me.'

'That *was* significant,' the priest agreed. 'Or at least I thought it was. When I heard that, I was sure that Baby Sharon, or whatever he's really called, was the murderer.'

'That's what I thought as well.'

'I reckoned that he'd murdered her, and taken her files to cover it up. But it was only later, in the middle of the night, that I realised the really important thing that had been said that evening. I'd hardly registered it at the time – it was something I'd heard so often before.'

A faint memory teased at Tessa's brain – something that Harold had said. She couldn't remember. 'Millions of times'?

'Baby Priscilla,' the priest went on. 'He started to tell a story. The rest of us shut him up, changed the subject. We were all sick of hearing about it.'

She remembered; it all clicked into place. 'About when Mummy laughed,' quoted Tessa slowly. She clenched her hands together, seeing Rob's tortured face in her mind's eye, hearing his voice. *She – laughed – at – me.* 'Tell me, Father Theo,' she demanded.

'It's not a very nice story,' he warned.

'Tell me.'

The priest shifted in his wheelchair, playing for time. 'I wasn't there myself. But Baby Priscilla was. So what I know is his version. Linda never talked about it, but I expect she felt guilty.'

'Tell me.'

He told her. Rob had been a young adolescent when it happened – thirteen or fourteen. At home during the school holidays, he'd had the bad luck to go into the front room to watch television, where he'd run into two of the babies who'd had a bit too much to drink. Bored and looking for a humorous distraction, the babies had marched him upstairs to the nursery, stripped him of his jeans and T-shirt, and dressed him in a nappy and a frilly dress. One of them had taken his photo. And when they'd shown the photo to Linda, in front of a mortified Rob, she had laughed. In spite of herself, but she had laughed.

'As far as I've been able to tell, it was why he left home as soon as he could, and severed all contact with his mother,' the priest finished.

'And refused to have his photo taken,' Tessa added slowly.

Father Theo went on, 'I remembered that story in the middle of the night. And I thought about how traumatised Rob must have been by the incident. He'd probably managed to suppress it, to keep it out of his mind, to pretend that it had never happened.'

Like she'd suppressed the truth about her mother's death, Tessa said to herself.

'But if something triggered that memory . . .'

'Yes,' said Tessa. 'That's just what happened.' Painfully, she recounted what Rob had told her of his final encounter with his mother. *She had laughed.*

Father Theo's face went as white as his bandages. 'Oh, poor Linda,' he said. 'Poor Rob.'

'You can say that?' Tessa blurted. 'After what he did to you? What he tried to do? You almost died!'

He gave her the ghost of a smile. 'Haven't you ever heard of turning the other cheek?'

'I always thought you had it in for Rob,' Tessa admitted. 'When we talked, I got the feeling that you didn't like him.'

Again Father Theo tented his fingers and looked thoughtfully at Tessa. 'Do you want me to be honest, my dear?'

'Yes, please.'

'It wasn't that I didn't like Rob. But I always had the feeling, from talking to Linda, and from the contact I had with him after her death, that there was something . . . damaged . . . about him. Something not quite right. It worried me. I never really connected it with that horrible story, but it nagged at me, especially after some of the things you let slip about his odd behaviour. I was concerned on your behalf.'

'Then why didn't you say anything?' Tessa asked.

The priest shook his head. 'You were in love with him. You wouldn't have listened to me.'

Tessa sighed. 'Probably not,' she admitted. 'So instead, I nearly got us both killed.'

'Nearly, but not quite.' His smile was affectionate, holding no reproach.

Melanie returned not long after Father Theo's visit had ended. 'You look tired,' she observed, concerned.

Tessa closed her eyes. 'I've just seen Father Theo, and it was wonderful to see him. But it ... wasn't easy. I learned some things about Rob that I didn't know, and if I had ... Well, never mind.'

'Do you want to talk about it?' Melanie, now more unwieldy than ever, lowered herself on to the chair by the bed. 'You don't have to if you're not up to it.'

Tears stung Tessa's eyes. 'I'm not sure,' she said. But after a moment she began telling Melanie the whole story, from her first meeting with Rob to that dreadful moment at the bottom of the stairs, informed with the insights she'd gained from Father Theo. 'He wasn't what I thought he was,' she finished miserably. 'I've been so ... foolish. I should have known. And I feel so ... guilty.'

'No.' Melanie squeezed her hand and echoed Father Theo's words. 'You were in love. And you might have been guilty of rushing into marriage a bit precipitously. But apart from that, there was no way you could have known.' She paused to give extra weight to her next words. 'Listen to me, Tessa. Rob was psychotic. The behaviour you've told me about – the charm when things were going smoothly, and the cold anger when he was crossed – all of that is entirely consistent with psychosis. And no wonder, given what you've told me about his mother,'

she added. 'None of it was your fault. Rob was a disaster waiting to happen. It was just bad luck that he had to happen to
you.'

Tessa took it all in, then spoke her thoughts aloud. 'But
now what?'

'Now you've got to put it all behind you and get on with
your life. Your baby—'

'Did someone mention babies?' said a voice from the door.

'Stephanie!' Melanie, smiling at the sight of the young
midwife, lumbered up from the chair and gestured. 'Come in.
Sit down.'

Making a grand entrance, Stephanie demurred. 'I wouldn't
think of taking a chair from one of my pregnant mums, and
besides, I can't stay.'

'You're all dressed up,' Tessa marvelled; she'd never seen
Stephanie in anything but the most casual of clothes, but this
evening she wore a short, sequined black dress, and her wild
red curls were held back from her face with a velvet band.

Stephanie struck a pose, arms outstretched. 'Tah dah! New
Year's Eve party,' she said. 'I'm meeting my boyfriend in a few
minutes, but I thought I'd stop by to see you on the way.'

'You look wonderful.'

'Wish I could say the same for you,' Stephanie grinned.
'Quite frankly, Tessa, white just isn't your colour.'

'You can always trust Stephanie to tell you the truth,' said
Melanie. 'Even if the truth hurts.'

Stephanie came up to the bed. 'Seriously, Tessa, how are
you feeling?'

'Tired, as I said. Apart from that, not too bad.' Tessa thought
for a moment, then added jokingly, 'But people keep treating
me like some sort of china ornament. "Take it easy", "Keep
calm", "Strict bed-rest" – all of that. The nurse won't even let
me out of bed. I'm beginning to think there's something wrong
with me!'

The midwife glanced at Melanie. 'Hasn't she been told?'

Melanie shook her head.

'Told what?' Tessa demanded, panic rising. There *was* something wrong with her, then.

'We didn't want to upset her,' explained Melanie. She frowned at Stephanie and shook her head again. 'The doctor thought it was best. I agreed with him, and so did Tessa's father. I believe in honesty as a general principle, but sometimes . . .'

Tessa's breath came in ragged gasps. 'Now you have to tell me!'

'Listen, Tessa.' Stephanie leaned over the bed and looked into her face. 'I think you need to know this, no matter what the doctor says.'

Tessa had a premonition. 'It's my baby, isn't it? Is she dead?' She was sure she'd felt the baby move, but . . .

'She's not dead,' Stephanie assured her. 'But she's in a very . . . fragile . . . state. You fell down the stairs. There appears to have been some damage to the placenta, and there is still a danger that it could detach.'

'So what does that mean?' Tessa gulped, staring into Stephanie's honest eyes.

'It means, Tessa, that you can't get out of bed until the placenta re-establishes itself. That might take a few weeks, or it might be up until the time the baby is born. We could be talking about more than four months of complete bed-rest.'

'Oh!' Tessa closed her eyes and her hands went to her abdomen.

'Look at me, Tessa,' Stephanie commanded.

Tessa obeyed.

Her voice was fierce, compelling. 'What this really means, and I can't say this too strongly, is that you have to fight for this baby. You have to want to hold on to her, more than anything else in the world. The doctor seems to think that it's a passive process – you just lie in bed for a few weeks or a few months and keep calm and everything will be fine. But he's a man,' she said. 'He doesn't really understand. It has to be active, not passive. You have to fight for her every second, every minute, every day. Or you'll lose her. I mean it, Tessa. You have to decide how badly you want this baby, how hard you're willing to fight to keep her. No one else can do it for you – not me, not Melanie. No one. It's up to you to hold on to her. If that's what you want.'

Was it what she wanted? Later, alone in the quiet darkness, Tessa faced up to that question.

Her baby. She folded her hands and cradled her abdomen, as she had done so many times.

Her decision. *Did* she want this baby?

The answer to that question had been easy at first. She had wanted the baby more than anything, enough to seek to get pregnant without telling her husband. Had she even then, she wondered, known subconsciously that he would be opposed to the idea? His negative reaction to the news had been upsetting, but there had never been any doubt in her mind that this baby was what she wanted.

Finding out about JoAnn's death, and the events surrounding that time, had been traumatic, but even that hadn't dissuaded her from wanting the baby.

But now . . .

It wasn't the prospect of four months flat on her back that daunted her. It wasn't even the idea of giving birth on her own, raising a child on her own.

This wasn't just her baby. It was Rob's baby as well.

Rob's baby. A murderer's baby.

She had been in love with him, yes. But she had been so wrong about him. All along, she'd been wrong. He wasn't the man she thought he was, the man she had needed him to be.

The Rob she'd loved was a fantasy, a reflection of her own needs. She had looked at him and seen him as she wanted him to be, not as he was.

The real Rob could be charming, yes. But that charm was a thin veneer, and she'd never wanted to see beneath that veneer to the troubled man inside.

Troubled, demon-ridden. Perhaps even mad, if Melanie was to be believed.

He had murdered his mother.

He had tried to murder an innocent priest.

He had, arguably, tried to kill his own wife and his unborn child.

And in the end he had killed himself. Was it really an accident, the car crash in which he had died? Tessa wasn't so sure.

Did she want his child? The child of a murderer? If the baby looked like Rob, with that black hair and those blue eyes, would she be a daily reminder of the terrible mistake Tessa had made in marrying this man?

Could she bear it?

Was she willing to fight to bring a murderer's child into the world?

Losing the baby now would be easy. According to Stephanie, she wouldn't have to do anything – not even get out of bed. All she had to do was to be passive, to let go. Then it would be over. Rob would be out of her life for ever, along with any lingering reminder of their intimacy.

What would be hard was the fighting, the holding on. Knowing, that at the end of it, she would give birth to the child of a murderer, a matricide.

The sins of the father . . .

She herself might even die, bringing Rob's child into the world. Die, as JoAnn had died, in a pool of her own blood.

Lying at the foot of the stairs, drowning in the pain of her injuries and the new and terrible knowledge of her husband, Tessa had welcomed the thought of death. She had thought that she wanted to die, that she had no reason to go on living.

Today, with its many revelations, had been painful as well. She'd had to face up to her own ignorance, her wilful misconceptions and her subconscious self-deception. She'd had to accept the knowledge of the man she had married, and her share of the blame for all that had happened as a result of that marriage.

And she knew, now, that she wanted to live. She'd never known until today how much she had to live for. For years she had felt herself to be alone in the world: solitary, isolated, unloved. Ian, and then Rob – she'd been seeking something that she hadn't found with either of them, some ideal of all-fulfilling love that didn't exist. The things that were important, the capacity for happiness, had been there all along, if only she'd known. Her father, who had always loved her; her friends – Melanie, Ned, the girls, Father Theo. Stephanie, even. And Andrew? Was there a place in her future for Andrew, eventually, as more than just a friend?

The baby.

Tessa felt a sudden sharp kick, and her heart lifted.

'Yes,' she said aloud, stroking her abdomen lovingly. 'Yes, baby. I want you. I want you to live.'

Her mind made up, Tessa slept.

It was the bells that woke her: a cacophony of bells, surrounding her, coming from all directions.

Tessa listened to the bells for a moment, wondering, her eyes still closed, then became aware somehow that she was not alone in the room. 'Melanie?' she queried.

'It's me,' said a male voice, apologetic.

Her eyes flew open. Andrew, sitting beside the bed, smiled at her.

'The bells.'

'The Millennium,' he said. 'Every church bell in the country is ringing in the new century – the new millennium.'

'The new year.'

'Happy New Year, Tessa,' he said. He took her hand, intertwining his fingers with hers.

She didn't resist. 'Happy New Millennium, Andrew.' Her free hand went to her abdomen. 'And to you too, baby.'

'Yes, we mustn't forget my goddaughter. Very appropriate, that – a new millennium for a new life.'

'"Should auld acquaintance be forgot, and never brought to mind",' she mused. 'I've never understood what that meant. Does that mean you're supposed to forget, or not?'

Andrew looked thoughtful. 'You should never forget,' he said. 'Move on, maybe, but not forget.'

'I think I'll call the baby Caroline Linda,' Tessa decided with sudden inspiration. 'After her grandmothers.'

Andrew smiled. 'I like that,' he said. 'For the sake of auld lang syne.'

UNRULY PASSIONS

Kate Charles

Margaret Phillips, Archdeacon of Saxwell, is in the prime of her life. She effortlessly combines her clerical duties in the church with a rock-solid marriage to the charming and devoted Hal.

Gervase Finch moves with his fiercely protective wife into the parsonage in the nearby village of Branlingham, before assuming the post as vicar. Although they love their spouses, Rosemary Finch and Hal Phillips are drawn together, both disturbed by ideals of womanhood: Rosemary competing with the ghost of Gervase's first wife, Hal married to a paragon.

Valerie Marler, a bestselling novelist, has also identified Hal as the object of her unruly passion, and strives to rewrite her past failures by pursuing her fictional ideal. But when Hal refuses to play his part in her love story, her revenge threatens to descend into tragedy.

'Compulsive reading' *Birmingham Post*

'Thoroughly entertaining' *The Times*

FALSE PRETENCES

Margaret Yorke

Recipient of the 1999 CWA Cartier Diamond Dagger

When her goddaughter is arrested during an anti-roads protest, Isabel Vernon is startled to discover that the fair-haired child of her memory has become an overweight, shaven-headed environmentalist and that Isabel herself is now regarded as Emily Frost's next of kin.

Emily, released on bail to the Vernons at their home in the commuter village of Fordswick, makes herself unexpectedly useful about the house and even finds a local job as a nanny to Rowena. But Isabel's unease about Emily's sudden reappearance in her life and her boredom with her own husband prepare the ground for a tangled web of menace, shot through with emotional and sexual tension.

Dissecting the fragile state of ordinary lives with chilling clarity, *False Pretences* reveals Margaret Yorke at her atmospheric, suspenseful best.

'Yorke has an extraordinary feel for the passions that lurk beneath unremarkable facades' *Sunday Times*

DEATH AND SHADOWS

Paula Gosling

A murdered nurse, disappearing drug supplies, a diminishing trust fund and the sudden death of two apparently healthy patients are just some of the problems confronting Blackwater Bay's leading private clinic.

Laura Brandon, recently arrived physiotherapist, niece of the owner of Mountview Clinic and self-appointed sleuth, realises that a lot of people have something to hide. Confronted by tight-lipped colleagues, inter-staff feuds, and strange tales about a shadowy evil that lurks in the woods, Laura begins to believe the theory of a psychotic killer on the loose. Then another, eerily similar, murder occurs and she knows the solution cannot be impersonal.

Fast-paced, entertaining, and full of misdirections, Paula Gosling's latest tale from the Great Lakes brilliantly confirms her mastery in the art of the murder mystery.

'Super, swift-sure characterisation, pace, high local colour: Paula Gosling has all the gifts' *Sunday Times*

Warner titles available by post:

☐ Cruel Habitations	Kate Charles	£6.99
☐ Unruly Passions	Kate Charles	£5.99
☐ False Pretences	Margaret Yorke	£5.99
☐ Death and Shadows	Paula Gosling	£5.99

The prices shown above are correct at time of going to press. However, the publishers reserve the right to increase prices on covers from those previously advertised, without further notice.

WARNER BOOKS

WARNER BOOKS
Cash Sales Department, P.O. Box 11, Falmouth, Cornwall, TR10 9EN
Tel: +44 (0) 1326 569777, Fax: +44 (0) 1326 569555
Email: books@barni.avel.co.uk

POST AND PACKING:
Payments can be made as follows: cheque, postal order (payable to Warner Books) or by credit cards. Do not send cash or currency.

U.K. Orders under £10	£1.50
U.K. Orders over £10	**FREE OF CHARGE**
E.C. & Overseas	25% of order value

Name (Block letters) ....

Address ....

....

Post/zip code: ....

☐ Please keep me in touch with future Warner publications

☐ I enclose my remittance £ .

☐ I wish to pay by Visa/Access/Mastercard/Eurocard

Card Expiry Date